The PROMISE of WONDER

ALSO BY KATHERINE WEBB

The Legacy

The Unseen

A Half Forgotten Song

The Misbegotten

The Night Falling

The English Girl

The Hiding Places

The Disappearance

PRAISE FOR KATHERINE WEBB

'Evocative. Totally transporting. This is a rich and delicious multi-layered read.'

—Eve Chase, on *The Disappearance*

'With marvellously atmospheric prose, she weaves a seductive spell around the reader and before you know it, you are captured in her world, captivated by her beautiful writing. Webb has a true gift for uncovering the mysteries of the human heart.'

—Kate Williams

'You know with a book by Katherine Webb that the writing will be impeccable.'

—Elizabeth Fremantle

'Katherine Webb has the rare gift of being able to create wholly convincing period settings and characters for whatever book she writes.'

—Historical Writers' Association

'So cleverly plotted, so perfectly pitched emotionally. It crosses genre between historical, psychological suspense, thriller, romance. An absolute triumph.'

—Iona Grey, on *The Disappearance*

'I couldn't have loved it more. Riveting, haunting, beautifully written . . .'

—Jenny Ashcroft, on *The Disappearance*

'Written with compelling precision, stunning elegance and remarkable insight.'

—*Lancashire Post*, on *The Hiding Places*

'A compelling and beautifully written tale of adventure, mystery and love, *The English Girl* enthralled me from the first page.'

—Santa Montefiore, on *The English Girl*

'This is an expansive piece of storytelling, full of adventure, betrayal, shocking secrets and passion.'

—*YOU* magazine, on *The English Girl*

'Haunting and atmospheric, the story and the characters stayed with me long after I'd read the final page.'

—Lucinda Riley, on *The Night Falling*

'I found it absolutely enthralling, and a guaranteed contender for one of my reads of the year. I can't praise this book highly enough – the sheer emotional power of the writing left me reeling.'

—BeingAnne.com blog, on *The Night Falling*

'Hauntingly good.'

—*Marie Claire* magazine, on *The Unseen*

'*The Unseen* by Katherine Webb has it all . . . it is a compelling read, and the political subtext about women's rights and social mobility is a delight.'

—Bertram Books, on *The Unseen*

'Brilliant and absorbing drama.'

—*Good Housekeeping* magazine, on *The Legacy*

The PROMISE of WONDER

Katherine Webb

LAKE UNION
PUBLISHING

This is a work of fiction. Names, characters, organizations, places, events, and incidents are either products of the author's imagination or are used fictitiously. Any resemblance to actual persons, living or dead, or actual events is purely coincidental.

Published by Lake Union Publishing, Seattle

www.apub.com

EU Product Safety Contact:
Amazon Media EU S.à r.l.
38, avenue John F. Kennedy, L-1855 Luxembourg
amazonpublishing-gpsr@amazon.com

ISBN-13: 9781662540844
eISBN: 9781662540851

Cover design by Will Speed
Cover image: © Artur Bociarski © nikkimeel © AnyaLis © AYDO8
© Peter J Barker © RAHADITYA15 / Shutterstock; © Collaboration JS / ArcAngel Images

Printed in the United States of America

That loss is common would not make
My own less bitter, rather more:
Too common! Never morning wore
To evening, but some heart did break.

—In Memoriam by Alfred, Lord Tennyson, 1850

PART I

Chapter One

Midsummer's Day

1889

Theo Hallewell woke to the subterranean light before dawn, and to the knowledge that today was *the* day. A day so long planned for, imagined and reimagined, that it was both terrifying and elating.

The house was still asleep; no muffled sounds of the servants getting up, just a few faint creaks from the old beams. A blackbird sang outside, and a dog barked in the distance. It would be hours before the guests went down for breakfast; hours before her mother would glide the length of the hall, asking after everyone's sleep and managing to appear interested in the replies.

Theo opened the window to the damp scents of stone, lawn, and the manure around the roses. Ordinary enough, on any other day, but now laden with potential. Like the whole world was holding its breath.

She had no idea what to wear on such a day.

Only recently had it started to matter. Theo had become visible, somehow, and had begun to sense other people's scrutiny. She'd preferred the anonymity of before, since there was really only one person she wished would notice her. Setting the small mirror from her dressing table on the windowsill, she brushed her hair out of its plait. Long, straight sweeps of mouse brown. Her mother, Diana, couldn't help making disappointed noises now and then, because it had been *such* a pretty colour when Theo was little. White-blonde, like her sister's.

She would turn sixteen in a couple of months, and wondered what that might mean. Her mother insisting she dress better, no doubt, *refinement* being the constant refrain. At least the longer skirts, which snarled around her ankles and ended up filthy, also hid the boots with the sturdy soles that she wasn't supposed to wear any more. There would be no being *out*, no launch into society, no parties or balls – not that Theo wanted any of that. But sixteen was surely a watershed. An acceptable age to court, and be courted.

She stopped brushing and stared into her own eyes, made greyer by the half-light. Widening them, she found it odd that *this* face was *hers*. Sometimes it felt like a mask; her body a machine she didn't know quite how to operate, prone to doing unpredictable things. She rose then, and moved silently past her sister's empty bedroom to the stairs.

Across the lawn and out of the garden gate, past the copse of elms with its noisy colony of rooks. Ahead of her, the ruins of Hallewell Castle sat up on their grassy mound, silhouetted against a sky now the colour of a starling's egg. As she climbed, a shaft of coral light caught a single broken tooth of battlement, creeping lower as the sun rose.

'"*The splendour falls on castle walls*",' Theo recited, walking a slow circuit of the outer rampart. '"*And snowy summits old in story*."'

She visited a few familiar places: the musket-ball holes that pocked the southern buttresses like acne; the murky guard room, all green and streaked with pigeon mess. The ruins were mostly Norman, but they sat upon much older things: an Anglo-Saxon stronghold, of which only the skeleton of a ninth-century chapel remained. Before that, the Romans had built a shrine at the spring below – the Holy Well that had given the ruins, the village and Theo's family their name. The castle had been built and rebuilt many times before being blown to pieces by Cromwell's Roundheads in 1646.

From the south-western side of the hill, Theo looked down at the only home she'd ever known. Hallewell House, built after the Civil War when the family had grovelled enough – and been penalised sufficiently – to be allowed to return. No more Lord or Lady Hallewells after that; just Mr and Mrs. They'd once owned vast swathes of Cranborne Chase, on the border between Wiltshire and Dorset; now the estate had shrunk to about forty acres of paddocks and gardens, the castle and the spring.

The house itself was a low, sprawling, many-gabled thing, some parts built of stone and others of half-timbered brick and render, all beneath an undulating roof. Like the castle, it had been added to and reconfigured many times. A Georgian forebear had added a boxy, double-storey entrance hall with big sash windows that looked wholly out of place.

The roofs of Hallewell village were dotted down the hill to the south. Theo's gaze settled on the thatched oblong of St Agnes's Caring and Preventative Cottage Home for Friendless Girls, and she wondered if Missy was awake yet. The matron ran a tight ship, but it was still so early that a skein of mist hung above the spring, and the chattering swallows seemed far too loud, skimming across the sky. Theo watched the spreading light paint everything with molten gold. She couldn't see Toby's house; it was hidden by trees. But she knew he'd be up.

'Auspicious,' she whispered. That was the word.

She turned east to her favourite view of all: an old drovers' route, away in the distance; a nameless green lane, sunken between high hedges, that crested the hill and then vanished. It reminded her of more lines by Tennyson: *And thro' the field the road runs by / To many tower'd Camelot*, and always gave her a powerful yearning to follow wherever it led. To see things she'd never seen. To be awestruck. She tried to ignore the thought that she probably never would. Society and responsibility, and being sixteen. And a girl.

There was a soft thump from below. Theo looked down and saw Kitty Shoat, one of the upstairs maids, yawning like a cat as she headed for the outhouse. The spell broke, and with a short sigh Theo made her way back. She needed to be washed and properly dressed in time to have breakfast with the guests. But the day *was* auspicious. Night would come, and her plan would work; Toby would *see* her, and everything would change.

In fact, Toby Meriwether had overslept. He surfaced with a start, got up too quickly, then had to wait, holding the bedpost, for the room to stop spinning. He was trying to cultivate the habit of rising at five in order to have at least two hours to study before Kit, asleep in the next bed, woke up and made it impossible. Their father taught at the national school in the next village – which Toby and Kit had attended – and he'd arranged for Toby to use an empty attic room there, during school hours. But Toby's conscience wouldn't let him stay there all day. His mother had enough to do, and tired easily, and Kit was adept at sneaking away and getting into trouble.

Once, Toby had spent five hours there, wrangling with a piece of algebraic logic that stubbornly refused to make sense. History, Ethics, Latin – these were all merely a question of quantity and retention. Algebra and Logic, however, were like tackling a puzzle with half the pieces missing. When he'd got home, Kit was up on the church roof again, throwing clods of moss at passers-by and hooting with laughter. It had taken Toby's direst warnings to persuade him to come down before the verger sent for Constable

Pryce, who'd been very hard on Kit ever since the incident with the horse manure.

The boys' mother, Mona, was kind and quiet, head and shoulders shorter than her sons, with fair hair and tiny hands. It seemed improbable that two such tall, dark-haired lads could have sprung from her. She loved them equally, it went without saying; and though she never lost patience with Kit, Toby knew that she worried. He worried too. He worried what would happen when he went up to university, because however much they loved him, Kit was a handful. Mona couldn't watch him all the time, let alone keep him occupied.

Kit had finished school three years ago, at fourteen, having got no further than Standard III. The headmaster had kept him on as long as possible – a gangling teenager surrounded by eight- and nine-year-olds, far too big and noisy as his frustration grew. Toby had been through all seven Standards by the time he turned twelve. At that point, the vicar had taken over his tuition in private and plundered various philanthropic bodies to fund his university entrance, since the fees for the first year alone would have outstripped his father's annual salary of a hundred and twenty pounds. But once he was away at Bishop Hatfield's Hall – *if* he passed the matriculation examination well enough to win the scholarship he needed – what then? Durham wasn't local; he could hardly nip home three hundred miles because Kit was in a fix. And in any case, the university was strict about away days. Once you were up, you were up.

Toby peeped out around the thick blanket at the window. The sky was an immaculate blue. He squinted at his watch, dismayed to find it gone seven already. Most days, panic roused him much earlier – the possibility of not having enough time to study, of not winning the scholarship, not being able to take up his place. Dreadful thoughts.

He dressed hurriedly, out on the landing, put off his wash and shave until later, and went down to where his parents were already at the breakfast table. Bread, jam and cocoa; a boiled egg each for Toby and his father, David.

'Stayabed,' Mona said, running a hand through Toby's scruffy hair as he bent to kiss her cheek. 'Thought you'd have been up with the lark again.'

'I wish you'd woken me.'

'You know I can't, without waking your brother. You'll have to tie a string to your big toe and leave the end outside the door so I can tweak it.'

'I'd only yell, and that'd be that.'

Toby reached out to grab a slice of bread but his mother slapped his hand away.

'Sit down. Eat a proper breakfast. You can't study on an empty stomach.'

He pulled up a chair opposite his father. There was just enough room for the four of them to sit down together, one at each side of the table, knees meeting in the middle. The parlour was their best room. It had a flagstone floor, green wainscotting, and a tidy hearth with a ring for the kettle. The fire had a settee to either side where they sat in the evenings, Mona sewing something, David reading the paper or carefully brushing his jacket and hat. Watercolours of plants and insects hung on the walls; a precious photograph of David's parents sat on the mantelpiece, along with an inherited silver snuff-box and Mona's Golden Jubilee souvenirs: three pressed-glass dishes, all with Victoria's cameo and crest. The cat was asleep in his customary sunny spot on the windowsill, tucked between the spider plants.

Next door, a coal-burning range and copper boiler for hot water were wedged into a far older inglenook, crusted with centuries of soot. A tin bath hung from a hook on the wall, and a large dresser held crockery, cutlery, and all the other things Mona used to conjure up their meals – Oxo powder, black treacle, Lea & Perrins sauce. Water from the Hallewell spring was fetched from a pump at the end of the lane. Upstairs were the two bedrooms, and downstairs, at the back, a lean-to with a tin roof and a stone sink, where garden tools were stacked and pots scrubbed. David's vegetable patch was easily the best-kept in the village. There he spent the quietly contented hours after school, usually with Kit to help him. The care of living things – pricking out seedlings, or treating the hens for mites and scale – was one of the few activities that could hold the boy's attention for any length of time.

Toby was on his feet as soon as he finished eating.

'Sorry. I'm so late already—'

David leaned heavily on his cane as he rose.

'Go on ahead, son. You needn't walk with me.'

'Of course I will, Dad.'

'Give me half a minute to pack you something to eat,' Mona said. 'And you're to study for as long as you need. Drop some eggs to Mrs Cooper on the way.'

Two miles of narrow lane ran between Hallewell and West End, their larger neighbour, which had the school, church, village hall and grocery. The road wound down the hill and across meadows where the Hallewell spring met several other streams, and regularly flooded. Trout wove in the current, and the air around the cattle thrummed with insect life.

Toby was careful not to get ahead of his father, or let his impatience show. David's right leg crumpled with the weight of every step, forcing his foot to drag on its side as he pulled it forwards. As a child, Toby had been fascinated by the ruination of that limb. He remembered poking small fingers into the mysterious twists and dents in the shin bone, and the strange protuberances of the knee, where the skin was all shiny and white. David had got the injury as a young man, in the Crimea, but there had never been any stories about his time as a soldier. A trunk in the attic contained a helmet, sabre, and heavy, brass-buttoned greatcoat, but, if asked, David would shake his head, or perhaps frown.

Only once had he let slip anything about his former life. They'd gone to the fête at the big house, and nine-year-old Theodora Hallewell, unable to look anyone in the eye but precocious with her reading, had been made to perform a poem. Perhaps Diana Hallewell had been hoping for something to do with God, flowers, or fair maidens, but her daughter had chosen Tennyson's 'The Charge of the Light Brigade': *Theirs not to make reply / Theirs not to reason why / Theirs but to do and die.*

Mona had cast a worried glance at her husband, so Toby had done the same. His father's face had been frozen, the muscles tight, eyes stark.

They'd left soon after that.

'Didn't you like the poem, Dad?' Toby asked.

'No.' A tone as close to anger as Toby had ever heard from his father. 'I did not.'

After an unfamiliar silence, he tried again. 'I thought it was—'

David rounded on him, bending down to his level. 'War is nothing to write poetry about, son.' His voice shook. 'There's no splendour in it, only senseless destruction. It serves nothing but the vainglory of powerful men. Do you understand? War is a hungry animal, and no good will *ever* come of feeding it.'

He had straightened and turned away, leaving Toby stunned. This was not what they'd been taught at school. After that, ever a fairly literal-minded child, Toby pictured mighty jaws, like the *jaws of Death* in the poem, biting down on his father's leg. David never shouted, nor wept, nor lost his temper, but he never laughed either. His smile never quite chased the shadows from his eyes. Toby didn't mention any of it again. He wanted his father's rare smiles and quiet approval, and never again to see that desolation.

Later at that fête, Toby had looked for Theo amongst the other youngsters, who'd ganged up and were busy stealing food. But when he found her, finally, she was up on the terrace with the well-to-dos. Sitting in silence, her back perfectly straight, gazing wistfully at the last egg sandwich on a three-tiered platter. Toby had caught her eye and waved, and Theo had darted a worried glance at her mother before raising her fingers surreptitiously. And Toby had understood three things that he'd only half grasped before: that Theo Hallewell was of a different breed to him; that the times she'd played with him in the village she'd probably done so on the sly; and that she must be lonely.

He remembered Theo's elder sister, Amy, as a smiling chatterbox whose prettiness had abashed him. Then she'd died, and Toby had known it was a terrible shame without really thinking about how sad it must be for Theo, or how odd to be the only child in such a huge house. Still, he'd also felt a prickle of resentment towards her, sitting up there in her frilly dress, with her white shoelaces and her hair in ribbons. He hadn't understood why, or even tried to; he'd merely stopped waving and turned away.

Two-thirds of the way up the hill on the other side of the water meadows, Toby paused to watch a pair of banded demoiselles, flying in urgent spirals with their brilliant blue bodies catching the light.

David caught up and leaned on his stick, breathing hard.

'Fighting?' Toby said. 'Or in love, do you think?'

'It's often hard to tell, in the young.'

'How do you know they're young?' Toby countered. 'Might be an old married couple.'

'Alas, nature tends not to allow such gorgeous things to grow old,' David said. 'Come along. Herodotus won't read himself.'

'It's Euclid today, in fact.'

'Ah. More dratted triangles? Bad luck, my boy.'

At the top of the hill Toby looked back across the valley again, at Hallewell's dun-coloured cottages. He liked to see the place he'd grown up in like this – small and hidden away, while the rest of the vast, wide world lay waiting. Waiting for *him*.

Theo was often out in the garden of Hallewell House, and even more often up at the castle: a solitary figure, lately grown willowy and almost graceful despite her untidy hair and practical boots. They saw far less of one another these days. Toby had serious work to do, while she apparently floated through her days, obsessed with her family's legends and flowery old Tennyson. All that *thou*-ing and *hath*-ing.

Then he remembered that it was Midsummer's Day, and he'd had a note a while back inviting him to a midnight gathering, the purpose of which remained a mystery. Nonsense cooked up by Theo's overactive imagination, no doubt; like the time she'd made their group of Sunday School companions lie in a circle around the spring, holding hands and chanting, for fully twenty minutes. He'd stolen a glance at Theo's face: eyes screwed shut, brows pinched, actually expecting something magical to happen.

He really didn't need a midnight gathering. What he needed was sleep, and to wake up early, and to study. But just then a whisper of breeze brought a gentle shiver, and he suspected he would do as she asked.

Chapter Two

In spite of waking so early, Theo managed to be late for breakfast. She made a beeline for Uncle Crudge. Timothy Ambrosius Crudge was not actually her uncle, but he'd been coming to Hallewell House as a paying guest since before she was born, and had never minded a small girl in a muddy dress tripping at his heels. He was an antiquarian and folklorist, a collector of the old and arcane. Many of the stories Theo knew about her own family had come from him. But as she approached, with her plate of bacon and tomatoes, he was dabbing at his lips and pushing back his chair.

'Ah! There you are, Theodora – Miss Hallewell, I should say.' He corrected himself, though it was unlikely Diana Hallewell could have heard.

'Hello, Uncle Crudge. *Bonjour*, Mr LeRoy.'

Crudge's new assistant gave her the briefest of nods.

'You've just missed us, I'm afraid. I want to make a start before it gets any hotter – the fiery chariot of Helios had the better of us by noon, yesterday.'

'Well, it *is* Midsummer's Day,' she said.

'Indeed.' After a beat, Crudge's eyes widened. 'Ah! Indeed! So it is.'

He tapped the side of his nose and gave her a wink.

'May I come and help you later, Uncle?'

'If your lady mother can spare you, then we should be delighted.'

Theo watched him walk the length of the room, saluting people here and there. Tall and slump-shouldered, with thick white hair and whiskers. Then, she had no choice but to sit next to the young couple who'd arrived the day before, whose names she had forgotten.

Diana had coached her thoroughly on what to say to strangers over breakfast, though she sometimes wondered whether they might prefer to keep their own company so early in the day. She knew *she* would. She missed taking her meals in the nursery with her bears, while her nanny read a novel and ignored her. An unwelcome fourteenth birthday present had been the end of that peaceful existence, and she'd eaten every meal since *en masse*. It was excruciating. *Practice makes perfect*, her mother often said.

Hallewell House was not *an hotel* of the common sort. The people who came to stay were *visitors*, guests of the house, even though they were strangers and paying. The hall, where the dining table was fully twenty feet long, was *not* a restaurant, let alone a *refectory*, so everybody in residence sat down to eat together, with the family. The guests were *invited*, sometimes via notices in the press. Accounts were settled with the utmost discretion, and there certainly wasn't anything as vulgar as a tariff card, let alone a front desk with a bell.

'Good morning,' Theo said. 'I trust you passed a restful night?'

The young couple stared at Theo. There was something still and serious about them.

'I don't tend to sleep a great deal, Miss Hallewell,' the woman said.

This explained the brown smudges beneath the woman's eyes. Theo still couldn't think of her name. She sipped her tea to buy time.

'Oh . . .' she said. 'Sorry.'

The husband glanced at Theo impatiently. He had a neatly clipped moustache, more gingery than the hair on his head, and tapped his thumb on his folded newspaper as though he wished to be allowed to read it. Theo tried to eat quickly without appearing to, and nearly choked on a piece of bacon fat.

'Are you here to solve the riddle?' she tried.

'The riddle?' The woman looked blank. 'Oh – the treasure?' She made it sound like a sweet absurdity. 'No.'

Diana appeared beside Theo's chair, much to her relief. Swathes of auburn hair piled high on her head, and her waist laced in hard. Diana was ageless and immaculate, and would remember the couple's name.

'Dr Mackie, Mrs Mackie, a very good morning to you,' she said. 'I trust everything is to your liking?'

'Very much so, thank you, Mrs Hallewell,' said Mrs Mackie.

'Theo, Dr and Mrs Mackie wish to tour the castle and grounds. I have told them that you are quite the best person to guide them.'

Her hand landed on Theo's shoulder – a gesture of apparent affection, though her grip said otherwise.

'Nobody knows more of our history, and our legends, than my daughter,' Diana went on.

'It would be my pleasure,' Theo said, sinking inside. 'Though I have promised to help Uncle Crudge, and—'

Diana tightened her grip. 'Mr Crudge isn't your uncle, dear. And he has his new assistant. I'm sure he doesn't need you.'

Theo surrendered. 'When would you like to go?'

Mrs Mackie cast her hooded eyes at her husband. 'As soon as you are free to take us, Miss Hallewell,' she said.

They took an hour to change their shoes and rest after breakfast, so Theo dawdled in the quiet parts of the house. A whole section of the building could only be reached through a single door beneath the east stairs. It wasn't a smart door – no reason to suppose it led anywhere but to service areas, but in fact it marked the boundary between the original dwelling and one of its less baronial additions, where she and her mother had their rooms. There were no dreary tapestries there; the floors didn't slope, and the windows let in a bit more light. It was where Theo's father, Seymour Hallewell, now six years in his grave, had made it his business to have as little to do with people as possible. Including his own daughter.

Theo drifted through the busy kitchen to the back door, hearing sloshing and chatter from the walled courtyard beyond.

Outside, she spotted Missy's dark curls and broad hips, which Cook called *saucy*. They swayed as she plunged a wooden dolly into the laundry tub. Theo had completely forgotten it was washday. A work party from the Friendless Girls' home was always sent up to help with all the bedsheets. Missy caught sight of Theo and grinned. Her face was built for a grin – short nose, round cheeks, a dimpled chin and a wide mouth with deep-red lips. The most beautiful lips, in fact, like one of Rossetti's paintings of William Morris's wife. Theo sometimes caught herself wondering what it might be like to be that beautiful. Cook – and if Cook had a proper name, Theo had never heard it – said it was no wonder Missy was trouble.

'What did you do this time?' Theo asked.

Missy gave a petulant shrug, then laughed. 'Seems someone put soap in Matron's tooth powder. You should've heard her cough and spit!'

'*Missy!*' Theo was shocked.

'*Someone* did, I said – wasn't me, was it?'

'Then how come you're doing laundry again, three weeks in a row?'

''Cause she says she *knows* it was me. Says she can see it writ large on my face, and I should be sure my sins'll find me out, and some other things besides. Which is rot.'

Missy scratched her forehead with a wet thumb.

'But, Missy,' said the other girl who was with her, 'it *was*—'

'What would *you* know?' Missy snapped.

She stopped plunging the sheets and put her hands on her hips.

Melissa Cartwright was actually a year younger than Theo, though she seemed older. Where she'd been before St Agnes's Theo couldn't guess, and nobody was willing to say. Nor could she find out who had found her a place at the home rather than leaving her to sink into ruin. Once, and only once, Missy had let something slip: caught by an unguarded memory, she'd said: *He never once let me—* But then her mouth had snapped shut, and Theo had been too afraid to ask who *he* was. *Mischief right down in her gypsy bones*, Cook said.

Theo didn't think it was mischief, but something far better than that – something that filled Missy up and spilled out all around her. Bravery, perhaps. Standing there now, with her wet arms alight in the sun and long curls of hair the colour of treacle escaping from her cap, Theo didn't see how anyone could think badly of Missy. Least of all if she really *was* a gypsy, which was impossibly romantic.

'Lord, I'm fagged,' Missy said.

Theo eyed the heap of laundry, and began to worry. 'I hope you won't be *too* worn out for . . . you know. Later,' she said.

It simply wouldn't work if Missy wasn't there. Missy was her armour.

She heard her mother calling. 'Meet me on the hill after lunch,' she begged, as she hurried away. 'I'll bring strawberries!'

Guests of Hallewell House didn't have to pay the ha'penny entrance fee to the castle, which day trippers dropped into a slotted box at the gate. Mrs Mackie, clinging to her husband's arm, was panting by the time they reached the ruins. The heaving of her chest was almost convulsive, and Theo looked away. She'd already relayed the chronology of the castle, and a few of the tales about her distant

Anglo-Saxon forebear, Lord Abrecan of Hallewell. He'd been an Aetheling, a kingling under Alfred the Great, and supposedly a sorcerer and alchemist.

She pointed to a spot on the wooded hill opposite.

'Over there, in an act of vile treachery, he was set upon by his own cousins while they were hunting. Bright light shone from his wounds, to banish the darkness, and—'

'Why were they hunting at night?' Dr Mackie said.

'Hush, Bertie,' Mrs Mackie whispered, but Bertie didn't.

'You said his blood banished the dark. So, it must have been night-time.'

'I don't know,' Theo said. 'Maybe they were hunting something that only comes out at night.'

'A unicorn, perhaps?'

Theo reddened, but pressed on. 'He fled towards the spring, but they never found his body. It is said that he did not die, and will return one day when—'

'When Albion has need of him?' Dr Mackie's tone tiptoed the edge of derision. 'Theories of magical hibernation seem common to many folkloric figures of the Dark Ages. In fact, a lot of the Abrecan legends sound rather familiar,' he said. 'Perhaps because King Arthur has come so much back into fashion of late. There are no written sources attesting to Lord Abrecan's existence, I suppose?'

'He's . . . he's mentioned in *The Anglo-Saxon Chronicle*,' Theo said.

'Indeed. Really, Rosalind, must we—'

'But your spring was sacred . . . before Lord Abrecan's time,' Mrs Mackie said. She was still out of breath, and though her face was damp there was no colour in her cheeks. 'As I understand it?'

'Oh, yes. The Romans, and the ancient Britons. The stone in the middle of the village green marks the way to it. Everyone calls it the Roman Cross, but Uncle Crudge says it's Celtic.'

Mrs Mackie perched on a broken wall to rest, and her husband looked weary. A different kind of weary.

'It was really the spring we were most interested to see,' he said.

'Oh. Well. It's this way.'

Back down the mound, and along a path into woods of beech and oak and holly. The spring emerged from a sudden jut of limestone, fell burbling into a pool below, then disappeared back underground. Theo had always found it mesmerising. The water seemed to bleed from the rock and then soak back into it, endlessly. It was ice cold, perfectly clear, and tasted – she liked to think – of the bones of the world.

Cut into the top of the outcrop was a pointed niche about a foot high, inside which was the carved relief of a face so worn it could have been anyone. The water goddess to whom the Romans had dedicated the spring, or some local deity whose identity had vanished with her followers. Crudge had unearthed enough pieces of dressed stone to indicate that there'd probably been an altar there, once. He'd also found a silver coin from the reign of Emperor Domitian, in the first century. It was in a locked display case in the house, along with the far more precious coin that Theo planned to steal later that day.

'Look, somebody's left flowers,' Mrs Mackie said. A small posy of limp violets had been tucked into the niche, and white rose petals were turning slowly on the water.

'The spring's a sacred panacea,' Theo said. 'And the village girls also think the goddess will bring them love, and grant them wishes, in return for votive offerings.'

'Does it work?' Mrs Mackie asked.

'I tried it once,' Theo said, her face growing hot. 'When I was much younger. But I can't say yet whether or not it has worked. Perhaps these things take time.'

'But you believe it could?'

Theo was about to deny it, too used to being teased, but Mrs Mackie's tone stopped her. She wasn't treating Theo as a silly girl telling stories, but as a person who knew things. Important things. The woman glanced at her husband, so Theo did too, and suddenly saw, in his motionless face, a deep and aching sadness. The shadows under Mrs Mackie's eyes; the way she couldn't catch her breath, and didn't sleep.

Theo's throat went dry.

'Yes,' she said. 'I believe it could.'

She searched for words, and found some of Uncle Crudge's: 'There's so much in the world we don't understand. Who's to say the Romans were *wrong*, or that what we dismiss as pagan profanity and superstitious "magic" can't have had some basis, if not in the supernatural, then in the *natural*? The human mind holds myriad secrets, and powers not yet fully understood . . .'

Dr Mackie turned away with a quiet snort, but Mrs Mackie took Theo's hand.

'I think you're right,' she whispered.

'What is it?' Theo couldn't help but ask.

'A tumour.'

Mrs Mackie's eyelids fluttered, as though saying the word caused the thing inside her to stir, to flex its terrible muscles.

'In my lung. The doctors say it cannot be helped – my own dear husband included. But perhaps they simply do not know *how* it may. So, perhaps there are other ways. Don't you think? Ancient ways.'

She wasn't that much older than Theo herself; perhaps nineteen or twenty.

'Yes,' Theo said. 'Yes, perhaps.'

Mrs Mackie turned towards the glistening limestone, and the pool where the trees and brilliant sky were mirrored.

'What do I do?'

Theo might admit that she didn't know, that there was no right or wrong thing. Or, she might give Mrs Mackie a fragment of the possibility she craved. She knew what it was like to need to believe in magic.

'A small gift would be ideal,' she said, with calm authority. 'It need only be a token. The ribbon from your choker would do it – it's such a pretty colour. Here . . .'

She helped unthread a pendant from the pale-pink ribbon. It was a butterfly of solid gold, weighty for its size and lifelike in every way but scale, from its hair's-breadth antennae to the veins on its wings.

'Oh – this is lovely.'

'It was a gift from my godmother,' Mrs Mackie said, her expression gently ironic. 'For my confirmation. Butterflies symbolise resurrection, as you probably know. And hope.'

Theo handed it back, then tied the pink ribbon in a bow.

'Put it up by the goddess – can you reach?'

'I think I can . . .'

'Be careful, Rosalind!'

'I'm fine, Bertie. Really. What comes next, Miss Hallewell?'

'Next, you should wash your face and hands in the pool, thank the goddess and ask to be blessed, say your wish, and then drink some water from your hands.'

'Is that all? Should I say it out loud?'

'I think perhaps it's better to. It . . . needn't be loudly, though. I'll go away a bit. You must hold the wish in your heart as you speak it – that's the most important thing.'

'Oh, it is in my heart.' Mrs Mackie smiled faintly. 'Have no doubt about it.'

Theo walked a short distance away, avoiding Dr Mackie's eye. But it might work, she told herself. It wasn't *false* hope, it was simply hope, and where was the harm in that? She heard faint sounds of splashing, and softly murmured words, and longed to be back out in the bright sunshine.

She'd felt so certain upon waking – the day and the world and her own self had seemed on the brink of some wild glory. But the young woman behind her was dying, and Theo's inner world was suffering a small quake that threatened to escalate. The undeniably real world around her came into sharp focus. It might *not* work. Neither Mrs Mackie's cure, nor her own designs for that night. And if they did not, then Toby Meriwether would leave Hallewell without a backward glance, and all Theo's hopes would go with him.

Sitting on the grass with Missy after the midday meal, their fingers pink from purloined strawberries, Theo saw Toby in the distance, walking home along the lane from West End. She surged to her feet, shading her eyes for a better view.

'"*She left the web, she left the loom; she made three paces thro' the room*,"' Missy quoted merrily, lifting from Theo's favourite poem.

Theo glanced back at her, cheeks blazing. 'It's Toby, not Sir Lancelot,' she said. 'And I'm not the Lady of Shalott.'

'You wish you were.' Missy was merciless. 'And he might as well be, for the way you swoon at the sight of him.'

'I do *not* wish I was the Lady of Shalott, else I'd be dying now because I've looked at him.'

'I think you *are* dying!' Missy cried.

Theo let her laugh. She turned to watch Toby again: his familiar outline, his familiar walk. She would have known him anywhere, at any distance.

'If he looks up, he loves me,' she whispered. 'If he looks up, and he sees me, then he loves me and will be mine.'

Toby didn't look up. He disappeared behind the trees at the foot of the hill.

'He's just a boy, Theo,' Missy said. 'There's plenty of others like him.'

'There aren't. Haven't you ever been in love, Missy?'

'Love's what men say to get what they want from you.'

This shocked Theo into silence.

Missy leaned back on her elbows with a sigh. 'He's nice looking, I suppose,' she said, perhaps deciding she'd gone too far. 'And he'd have to be as big a dunce as his brother to turn you down.'

Theo snatched gratefully at the words. 'Do you think so?'

'Well – we'll see tonight, won't we?'

'Tonight is about summoning Lord Abrecan, and the ancient—'

'Oh yeah?' Missy cut her off. 'Nothing at all to do with being up close to Toby Meriwether in the dark, then?'

'Not at all.'

Missy laughed again. 'Ha! Will you let him kiss you?'

'Missy!'

'Will you?'

Theo didn't reply – she couldn't, given the way her lungs had emptied out at the thought.

'Want me to tell your fortune?' Missy said then, and Theo nodded.

She ran her index finger across Theo's palm, and looked closely.

'Your lifeline is long, like your bloodline. You shall know a love the likes of which you've never dreamed. And you shall be loved, and you shall marry.'

'Who? Who shall I marry?'

'Difficult to see. But it's someone you already know . . . and he has a handsome face.'

Theo beamed. 'Will I leave Hallewell?'

Missy squinted, checking. 'Yes. And you'll forget all about your good friend, Missy.'

'I won't. Not ever.'

◆ ◆ ◆

Toby got home with the bones of his backside bruised and his head overstuffed with geometry, to find the table covered with newspaper and a strong smell of lanolin in the air. Kit, his knees bobbing impatiently, was doing his best to clean his shoes without getting dubbin all over himself. He was fighting a losing battle.

Kit flashed a smile. 'Toby's back.'

'So he is,' Mona called from the kitchen. 'But you carry on brushing your shoes, please, Christopher.'

'I am.'

Kit nipped the end of his tongue between his teeth, scrubbing even harder. He could be so delicate with certain things, yet so cack-handed with others. Toby picked up the shoe Kit had already done and reached for a cloth.

'I'll buff it for you, shall I?'

'Yes,' Kit said. 'Thank you, yes.'

Kit's shoes were enormous, like his hands and his ears. He and Toby were the same height, with the same dark hair, but were put together very differently. Kit was skinny and all angles, his knees and elbows like knots in string; and he was never still except in sleep.

Wearing a pinafore over her dress and smelling of bread dough, Mona came to inspect the finished shoes.

'That's a grand job, Christopher,' she said.

'Can you see your face in them?' he demanded, since no lesser praise would do.

Mona took them over to the window. 'Why, I certainly can!'

Kit thumped the table in delight and rocketed to his feet.

'Then let's go, Toby!'

'Are we going somewhere?'

'Yes. To the castle.'

'The castle again?' Mona said. 'Aren't you ever tired of it?'

'No! Come *on*, Toby. Are we going?'

Toby stretched his shoulders. 'We're going,' he said.

Kit rushed for the door.

'Christopher! Socks and shoes!' Mona called after him. 'No child of mine will run barefoot like a savage.'

'Aren't we all savages, Mum?' Toby said. 'Isn't that what the good reverend said last Sunday?'

'Some more than others.' She swiped at him with her cloth.

Toby ducked up the stairs to get his notebook, which he always took with him to the castle, then followed his brother out.

The castle mound was swathed in daisies and red clover, and Kit was already halfway up it, swinging a stick he'd picked up, as Toby dropped their ha'penny into the box by the gate. The afternoon was as hot as the morning had promised, the sky buoyantly blue with a few faraway scuffs of cloud. Toby rolled up his sleeves, damp around his collar and waistband.

He spotted the antiquarian, Timothy Crudge, in a shallow ditch in the north courtyard, and walked over to him as Kit ran around, swiping gleefully at imaginary foes.

'Found anything, Mr Crudge?'

The older man squinted up at him. 'Ah! Toby, my boy. Alas, no, not a dickie-bird thus far.' He wore a curious outfit of beige canvas, with an apron of pockets for his trowels and brushes and picks. He wiped his hands on it and offered one to Toby to shake.

'Arnaud, come and meet Toby Meriwether, local scholar and gentleman,' Crudge said.

The quiet young man, who had been diligently scraping at some broken bricks, rose to his feet. 'A pleasure to make your acquaintance.'

'How do you do? Hot day for it,' Toby said.

'I was told it only ever rained in England.' Arnaud took off his hat and rubbed his hairline.

'Ah ha, you see!' Crudge raised a finger. '*Prejudice*. The French really are terribly superior, when it comes to the English.'

Arnaud gave a small smile, and at that moment Kit came jogging towards them. Crudge spread his arms to intercept him.

'Hold, there! *Around* the diggings if you please, young man – I thank you!'

Kit grinned. 'But I'm the *king* of this castle!'

'Well, kings can still sprain their ankles. Not to mention trample archaeological evidence.'

'Sorry,' Toby said, as Kit jogged on.

'For what?' Crudge waved a hand. 'I should have erected a cordon.'

'What is wrong with that boy?' Arnaud asked.

Toby bridled. 'Not much at all, in fact.'

'That's Toby's younger brother, Christopher,' Crudge said. 'A pure soul, as innocent as the day he was born.'

Stiffening at the rebuke, Arnaud returned to his work.

Crudge nodded at Toby's notebook. 'Did you come to study the symbols?'

'I supposed I might. Though I already have drawings of all of them – that I can find, anyway. Unless you've found any more?'

'And not told you? Hardly.'

'Somehow, they make more sense when I see them actually in the stone. As though something about their *exact* setting might be relevant. Does that sound bizarre?'

'It sounds quite logical to me, in fact. The symbols are distributed throughout the castle – if their positions *weren't* relevant, surely their author would have simply written them all out together, in a convenient line?'

Toby had worked at it since he was ten years old, and knew the symbols better than anyone. Common enough in medieval buildings, they were originally thought to have been stonemasons' so-called banker marks, to identify who had worked what. Then Theodora Hallewell's great-grandfather had found some lines written in the margin of an eleventh-century tome, long forgotten in an attic, that implied the symbols spelled out the location of some kind of treasure.

The lines had been published in *Notes and Queries* in 1832, with a pledge from the Hallewells to split the value of any finds with the finder. Fortune-hunters had been coming to the castle ever since. Toby had the magazine clipping in his notebook. He'd also written it out more times than he could count, hoping for some new insight: *Let the treasure of the Holy Well, from the blood of Abrecan who was called Wolf, be found by the marks in the stone and the knowledge thereof.*

Some respected scholars denounced it all as a hoax, but the legend of Lord Abrecan's not-quite death encouraged others to believe that the 'treasure of the Holy Well' was the secret to eternal life, a bit like the Holy Grail. That attracted a handful of swivel-eyed, mystical types every year, alongside the more erudite. But Toby had noticed something about the marks, something he didn't think anyone else had.

He crossed to the broken arch of a Norman window. There, tucked below the embrasure, was one of the symbols that stood out to Toby as incongruous, and highly unlikely to be a simple banker mark: a perfect circle, with a dot in the centre. Or so most people, including himself, had thought. In alchemical notation it was the symbol for the sun, and therefore for gold; a few outliers thought it was an eye, and tried to follow its gaze towards a geographic location.

Toby thought something else altogether. He suspected the central dot might in fact be frost damage. And when the sun caught it from a very particular angle another detail emerged: two tiny cuts either side of the circle, angled to meet on its surface, like an arrow pointing the direction in which the circle might turn. Or like a mouth – the mouth of a serpent, eating its own tail. Uroboros. A symbol of eternity that had made its way from prehistoric Egypt into the alchemical writings of the ancient Greeks at Alexandria. A representation of endless return . . .

He straightened up in surprise at the sight of Theodora Hallewell, carrying three glasses and a jug on a silver tray, and staring at him as though dumbstruck. He cleared his throat to say hello but somehow ended up not saying it. Her hair was loose, held back at the sides with combs that looked ready to fall out, and she wore a striped grey dress, boned and buttoned, with long skirts. They saw much less of each other these days, and he was always surprised by the changes in her. The elongation of her face and steeper contours of her cheekbones; the way her dress no longer clad the body of a child. Only her demeanour – one of lively animation coupled with an air of diffidence and perpetual distraction – was unchanged.

'I've brought lemonade for Uncle Crudge and Mr LeRoy,' she said, when the moment for a polite greeting had passed. 'But you can have some too, if you'd like?'

'Capital,' Toby said, a word that Crudge often used, though *he* didn't sound like a pompous idiot when he did.

The trace of a smile touched Theo's lips. She looked down at the tray she was holding. Each glass had a splash of water in the bottom. 'There was ice, but it's melted.'

Toby was suddenly intensely thirsty. 'That's a pity. But never mind.'

Again, he sounded like a bad actor.

Theo waited a moment longer, then carried on towards Crudge's dig. Toby watched her, annoyed. Since when did he act like an idiot in front of her? Since when did his every word and gesture feel so ill-fitting? Perhaps it had to do with his leaving, and the feeling that he ought to say something to her before he did. Though he had no idea why, really. Or what.

Squaring his shoulders, Toby turned to follow her.

Kit appeared, as if by magic, to claim one of the glasses of lemonade. He gulped it down, then belched and yelled, 'Sorry, thank you!' as he cantered away again, making Theo laugh.

Usually, Toby hated it when people laughed at his brother, but Theo only did it because Kit delighted her.

'And for you?' she said to Toby, refilling the glass.

'Wasn't the third glass supposed to be for you?'

'I had some before I brought it up. And I haven't been running about as much as Kit.'

'Now, Toby,' Crudge said. 'I hear you will be attending Theodora's midsummer rite this evening?'

Theo put the jug down with a clatter, then had to steady the tray.

Toby became very aware of her penetrating gaze.

'Gosh – I'd clean forgotten about it,' he lied. 'I've got an awful lot of reading to do tomorrow, so perhaps—'

'But you *must*,' Theo burst out, patches of pink appearing on her cheeks. 'It . . . it won't work without enough of us there.'

'It won't work because, well – because it obviously *won't*,' Toby heard himself say, as though vaguely amused by the idea.

Theo stared in silence at the bricks in Crudge's trench.

'I'm surprised to find you such a sceptic, young man,' Crudge said reprovingly. 'Especially given the contents of your notebook.'

'That's different,' Toby said, sounding like a child again. 'But you're right – I ought to keep an open mind.'

'Then, you'll come?'

'Yes. I'm sure I said so, already.'

Theo relaxed, visibly, then her eyes found Kit, who was scaling one of the broken stacks. It was only about eight feet high, so safe enough.

'Will Kit come?' she said.

'If he wakes up, I'll have to bring him.'

'Well. Perhaps he won't wake,' she said, though not unkindly.

Toby knew she was fond of Kit, but his brother was unsuited to certain things, and being quiet for a secret – and entirely pointless – ritual was likely to be one of them.

On cue, Kit hallooed them from the top of the stack, waving his arms. The sun caught in the creases of his gleeful smile, and Toby realised he was going to have trouble getting him to come home – particularly while Theo was there to show off to. Glee could quickly turn to frustration, to anguish and tears. But Theo was watching Kit with a smile of her own, and returned his wave, and a strange pang made Toby look away. He felt exposed, and when he looked at Crudge for distraction he found the old man watching him shrewdly. As though seeing something Toby was unaware of.

'I ought to get him down, I suppose,' he said, to cover himself.

'Oh, why?' Theo said. 'Look how much fun he's having.'

But at that moment Kit went too close to the edge and teetered, arms wheeling.

'*That's* why,' Toby said, far more sternly than he'd meant to.

Her face fell.

He spent the next ten minutes trying to persuade Kit to come down. Crudge, to whom Kit would sometimes listen, soon came to join him at the foot of the stack, and shortly after that Toby saw Theo making her way back to the house, her hair swinging behind her. With her gone, Kit was finally swayed by the prospect of bread and jam, and slithered back down to earth.

Crudge touched Toby's arm as he turned to go. 'Please, be kind to her, young Toby,' he said.

'Kind? To whom?'

Crudge smiled tolerantly. 'Soon you'll be off to university, and then to wherever else your ambitions take you. But this . . .' He gestured at the castle, the hills, the house. 'This is all she has. It isn't easy to be left behind.'

Chapter Three

Theo abandoned the tray on a sideboard in the entrance hall, and stopped to stare into the big, speckled mirror. What did he see? What had he *seen*? The need to know was excruciating. The sun had picked out the freckles over her nose, but, washed silver by the mirror, she hardly recognised herself. The truth was, if she didn't know how Toby saw her, then she wasn't sure how to see herself.

They'd held hands, when they were little – a simple, tacit acknowledgement that here was a kindred spirit. They'd talked about being grown up, and getting married. It had been as natural as breathing. When had that ended? Had it been when Toby turned twelve, and the vicar took over his schooling, and spoke of *going up*? Toby had always been the serious sort, his straight brows and dark eyes giving him a hawkish look. Since early childhood Theo had loved his sudden, beautiful smiles; she'd loved being the cause of them. Then one day, around the time he suddenly shot up in height, they'd been walking along the lane hand in hand when one of the farmers came by on his cob. Toby had shaken her off abruptly. She remembered it clearly – the sting of it, and not understanding why.

She took a deep breath, stopped staring in the mirror, and went to her father's study. Behind its heavy oak door lay a realm of shadows and silence. Seymour Hallewell had been a scholar of sorts, a man of many hobbies, who'd written undistinguished books on all sorts of subjects.

From a long time ago, before her sister's death, Theo remembered a man with gentle hands, who'd carried her on his shoulders and sung songs about dragons. He'd been more or less a recluse by the end, rarely venturing from his room. When he'd died in there, it was two days before anyone realised. The room had simply been abandoned after that; Diana never went in, so the servants hardly bothered to.

But Theo knew where to find a few useful things: in a pile of pennies and pencil shavings on Seymour's desk sat a silver half-crown. She snatched it up. One of the things she needed for her ritual to summon Lord Abrecan. To summon him, and Toby Meriwether.

It won't work, Toby had said, *because it obviously won't.* How sharply that had cut. How painful it was to feel the edges of her make-believe world, her own sense of wonder, threatening to crumble.

Dinner that night was a painful affair. Theo's mother seated her far enough from Uncle Crudge for it to be impossible to join in his conversation with the Misses Hart – a pair of bookish spinster sisters – and close enough to Dr and Mrs Mackie for it to be obvious that she couldn't think of a single thing to say to them. What could one politely enquire of a person who was dying, and of the person having to watch her do so? Their end of the table was a stiff, uncomfortable place, where the sip of asparagus soup and the crunch of radish salad made Theo's skin crawl. She longed to escape.

Later on and finally free, Theo loitered by the display case in the corner of the long hall. In it were the best of the Hallewell artefacts unearthed over the years. There were several coins, and a medieval gold posy ring shaped as clasped hands, with a French inscription meaning: *My Heart is With You.* A lot of musket balls, arrowheads, shoe buckles and clay pipes; and the top half of a lead statuette of a woman, a devotional piece dating from the eleventh century.

Hearing murmured voices, Theo glanced up to see Crudge and Arnaud heading upstairs to their rooms. They did not see her. Her uncle carried a newspaper under his arm, and when he reached for the banister, he dropped it. Arnaud picked it up and tucked it under his own arm, and the way he looked at Crudge had none of his usual *froideur*. His smile was unguarded, and charming, and Theo felt oddly relieved. Crudge rested an affectionate hand on Arnaud's shoulder as they climbed.

When they'd gone, Theo returned to the display case. The coin she needed was more or less the same size as the half-crown in her pocket, and even though it'd been buried for more than a thousand years, the silver was still bright. The words *Elfred Rex* were clear. King Alfred the Great, who ruled the kingdom of Wessex at the end of the ninth century – when Abrecan was at Hallewell. It was very rare, and very valuable, and Abrecan *must* have touched it . . . The thought awed Theo far more than any saint's finger bone or scrap of nun's robe.

The key to the display case was kept in the safe in Diana's dressing room. Theo knew the combination, and had fetched it while her mother gossiped with the ladies in the small drawing room. Ears straining, she switched the coins. The half-crown looked far too big and smooth once it was in position on the purple baize, but it was better than leaving an empty space. Abrecan's coin seemed to heat the skin of her palm. She held it tight as she relocked the case, used her cuff to buff her fingerprints from the glass, and ran.

She replaced the key and darted into her sister's room. It was where she went when she needed to calm down, gather herself, be invisible again. Nobody would find her there; no one ever came in. It was another forgotten, untouched place. A teal eiderdown was still on the bed; brushes and combs still on the dresser; fine woollen undergarments still packed in the trunk with sachets of camphor and lavender. The air so very still.

Their part of the house was as populous with the dead as it was with the living.

Theo stared at the single, small thumbprint on the mirror of the dressing table set, remembering the horrible day she'd been made to pose with Amy's lolling head on her shoulder, holding her cold, lifeless hand for the camera. Amy hadn't smelled right. All Theo had wanted was to push her away and run, and being forbidden to do so had brought her close to hysterics. She hadn't seen her mother's face for months – just its vague shape behind a heavy black veil. Theo had felt like she was trapped, alone, at the bottom of a well. It had only got better when Uncle Crudge came to stay, and they'd sat together in the library, poring over the atlas for hours at a time. *Ah, Mesopotamia! Fascinating, fascinating. King Sargon and the Akkadian Empire, and the Hanging Gardens of Babylon! All gone now, sad to say, and nobody's quite sure where they were. But perhaps we'll go there one day and find them, shall we, Theo? You and I?*

Her mother had loved her better before Amy died. And Theo dreaded her own tendency to panic, which she was sure had begun around that time. Perhaps the day of the photograph.

Once her heart had slowed she went back to her own room, undressed partly and lay in bed, in case her mother looked in. Now that the time had almost come, the nerves were like a creature worming in her stomach. She felt sick, and there was no danger of her falling asleep. Much later, she heard the soft creak of floorboards as the servants finally retired, and after that was silence. Theo watched the hands of the clock tick slowly towards twelve.

Toby couldn't risk shutting his eyes; there was no hope of waking again if he drifted off. He sat on the floor of their room once Kit was asleep, silently revising the events and place names in the Bible.

When the stories began to muddle with fatigue, he switched to conjugating irregular Latin verbs, because the drill was so familiar to him, and proceeded in so orderly a fashion, that mere tiredness couldn't derail it. *Sum, es, est, eram, eras* . . . He'd got all the way down to the third person pluperfect when he was interrupted by Kit, turning and mumbling in his sleep.

It was hot and stuffy in their room. Toby got to his feet in silence, and almost changed his mind at that point. The pale shape of his still-made bed was a siren's call to his weary brain. But he couldn't help thinking about earlier, at the castle, and the way he'd snapped at Theo because he'd annoyed himself by being gauche. *Be kind to her*. For some reason, the implication that he'd been *un*kind was intolerable. Because, now he came to think about it, Toby couldn't remember a single occasion when Theo Hallewell had said or done an unkind thing. Was that even possible? Surely everybody lost their patience or good humour at times? But perhaps it was easier not to when your life was one of carefree idleness and make-believe.

He sighed. He'd said he would go, so go he must. And he'd probably be home again by a quarter past twelve, when it turned out everyone else had slept through it. He'd been staring at Kit's half-visible form in the darkness, and jumped when his brother spoke.

''S'it morning, Toby?'

'Hush, no, it's not morning.'

There was a chance Kit would slip back into sleep as easily as he'd slipped out of it. Instead, he sat up.

'Where are you going?'

'Nowhere. Downstairs, to study.'

'But it's night-time.'

'Just . . . go back to sleep, Kit. Everything's fine.'

'You're going somewhere!'

'Shh! Be quiet, or you'll wake Mum and Dad.'

'Can I come?'

Toby hesitated. If he insisted, Kit might stay put. Or he might try to follow Toby in secret, which would end in chaos. He cursed inwardly as Kit hurried over to him, bringing the warm, feral smell of sleep.

'Please can I come?'

Toby sighed again. The castle in darkness was no place for Kit; but then, it was no place for any of them, really, and it would be so much easier not to have to insist. 'Can you be quiet?' he said.

Kit danced from foot to foot.

'I mean it, Kit! Not just normal-quiet, but *extra* quiet. Otherwise it will all be spoiled.'

Kit nodded, but Toby could feel his excitement. He wavered a moment longer, doubting it all again. 'Come on, then,' he said, then waited while his brother struggled into his trousers and shirt, moving with excruciating slowness and exaggerated care.

The muffled bell of St Mary's in West End struck the half hour.

'Quiet but faster, Kit,' Toby whispered.

Once they were on the path, they hardly needed a lamp. The moon had risen bright white, and it outlined the familiar route with silvery shadows. The night air was soft on the skin, and Toby smelled the warm stone of the castle before they reached it. His fatigue and misgivings faded. There *was* something thrilling about being there in the middle of the night – as though the place *were* actually liminal, or had some magic about it. A dry corner of his mind observed that these were hardly the thoughts of a rational man of letters, but they were no less seductive for that.

He heard whispers ahead, quiet female voices from the old chapel, and Kit made an excited little sound when he recognised Theo. He ran ahead into the soft glow of candlelight. Toby walked more slowly, and saw Theo, Missy Cartwright and a girl he didn't recognise, sitting on the rabbit-shorn grass in the circle of light thrown by four tiny wicks in glass dishes. Theo was dressed in white, her hair hanging down over her shoulders. She'd arranged a few things in front of her – a silver cup, a curl of paper – and when she looked up at him her face reflected such simple, uncomplicated happiness that Toby couldn't help but feel its echo.

She was beautiful, he realised. Like something an artist would paint. Perhaps it was the moonlight, and her luminous expression. Or perhaps she'd always looked like that.

'Hello,' he said, blood racing, as he stepped into the golden glow.

Theo had brought water from the spring in her silver christening cup. On a scrap of paper she'd written out her invocation – with a little help from Tennyson. Abrecan's coin was in her hand, and the ruins of the castle stood sentinel all around, black against the gauzy sky. The night was mild, still, and completely perfect. Despite the tingling all over her, Theo was suddenly completely calm. It actually didn't matter if the ritual worked, or what happened next: Toby was there, and looked happy to be. He would *see* her again, and realise.

'Do sit,' she said. 'Quickly, it's almost midnight.'

Kit bobbed and fidgeted; undone, as always, by Missy's prettiness. He dropped abruptly to his knees in front of the girl she'd brought with her, and held out one long, knobbly hand.

'Who are you?'

The girl tucked her knees in tighter. 'Joanna Bowen.'

These were the first words Theo had heard her speak. She had mistrustful eyes and a scattering of acne on her cheeks.

'I told her to come with me if she wanted to meet two handsome young men tonight,' Missy said, dipping her eyelashes at Kit, who flushed, and fidgeted even more. Theo wished Missy didn't have to act that way with men. And it was *all* men – she'd even seen her look through her lashes at Uncle Crudge, though he'd gallantly ignored it.

Joanna didn't take Kit's hand, and he glanced at Toby for guidance.

Missy elbowed Joanna none too gently. 'Well, shake his hand then, don't be rude.'

The girl did as she was told, not meeting Kit's eye, and Missy flicked her skirt aside.

'Come and sit here, Kit.' She patted the turf beside her. 'You'll protect me if the ghost of Lord Abrecan does come, won't you?'

'Yes. Yes, I will.'

'It's not his ghost, it's really *him*,' Theo said. 'In spirit form.'

'I'm not sure I understand the difference,' Toby said.

He sat down near to Theo, and caused the very air to change.

'A ghost is just a shadow, left by a person who's died,' Theo explained. 'Abrecan didn't die. He took spirit form. It's different.'

'If you say so.' Toby was teasing, but only gently.

'Well, it won't work if we don't at least *try* to believe in it,' she said.

'Look, Kit,' Missy said, reaching behind and tapping her fingernails on an earthenware jar. 'Lugged it all the way up the hill, I did. Pat Meecham's finest.'

Theo had wanted to object to the cider, but it was hard to argue with Missy.

'A good drop to wassail the ghosts,' Missy said. 'Abrecan'll be thirsty after such a long kip.'

'And what did Pat Meecham want for it?' Joanna asked, a bit cattily.

'To meet me at the castle to drink it, tomorrow night.' Missy grinned, deepening the dimple in her chin. 'He's in for a lonely time of it, mind.'

'You *are* wicked, Missy Cartwright.' Joanna's disapproval teetered into admiration.

'Kit is not to have any of that,' Toby said sternly.

'Why not? Why can't I?' Kit said, and Missy laughed.

'He's not your captain, is he?'

'He's not my captain!' Kit agreed, too loudly.

'Shh! Kit, shh,' Theo soothed him, and to her slight surprise he *was* soothed. 'It's time to begin.'

She tried to sound serious and authoritative. She'd rehearsed this in her head so many times that it now seemed to be happening to somebody else, with her merely watching. The candles fluttered in a wisp of breeze. Toby's shadow reached right up to the sky.

'We're sitting in the ancient chapel where Lord Abrecan's feet once trod.' She held up the silver coin. 'This coin carries the touch of his hand from a thousand years ago, when he was flesh and blood like us.'

Next was her christening cup. 'In this cup is water from the holy well, which rises and sinks endlessly, and into which his mortal remains fell, and were taken utterly. The water became his blood, and his blood became the water.'

A flutter of worry, only now, that there was something a tiny bit blasphemous about that part. She held up the scrap of paper.

'Here are the words to call him forward. For it is said that his spirit will visit this place at midnight each Midsummer's Night. By these things – the coin, the water, and the words – we shall see him. Or . . . hear him,' she amended, to widen the net. 'As the clock strikes, I will say the words, and bring all these things together, and then . . .'

She wasn't sure how to finish, but St Mary's first chime came to her rescue.

Theo looked around the little circle, as gratified as she was terrified that they were all paying attention, all waiting. Missy drew her shawl in tighter; Joanna looked anxious. Kit was wide-eyed, and Toby . . . she couldn't look at Toby.

'"*Nothing will die.*"' Theo owed Tennyson for this first part. '"*All things will change Through eternity.*"'

Next came her own composition. She spoke it slowly, rhythmically, like a poem.

'Nothing will die, but return, unceasingly. Then let the circle turn, and all the countless years of men. Come back again.'

It had taken her weeks to get right. Not too fey, or too ghoulish. Resonant, she thought – portentous. She reached out and let the scrap of paper catch fire on a candle, momentarily blinded by the flare.

'Come back again.'

She dropped the coin into the cup, and then the burning paper, which hissed and went dark.

'Come back again.'

She timed the third repetition with the final toll of the church bell, and afterwards came a moment of perfect stillness, suspended in time.

A pale shape rushed over their heads, silent and quick. Missy squawked and Kit scrambled to his feet, giggling nervously. Joanna cowered, hiding her face in her hands; Theo gasped, glancing incredulously at Toby. Then the owl, which had alighted in one of the trees near the spring, whistled mournfully for its mate.

'Ha!' Missy burst out, and Toby laughed softly.

'Abrecan the owl!' Kit said, and Missy laughed, which made Kit grow several inches taller. 'Abrecan the owl!' he said again.

'Abrecan the bloody owl!' Missy said. 'I thought he was supposed to be a wolf?'

'Well . . .' Theo thought fast, and at that moment a dog began to howl, down in the village.

The song was picked up and echoed by another, out on one of the farms. And then another. Their plaintive voices sent shivers over the skin. Theo met Toby's eye, and they shared a smile.

'I wonder what's set them off?' he said.

Theo felt a flicker of hope – the possibility that he understood. Understood *her*. Understood that if there wasn't to be magic and stories in the world, then the world would be desolate indeed. And if *he* wasn't to be in her world, then she would be desolate too. That when she'd said *come back again*, she'd meant him as much as Abrecan.

'Black magic! That's what this is!' Joanna quailed, backing away.

'It's an owl and some dogs barking at the moon, you lummox,' Missy said. 'Kit's supposed to be the idiot round here, not you.'

'You heard her! That was a *spell*. You never said anything about casting *spells*!'

'My brother is not an idiot,' Toby said.

'Is he not?' Missy smirked.

Kit was swooping around them haphazardly, arms wide, hooting like an owl.

'I want to go home!' Joanna said.

'Christ's sake.' Missy rolled her eyes and sloshed the cider towards her. 'A gulp of this'll sort you out.'

Toby stood as well, and Theo found herself the only one still on the grass. She reached into the cup to fish out the coin, and her fingers came up flecked with ash. The spell, if such it had been, was thoroughly broken.

She got up and took Joanna's hands.

'Please don't be frightened. It was only a game. It was just for fun; you're perfectly safe.'

And whether it was because Theo was from the big house, or because she was older or because she was gentle, Joanna relaxed.

'I never meant to call you a witch or nothing,' she said. 'Beggin' your pardon, miss.'

'Let's not worry about it.'

'Nice try though,' Missy said. 'I nearly died when that owl went over.'

She wrenched the cork out of the cider bottle with her teeth, took a long swig and then offered it to Theo.

Wanting to recapture her momentary elation, Theo took it. The cider was warm and sour.

'Who's to say it didn't work?' she said. 'Who's to say that wasn't him, watching from behind the owl's eyes? And making the dogs howl?'

Missy laughed again. 'I think maybe *you're* a bit of an idiot, an' all.'

She looked past Theo to where Toby was standing awkwardly, hands in his pockets, keeping an eye on Kit. She pushed Theo towards him.

'He looks thirsty,' she whispered.

Theo took the cider over to him, but Toby shook his head.

'I have to study tomorrow.'

'Like every day, I suppose,' Theo said. 'Every day until you go.'

'And every day after that.'

Toby's eyes had the fierceness she found both mesmerising and alarming. But she held his gaze, having looked away a thousand times before.

'Then, a toast to your studies, present and future, far from Hallewell,' she said.

The words seemed to strike home. Toby softened, took a drink, and grimaced. 'That's horrible.'

'Isn't it?'

There was a pause. Kit was still swooping. 'Look at me, Missy!' he called. 'Missy!'

'Hush, Kit!' Toby said. 'Quieter – unless you want Constable Pryce to come.'

Kit's arms fell to his sides. He'd been frightened of the policeman ever since he'd been put in manacles and taken halfway to West End in the back of a cart, after the incident with the horse manure.

'Poor Kit,' Theo said. 'He's so full of joy, isn't he? And every day is long, and full of moments to rob him of it.'

'Sadly, his joy can quickly take him into danger.'

'I know. I meant no criticism. No one was ever a better, more devoted brother than you, Toby.'

'Well.' Toby looked away. 'Perhaps a better brother would stay at home to help him.'

The darkness made her bold: 'Kit will understand, you know. Your going. He won't like it, but he'll understand, and he'll know that . . . that you'll come back to visit. You will, won't you?'

'Of course. When I can.'

'Then . . . not very often?'

'It can't be. *If* I get my place, I'll only be able to travel down between terms. And that will seem an age, to Kit.'

'Perhaps not only to him.'

Theo wasn't sure if he'd heard her. His eyes sought his brother again, indistinct in the smudged light. They heard his nervous laughter, and Missy's drawl.

'You'll get your place,' Theo said. 'I know you will.'

'Missy isn't a good friend for you, Theo,' Toby said abruptly.

'What do you mean?'

'The way she is. The way she . . . flirts . . .'

Theo stiffened. 'It's not her fault. It's just . . . how she was raised. She's truly good, at heart.'

'That may be so, but others won't see it. She already has a reputation; you must know that.'

'Then . . . perhaps my being her friend will help to steer her, and keep her safe.'

'Perhaps. But . . . she could taint *you* with that reputation, Theo. It's different for women.'

'Is it?' Theo hated his lofty tone, though she couldn't have explained why, exactly. 'Now you sound like the vicar.'

'Then I apologise wholeheartedly.'

Theo didn't want to talk about Missy, not with Toby. Not when he'd noticed Missy's flirting; not when he'd described the two of them as *women*, in that discriminate way. Had he learned about it in one of the many books he'd read? The topic of *women*? She sought to change the subject.

'What was that symbol you were looking at earlier? When I brought the lemonade?'

'I'll show you.'

Toby picked up one of the candles, shielding it with his hand as he led Theo beneath broken arches to the window with the circular mark.

'It's difficult to make out.' He moved the light around. 'Here – do you see?'

Theo bent closer. The flame picked out every eyelash and tiny brow hair, and the gleam along the inside of her lower lip. Her hair swung forward and brushed across his wrist, and he caught the scent of her breath – apples, from Missy's scrounged cider.

He swallowed. 'I think it's the snake who eats his own tail, Uroboros. It's the symbol of—'

'Eternity,' Theo whispered.

'Yes.'

Toby wondered how she knew about it. There were plenty of esoteric books in the library at Hallewell House, but he'd never imagined Theo would bother to read any of them.

'Endless return,' he said. 'I was reminded of it during your invocation.'

'What does it mean? Is it part of the riddle?'

'I don't know, yet. But I think it could be significant. An intimation of immortality.'

Theo didn't answer, and Toby heard how pompous he sounded, yet again. Saying what he had about women. He'd meant to sound wise and grown up, but Theo had recoiled and only then had he realised how it might feel to have your whole existence reduced like that. Theo was not *women*. She was female, but that hardly said everything about her. It hardly said anything about her at all.

He tried to follow the line of thought, unsure where it was heading, but it dwindled to a dead end. He was right about Missy Cartwright, though. Whether or not she was good-hearted, she would get herself into trouble one day. Only last week, he'd seen her stop to drink from one of the village pumps, and when she'd noticed Toby and Kit nearby, talking to the grocer's boy, she'd washed her face as well – splashing water on to her neck and blotting her cheeks with wet fingers. Opening the top buttons of her dress to let it run down over the flushed skin of her chest.

It had been a blatant display. Later that night, Toby had heard Kit whimpering in his bed as his hand worked frantically at his crotch. The vicar's dire warnings against the solitary vice – of spent life force, epilepsy and the inevitable descent into homosexual debauchery – made no impression whatsoever on Kit. But Toby didn't like to be reminded that although Kit's mind remained childlike, his body had all the usual male instincts. *Innocent*, Mr Crudge had called him, earlier that day. Toby wasn't sure how long Kit could stay that way.

'If anybody can figure it out, Toby, it's you,' Theo was saying, and it took him a second to realise she meant the Hallewell riddle rather than Kit's passage into manhood.

'It's quite rare for banker marks to include curves, or circles,' he said.

'Yes, Uncle Crudge told me. They're much harder to carve than straight lines.'

'Right. So, I think perhaps the more elaborate symbols, and the ones with curves and circles . . . perhaps *those* are something more than masons' marks. And to have a hope of gathering a meaning from any of them, I need to identify which is which.'

'You must find the right pieces of the puzzle before you can solve it.' She maintained her scrutiny of the snake symbol.

'Theo . . .'

Her grey eyes turned on him, a tiny candle flame reflected in each.

'Do you . . . do you know it?'

'What do you mean?' she said.

'The symbols. The riddle . . . the clues to the Hallewell treasure . . . Do you know the answer?'

'Of course not!' She moved back, eyes widening. 'You can't think that if *I'd* deciphered it, I wouldn't have told you?'

'No . . . I know you would. I just meant that . . . perhaps it's all a joke. A Hallewell joke.'

Theo stared at him. 'You don't think very much of us, do you?'

'No, I didn't mean that. I don't think badly of you at all, Theo.'

'But do you think of me at all?'

He didn't know how to reply. He pictured himself looking back from the lane on the way to West End, trying to spot the pale mote of her dress in the distance.

'It will be so strange when you've gone,' she said. 'Strange to know you've done what I so wish I might.' She glanced at the coin glinting in her palm. 'There's a green lane to the east of here – have you ever noticed it? It climbs over the hill, between two fields. Every time I see it, I get this terrific longing to explore it. I know it probably doesn't go anywhere very special, but that isn't the point. The point, I suppose, is not knowing *where* it goes. I wish my life could be like that.'

Toby had never before heard Theo say anything that resonated so closely with his own feelings.

'Never mind,' she said, closing her hand again. 'I don't blame you, that's all. I . . . I think it's wonderful, your going up to Durham. I'm sure you'll have such an exciting time, and forget all about the castle, and the puzzle.' She paused. 'And about me.'

Toby took her hand, which he hadn't done since they were children. The sight of her downcast dismayed him, when not ten minutes earlier she'd lit up the night. Slowly, almost painfully, understanding crept into him. He put his other hand up to her face, struck by the warmth of her skin. She turned her cheek into his touch in a way that made his muscles clench.

'I'll write,' he said, leaning closer. 'And I will come back.'

All he wanted to do then was kiss her. Her mouth, familiar but now utterly unknown as well, was inches from his. Her lips would be warm, and soft. Toby's hands started to tremble, and the blood rushed inexorably to his groin so that he didn't dare to move, however badly he wanted to.

'Missy, *look*!' Kit's voice echoed in the night.

Toby blinked. Then again, even louder: 'Missy! *Missy!* Look – I told you I could! I said I could do it!'

Clenching his teeth, Toby turned and hurried towards Kit's voice. Anger at the interruption, at his brother, flared and then died, leaving an aftertaste of shame.

Back in the main courtyard, he searched the darkness with mounting unease. He saw the two girls, arm in arm, by the ruined west wall. Their shadows danced, confusing him, but a second later Toby spotted his brother. He froze. Theo came up behind him; she gasped and grabbed his sleeve, but Toby couldn't move. The blood hammered in his ears.

Theo ran across the courtyard with her heart in her mouth. Kit had climbed a section of the ruined wall. Far, far too high. Earlier that day he'd come close to falling. If he did so now, there was no hope of landing without injury.

'Missy!' Kit waved his arms. 'Missy! Look – I said I could do it!'

'Kit!' Theo called. 'Do come down, at once!'

He didn't seem to hear, or even to notice her. She barrelled into Missy and Joanna, who were arm in arm, heads together, whispering.

'Watch out, clumsy ox,' Missy said.

'Missy! *Missy!*' Kit called.

Missy took another swig of cider and walked away.

'Kit, listen to me – *please* climb down!' Theo cried. 'It isn't safe – the walls aren't solid!'

Kit made a small, desperate sound, his eyes fixed on Missy.

'Missy! Help me!' Theo hissed.

Missy looked at her blearily. 'What do you expect *me* to do? He got himself up there . . .'

Theo stared at her, aghast.

Missy rolled her eyes. 'If we all go off over that way,' – she pointed – 'he's bound to come down and follow us, isn't he?' She linked arms with Joanna again. 'Come on. You'll see.'

Theo couldn't. On the other side of the courtyard, Toby was still rooted to the spot. *Why* didn't he come and help?

'Kit, *please* come down!' she begged. 'Stop waving your arms about – you'll fall!'

But Kit only had eyes for Missy, now holding hands with Joanna and spinning her around. His mouth worked in silent anguish. Theo's heart was pummelling. She glanced over her shoulder again and saw, with a burst of relief, that Toby was finally on his way over, sprinting through the darkness. It would be unimaginably awful if Kit got hurt. Toby would never forgive her – she would never forgive herself. Her throat was too dry to swallow.

A small chunk of masonry hit the grass behind her.

She looked up, and saw Kit crouching, searching. She thought for a moment that he was readying himself to climb down, and that his feet had dislodged the loose piece of stone. But then he straightened again.

'Missy, *look at me*!' he cried, raising his hand.

'Don't—' Theo began.

The stone described a smooth arc against the stars. Theo lost sight of it before it landed, but she heard the quiet, muffled percussion when it did.

Missy sank to the ground as though her strings had been cut.

◆ ◆ ◆

Toby reached the foot of the wall with his skull buzzing. After the horribly long time he'd been paralysed his mind was now clear, and focused completely on getting his brother to safety. Kit had stopped flailing his arms, at least. He gathered himself.

'Christopher Meriwether.' He used the tone that said he wasn't playing any more, that the fun was definitely over, that Kit had overstepped the mark. 'Come down from there, *immediately*.'

With a whimper, Kit looked down at him and then back at the trio of girls, two of them fussing over the third. He wobbled, and Toby held his breath. If Kit stepped backwards for balance, he would fall. Toby's knees ached. He felt sick, and fought to keep the right tone of voice.

'Now you listen to me, Kit – look at *me*, not at them. Good. Crouch down and take hold of the wall with your hands.' Toby paused, swallowing hard. 'Can you remember the way you climbed up?'

Kit nodded.

'All right. You're going to climb back down the same way. Exactly the same way, but in reverse. Start right now, Kit.'

His brother finally did as he was told. Crouching, finding handholds, and inching his way back down the jagged edge of the wall. Toby watched in silence, willing him to safety. A toehold disintegrated into a shower of gravel; Kit slithered perilously, hands clawing for purchase.

Toby's heart stopped.

Kicking and scrabbling, Kit found his grip, and was soon only twenty feet up, instead of thirty or more. Then ten. Then he was jumping down, and landing on the turf.

Toby shut his eyes for a moment, weak with relief. 'Come along, Kit,' he said. 'We're going home. Right now.'

Kit ignored him and headed towards the girls, tiptoeing, his hands flexing at his sides. Why *was* Missy still on the ground? She couldn't be that drunk. With the sick feeling returning, Toby followed.

She seemed to have fainted. Then he saw blood on her face, dribbling from a cut on her forehead. Her cheeks were pale, her eyes closed. Theo's eyes were glassy with shock, and horror emptied Toby's head of everything else.

'Wh . . . what on earth—?'

Then Missy opened her eyes and swore. Gingerly, she sat up. A second rush of heavenly relief for Toby, again with anger at its heels.

Missy touched her head and winced. Her eyes found Kit. 'What did you do *that* for?'

Theo's relief was palpable. 'Missy, are you all right?'

'What happened?' Toby snapped.

'He threw a rock at her!' Joanna said. She looked around for it, and pointed. 'That one there!'

'No.' Kit shook his head. 'No, I . . . I never . . .'

Toby's reply was automatic. 'He would never do that.'

'But he did! Look – look at the cut on her head!'

Kit whimpered.

Joanna reached out her fingers but Missy jerked her head back. 'I don't need you poking it,' she said, then did exactly that herself. '*Ow!*'

'But are you all right?' Theo said.

'I suppose I am, since I'm sitting here telling you so. It'd better not leave a scar or I'll have your guts, Kit Meriwether.'

'I expect there are a lot of loose stones up there. It was an accident, that's all.' Toby heard how strangled the dishonesty made him sound. He remembered the time Kit had got on to the church roof and thrown clumps of moss at the verger.

'It weren't no accident!' Joanna cried.

Missy raised her arms. 'Help me up, then.'

Theo and Joanna grabbed a hand each and hauled.

Missy staggered a bit once she was on her feet. 'I've gone all giddy.'

'I'm sure you'll be all right,' Theo said.

'Well,' Toby said. He felt oddly breathless. 'I need to get Kit home.'

He almost left it there, but Missy was dabbing at her head and shooting daggers at Kit, who was pacing like a cornered animal, in obvious distress.

'Did you tell him to climb that wall?' Toby snapped at her.

'It's not *my* fault your brother's such a ninny,' Missy said. 'Who knows why he does anything?'

'*Missy!*' Theo gasped.

'Kit? Did Missy tell you to climb the wall?' Toby asked.

Kit shook his head. 'She said . . . she said, "Bet you can't."'

Toby rounded on Missy, outrage swelling in his chest. 'There! He could have been *killed*, you stupid girl! Come on, Kit. We're going home.'

'Wait!' Theo sounded stricken. 'Toby, don't go – please.'

'Why in heaven's name not? If Kit had fallen . . . if he'd fallen—' Toby couldn't finish the sentence. 'Just . . . take Missy back. Go to bed, all of you, and let that be an end to it.'

'But . . . they'll ask how she hit her head. They're bound to ask!'

Toby hesitated. 'And what will you tell them?'

Theo glanced back at Missy and Joanna.

'We can't say what really happened, can we? Any of us. We can't say that we were here.'

'You'd be in trouble, I suppose? The pair of you?' Toby said.

Joanna looked terrified; Missy's frown deepened.

'I think we all would,' Theo whispered.

'You'll have to invent some story,' he said. 'Just say that you fell on the stairs at the cottage. Can you do that, at least?'

Toby marched down the castle mound with Kit at his side, tripping now and then on tussocks of grass. The night had no glamour any more, no hint of the ethereal. It was all too real – the danger Kit had been in, the terrible clarity of what might have happened. Toby held himself tight inside. It had *not* happened. And he would never, ever put his brother in such danger again.

'Kit, you mustn't tell anyone about *any* of this,' he whispered hoarsely. 'Do you understand? Not anyone.'

Kit nodded, his face a mask of unhappiness. 'Toby, did I hurt her?'

'No,' Toby said at once.

'I never meant to!'

'You didn't,' Toby said tersely. 'It was her fault.'

'S-sorry, Toby.'

'Don't say sorry, you didn't do anything wrong.'

But once they'd sneaked back inside and he'd got Kit into bed, and much later, when Kit had gone to sleep, Toby lay awake. He needed to rest, to be able to study in the morning, but the scene kept playing in his mind. Seeing Kit from across the courtyard, so close to disaster, and being helpless, rooted to the spot. Then the blood on Missy's forehead. When he finally dozed off it was only to fight himself awake again, gasping, having relived in a dream the worst part: Kit about to fall, and himself powerless to do a single thing about it.

Chapter Four

Theo hated secrets. This one had been easy enough to keep, so far, since nobody had asked her anything about it. Nobody *knew* to ask her anything, except Uncle Crudge. Still, her knees wobbled as she climbed the narrow stairs of the Cottage Home to visit Missy. She had pins and needles in her hands, and knew that the nerves were all to do with what *might* have happened. The thought of it was following her around like a shadow.

St Agnes's occupied an ancient, thatched longhouse with five bedrooms all in a row. Only the matron, Mrs Vine, had one to herself, and up to twenty girls lived there at any one time, being saved from themselves – from poverty, temptation, dissolution and all the rest. Besides Mrs Vine, who was appointed and paid by the Ladies' Association, they had a local woman who came to teach them the basics of cookery. The girls did everything else themselves, as well as laundry and sewing for third parties. A bed became free when a girl turned fifteen, as long as she was going to a position, or a marriage. Otherwise, she could stay on till eighteen, at which point she'd be out on her ear, albeit with a good reference.

The mattress on which Missy was sitting would sleep four, top to toe, come night-time. The whitewashed walls were flaking; the floor was bare but for a rag rug either side of the bed. There were no personal possessions anywhere, just a shared jug and bowl on the washstand, and hooks along one wall for clothes.

With a bandage around her head, holding a wad of gauze above her left temple, Missy looked cross. 'Thank God you're here,' she said. 'Who ever knew being idle was so bloody *dull*? Why didn't you come yesterday?'

'Well, I . . . I thought it might be better to let news of your fall get about, first. It might have looked suspicious if I'd come the very next day.'

'Oh yes.' Missy smirked. 'My *fall*.'

Theo faltered. 'You *have* been telling people that you simply fell on the stairs, haven't you? If my mother knew that we . . . that I'd—'

Missy waved her quiet. 'Yes, yes, don't bleat.'

'How are you? Is it very painful?'

'Not so bad,' Missy said. 'Better than yesterday. If I move about too much it aches. I was up and at my chores this morning but it made me so giddy I got seasick, so matron sent me to lie down.' She sighed. 'Every working hour I dream about resting, and now I'm resting, turns out I'd far rather be up and doing. Ma always said I was contrary.'

There were no chairs, so Theo perched on the edge of the mattress and reached for her friend's hand. 'Oh, Missy, why on earth did you goad Kit that way?'

'I didn't *goad* him, I only said I didn't think he could do it.'

'But you know that's the same thing!'

Missy pulled her hand away grumpily. 'It wasn't my fault. The cider got me all silly . . . I didn't know what he was up to! In any case, *I'm* the one with a lump on the head, not him.' She brightened. 'But never mind that. Tell me what you and Toby said to each other – or better still, what you *did*.' Missy grinned. 'Did he promise anything? Is there an *understanding*?'

Theo could still feel his hand holding hers, and touching the side of her face. She could still see his eyes, burning into hers. But then he'd been so angry at the end; as angry with her as with Missy. 'He said he'd write to me,' she said, hoping it still stood.

Missy's face fell. 'Is that it?'

'But that's a lot, Missy! It means I'll still hear from him. That he'll . . . miss me. He won't forget about me.'

'But he didn't kiss you?'

'I thought . . . I think he was going to.' She gazed up at the wonky ceiling beams. 'He held my hand, and my face – like this – and he looked at me like . . . Oh, I don't know how to describe it!'

'Then what?'

'Well . . . then we heard Kit shouting, and Toby ran to see what was up.'

'Oh. Pity. So, what'll you do now?'

'What do you mean?'

Missy rolled her eyes. 'Well, he doesn't go up north for months, does he? You'll see him before that, won't you? Before all this very important letter-writing starts?'

Theo nodded.

'Maybe a few more midnight trysts?'

'Missy!'

'What is it you upper-types do, then?'

Theo had no idea. In truth, she hadn't thought past getting to talk to him by himself. Getting him to notice her again. Now, having done that – at least, she thought she had – *What next?* was daunting. She was saved from having to answer by the creak of footsteps on the stairs, and a knock at the door.

Missy pulled a haughty face and did her best impression of a lady. 'Come.'

The door opened and a man ducked beneath the jamb. He had a head of thick, light-brown curls, and straightened up with a smile for each of them. Theo recognised him – the physician who'd been called out to Hallewell House the winter before, to see one of the guests.

'Well, now,' he said. 'I know that you are Theodora Hallewell – how do you do? So, you must be Melissa Cartwright.'

He held out his hand and Missy shook it, looking a little undone. Theo went blank for a moment, but then remembered his name.

'Dr Anscombe. It's nice to see you again.'

'Is it? Oh, good.' A smile crinkled the corners of his eyes. 'I often think – in my line of work – that I must be the very *last* person people wish to see.'

The doctor set his bag down on the floor.

'Missy,' Missy said quietly. 'Everyone calls me Missy.'

'Very well, then.'

She looked astonished. 'Matron never went and called you?'

'She most certainly did, and she was quite right to.'

'But I'm right as rain, really. It only hurts if I poke it, or bend over.'

'Head injuries can be unpredictable.'

Dr Anscombe undid his cuffs and turned them up.

'Should I . . . leave?' Theo asked.

Missy nodded, but the doctor spoke over her. 'There's no need, Miss Hallewell. I'm sure it does Missy good to have a friend standing by.' He turned back to the patient. 'Now, if you wouldn't mind angling your face towards the window – yes, I know it's bright. I'm going to cover your eyes one at a time, but please keep both of them open, so I may see the effect of the light upon your pupils.'

Missy did as she was told, following the doctor's every move with none of her customary archness.

'Very good. Now, to the wound itself.'

He sat down on the edge of the bed, and began to unfasten Missy's bandage.

'Are you dizzy? Mrs Vine said you'd been feeling sick? And is it hurting less now than before, or more? A tumble on the stairs, wasn't it?'

'That's right,' Missy said, her big eyes fixed on his.

'They are so very narrow and twisting in these old cottages, it's hardly surprising.'

Missy winced as the gauze fell away. The doctor held her head steady and peered at the wound, and Theo craned forwards. In truth, there wasn't much to see. A graze with a cut at its centre, that started at the top edge of her forehead and disappeared into her hair. It didn't look very deep, though it had bled enough at the time, and the whole area had swollen into a greenish egg. Theo stared at it and began to feel sick herself.

'It has been well cleaned,' the doctor observed.

'Matron did it,' Missy said. 'And she was none too gentle.'

'And were you actually unconscious for any length of time?'

'Well . . . one of the other girls came when she heard me fall – Joanna. She says it was only for about a minute. Not even that.'

'Any loss of consciousness could be serious, Missy. However, I suspect it is a common enough concussion, and nothing more.'

'Oh.'

'But, pay attention now, because this is very important: if you begin to feel any worse you must either call me again, or come to see me at the hospital in Shaftesbury – I am the in-house surgeon there. If the nausea continues, or your eyes become sensitive to the light, or you feel dizzy or very sleepy. All right?'

'Yes, Doctor.'

Now Missy found her smile again, and that artful dip of her eyelashes.

'In fact,' he went on, 'perhaps I should see you again in any case. In two or three days' time, just to check that your symptoms have abated and there is no infection. We should be able to leave the dressing off at that point, but I'll redo it for now.' He thought for a moment. 'Yes. I will ask Mrs Vine to excuse you on Saturday. How's that?'

'All right.' Missy beamed. 'Thank you, Doctor.'

'I could ask Mama if Peterson can take you in the dog cart,' Theo said.

'That would be most kind, Miss Hallewell,' Dr Anscombe said. 'Far better for Missy not to have to walk – it must be ten miles, there and back again.'

He refastened the dressing, and his cuffs, and took his leave. Missy waited until they heard the front door thump behind him before sighing extravagantly.

'Holy Jesus and all the flaming saints!' she swore. 'Did you ever see a more *beautiful* man?'

Theo couldn't help but laugh. 'Did you think so?'

'Did you not?'

'Not especially.'

'You only have eyes for your Sir Lancelot, I suppose.' Missy laced her fingers across her lap in a determined sort of way. 'So much the better, as we shan't come to blows. For I shall marry that man or die in the attempt.'

'*Missy!* What if he already has a wife?'

'The world wouldn't be so cruel – but if he has, she'd better watch out!'

Their laughter soothed Theo's nerves.

'Dr Anscombe is very good,' she said. 'One of our guests had such a nasty turn last winter. He looked so bad I thought he must die, but Dr Anscombe knew exactly what the problem was, and what to do about it.'

'What was it?'

'A stone in his kidney. Dr Anscombe took it out, and the man was right as rain.'

'He cut into him to take it out? Into his *kidney*?' Missy was incredulous.

'Yes. Imagine that?'

'How . . . How on earth does a stone get into a kidney?'

'Well . . . I haven't the faintest idea. But there it was.'

'And however did the doctor get it out without killing him?'

'I don't know that either; but he did.'

They were both quiet as they tried to fathom such a thing.

'So, you are in safe hands.'

'I certainly hope to be.' Missy grinned. 'Come again before Saturday – before I go to Shaftesbury to call upon my intended. Just in case we wed at once, and I don't come back.'

'Mind you follow doctor's orders, now,' Theo said.

'No need to worry. I'd do *whatever* he told me.'

Theo didn't go home directly, but walked slowly through the village. She'd been avoiding Uncle Crudge because she knew he'd ask how the ritual had gone, and she hated to lie. People always saw straight through her, and she couldn't bear the shame of it. It was a cooler day. A breeze pestered at her hair, and turned the poplar leaves silver side up. With a start, she remembered that she still hadn't returned Abrecan's coin to the display case. It had gone clean out of her head. Her heart thumped disproportionately.

But it was *all right*, she repeated to herself. Everything was going to be all right.

Passing the Meriwethers' cottage, Theo saw Kit in the vegetable patch with a heap of newly dug weeds beside him. She toyed with the idea of calling in, but what on earth would she say? At that moment the door opened, and Mrs Meriwether came out with two doormats and a beater.

'Miss Hallewell!' she said. 'You nearly gave me a turn, standing there.'

'Sorry, Mrs Meriwether.'

There was a pause.

'Are you well? And your mother?'

'Oh, yes, thank you.' Theo's breath was too high in her chest. 'And you? All of you?'

'Well enough.' Mona's forehead creased. She draped the mats over the front wall and put her hands on her hips. 'Though something's worrying our Kit, and I wish I knew what.'

'Is he . . . ill?'

'Not that, exactly; but he's sorrowful, and full of nerves.' She shook her head. 'He won't tell me what the matter is, and Toby's none the wiser.'

The ground tilted beneath Theo's feet.

'Oh! Dear me, you've gone as white as a sheet!' Mona hurried over and took her by the arm. 'Come inside and sit down.'

'Oh, no, thank you. I'm perfectly—'

Mona lowered her voice. 'Is it the curse? I was forever fainting when I was your age. Something sweet is what you need – a scone with honey, perhaps?'

Theo was desperate to sit down and be mothered. But what if Toby came home? He would feel intruded upon. And what if Kit burst into tears at the sight of her?

As politely as she could, Theo pulled her arm away. 'You're quite right, Mrs Meriwether – I think I do need a lie-down. I'll carry on home and go up to my room. Thank you so much. You're very kind. Good day to you.'

She sensed Mona's gaze following her as she walked away.

Uncle Crudge waved, grinning his big, horsey grin, as she crossed their own lawn. 'Ahoy there, young Theo!'

Theo knew she'd cry if she stopped to talk to him, or if she even looked at him, so she hurried inside, and didn't need to see his face fall to hate herself for it.

Peterson had far too much to do, Diana declared, to be ferrying the likes of Missy Cartwright about the countryside.

'Doesn't matter,' Missy said, when Theo went down on Saturday to see her off. 'I'd walk *a hundred* miles to see Dr Anscombe again, never mind five.'

Her prettiness was unearthly in the silver-green of the morning. She'd taken off her bandage, and the scab on her head was hidden by a frilled cotton cap, worn beneath her straw hat. It made her look younger.

'But I should have liked to have gone with you, and saved you the walk,' Theo said. 'Are you sure you'll be all right? Is it still very painful?'

'Hardly at all – don't get in a stew. I'm following doctor's orders, aren't I? He'll soon sort me out. And the Charitable Ladies are paying, after all.' Missy thought about that for a second, then laughed. 'Paying for me to try my luck with that heavenly man – there's a turn-up!'

'Missy, really!'

'I might make a respectable marriage, Theo. Imagine that? *Me.*'

This time her smile was tentative, and betrayed the dreams she hid behind her brazen front.

'Of course you might.'

'Plenty of men like a simple country girl,' Missy said, as though hearing an unspoken doubt. 'A strong constitution and good hips for making lots of babies, that's what Ma used to say. Not all of them's after a dainty gentleman's daughter.'

'I'm sure you're right.'

'Wish me luck, then.'

They hugged goodbye. Missy's hair smelled of rosemary, her skin of spring water.

'How could he not fall in love with you?' Theo said.

Five days came and went after midsummer, and neither of the Meriwether boys went up to the castle. Kit stayed at home, and Toby stuck to his books. He looked for Theo everywhere, to be sure of avoiding her; half expecting to bump into her in the lane, or to find her waiting on a wall in the village, kicking her heels, like when she was little. His disappointment when no such meeting occurred weighed exactly the same as his relief.

On Sunday, as usual, they went to the service at St Mary's. Kit, who normally began to fidget after ten minutes, sat unnaturally still, with his head down. Anyone looking closely would've seen his lips muttering silently, and a small muscle in his cheek twitching intermittently. Toby saw it, and worried. He knew his mother did too.

'Toby, you *must* know what's up with him,' Mona said, on the walk back. 'He tells you everything.'

She chose her next words carefully.

'I know you're both of an age when . . . girls can . . . cause a distraction—'

'Mum—'

'There's nothing you can't say to me, Toby. I shan't be embarrassed.'

'But perhaps I might.'

‘Is that it, then? Is he lovesick?’ Mona shook her head. ‘I always knew it’d be hard for him when he got older. Not finding a sweetheart, never mind a wife.’

Toby clenched his teeth. The truth was, Kit couldn’t cope with unfairness. He hated secrets, too. *What did you do that for?* Missy had said. All the blame on Kit, just like that. As though he’d done it on purpose, out of mischief or malice. As though there were any malice in him whatsoever.

◆ ◆ ◆

On Sunday afternoon, Theo caught a lift into Shaftesbury with Cook, who was visiting her elderly aunt. Confusingly, the hospital was called the Westminster Memorial, after the Marquess of Westminster, a local bigwig whose widow had donated the land in his memory. It was a charitable institution, which charged fees only to those who were able to pay. Theo stood looking up at the place, clutching a paper bag and an entirely unnecessary shawl. It was two storeys high and not twenty years old, built of stone in the Gothic style. The central portico had an oriel window above it, and there were matching chimney stacks at either end of the roof. Inside were beds for eight patients and sixteen nurses, and a small operating theatre.

Theo shuddered at the thought of it. There were books on surgery and anatomy in the Hallewell library. Drawings of the sunken cheeks and eyes of cadavers, of gaping wounds, and saws biting into bone. But then, the operating theatre must be a place of wonders too. After all, it was where Dr Anscombe had retrieved the stone from that man’s kidney, saving him from an early grave.

A young nurse was at a desk. She’d been counting entries in a long, tabulated list, but hurried to her feet as Theo approached.

'Good morning, miss,' she said, in a soft local accent. 'How may I help you?'

'Good morning. I've come to visit Melissa Cartwright. She came in yesterday, from Hallewell?'

The nurse smiled. 'Oh, yes. I've met Melissa.'

'She was to be examined by Dr Anscombe, but then I heard she'd stayed overnight?'

'Yes, that's right. Only . . . well, it's not visiting hours, you see.'

'Oh.'

Theo was crestfallen. She hadn't thought of that.

The nurse chewed her lip. 'But since you're here . . . It's Matron's afternoon off, by lucky chance. And it can't do no harm, just for a minute.'

'Oh, thank you! I've brought some oranges.'

The nurse took her along a corridor to some double doors with little windows, through which Theo glimpsed a row of tidy beds, each occupied by a prone figure. Then the view was blocked by Dr Anscombe, who gazed at Theo in incomprehension for a second before recognising her.

'Miss Hallewell!'

'Oh, Doctor,' the nurse said, flustered. 'I know it's not visiting time, but I thought . . . The young miss has come all the way to see Melissa, and brought her some oranges. I didn't think it would—'

'I see.' The doctor looked troubled. 'Thank you, Nurse Webster.'

Wide-eyed, the nurse bobbed and left them.

'Miss Hallewell, I wonder if I might perhaps have a word?'

He took Theo's elbow and led her away from the door. Theo felt the strength of the hand that had guided her, and, standing close, noticed how tall he was.

'I'm afraid I can't allow you to see Missy just now,' he said. 'It's very important that she be allowed to rest.'

'But . . . isn't she better?'

'I've no wish to worry you unduly, but I do have some concerns. Her symptoms appear to be worsening by degrees, rather than improving. She complains of a headache again, and seems drowsy.'

Theo stiffened. 'Oh.'

'My fear is that the injury may not be as superficial as it first appeared.'

'She seemed so well . . .'

'Indeed. But the damage may be worse than we apprehend.'

'But she . . . she will be all right?'

'She will receive the best possible care, I assure you. Sometimes, with a head injury, an operation is required in order to . . . How best to explain it? Well, you saw, for example, that her head had swollen, at the point where she struck it?'

Theo nodded.

'Well, upon occasion, a swelling like that can occur on the *other* side of the wound as well. On the *inside* of the skull. And, if so, a small operation is needed to release the pressure. Do you see?'

'You mean a . . . trephining?'

Theo had seen it in one of the books: a hole cut into the skull. In those drawings, the patient was always strapped into a chair while the surgeon screwed down into his head. She swallowed. It had never seemed something that might happen in real life.

Dr Anscombe smiled. 'Exactly that, Miss Hallewell; you are better informed than many young women. I very much hope it won't come to that, of course. Time will tell.'

He squeezed her arm, just below the shoulder. 'I shall take the best possible care of her, I promise.'

'Thank you, Doctor,' Theo said.

But she couldn't help being frightened, when *her* plan had led to this.

'Go home, Miss Hallewell, and rest easy. Whatever happens, I will be here for Melissa. I give you my word.'

Theo handed over the bag of oranges, and let herself be reassured. As the doctor steered her gently back towards the foyer, she lost herself to wondering whether it was harder to fetch a stone from a kidney or to cut a small section from a skull.

'Shall I come again tomorrow?' she asked.

'Perhaps wait, and I will send word.'

'Do you promise?'

'Of course.' He smiled down at her. 'Have no fear.'

So, Theo dawdled back to the trap, via the sweetshop for a quarter pound of Unclaimed Babies, and waited while Cook finished her visit. The worrying thought of it all remained. She bit the head off one of the jelly sweets, then another, and another, until the sugar made her throat raw. But Dr Anscombe would look after Missy. She would soon be home, swaying her hips up the hill and making all the boys stare.

The four of them were sitting down to supper on Monday evening when they came for Kit. Mona had David's plate in one hand and a ladleful of rabbit stew in the other, and the sudden knock at the door startled them all. Unease flooded the room. Nobody came knocking in the evening, unless there was trouble. David struggled to rise.

'Don't get up, Dad,' Toby said. 'I'll see who it is.'

Kit stared at Toby, his mouth falling open. As though he knew.

Toby opened the door to find two men on the step. His muscles tightened, one by one. Calves, thighs, stomach, arms. His hands curled into fists.

'Constable Pryce,' he said stiffly. 'Good evening.'

Kit scraped his chair back, kicking the table as he surged to his feet.

'Steady now, Kit . . .' Mona said. 'Forgive him, Mr Pryce. He jumps at the mere mention of you, after all that to-do last year.'

'Evening, Toby. Mr and Mrs Meriwether.'

The policeman had the decency to look uncomfortable. But he also had the jutting chin and steady eyes of a man set upon doing what he had come to do.

'It's the lad I've come for, so let's not have another to-do. Let's keep it quiet and civilised, shall we?'

David looked perplexed. 'Which lad?'

'Christopher.'

'What do you mean?' Mona said.

She got up, putting herself between her son and the door. Toby stood rooted to the spot.

'Seems there was an incident. Up at the castle.'

'What incident?' Mona said. 'Kit's been at home with me these past six days or more . . . Whatever has happened, he can have had no part in it.'

'Yes, well, the incident took place on Monday night last, as I understand it. A girl was—'

'What has she said?' Toby blurted.

'What has who said?' David asked anxiously.

'Missy Cartwright,' Toby snapped. 'It wasn't Kit's fault. He never meant to harm her. She goaded him – deliberately.'

'Toby, what is this?' Mona's voice shook.

Kit kept whimpering, then put his head in his hands and shook it. Harder and harder, until he was hitting himself.

Mona grabbed at his hands. 'Stop, Kit! Oh, stop it!'

'It was *not* Kit's fault,' Toby said. 'You can't take him; you can't blame him. You can't believe a word she says.'

A black feeling like anger filled his head, but it might also have been fear.

'So you say,' Pryce said. 'But no one shall hear a word of hers again, whether to believe it or not.'

'*What?*' Mona said.

'The wound . . .' Toby's mouth was dry, his tongue sticky. 'The wound was not serious. A glancing blow . . .'

His head was bursting now, the pressure unbearable. Kit had started to cry.

'Wound?' Mona whispered. 'What wound?'

'Then you admit that you were there, and saw it happen?' Pryce said.

Toby was silent.

'Well,' the policeman said. 'The lass is dead of it.'

'Who? Who is dead?' David's words echoed in the silence.

'Melissa Cartwright. And I'm to take Christopher into Shaftesbury to be charged for her murder.'

Dr Anscombe appeared shortly after eleven on Tuesday morning. The guests were being refreshed out on the terrace, and Theo was sitting in almost companionable silence with Dr and Mrs Mackie. She certainly couldn't have managed a polite conversation with anybody else, not with Missy still at the hospital and no word since her Sunday visit. She just wanted it all to be over. Missy healed, Kit happy, all forgotten. Well, not *all*. Not Toby's almost-kiss.

She watched the doctor pushing his bicycle up the hill and knew it must be important news for him to have come all that way. She stood wordlessly as he reached the house, and turned to go indoors. *The injury may not be as superficial as it first appeared.* There was a weight at the centre of her chest.

Her mother joined them in the drawing room, in high dudgeon at having been circumvented.

'Have you a private appointment with my daughter, Dr Anscombe?' She used her iciest tone. 'Theo, are you ill?'

'Mrs Hallewell, please forgive me. I'm terribly sorry to call so abruptly. But I . . . I wanted to come in person, since I know your daughter to be a good friend of Miss Cartwright—'

'Who? Melissa Cartwright?' Diana made a face. 'I hardly think so. A most unsuitable girl.'

Theo wanted to tell her to shut up. To listen.

'What's happened, Doctor?' she asked, in barely a whisper. 'How is she?'

He hadn't told her not to worry. He hadn't smiled. Theo gripped her hands together so hard it hurt.

'I wanted to come in person . . .' he said again. 'I'm most terribly sorry to say that . . . that Miss Cartwright succumbed to her injury. Yesterday, in the afternoon.'

Diana stared. Theo didn't understand.

'Succumbed . . . ?'

'Yes. I'm most terribly sorry.'

'She's *died*?' Diana was incredulous. 'Of a trifling knock on the head?'

'What seems trifling can, in fact, be very serious . . . The brain may be injured, all out of sight, behind the smallest of wounds.'

Theo shook her head. She refused to allow it.

'No. She was fine! She . . . she *walked* the five miles to see you! Gladly! She was *fine*!' Her voice climbed in desperation.

'Theo! Lower your voice!'

'I will not! Missy was perfectly well – she *can't* have died!'

'I understand how difficult this must be.' Dr Anscombe looked wretched. 'And I quite agree, she did seem much recovered when she arrived at the hospital on Saturday. But soon afterwards she complained of an intense pain in her head, and of drowsiness, and disturbed vision. Her condition worsened. I suspected swelling within the skull, just as I told you, Miss Hallewell. Yesterday morning I performed an operation to relieve it, but . . . the fracture to her skull was more severe than it had appeared. The operation itself was a success, but she . . . she did not reawaken from the chloroform narcosis.' There was a moment of silence. 'She passed away at around three o'clock in the afternoon. It was very peaceful.'

'*Peaceful?*' Theo's mind got stuck on that one word. 'No. Missy wasn't *peaceful* – not ever!'

She sought a toehold of any kind – a way to escape what she was being told. The doctor was lying, or mistaken. He'd got the wrong person. Dark blotches crowded her vision, and Diana's voice was the last thing she heard.

'Theo!'

She lay for a long time in the quiet of her bedroom. The doctor had carried her up, apparently, and Theo's first thought was how envious Missy would be about that. Then came the realisation, and the shock, and a fresh storm of sobbing that made her head pound. She wouldn't eat, or drink, or talk to anyone. Her face had patterns of dried salt; her eyes were bloodshot. But when Uncle Crudge knocked gingerly at her door on Wednesday morning, she didn't send him away. He sat down beside her and she curled herself against him. Sadness made his face heavy.

'There, there, little one,' he said.

'It's all my fault, Uncle,' Theo said eventually.

'Nonsense. How can it be?'

'It was all my idea! I made us all meet up that night – I insisted they all come, when nobody truly wanted to.'

'But you might as well blame the weather, then, for not raining you off. Or the castle, for being made of stone.'

'And I left the others. I wanted to talk to Toby, so I . . . I made him come away. He *always* watches Kit! He *was* watching him, until *I* took him away. And now Missy is dead. Missy is *dead*!'

'And I'm sure young Toby will be castigating himself just as severely – and unfairly – as you are, for what has befallen his brother.'

Theo wiped her eyes. 'Why? What has happened to Kit?'

'Oh, my dear girl.' Crudge sighed. 'I didn't want to have to tell you, but I didn't want anybody else to, either.' He held her hand tightly. 'Christopher has been accused of causing Missy's death. Of her . . . murder. Worse than accused – he has been arrested, and taken to Shaftesbury.'

Theo was stunned. 'But – no!'

Only now did Theo realise that she'd told him what had actually happened at the castle, rather than the agreed lie. Only now did she realise that Crudge hadn't queried it. She stared at him, bewildered.

'Missy fell on the stairs, at St Agnes's,' she said weakly.

Crudge shook his head. 'There was another girl with you that night, I believe.'

'Joanna.' Dread and realisation tumbled through her. 'Joanna Bowen.'

'When Joanna heard that Missy had died she became quite hysterical, apparently. She told the matron all about the midsummer ritual, and that Christopher was responsible for Missy's injury. Constable Pryce was called at once. I'm so sorry, Theo. Forgive me for bringing you such terrible news.'

'But they can't *believe* that? They can't think he meant to hurt her? *Everybody* knows there's no more harm in Kit than in a . . . a . . . puppy!'

'I fear that both the matron and Constable Pryce *do* believe her. Other girls at the home heard them sneaking back in that night, you see, yet nobody heard any kind of disturbance on the stairs.'

'But to blame Kit on that one girl's say-so? They mustn't! Oh, Uncle! You have to help me – what should I do?'

But Crudge had no answers, only arms to hold her until, at length, she fell asleep.

'Black magic. Drunkenness. Midnight assignations. Shameless flirtation.'

Diana paced in front of the fireplace with her eyes fixed on the floor. The tendons of her neck were standing out as though invisible hands were wringing it. Theo was feeling something similar – a choking sensation that wouldn't let up. *It wasn't black magic. I wasn't drunk. It wasn't flirtation, it's love.* The effort of speaking was far too great.

'Theodora? Have you nothing to say?'

Her mother looked exhausted – her lips were dry and pallid.

'A daughter of this house, behaving like the worst kind of . . . *delinquent.* Half of the guests are leaving! And who can blame them? A *murder*? On our very doorstep – and my own daughter involved!' She raised a hand to her forehead. 'The papers will print it all. We are quite ruined.'

Theo had no words of comfort or defence to offer.

'So, you will remain silent,' Diana said. 'Very well, then. Perhaps it is not the worst way to proceed. You must make your testimony to the police, but that will be the end of it. You will not speak another word about this. I shall deny your involvement to any person who has the temerity to mention it, and God help you . . .' She glared at her daughter. 'God help you if you ever contradict me.'

Diana let the words hang.

'Do you hear me, Theo? Our only hope is for this to pass, and for our association with it to be forgotten.'

Theo heard her, but couldn't respond. She was overwhelmed just then by the thought of how frightened Kit must be, locked up in gaol without his family. She saw again the chunk of stone sailing through the air. It was blind ill luck that Missy had been struck; Kit would never have wanted to cause her harm. Somehow, the police – and everybody – must be made to see that.

Theo's head felt numb, and her heart tripped whenever she thought about it, whenever she remembered. At the end of the week she walked back to the hospital. Heavy legs, heavy steps; the journey took her two hours. She was light-headed by the time she arrived, and half stumbled into Dr Anscombe's arms.

He deposited her in a small room out of the way. White walls and a dark-red floor, acrid with the smells of carbolic and vinegar. A desk held neat stacks of paperwork; there were metal filing cabinets, and a safe in the wall.

The doctor's concern was clear. Gently, he lifted each of her drooping eyelids in turn.

'You are stricken, poor girl. Have there been other fainting fits?'

'Not since you first told me,' Theo said. 'But I wish I *would* faint, and wake to find it all a bad dream.'

He held her wrist with two fingers and counted against his watch.

'The events have put a terrible strain upon you. You must rest, and allow your mind to quieten.'

'I . . . I don't see how it ever can.'

He gave her a questioning look.

'It's all my fault, you see,' she said. '*I* brought us together at the castle that night.'

The doctor nodded. 'Yes. I have heard that the tale about a fall on the stairs was a lie.'

Theo flushed guiltily.

'It was a shock to hear that a young boy had been arrested.'

'Kit would never hurt a fly! It's all so *awful*, Dr Anscombe!'

'But he did throw a stone at her?'

'Not on purpose! Please, you must understand – Kit's . . . different. He's still like a child, on the inside.'

'You mean, he's an imbecile?'

'Not that, exactly. But he never meant to hurt Missy. I *saw* what happened!'

'Well, if you tell all this to the police, I'm sure the boy will be let off.'

'But Constable Pryce hates . . .'

The doctor waited, but she didn't have the heart to go on.

'I'm so dreadfully sorry that I couldn't save your friend, Miss Hallewell,' he said. 'I did everything I could, but . . . the brain is not like any other part of the body. Damage might occur to some part of the liver, or lung, and yet the rest be restored to sufficient function for the patient to continue in good health. But when damage occurs to the brain the outcome is always unpredictable, and usually far more grave. I . . . I wish I could have done better. Alas, I am not infallible.'

Tears blurred Theo's vision. 'But you are not to blame,' she said. 'I . . . I came to ask . . . may I please have a snip of Missy's hair? For a keepsake.'

Dr Anscombe crossed to the window and stared out for a moment. Then he said: 'I'm terribly sorry, but that won't be possible. Melissa is already with the undertaker.'

'Oh.' Theo wiped her wet face with her hands. 'But . . . if I went there and asked them, surely they would—'

'A mortuary is no place for a young girl.' He turned. 'I will go on your behalf, and make the request.'

'Thank you, Dr Anscombe,' Theo whispered.

She didn't want to see Missy. Not now. She remembered all too dreadfully having her photograph taken with Amy's empty shell. But she needed something of Missy; something to keep hold of, because otherwise she would vanish altogether, and that was unimaginable.

The doctor came and handed her his handkerchief.

'What a sorry thing it all is,' he murmured. 'What a dreadfully sorry thing.'

He took her home in a cab.

Later on, Theo eavesdropped on the servants. It was how she usually found things out. Peterson said that they would most likely move Kit from the police station in Shaftesbury to the gaol in Dorchester to await trial. *The poor mite*, Cook muttered. Theo didn't understand how it all worked – the different courts, the different judges. But she had read about Dorchester Prison: a maze of cold stone behind a grim edifice, populated with the poor, the brutal and the hopeless. It was a hanging prison. The gallows had been built in plain view of the inmates, to dismay them into repentance and obedience.

There wasn't much time, but Theo knew she *had* to prevent Kit being taken there. She had to find some way to halt this catastrophe.

Chapter Five

Toby stood at the front gate and watched his father make his slow, uneven way towards the school. The view was as beautiful as it had always been, the sky as blue, and yet the morning of Midsummer's Day, when Toby had walked to West End with his father, seemed to have happened in another lifetime, to an entirely different person.

They ought to spend the money saved for his education on a dog cart and pony, he thought. If it wasn't enough, Toby could get a job and make payments. He realised how selfish he'd been to aim so high; to gobble so much of the family's income when his father was in pain, every single day. And now, when they needed to travel to see Kit, they could not. Not easily. Toby might be able to borrow the vicar's bicycle from time to time, but neither of his parents could ride it. They just had to wait, and hope to catch a lift with a neighbour.

Kit was to appear in front of the magistrate at the county court in Shaftesbury Town Hall at the end of the week. If the charge of murder were upheld there, the case would be passed at once to be tried at the assize court, and that meant a move to Dorchester. The assize court, held twice a year by a visiting judge, would sit in September. So, Kit might be held in a prison thirty miles away for the next two months, and they certainly couldn't afford to take rooms to be nearer to him.

Toby tried to believe it wasn't going to happen. The magistrate would see Kit's goodness, his distress, and his . . . reduced capacity. Everyone in Hallewell would speak for his character. Then Kit would come home and they could focus on settling him down again. Toby didn't think about Durham University, or his degree, or his brilliant career. He focused on the present, and did his best to ignore the despair in the pit of his stomach.

Once his father was out of sight, Toby went back indoors.

Mona now went about her work with her mouth set. Scrubbing carrots and thumping her fist violently into bread dough; plucking the bird for dinner and sweeping the floors with short, angry strokes. She continued to cook for four people, as though she couldn't conceive of Kit's absence. Toby had taken over his brother's gardening duties, and was standing between the runner beans and the Brussels sprouts when, at eleven o'clock, the bell of St Mary's began to toll. Mona froze at the washing line, a wet vest gripped in her fist. Toby straightened, and their eyes met.

They were burying Missy Cartwright that morning.

Toby supposed Theo would be at the graveside, all watery-eyed and remorseful. His jaw clenched. When the tolling stopped, it took a while for them to resume their work. Wordlessly hoeing, and hanging things to dry. Toby was invaded by a memory of the dimple in Missy's chin, and of her lazy, mischievous smile. Dead and gone. His mind reared back from the impossibility of it all, and for a second his head was quite empty. Scoured out by shock.

Timothy Crudge called at teatime, dipping his grizzled head so as not to bash it on the door jamb. He was sombreness itself, from the stoop of his shoulders to his bloodhound eyes, and even that put Toby's back up. Crudge had always indulged Theo in everything. He'd known about the midsummer gathering, and could have put a stop to it as sheer tomfoolery. Toby didn't want to sit down and have *tea*, not with Mr Crudge, not with anybody. He glared down at his clasped hands as the kettle boiled and Mona brought out a plate of scones.

'And the . . . funeral?' David asked.

'It went as well as anything so sad may go. Her fellows from the girls' home were distraught; it was pitiful to see. And Reverend Nimrod forsook his usual fire and brimstone. He talked a great deal about rebirth, and the gathering in of little children.'

David was sceptical. 'Missy was almost fifteen, I think. Hardly a child.'

'Well,' Crudge said. 'Perhaps he chose to allow, at the end, that she'd been more sinned against than sinning, in her short life.'

'Ah.' Mona watched the old man with eyes full of shameless need.

'I received your letter,' Crudge said. 'And of course – of *course* I will speak for Christopher before the magistrate.'

David sagged, and Mona reached for Crudge's hand. 'You are very good. Thank you.'

'There's no need,' he said. 'The thought of any misfortune coming to that sweet boy . . .' He shook his head slowly. 'Missy's death was tragic, but nothing can be done for the poor girl now. To punish an innocent party would merely compound the tragedy with an outrage. I find myself at a loss to understand how the lad came to be accused in the first place, given that the blow was clearly accidental.'

'Is that what Theo says?' Toby broke in.

'Yes, naturally.' Crudge looked at him with mild perplexity. 'Toby, you cannot imagine *Theo* would ever think ill of your brother?'

Toby returned his gaze to his knotted fingers.

'Of course not,' Mona answered for him. 'It's just . . . if *only* she hadn't thought to bring them all together that night—'

'Don't blame her, Mrs Meriwether,' Crudge said. 'I beg of you, don't blame her. The poor girl is already tormenting herself.'

Tears started in Mona's eyes. 'Oh! I don't blame her. Not really. It's just so difficult not to think . . . it might have happened differently. Or better yet, not at all.'

'We are where we are,' David said quietly. 'It won't help to dwell on what might have been.'

'You're quite right,' Crudge said. 'And I have a proposal to make, which I hope might lessen your fears somewhat.'

Three pairs of Meriwether eyes lit upon the old man in hope, and he found the trace of a smile for them.

'There can be no guarantee of success, but . . . I have a brother – Augustus – whom I love dearly. I do not see him often. There were certain things . . . certain failings on my part, that drove a wedge—' He cleared his throat. 'In any case, though he is the younger of us by six years, he became the sole beneficiary of our parents' estate when I failed to marry by the age of forty. He pays me a perfectly adequate allowance, and from time to time has also been persuaded to fund specific expeditions, and other, more unforeseen expenses . . .'

Crudge looked around the table, and was met with incomprehension.

'Indeed. Let me speak plainly. My brother is a barrister at law, in London; rather an influential one. I wrote to him immediately upon Christopher's arrest. Now, whilst he is unable to come himself, he is sending a colleague from his chambers, by the name of Noah Cornwallis. A junior, but a keen and wholly competent one.' Crudge checked his pocket watch. 'He ought to be boarding the train at this very moment, in fact.'

'Your brother is sending this man . . . to what end?' David said.

'To advocate for Christopher before the magistrate, and at any subsequent trial – though, let us hope no such trial occurs. There will be no charge – Mr Cornwallis will act *pro bono*, in the pursuit of justice. It is all arranged.'

'Oh,' Mona said.

David looked lost. 'My dear Mr Crudge, that is *very* good news! How can we ever repay such generosity?'

Crudge shook his head emphatically. 'My wish is to do all I possibly can to help Christopher. There is to be no sense of indebtedness whatsoever.'

Mona wiped her eyes with her fingertips. 'Well, I shall feel indebted, whether you like it or not. You kind, *kind*, most generous man.' She gripped his hand again. 'Thank you.'

None of them could think of anything else to say, and after a while Mona brightened. She sat up taller, reached for the pot and poured the tea.

'Have a scone,' she told Crudge. 'Have all the scones!'

Once again, Theo walked in Missy's final footsteps to the hospital. And there, she halted at the last doorway Missy had ever walked through – flushed from the exercise, eager to see Dr Anscombe again. The building swam before her eyes. However much she owed it to Kit, the mission seemed hopeless, and she longed to go home. Her hat was squeezing her head, her armpits were wet, and she didn't know what she would say. She struggled to marshal her thoughts; it had been days since she'd managed to sleep or eat properly.

The doctor hadn't managed to get her a lock of Missy's hair. He'd confessed as much at the funeral. *Forgive me. It simply wasn't possible.* So, Missy was gone. Completely gone; underground, in darkness.

Woodenly, Theo carried on inside.

In the sudden cool of the foyer she was met by a woman with steel-grey hair, hard cheekbones and an immaculate uniform. 'Excuse me, do you have an appointment?'

Theo shook her head.

'Visiting hours are from two o'clock until three on Tuesday and Friday afternoons.'

The nurse put her hand on Theo's shoulder, turned her, and she was almost outside again before she found her voice.

'M . . . Melissa Cartwright,' she said. 'Please, I . . . I wanted to ask the doctor . . . The thing is, I know the young man who stands accused, you see, and he . . . I don't believe he killed her, not at all! But he stands accused and I need to . . . I need . . .'

She ran out of breath, and clutched at the woman's sleeve.

'Young lady, that's quite enough of that,' the nurse said. 'Calm down. I'll get you a glass of water.'

The nurse sat Theo on a hard chair in the same comfortless room she'd been in before, and fetched the water, appraising her carefully all the while. 'Now then,' she said. 'I am Sister Hendry, the matron here. And who might you be?'

'I'm Theodora Hallewell.'

'A friend of Melissa Cartwright's, you say? We were all saddened by her sudden decline.' Sister Hendry didn't blink, but the hardness in her face, which must have been habitual to have left such lines, softened fractionally.

'I waved Missy off, that morning,' Theo said. 'And she was quite well. So, it is very difficult . . . Dr Anscombe explained that she worsened soon after that, and that that's the way it may go, with injuries like hers, but . . . I wanted to ask . . . if . . . whether something else could have happened?'

'Something else?' Sister Hendry's tone flattened. 'Miss Hallewell, are you suggesting that some fault lies in the medical care she received here?'

Theo was dismayed by her frigid indignation. 'Oh, no! No, not at all—'

'Because, I assure you, she received the best *possible* care from the doctors and from my nurses.'

There was a soft knock at the door and Dr Anscombe appeared. His face lifted at seeing Theo, then fell again.

'Miss Hallewell! I wasn't expecting you. Are you well?'

'The lass was just asking whether there was more we could have done to save Melissa Cartwright,' Sister Hendry said.

'Oh, no – I didn't mean that at all! Only that . . . with Kit accused of murder . . .' Theo cast about desperately. 'Mr Brownlea out at Hilltop Farm – he dropped dead the year before last. He wasn't as young as Missy, but he wasn't an old man. Thirty, or thereabouts. Apoplexy, they said, when he'd been strong as an ox until that moment—'

'Melissa didn't suffer an apoplectic fit, she—'

'But *something* else? Something that might make them see . . . Kit was not to blame?'

Dr Anscombe and Sister Hendry exchanged a look, then the doctor pulled up a chair and sat down, steepling his fingers. In his face she saw the echo of her own anguish.

'My dear Miss Hallewell. I understand how difficult this is, but please believe that Melissa died of her head injury. There was no other cause. The pressure beneath her skull would have proved fatal within hours had I not attempted to relieve it. It . . . it may be that the strenuous walk from Hallewell caused the swelling within the skull to increase. We cannot know for sure.'

Theo's throat ached. 'Then, if Mama had let Peterson drive her after all—'

'Please, do not seek ways to castigate yourselves. Nobody could have foreseen the consequences.'

Theo stared at the doctor's hands. Broad, appealing hands, the nails clipped short and spotlessly clean, apart from a crescent of something dark beneath one little fingernail. Unsteadily, she got to her feet.

'Thank you,' she whispered miserably. 'Good day to you.'

She walked a short way from the hospital and sat on a bench beneath a chestnut tree.

Kit was in a cell at the police station on Bell Street, a short walk back into town. Theo knew if she went home again without even trying to see him she would hate herself even more, but at the same time she recoiled. She took Abrecan's coin from her pocket, studying its strange lettering as she turned it to the light. Nobody had noticed it was missing. How frightened she had been about taking it; how riddled with pointless nerves. She understood better, now, the scale of a thing worth worrying about. She got up, and forced her feet towards Bell Street.

The station was built of brick, with stone window dressings, and might have been somebody's unlovely home but for the large police lantern by the entrance. Constable Pryce would not be there – he lived in a tied cottage in West End – which was good, since he was unlikely to be any help. Theo would be seeing him later to give her sworn testimony, and was dreading it. So desperate to say the right thing that she wasn't sure what to say at all.

Some of Shaftesbury's ten constables – the unmarried ones – had rooms at the police station; the rest, along with the sergeant and superintendent, lived nearby with their wives. Theo was in luck that day: the young constable minding the front desk was a sympathetic sort.

'Be as quick as you can, miss,' he said. 'Sarge'll be back from his lunch before long. Only don't go riling the lad up, will you? He's been nice and quiet a good few hours now.'

He took Theo through to the cells at the back of the building, and there, through a hatch in a metal door, she saw Kit. He was lying on a mat on the concrete floor, with a covered bucket in the corner, a three-legged stool, a Bible, and nothing else. Thick layers of shiny paint caked the walls. The cell smelled of urine and sweat.

'Kit!' she called softly. 'It's Theo.'

At the sound of her voice he struggled up and came rushing to the door. He was pale, and the little muscles in his face that ticked when he was upset were all doing so. His gaze roamed constantly, never resting for more than a second.

'Have you come to take me home?' he asked.

'I wish I could, Kit,' she said. 'I do so wish I could! But not just yet.'

His mouth drooped. 'Soon though? Swear?'

'I swear.'

It was wrong to promise him, but perhaps there was a way. Somehow, she *had* to find a way.

'Did you bring any supper?' he asked. 'Did you bring a cake?'

'No. Sorry. I . . . I forgot.'

'It's cold in here. Mum said, "It's summer, son," but I said, "It's still cold, Mum, there on the floor."'

'I believe you. She'll bring you a blanket next time, I'm sure.'

'Dad said, "Jump about a bit, son." So I did that for a while.'

'Are the policemen being kind to you, Kit?'

'Constable Philpott brings me biscuits and tea.'

'Does he? That's nice. Was that Constable Philpott who came in with me just now?'

'Yes. But I can only sleep in the daytime because of the ghost.'

'The ghost?'

'Yes. The ghost. Constable Hickey says there's a ghost of a man who was hanged in here and he walks about at night-time, and if you fall asleep he steals your teeth.'

'Well, Constable Hickey is a rotten liar. There were no men hanged here, and there are no ghosts, and even if there were they couldn't steal your teeth because they've got no hands.'

'Oh.'

'That's the truth, Kit. It's perfectly safe to sleep at night.'

'Do you promise?'

'I promise.'

'All right then. That's good then. When can I go home?'

Theo swallowed. 'Soon, Kit.'

'Constable Hickey says I should confess my sins if I want to get into heaven when I'm dead, but I never meant to hurt Missy.'

'Of course you didn't! We all know that, and you mustn't listen to Constable Hickey – he sounds like a troublemaker to me.'

'Does he?'

'Most definitely.'

'All right. All right then, I won't.'

There was a whistle from the front, and Constable Philpott jerked his head for Theo to go. She forced her arm between the bars.

'Shake my hand, Kit,' she said desperately.

He did as he was told. His skin was gritty with dirt, and very cold. She pressed Abrecan's coin into his palm. 'I'm *so* sorry about all of this, Kit. You'll be home soon.'

Kit looked down at the coin, puzzled.

'Put it in your pocket, Kit – quickly! It's Lord Abrecan's coin. Remember? It will keep you safe – no ghosts or anything like that can bother you while you've got it.'

Relief washed over Kit's face. 'Lord Abrecan's magic coin?'

Theo felt weak. 'I'll come again soon,' she said.

And then wept all the way home.

◆ ◆ ◆

Toby had been dithering in the front garden, annoying himself. He wanted to talk to Timothy Crudge about the barrister at law, but didn't want to go anywhere near the big house. Then he saw Theo trudging up the hill. The gate clanged behind him as he set off towards her. She looked up and her expression changed, but not to the joyful welcome of Midsummer's Night. He knew he would never see that again, but didn't pause to decide how he felt about it.

Closer to, he spotted scraps of goosegrass caught on her skirt. He saw her red eyes and tear-streaked face, and the sad slump of her shoulders.

'I've been to Shaftesbury,' she said. 'To the hospital. I tried to find out if . . . if it could've been something other than the bump on Missy's head that . . . did it.'

Toby wondered why he hadn't thought of that. 'And?'

'They said no. I tried my best to make them think of something, but—'

'So, it's all on Kit,' Toby said.

Theo wiped her nose with a balled-up handkerchief. 'Dr Anscombe said she died of the blow to her head, and nothing else.'

'But perhaps we should ask a different doctor? Difficult, now she is buried. But I will speak to Mr Cornwallis.'

'Is that the lawyer Uncle Crudge has—?'

'Yes,' Toby said stiffly.

Somehow, he'd hoped that the arrangement might be kept private. But no. Of course not. The Meriwethers had become news.

'I . . . I went to see Kit, too,' Theo said.

'Good.'

Pressure was building in Toby's head again, making it hard to think.

'He was . . . fairly well,' she said. 'He was trying to sleep, because one of the officers had told him a ghost story that kept him awake all night – I talked him out of it, though. But he did keep asking when he could come home. Oh, Toby! It was awful!' She started crying again.

'It was awful for *you*?' The words pushed their way out; he couldn't hold them. 'If it hadn't been for your foolish game—'

Toby cut himself off.

Theo looked stricken. 'Then you *do* blame me. Uncle Crudge told me you would not, but of *course* you do!'

'If you hadn't asked me to explain that symbol . . . if you hadn't taken me away, so that I stopped watching him—'

'I *wish* I could undo it all! I'm so very, very sorry . . .' She hesitated, then said quietly: 'Constable Pryce is coming to take my deposition later this afternoon.'

'But you will stand witness for Kit, as well?'

'My mother does not wish . . .' Theo twisted uneasily. 'The guests . . . she fears—'

'The *guests*? What in God's name have the wretched *guests* to do with anything?'

Toby glared at her, feeling, for the first time in his life, that he wanted to hit someone. He jammed his hands into his pockets before that someone became Theo.

'People can always tell when I am lying, Toby,' she said.

'What?'

'*You* saw what happened, as well as I did.'

'I . . . it was dark,' he said.

The crucial moment at the castle was fragmented in his memory. He couldn't say for sure what he'd seen, or where he was looking when Missy was struck – he'd been running – but he'd already decided to say whatever was needed.

'I didn't see clearly, but it doesn't matter because I know my brother.'

'Yes, but . . . he . . .' Theo looked lost, and it sent a needle of fear through him.

'Kit *never* meant to harm her – or anyone,' he said. 'You know that.'

'Yes. Yes, I know.'

'Then you needn't lie. Even if . . . even if you do not describe *exactly* what happened, it won't be a lie.'

Theo wrapped her arms around herself. 'Toby—'

'For pity's sake, Theo! He needs your help. Do you think for one moment that if it had been *you* who'd climbed up there, *you* who'd . . . dropped that stone, you would have been arrested? And charged with murder? Of *course* not! But because Kit is different, and because he is lower class . . .' He took a breath. 'You're his friend, aren't you?'

'Of course I am. His and yours! But . . . I'm afraid. I'm afraid to make it worse.'

'Worse than him being accused like this? Worse than him being—?'

She flinched. 'Don't! Don't say it.'

'How afraid do you think Kit is? How afraid do you think my mother is?' Toby tried to swallow but his throat was too tight. 'We're *all* afraid. But you *must* help him! Constable Pryce has always been against him. And that girl, Joanna . . . she makes him sound like the devil incarnate!'

'She just doesn't know him . . . Perhaps I could explain, and convince her otherwise?'

'Do that. Make her see that what happened was *accidental.* My testimony will never be taken as impartial, but *yours* will count for a great deal, Theo.'

She nodded, her face pinched.

Toby turned away abruptly, so that he wouldn't be tempted to comfort her. To reach out and touch her.

That evening, the Meriwethers sat as usual on the narrow settees either side of the hearth. Every now and then ash sifted through the grate, David turned a page of the Thompson & Morgan seed catalogue, and Mona tutted quietly as she dropped a stitch. The cat sighed.

Toby flicked through his notebook of the castle's symbols. It soothed him, somehow, to move the pieces of the puzzle around with no real expectation of solving it. He'd identified another symbol linked to infinity: Uroboros again, this time in the form of a horizontal figure of eight. Endless life. He saw Theo's face in candlelight, bent close to study the circular symbol: each tiny golden eyelash, each small movement of her mouth. The way she'd turned her face into his hand. He blinked, his eyes dry as he forced himself back into the present.

They each did this – he'd seen it: stopped what they were doing to stare, carried away by a thought. He knew his parents' thoughts were all for Kit. His ought to be, too. He glanced across at them, guiltily. They were paler, slightly shrunken versions of themselves. His mother, in particular, had lost weight. His father looked up so Toby pressed his lips together, which was what they did now instead of smiling.

David cleared his throat softly. 'Toby, I know it's a difficult time, but you mustn't neglect your studies.'

Mona let her knitting rest in her lap.

'My *studies*?'

Behind his round spectacles, David's gaze was perfectly steady.

'I haven't seen you pick up a proper book since— I know you've prepared well, but you must keep what you've learned fresh in your mind.'

'Whatever for?' Toby said.

'The last thing you want, before matriculation, is to feel you must cram at the last minute – losing sleep and overfilling your head could be disastrous. A fall at the final hurdle.'

Toby was silent for a long moment. 'You . . . you can't imagine I'll be taking up my place? Not now?'

'Why ever not?'

'Because . . .' Toby clenched and unclenched his hands. 'Because of Kit. Because of what's happened. Because of my *stupidity*, and the trouble it has caused.'

Mona and David exchanged a look.

'You see?' Mona said.

'Yes,' David said. 'I do now.'

He leaned towards Toby, hands resting on his knees.

'Son, you *are* taking up your place at Durham. We simply will not have it that you don't.'

'But—'

'Kit may be home with us by the end of the week. We all hope so, and Mr Cornwallis is optimistic. Or, it may be many weeks before he is tried. After which . . .' David twitched, as though distracted by a passing shadow. 'After which time, he will come back to us, God willing.'

'He'll be so unsettled,' Toby said. 'He'll need—'

'He'll need us, yes; more than ever. He will have your mother and me, and, come the end of the Michaelmas term, he'll have you, too.'

'But the money . . .' Toby's voice was tremulous. 'The money would be far better spent on a pony and trap. To travel to Shaftesbury, and to the station, for Dorchester. And to school, Dad.'

'A pony and trap?' Now David did smile. 'You suggest we spend the money we have painstakingly saved for years – and which the vicar has painstakingly begged – on a pony and *trap*?'

'But I *can't* go!' Toby burst out. 'Not after what's happened – not after what I've done!'

David sighed. 'Toby. Was it wise to take your brother out at night? No. It was not. Was it wise to leave him in the care of Missy

Cartwright, who was scarcely a responsible person even without a drink of cider? No, son, it was not. But was it wicked? Of course not! You are eighteen, and cannot be expected to be wise at all times. There was simply no way you could have foreseen the events as they unfolded, and it would be foolish indeed to let them direct the course of *your* life, as well as Kit's.'

He held Toby's gaze.

'I wasn't there to prevent what happened that night, but I *am* here to prevent this. And prevent it I shall. You *will* take up your place at university.'

'Do listen to your father, Toby,' Mona said softly. 'I hate to part with you, but I shall hate it all the more if you *don't* go.'

'And if it goes to the assize? And if they . . . if they *hang* him?'

Toby could hardly speak: he *was* going to Durham after all, and was awash with such towering relief and such terrible guilt that it felt like they'd tear him in half.

'They will not hang him!' Mona said.

David said nothing, so she said it again.

'They will not.' She came and put her arm around Toby. 'Love, they'll let him come home. You'll see.'

Joanna Bowen backed away from Theo as though she'd come wielding a knife. Theo had gone around the side of St Agnes's rather than knocking at the door, hoping to avoid Mrs Vine, and had spotted Joanna out in the orchard.

'I know what I saw!' Joanna was shrill.

'But it was very dark, wasn't it?' Theo said. 'And Kit would never have meant to hurt *anybody*, let alone Missy. He's really very gentle. And he was always soft on Missy—'

'But he *did* hurt her, and I saw him do it! And Missy saw too – she said it, soon as she woke. "What did you do that for?" she said!'

'But it wasn't *murder*, Joanna, you must see that.'

'What do you call it, then? She died 'cause of what he did, so what do you call it? We should never have gone there – I wish I never had!' Her face writhed. 'It weren't right – none of it. That dark spell you made . . . Who's to say you didn't bring it all about? Who's to say you never meant for it to happen?'

'Missy was my best friend!'

'Well, maybe it went wrong then, your spell.'

'It wasn't a spell! It was just . . . I was just . . .'

'Oh! Mrs Vine – come and help me, I beg you! Miss Hallewell's come to silence me!'

Theo hurried away, cheeks flaming.

She gave her testimony to Constable Pryce at the walnut table in the small drawing room, with the manic *tick tick tick* of the carriage clock in her ears. Every part of her yearned to be elsewhere. To be invisible. In essence, Toby had told her to lie to prove a greater truth. *Even if you do not describe* exactly *what happened* . . . But Kit *had* thrown the stone, and she had seen him do it.

The policeman had reminded her that to be dishonest in a sworn testimony was a criminal offence. He was staring at her, her mother was staring at her, and Theo had sworn on the Holy Bible, so God was staring at her too. The pen, hovering over the empty sheet, shook visibly. But she owed it to Kit, and she owed it to Toby. What she owed Missy, she wasn't sure; but Missy would never have wanted Kit punished. She'd been moody, but never vindictive.

Theo tried not to think about standing witness at the courthouse. About telling this same lie again, to the magistrate. He would see through her. They would all see through her. They would doubt her and question her and she would crumble. She felt physically sick at the thought.

'Miss Hallewell?' Pryce said, when a minute had ticked by and she had not made a mark. 'Is there some problem?'

Theo shook her head. She clenched her teeth, and wrote:

> *It was very dark, and difficult to see clearly. With Melissa's encouragement, Christopher climbed high up on to one of the walls of the castle. He wanted Melissa's approval very much. He called and gestured to her, and I believe that the stone was dislodged accidentally by his foot. It was by ill luck that it struck Melissa. The castle walls are not stable and Christopher should not have climbed so high, nor should Melissa have urged him to. They were both in error but the wounding was wholly accidental. I have known Christopher all my life, and know him to be a gentle person with no violence in him.*

Pryce tapped the page when she'd finished. 'Don't forget to sign your name just here.'

'There, then.' Diana stood, hands clasped. 'Let that be an end to it.'

'I shall present myself at the courthouse on Friday,' Theo said, as steadily as she could.

'You will do no such—'

'I will present myself, and I will vouch for Kit,' Theo interrupted breathlessly, then risked a brief glance at her mother. She had never defied her before; it was unknown territory for both of them. Diana's face was unreadable.

'It is my right,' Theo added, though she did not know if that were true.

'In fact, given your tender age, Miss Hallewell, the decision rests with your mother,' Pryce said.

Again, Theo met her mother's eyes. They were stony.

'Please,' she said. 'I must speak for him. I have a duty.'

'Go to your room, Theodora,' Diana said. 'You are overwrought.'

Theo went to Amy's room instead, and passed several hours in solitude. She thought back through each moment of Midsummer's Day, noting every incident and decision – every chance she had missed to make things go differently – until there was a quiet knock at the door.

'Theo? Are you in there?'

Uncle Crudge came in on soft feet, tweaked his trousers and sat down next to her, on the floor beside the bed. He was all knees. Theo risked a look at him – his kind face, his eyes of washed-out blue. She rested her head on his shoulder.

'I've always been able to tell when you're leaving,' she said.

'Your lady mother feels, perhaps, that I have been a negative influence upon you.'

'Oh, sometimes I hate her!'

'Do not say so. Anger and hatred are not the same thing, and a hard person is simply an unhappy one. Try to remember that. And that you are all she has.'

'She's found out that you knew about midsummer beforehand, hasn't she?'

He nodded sadly.

'Can I come away with you? You promised to take me to Mesopotamia.'

'Did I?'

'Yes! After Amy died, you said you would.'

'Then I must make good on that, one day. But now is not the time, Theo.'

Theo put her arms around his neck and held tight, taking deep breaths of his linen and whiskers and Pears soap smell.

'This will never go away, will it?'

'No.' He sighed. 'But there *will be* an afterwards. There always is, however impossible it might seem. One has simply to hold on until then.'

'How do I hold on, Uncle?'

'Any way you can, my dear girl. Any way you can.'

Crudge patted her lightly, and she tried not to think about the time that was coming – the time between now, and afterwards.

Chapter Six

The magistrate took his place on an ornate chair beneath a wooden archway bearing the Shaftesbury coat of arms. The clerk had a desk to perch at, and the fifty-strong audience were seated on crowded pews. There was much scuffing of boots on floorboards, much murmuring; a smell of wax polish, hair and warm bodies. David and Mona sat with their arms linked, as a single entity, and Toby was to one side. He had never felt so alone, and was so tense he had to remind himself to breathe. The bailiff cleared his throat.

The prosecution had the first witness: Joanna Bowen, with her sharp-edged condemnation. Noah Cornwallis, in Kit's defence, demanded to know whether she had been looking up at the crucial moment; whether she had actually *seen* and not extrapolated, due to the darkness and the cider, Kit take aim and throw.

'As surely as I see you now,' Joanna said, narrowing her eyes.

They had Constable Pryce, who testified to several incidents of trespass and dangerous climbing, and to Kit's history of throwing things at people. How Kit had been arrested for assault only the year before, after pelting the constable with farmyard ordure. How he would have been prosecuted for causing bodily harm then, had Pryce himself not condescended to drop the charge.

Toby loathed the man, and fantasised about causing him some actual bodily harm.

There was also one of the farm boys, who described catching Kit in acts of degrading self-abuse on more than one occasion, including one time when he found Kit spying from behind a tree as he and Missy kissed.

The coroner described Missy's head injury and the effect of it in general terms. He stated that there was no way to tell from the injury whether the stone had been thrown by accident or design. Dr Anscombe, the surgeon-physician, described the treatment Missy had received at the Westminster Memorial with considerably less *sang froid*. He seemed almost distressed, in fact.

On Kit's side were his family – respectable, well liked. The school's headmaster, Mr Coniston, testified that despite Kit's behavioural abnormalities and low intellect, he had never once lashed out at another child in all his years of attempted schooling. Next stood Timothy Crudge, another respected gentleman, who had known the accused from birth; then – to the surprise and delight of the Meriwethers – the Reverend Anthony Nimrod, who spoke to the assembly as though the whole thing were an astonishing waste of time and public money.

'I hardly think lobbing a few horse-apples at a policeman makes the boy a murderer,' he said.

Toby could have kissed his sour old face.

Noah Cornwallis argued that, in the dark, Kit could have had no real hope or intention of actually hitting Missy – or anyone – with the stone, but the magistrate gave no quarter there.

'He was calling her name, Mr Cornwallis, and gesticulating for her attention. The intended target of his missile can scarcely be in any doubt.'

'Then let us bear in mind Christopher's reduced intellectual capacity, Your Worship; for it seems to me that he remains, in many ways, a child, and a child cannot be expected to fully understand—'

'A *child* does not spy upon a maiden out courting; nor is he driven so wild by the sight of her that he must abuse himself publicly in the most obscene manner.'

'What is this?' Toby whispered furiously to his father. 'He speaks as though he has decided already!'

David didn't reply. A sharp smell of sweat was coming off him.

But they had Theo. Cornwallis had warned them that in cases like this, where there was no material proof and only the testimony of witnesses to rely upon, it was impossible to be assured success. Only five people had been at the castle that night, and given that Toby's account had been all but dismissed, it came down to Theo's word against Joanna's. She would be the last to speak for Kit – the last of all the witnesses, in fact, because she was nowhere to be seen. Toby checked his watch – she'd known the session began at nine-thirty; it was now a quarter past ten. He caught Crudge's eye; the old man looked troubled, and gave a shake of his head, so Toby turned to stare at the panelled door through which Theo would walk. Through which she *must* walk.

Theo had hardly slept. When she'd dozed it was to lurch awake moments later, from chaotic dreams of onrushing disaster.

The night terrors receded once she was up and dressed, but fatigue made it hard to think clearly. Every time she told herself she would do what needed to be done – stand up and speak and not be unnerved – a hundred doubts argued loudly that she would fail. That she would be caught out in her lie, and that Kit would be punished for it in the worst possible way. She couldn't touch her breakfast, and wished with all her heart that Crudge could have come to fetch her and go with her to the Town Hall for courage.

'You look ill, Theo,' Diana said. 'And your hair is lank. Perhaps you shouldn't go after all.'

'I must go.'

With an air of perplexed indignation, her mother had eventually consented to her attending the hearing, on the condition that Theo kept to her room until then and spoke of it to no one. The remaining Hallewell guests were told that she was unwell. Theo had written to Crudge and the Meriwethers to expect her, and when Peterson drove her into Shaftesbury it would be on the pretext of her seeing a doctor.

'Well, you will make a pretty fool of yourself if you faint at the feet of the Justice of the Peace,' Diana said.

In the tilt of Diana's chin Theo saw that she half wanted that to happen. For Theo's unexpected wilfulness to end in humiliation. In response, her resolve stiffened a fraction. She met Diana's gaze more steadily. 'I won't faint.'

But on the drive into Shaftesbury, any such certainty deserted her again.

Her head thumped with the beat of her heart. The lane out of West End was blocked by a flock of sheep refusing to be moved from one field to another. Minutes ticked by while the collie dodged, the sheep milled and the shepherd cussed, and even as Theo fretted about it she felt a pathetic rush of hope that she might be saved from having to speak by something out of her control, some act of God. But the sheep cleared eventually, and Peterson geed up the pony.

'Never fear, Miss Hallewell,' he said. 'I shall get you there.'

And then they were outside the Town Hall, with its faux crenellations and its three-tiered portico, where the huge clock showed that the session had started almost an hour ago. Peterson handed her down and her head swooped. As though her mother had cursed her with prophecy, Theo was certain she *would* faint. They would find her out. Nausea swelled and sank in horrible waves.

'*It won't be a lie.*' She whispered Toby's words to herself as she forced her feet across the cobbles, into the building and up the stairs.

She gave her name and was admitted to the council chamber. The murmur of voices lowered. She could feel their eyes – so many eyes. All those people watching her, and judging. She didn't dare look at any of them. Noah Cornwallis took her elbow, guiding her to stand beside the clerk's desk and face the magistrate in his scarlet leather chair. She glanced at him, and where she'd expected to see long robes with ermine, and a face of owlish wisdom, she saw rolling chins beneath a battered wig, and small, dispassionate eyes.

'Please accept our apologies, Your Worship,' Cornwallis said. 'Miss Hallewell was unavoidably detained upon the journey.'

Theo had no memory of telling him that, if she even had.

'Indeed,' the magistrate grunted. 'Well, child, what have you to say?'

Theo looked up. She felt naked. She tried to speak but her throat was closed. The excruciating silence seemed to go on for hours. She knew Toby was there, in one of the seats behind her. His parents too, and Crudge. The vicar. Joanna Bowen. Her skin crawled; she longed to disappear.

The fat magistrate seemed to take pity on her. He shifted in his seat.

'Now, now, have no fear. I shan't bite you. Can you tell me what happened on the night in question? The night Melissa Cartwright received her injury?'

'It was an accident,' Theo managed to say.

'You'll have to speak up, child.'

'I . . . Kit . . .'

Her voice shook, and her head felt far too hot.

'He . . . Kit didn't mean to hurt anyone.'

'That is for me to decide, young lady. What I would like to hear from *you* is precisely what you saw, with your own eyes.'

Again, the silence stretched. 'I . . . I saw . . . Kit didn't . . .'

She cast back desperately, trying to recall the wording of her written testimony. But the memory bubbled up, inexorably, of Kit's hand finding a loose stone and casting it through the darkness. *Look at me, Missy!*

'It was dark, and I saw him . . . It wasn't his fault, and it . . . it's not a lie,' she stammered.

Any softness vanished from the magistrate.

'Well, thus far you have said precious little that may or may not be taken as a lie, Miss Hallewell. But I wonder why you should feel the need to make that assertion?'

He stared at her. The floor pitched and Theo staggered slightly for balance. It was happening: he *knew*. She could think of nothing beyond making her escape.

The magistrate addressed the prosecution lawyer. 'Mr Beavis. Perhaps you might have better luck with this witness?'

Cornwallis was at Theo's elbow again in an instant.

'Your Worship, forgive my interruption – it seems clear that Miss Hallewell is not well. I request she be excused, and taken outside for fresh air.'

'Indeed.' The magistrate waved a hand. 'In any case, I have heard enough.'

Theo's relief at being outside was so great that twenty minutes passed before she began to grasp how badly she had failed. They were on their way back to Hallewell before the Meriwethers had even emerged, and Crudge went with her this time.

'Did it finish?' she asked him, her voice dull with exhaustion. 'Or must I go back again?'

'It finished, dear one,' Crudge said.

'And . . . the outcome? Is Kit to be allowed home?'

She knew the answer before it came. Only the feeblest of hopes made her ask.

'No, Theo.' Crudge could not soften the news. 'The charge of murder stands. The case now passes up to the Court of Assize.'

◆ ◆ ◆

Toby had never walked up the path between the box hedges of Hallewell House before, nor across the terrace to the huge doorway. He felt watched, and unwelcome.

'Your card?' said the young manservant who answered his knock, once he'd explained that he wasn't a guest, nor expected. He swept his gaze over Toby's worn shoes and ill-fitting jacket, then shut the door in his face. Toby stiffened his spine. Anger churned as he waited.

'Mrs Hallewell is indisposed,' the servant said stonily, on his return.

He started to close the door again, but Toby stopped it with one hand.

'It was Miss Theodora Hallewell, rather, that I'd hoped to speak with,' he said. 'On an important matter.'

The servant rolled his eyes impatiently. 'Well, what do you think she'll say to that? Take a hint, fella.'

Toby beat his retreat with as much poise as he could, stopping halfway home to lean against a wall until he'd quietened the fury of unsaid things in his head.

Cornwallis had won one important victory at the Town Hall. Given Kit's handicap, the magistrate had been persuaded to let him await trail where he was, at the police station, rather than transferring him to Dorchester Prison. And they'd been allowed to take him extra blankets and food.

One day, Kit showed Toby the lucky charm Theo had given him: Abrecan's coin.

'She says no ghosts can come while I've got it. She says I'll be safe while I've got it.'

'That's a very special thing,' Toby said, desperate to believe she was right.

At home he struggled to focus, his attention wandering from his books, over and over, as he reminded himself to have faith in the judicial system. But then, as September began and the date of the trial was set, Noah Cornwallis discovered which judge would be sitting. And Toby saw the blood drain from his face.

Lord Humphrey Paxton-Nevis was an unyielding man by reputation; a man of almost no fellow feeling, known to come down particularly hard on men who'd harmed young women.

'Try not to worry,' the barrister said. 'Christopher is only just seventeen. He would not condemn one so young.'

But it sounded to Toby as though he were trying to convince himself as much as anyone else.

Theo came down with a fever soon after her encounter with the magistrate. Her sixteenth birthday came and went without notice. Cook made her endless cups of beef tea, and her mother dosed her with Eno's Fruit Salts and purgatives. The fatigue of hopelessness smothered her will to do anything, and she lay in bed for long hours, damp and silent, while the glorious summer ripened and faded. When Theo saw the first rusty blotches on the horse chestnut trees she wept, because everything was dying, and everything would.

Diana called Dr Anscombe. Theo had no idea of the day, or the date. The curtains were drawn in her room, and his face loomed towards her, lit by a candle. He looked so handsome, so calm and concerned. *Did you ever see such a beautiful man?*

'How do you do, Miss Hallewell?'

Theo stared at him and thought of Missy. Her instant infatuation; her sudden, tenuous hopes. 'Missy wanted to marry you,' she whispered. 'That's why she came to see you at the hospital. I don't think she'd have bothered, otherwise. And I wish she hadn't.'

He drew back a fraction. 'As do I, upon occasion. Yet, I still believe I was her best chance.'

Dr Anscombe laid his palm on Theo's forehead, then checked her pulse. His fingers were warm. He fetched a stethoscope from his bag. 'With your permission, I will listen to your heart?'

He moved the collar of her shift aside and reached in delicately. Theo awaited his verdict with disinterest. She knew her heart was still beating.

'I can't seem to understand it,' she murmured. 'That Missy's heart isn't beating any more. It was so strong – *she* was so strong. She seemed to be—'

'Even the strongest among us are but flesh and blood.' The doctor gave a small frown. 'You dwell upon it, Miss Hallewell?'

'I can't stop thinking about her. Or about Kit. Poor, poor Kit!'

'You are young to be faced with so much mortality,' he said softly.

He leaned away and began to coil his stethoscope, and Theo grabbed his arm. In the sudden, unexpected intimacy of the examination, she saw a chance.

'Could you not say it was something else that killed her? Oh, *please*, Dr Anscombe, I beg you . . . It would not be a lie; not if it told a bigger truth.'

'Whatever do you mean, Miss Hallewell?'

'Kit *never* meant to hurt her! The judge and the jury will not know that, but we do. *I* do! With all my heart.'

The doctor studied her again, face troubled.

'I heard about your collapse at the magistrate's hearing,' he said gently.

Theo shrank back.

'You were not able to say your piece. It must weigh heavily on you.'

'I failed him utterly.'

The doctor reached out and took her hand in both of his.

'You did not. The events . . . the evidence is clear. You must trust to the wheels of justice, and to God, that the outcome will be all that it should be. However painful that may be.'

Theo hesitated. He sounded so certain that she was tempted to believe him. A man such as he must understand it better.

'But they do not know Kit,' she said. 'How can they judge him fair?'

'They will judge him fairly *because* they do not know him. Please, Miss Hallewell . . . you have done all you can for him. All any of us can do, in any situation, is speak truthfully. You are not to blame.'

Theo lay back, the desperation to make him understand fading into hopelessness. A wave of despair was dragging her away, but then a sudden movement across the room caught her eye. She heard the familiar rustle of her mother's dress and realised, with a shock, that Diana had been there all along.

'Well, Dr Anscombe? What is wrong with her? Is she hysterical?'

'It is entirely possible to die from a broken heart, Mrs Hallewell, however unscientific that may sound.'

'You suggest that she may *die* of this?' Diana sounded more outraged than afraid.

'Forgive me, no, I am not making myself clear. But – perhaps we should discuss the matter elsewhere.'

He glanced back at Theo, then came a step closer and lowered his voice.

'Rest, Miss Hallewell. You are young, and very sensitive, but you *will* recover from this. Stay in bed a while longer, but not for too long. You need fresh air; a change of outlook. You must give your mind other things to do.'

Theo made some effort to do as he said, but it felt impossible.

'If this carries on, I shall have to send for the doctor again,' Diana said one day, pushing back the curtains and standing with her hands on her hips, a crisp silhouette against the sudden light – the long line and tight sleeves of her dress, her hair coiled on top of her head.

At length, she came to the bedside and laid a hand on Theo's clammy forehead. Their eyes met, and Theo thought she saw something stir beneath her mother's hard surface. Concern, perhaps even a momentary flash of unease. A far-off memory surfaced, of her mother at Amy's bedside as she lay dying. Of the frightening agony on Diana's face, and the way her eyes had skimmed over Theo, unseeing. Theo searched for that look of care again now: the chance of sympathy between them. But it had gone.

Diana gripped her arms tightly. 'This solves nothing, don't you see? You cannot simply . . . *give up*, and take to your bed when things are difficult. You're far too much like your father – you always have been. You may think yourself apart from this world, but you aren't. You're *here*, Theodora, and you have a role to fulfil. You're not a child any more; you can't just stamp your foot and say you don't want to play.'

Theo said nothing, so Diana got up and went back to the window.

'I need you to rally, and be well,' she said quietly, almost to herself. 'I need you to forget about what happened, and about Missy and that boy. Both of those boys.'

'I can't,' Theo said.

'You must. Or at least pretend to.'

Diana fetched an envelope from her pocket.

'This arrived for you. Once you've read it, have a bath and get dressed. We will see you on the terrace for afternoon tea.'

Theo studied the writing eagerly, but it wasn't from Toby, nor Crudge. When she opened it, a small velvet bag dropped on to the bedspread. It contained a gold pendant in the shape of a butterfly, the veins of its wings and the buds on its antennae picked out in perfect detail. She knew at once where she'd seen it before, and what it must mean.

3, Springfield Villas,
Church Lane,
Chobham,
Surrey

Wednesday, 18th September, 1889

Dear Miss Hallewell,
I trust this finds you well. I am sorry to be the bearer of sad news, but must inform you that my beloved wife, Rosalind, succumbed to her illness and passed from this world some weeks ago, on the twenty-fourth of August. Two months to the day since we met you, and visited the spring together. I apologise for not writing sooner but I have been indisposed. A death long foreseen is nevertheless a shock, when it comes to it.

As I am sure was apparent when we met, I set no store by magical theories or the supernatural, least of all as a way in which to restore health when medical science has failed. The 'mystical' waters of the Hallewell Spring did nothing to cure Rosalind of her disease. When one so young and so very good is taken, it is hard to believe in anything much at all, truth be told. Yet my wife did believe that the waters and the prayers might save her. I would say she was happier during our stay with you than at any other time this past year.

She went to the spring every day – did you know? To perform the ritual you taught to her. She took flowers as an offering, and a handkerchief, and even a small cup of wine. Though it seemed preposterous to me, she said it gave her hope – as though hope were a cure in itself, which, assuredly, it is not.

In any event, she bade me send you her pendant to show her gratitude, and to remind you that there is always hope of a reprieve. She was quite taken with you, Miss Hallewell. She liked the way you did not speak if you had nothing to say – so few people will not simply fill a silence with empty prattle, young women being particularly guilty of this. Around the time we left Hallewell we heard whispers of a tragedy, and Rosalind noticed a change in you. She was concerned for you. Have her necklace then, and if there has indeed been some unfortunate happening there, then I hope it will turn out well enough in due course. Rosalind would have hoped it too.

Yours et cetera,

Dr. Albert M. Mackie

P.S. It occurs to me that Rosalind died with no knowledge of the end being upon her. She went to sleep secure in the belief that she would wake again, and so wasn't in the least bit afraid. Perhaps that was what hope did for her, and perhaps I am merely angry and in despair to dismiss it so.

Theo read the letter three times. She tried to imagine Rosalind Mackie dead and cold and underground, just like Missy. She remembered the exaggerated heave of her ribs as she'd fought for breath, and pictured those ribs now stopped, still, forever. She could make no sense of it. She put her fingers between her teeth and bit down until it hurt. How could it ever be that her fingers would feel nothing? That they would be bloodless flesh, shrinking to the bone and then dropping off it, without the power of touch or movement?

But it had happened to Missy; it had happened to Rosalind.

Theo caught the stale smell of herself, and her sweaty nightdress. She got up, revolted, and rang down for Kitty to draw her a bath.

She didn't wait for more than two pails of hot water, so the bath was cool. It sent shivers all over her, stirring the blood in her veins. She looked down at her pale body, distorted beneath the surface – a woman's body. Narrow in the hips and small-breasted, but definitely a woman's, not a child's. She tried to grasp the meaning of it; she tried to understand. Missy had been granted fewer years than her; Rosalind Mackie only a handful more. Amy far, far fewer.

'"*The stream will cease to flow*",' she murmured, '"*The wind will cease to blow; The clouds will cease to fleet; The heart will cease to beat.*"' She sank to her chin, and her breath made tiny ripples on the water. It was one of the first poems she'd memorised, a mirroring partner to the one about endless life that she'd stolen for her midsummer invocation. As a child, she'd given no thought to the meaning of the words, only to the sound and rhythm of them. '"*We are call'd – we must go. Laid low, very low, In the dark we must lie.*"'

Theo sank beneath the surface. The world blurred, booming with the sound of her blood, crackling as her ears filled with water. Lungs straining, body craving air, she clenched her fists and weathered it. Ophelia had died like this; and Maggie Tulliver; and countless shipwrecked sailors. When she could stand it no longer she sat up violently, slopping water on to the floorboards. She was not dead, or dying, so perhaps there *was* still hope – hope of a reprieve, for herself and for Kit. Perhaps there *were* things she could do; ways in which Toby might come to forgive her, and all could be made right. And none of it could be done by lying in her bed, paralysed with misery. Her mother was right about that.

She still felt weak but she scrubbed herself clean, got dressed, and styled her hair as best she could without help – parting it in the middle, twisting the side portions into ropes and fastening them at the nape of her neck. Then she rummaged through the drawers of her dressing table until she found a pale grey ribbon, and tied the butterfly pendant around her neck. A neck in which the blood was still quick, and warm. Looking closely in the mirror, she saw the subtle twitch of the pulse beneath the skin.

Hunger knotted her stomach. She would write back to Albert Mackie, and she would go to see the Meriwethers, even though she shrank from the pain she'd caused them. Uncle Crudge had written to tell her about the judge's arrival in Dorchester, and the date on which Kit's trial would begin. It was fast approaching; time was short.

Toby had a clear memory of Theo swaying on her feet in front of the magistrate. He hadn't tried to see her again since being turned away from the big house. The rumours, which always leaked from any house with servants, were that she was still ill, and in bed. That she had been driven mad by what had happened. He didn't believe that; it was most likely just embarrassment at losing her nerve in public. Impatience gnawed at him – time was running out. He needed her to get well, and practise her testimony.

So she was overdue, when she finally turned up. She came after school hours, when all three Meriwethers would be home, and though her clothes were smart the rest of her was not. Sallow skin, dull eyes, cracks at the corners of her mouth. She and Toby simply stared at one another from either side of the doorstep, neither smiling nor speaking, until Mona came to see who it was.

'Miss Hallewell!' She seemed taken aback. 'Won't you come in?'

The four of them sat on the small settees, and Mona didn't offer tea. Toby noticed that Theo couldn't look his parents in the eye. That she looked wretched, and unwell. The prickle of sympathy he felt only made his anger stir.

'It's nice to see you up and about,' Mona said. 'Are you recovered from your bout of illness?'

'I . . . I cannot say,' Theo said, with a tremulous hint of a smile. 'But since resting has not worked, perhaps it is better to try a return to . . . activity.'

Toby wondered if she'd been about to say *normality*. They could never go back to that.

'At least, that's what the doctor says,' she added.

'Well, he probably knows best.'

Silence fell. Toby fought to keep still. He felt like Kit must always have felt, with his fidgeting and his sudden explosions of movement. There was too much to do, too much to contain. Theo kept touching a gold pendant that hung between her collarbones, and it irritated him. Such trinkets hardly mattered. Such girlish vanity.

'My uncle wrote to tell me the date of the trial,' she said quietly. 'The seventh of October.'

'Yes,' David said.

'Kit is quite looking forward to the train ride,' Mona said. 'He's never been in one before.'

He would be taken by wagon to Semley station, since Shaftesbury was too steep to be on the railway, and then to Dorchester via Yeovil Junction. Mona clasped her hands in her lap, then unclasped them and laid them flat.

'Of course, he doesn't really understand—'

'I wanted to ask if there is anything I can do to help,' Theo blurted. 'Anything at all. You must please let me know, however small or large it may seem.' She took a breath. 'I am so very sorry for the way I failed with the magistrate. I cannot explain what happened. Only that I . . . I have never been able to . . .'

Toby held his breath but she stopped short of telling his parents she had lied in her statement. That she had, in fact, seen Kit throw the stone. He hadn't told them – he couldn't bear to – and had no idea if they suspected as much.

'Noah Cornwallis suggests that you practise what you will say at the trial,' he said. 'So that nerves will not be such a factor, when the time comes.'

Theo turned to stare at him. 'I . . . I *cannot* speak at the trial!'

'But . . . you *must*,' Mona said.

'My dear.' David laid a hand on his wife's arm. 'Let's hear what Miss Hallewell has to say.'

Theo looked stricken. 'You were all there,' she said. 'You saw what happened. I *cannot* speak before the judge; I would make it so much worse for Kit if I did. If . . . the same thing happened again.'

'Perhaps it would not, if you were to prepare in advance as Mr Cornwallis suggests,' David said encouragingly. But Theo was shaking her head, her gaze darting from one face to the next as though too afraid to land.

'You just asked what you could do to help Kit,' Toby burst out. 'You were there that night. The best – the *only* – thing you can do is speak up for him!'

'No – don't you see? I can't! I would get it all wrong again, I know I would! I would make it worse for him, and I couldn't bear that. Please believe me—'

'Then you will let Joanna Bowen's account go unchallenged?' Mona said.

'They . . . they have my written account.'

'That will not carry the same weight with the jury! How could it?' Toby snapped.

'They will find me out,' Theo whispered.

There was a hung moment. Toby shut his eyes. He felt the realisation settle on to his parents. David cleared his throat. 'You mean to say that your written version is . . . skewed, in Kit's favour?'

Theo stood abruptly. 'Forgive me. I shouldn't have come.'

She rushed from the room, and Toby went after her.

'Theo, wait!' he called, and she froze.

He took her shoulders, turned her to face him. 'Theo, *please*. Without your word against Joanna's . . . don't you see?'

Tears flooded her eyes. 'You *saw* what happened at the Town Hall, Toby! I can't do it!'

'You mean you are afraid to, and too cowardly to try!'

Her fingers went to her necklace again. He fought the urge to slap her hand away from it.

'The magistrate *knew* I was lying, don't you understand? People always do! If I do not speak, if I do not give myself away, then my written statement will stand.' She stared up at him, beseeching. 'If

I go, I will make it *worse*. Ask anything else of me, Toby! Anything but that!'

'There *is* nothing else!'

'I . . . I begged the doctor to lie. I asked him outright to allow for some other cause of Missy's death—'

'But don't you see? You were *there*, Theo. Nothing matters except your word against Joanna's!'

She shook her head wretchedly, but he refused to allow it.

'Practise. Rehearse what you will say. Rehearse how you will answer to anything you might be asked. Summon the courage, Theo! It's a simple enough thing to do.'

'Toby, please—'

'You *must* do this. You must. They will believe you. You were Missy's friend as well as Kit's, and you are the more respectable by far. They will believe *you*, if you say it was an accident!'

Theo's head drooped. She swayed again, just like at the Town Hall, and Toby realised that she meant it. She would not speak at the trial. He took a sharp breath: her refusal was causing an actual physical pain somewhere near his heart. He felt betrayed, and realised that he'd thought Theo would do *anything* for him. He'd thought she loved him – had known it, in fact. That sudden feeling at the castle, when he'd yearned to kiss her . . . But he'd been wrong. About all of it.

'If you do not . . .' He struggled to finish the sentence. His head was roaring. He didn't know what he would do. 'If you do not, then you were never a friend. Not to Kit, and not to me.'

Toby had never been sure how well Kit understood time. He seemed to have kept a young child's view of it – either something was happening right now, or it wasn't happening. He didn't appear to differentiate between something due in five minutes, five hours, or five weeks. And yet, as the trial date approached, Kit grew more agitated. Restlessly pacing his cell, unable to keep still even when they brought him his favourites – jam sandwiches and shortbread fingers. Toby wondered if some of the officers were goading him about the upcoming trial, but Constable Philpott didn't think so. They'd all grown fond of Kit, he said; even Constable Hickey, who didn't like anyone much.

With a sinking feeling, Toby could only suppose Kit understood his situation better than they realised. His suspicion was confirmed as he got up to leave after visiting on the second of October, three days before Kit was due to be moved to Dorchester. Kit had fidgeted throughout the visit, his face twitching even though Toby had been careful not to mention anything about it. Lord Paxton-Nevis had arrived, and all was running to schedule; Kit's would be the first case heard, and the only charge of murder on this assize.

'Has Mr Cornwallis been to see you?' Toby asked, wondering if that were the cause.

Kit shook his head rapidly.

'Kit – come and sit down, calm down. Steady the breathing, remember?'

He did a few himself, to lead the way, exaggerating the slow inhalation, the even slower exhalation. But Kit surged to his feet again, pacing from one corner of the cell to another.

'I don't want to go there!' Kit said. 'Not even to ride on the train. I don't want to go, and be hanged!'

Toby closed his eyes. He went to stand in front of Kit, putting his hand on the back of his neck and pulling him closer until their foreheads touched. Breathing in Kit's unwashed hair and the sourness of his unbrushed teeth; the same softly animal smells he'd always had.

'They aren't going to hang you, Kit.' Toby's voice didn't sound like his own.

‘But they might! They might!’

‘They won’t, Kit.’

‘Do you promise?’

‘Kit . . .’

But Toby couldn’t promise. The words wouldn’t come.

‘We all know you didn’t mean to hurt her,’ he said instead. ‘You’ll be home soon. Please don’t worry. I need you to be brave. Be very brave, and do as you are asked, and leave the rest to me.’

They stood with their heads together for as long as Kit could tolerate it, and when he broke away to pace again Toby kept his eyes shut, because he hated the world and everything in it, and he didn’t know what to do.

Chapter Seven

The trial was not mentioned at Hallewell House. The newspaper was mysteriously not delivered that week. Still, the night before it was due to begin Theo's pulse picked up, and would not slow. It was the thought that she *could* still go to Dorchester; that she *should* go. That she might hold her nerve and lie through her teeth, and somehow save Kit. *If you do not, then you were never a friend.*

Her heart vibrated. She panted as though she'd been running, and her muscles spasmed uncontrollably. Dr Anscombe had travelled to Dorchester for the trial, so another doctor came. A man named Fortescue, with a granite face and lifeless eyes, who looked at Theo as though she were a specimen in a jar. He gave her drops of something in water that slowed everything down, drawing a thick curtain between her and the rest of the world. She drifted, dimly grateful that the decision had been taken out of her hands.

The courthouse in Dorchester Shire Hall was several times the size of the council chamber in Shaftesbury, the ceiling three times as high. Lord Paxton-Nevis sat beneath a far grander canopy, behind a properly constructed bench. Witnesses spoke from a raised box, and spectators sat in two tiers of galleried seating. Cold October sunshine lanced through windows ten feet tall. Kit stood in the dock, his skinny wrists manacled. He was not permitted to sit, and rocked from foot to foot. Now and then he looked up at David and Mona, who blew him kisses and tried to smile. Then his wide, restless eyes moved to Toby, and all Toby could do was nod. In quiet moments they heard Kit's murmurs and hums of distress.

The room smelled just the same – of wood and hair and breath. And, besides a crowd of curious strangers and a brace of journalists, most of the same people were there, too. The same witnesses gave their same testimonies. All bar Theo, of course. Toby had asked Mr Crudge if she planned to attend, and guessed the answer from the way his face fell.

'She really isn't well, Toby,' he said. 'Please try to forgive her.'

'But is she *really* ill, or is it just . . . girlish hysterics?'

'Well, I haven't been permitted to visit for a fortnight or more. I have written for news, but Mrs Hallewell is very keen for nothing to disturb her daughter. The doctor has prescribed rest, and I am sure—'

'I'm sure she's hiding her face, nothing more,' Toby snapped.

'*Toby*,' Crudge admonished. 'She feels it very deeply.'

'What's the use in her feeling it, if she does nothing?'

He turned away before Crudge could reply. Yet he couldn't shake the idea that Theo *would* appear, in the end. Just like she had at the magistrate's hearing: late, and half shot with nerves, but there. She would sneak out of the house, and come to speak for Kit. He could picture it clearly: the clerk whispering to the judge; Noah Cornwallis pricking up his ears; the door opening and all of them turning to see a breathless Theo rush in. Anxious, perhaps, but ready to say what needed to be said. Ready to save Kit from the calumny of Joanna Bowen and Constable Pryce.

Toby's own testimony served only to worsen his frustration.

'You say the stone was dislodged accidentally by your brother's foot, as he fought for balance?' the prosecutor said.

'Yes. After Missy herself had goaded him to—'

'And yet, we have it from another eyewitness that Melissa was some forty feet clear from the base of the wall when the stone struck.' He checked his notes. '"The length at least of two coaches and four" has been attested to. You dispute that?'

'I . . . yes. It wasn't that far.' The lie made his pulse tick in his throat.

'Because it seems *highly* unlikely, does it not, that a stone merely *dislodged* would fly so far, even from height?' The prosecutor gave him no time to reply. 'So, in whom ought the court to put their faith, Mr Meriwether? You, who, it seems to me, would say anything at all to assist your brother in his predicament, regardless of the oath you have sworn upon the Holy Bible; or Miss Bowen, who was at Missy's side when the blow landed, and has no cause to lie whatsoever?'

'No cause except her spite. She took against Kit from the very start, because he was different, and—'

'Young man, I think you have said enough.'

Toby looked at Cornwallis, who gave a terse nod. He stood there a few seconds longer, boiling with the need to say more, to shout, to force them to *listen*. Then, rigid with stifled desperation, he had no choice but to step down.

Dr Anscombe took the stand, and Cornwallis did his utmost to prod the man into allowing even a chink of doubt.

'There could have been an entirely unrelated infection of some kind, could there not?' Cornwallis said. 'Some hidden illness or congenital fault, which, once the girl was in a weakened state, conspired to overcome her?'

'I assure you, Mr Cornwallis, that any doctor worth his salt would notice the signs of such a malady. Melissa Cartwright displayed none. And the very manner of her death – her having first fallen into an unresponsive state – testifies to the damage to her brain being the cause of it.'

'You are entirely certain of that? There was no irregularity to her heart, or propensity to—'

'The blow to her head caused her death, Mr Cornwallis,' Anscombe said. 'My operation was her best and only chance of survival, but the damage had already been done.'

'Was she given some medication, perhaps, to which she may have reacted adversely—'

'Mr Cornwallis,' the judge interrupted. 'There are only so many times we may expect the good doctor to repeat himself. Move on.'

Toby stared at Dr Anscombe and hated him, with his handsome face and kindly eyes; his curly hair and Greek nose lending him a hint of Lord Byron. What would it have cost him to admit that there *might* have been some other cause, even if he didn't think it were true? To allow some hint of mitigation?

Lord Humphrey Paxton-Nevis had not seemed so very bad, on first inspection. His reputation was such that Toby had half expected him to have mad eyes and the blood of innocents on his chin, but instead he was a man of around sixty, of medium height and build, with a not unpleasant face that gave little away. He appeared cool, certainly; but that was appropriate to the gravity of his station. Toby had felt a glimmer of hope. Here was a rational man, an intelligent man. A man who would see through all the blether and recognise the absurdity of calling Kit a murderer. But then, during Joanna Bowen's spiel, he'd interrupted her to ask of Missy, tenderly: *Pretty, was she?*

Timothy Crudge spoke so warmly about Kit that Toby felt bad for having put him on the spot over Theo. But, as the prosecutor pointed out, Crudge had not been there to see what happened that night. The trial progressed quickly. Toby watched for the clerk's whisper; for the judge's nod; for Theo to make her entrance.

On the second day, Cornwallis called Dr Heinemann, a practitioner in the new field of psychology, who – his fee paid by Crudge – had assessed Kit. He testified to his conclusion that Kit was suffering from a form of foreshortened development, which had halted his intellectual growth at around the age of seven. He recommended that Kit be admitted to a clinical institution for further assessments to take place. He had observed, during his examination, no murderous or violent urges in him.

Lord Paxton-Nevis was unconvinced. He leaned forward and fixed Heinemann with a stony eye.

'Either the young man is of sound mind, and knew precisely what he was doing in throwing that rock, and is therefore a murderer through and through; or else he is a cretin, who had no understanding of the consequences of his outburst of temper, in which case he is a danger to all who encounter him and must not be allowed to go free. But he cannot be both, Dr Heinemann.'

'My Lord,' Cornwallis protested, 'Dr Heinemann—'

'Move on, Mr Cornwallis.'

Toby became aware of the loud thump of his own heart. That same sharp, animal smell, coming from his father. He realised that they were all falling. The ground beneath them was cracking, and no matter how they struggled, there was only one direction in which they could go.

His pulse accelerated by increments. His hands began to shake. He knew he had to do *something* – that he *must*, because they were careening towards Kit's committal, and it was all because Toby had gone along with Theo's foolish game and had taken Kit with him. Because he'd let Theo distract him, and lead him off into the beckoning darkness of the castle.

He needed to act, but he was paralysed. It was *exactly* like seeing Kit high up on that wall, and being rooted to the spot. The terrible impotence was just the same. He thought it might drive him mad. Something was building in his chest and he clenched his jaw to keep it in. He watched with increasing desperation for Theo to rush in, frightened but resolute, and declare to them all that she had been there, that she had *seen*, and that it was not murder. Even as the testimonies ended, and Kit fidgeted his manacles. Even as the judge directed the jury, in the worst possible direction.

'The defence have called this case "a tragedy", but do not be distracted by the prickings of pity, unless they be for little Missy Cartwright. A child even as young as seven years is well aware that if he throws a missile, and that missile strikes true, he will doubtless cause an injury. Let me remind you that whether or not Christopher Meriwether intended to kill the girl is not relevant. The evidence, to my mind, indicates that he *did* indeed kill her, and, if you are in agreement, you must find him guilty.'

The courtroom emptied; the spectators filed out in search of refreshment. And there was nothing whatsoever Toby could do about it. Theo was not there. She had not come.

The jury deliberated for less than an hour. Fifty minutes, to be precise.

Kit was brought back in, shuffling, hunched. When he looked up again, Toby found his gaze unbearable. There was fear in his little brother's eyes, of course, but there was also trust. Kit trusted him to *do* something. To fix it somehow, and take him home. *Be very brave, and do as you are asked, and leave the rest to me*. There was such a roaring in Toby's head that he didn't hear the verdict as it was read out. He didn't hear his parents' cries, or the tumult that broke out along the galleries. He saw only Paxton-Nevis, reaching for the black square and draping it solemnly, absurdly, over his wig, as he sentenced Kit to death.

Then he wasn't paralysed any more.

'This is rubbish!' He surged to his feet. 'It's *rubbish*! You're *murdering* him! You're murderers, all of you!' He pointed wildly at the jury.

'Young man,' Paxton-Nevis barked. 'Remove yourself, or I shall hold you in contempt!'

'He's innocent, damn you!' Toby shouted. 'This is all wrong – you must let him go! God damn you all to *hell*!'

On and on he went, hardly aware of it, until the bailiffs were sent up to eject him. Kit was pulled the other way, through the doorway down to the cells. He didn't struggle; he behaved himself, and did as he was asked. Just as Toby had instructed him to.

'Kit! *No!* You must listen to me! You *must* let him go!'

Toby kicked and fought, but he was no match for his captors.

When he came to his senses, he was sitting on the kerb outside the courthouse with his head between his knees. He looked up and saw his mother weeping, and his father talking earnestly to Cornwallis, his face slack with disbelief. Toby felt hollow. If he'd reacted at once, on seeing Kit up on the castle wall – if he'd run straight to him, instead of freezing like a rabbit, he might have reached him before the stone was cast. He might have prevented it all. And now, *this*. And no way to undo any of it.

They had to bribe the governor of Dorchester Prison to be allowed in to see Kit. It was money at first, for as long as they could find it; then the governor took the apple cake Mona had baked for Kit instead. He was a mean, grasping man, but after a while he always let them in, and accepted whatever they offered: half a dozen eggs, biscuits, jars of piccalilli. Kit always wanted to know what they'd given him; David turned it into a game, and made him guess.

The prison was bleak, hardly a place for games. Narrow corridors of small, frigid cells, in which the inmates spent twenty-three hours of each day and weren't permitted to speak. It stank overwhelmingly of bodily fluids. The gallows were at the connecting hub of several corridors, with every hanging either visible or audible to most of the men. Now and then a babbling voice echoed along the halls and stairwells, until it was cut off short. Once, while Toby was there, an unholy chorus of howls and banging and whistles broke out for no discernible reason, after which three men were dragged into the courtyard and flogged.

Kit's cell was at the end of a row, and his only neighbour was a Devonshire man named Oxcott. Soft-spoken, with grizzled hair and a ruined, bulbous nose, Oxcott was awaiting transportation to Tasmania for the theft of a wheel of cheese. After dark, when the warders patrolled less often, he taught Kit silly songs, like 'If You Want To Know The Time, Ask A Policeman' and 'Where Did You Get That Hat?'

'Bey shouldn't be 'ere, should 'ee?' Oxcott said, when Toby thanked him. 'Don't matter what 'ee done. Geddon?'

'I completely agree,' Toby managed to say.

David took in a packet of Player's Navy Cut for Oxcott, every time they went.

Whenever they visited, their mission was to distract Kit; to make it as normal as possible that he should be staying there for a time, and to give no reminders of what was coming. They took him paper and pencils for drawing, which they had to take away again when they left. They took a deck of cards, and played snap. They asked around Hallewell for old postcards and greetings cards to show him. When there was nothing else, they told him stories. What was new with the hens and vegetables – their bumper crop of autumn raspberries. Toby entered into the spirit of the game wholeheartedly. It was a relief to pretend nothing bad was coming, and if it was supposedly for Kit's benefit, he knew it was for theirs, too.

At home, Toby found it physically difficult to swallow. None of them had much appetite anyway, and pushed the food around their plates until it went cold. The time between their visits to Kit was tense and aimless, numbed by dread. David still taught, Toby still studied; Mona still cooked and cleaned and cared, all by rote. The date of Kit's execution was set for the fourth of November. A Monday.

Sometimes, Toby went to Dorchester by himself, when his parents couldn't get away or they were trying to eke out the rail fares. Alone, he found it far harder to keep the fantasy going. He didn't have his mother's strength, or his father's self-possession. It was impossible to forget that it was all because of him. Him and Theo and Missy.

'What was it for dinner last night?' he asked Kit, one week before.

Seven days. One hundred and sixty-four hours, given that it was one o'clock by his watch, and Kit would hang at nine in the morning. Toby's mind searched constantly for an escape, a reprieve, a reason to hope; just as it had conjured Theo to the courthouse. But there was still nothing he could do. He was still helpless.

'Stew,' Kit said.

'Turnips again?'

'Carrots and swede.'

'Ah, well. It's good to ring the changes,' Toby said.

'I hate swede, though.'

'Me too, Kit.'

They were sitting side by side on the floor of the cell. Knees bent, backs to the wall, with the cold stone pressing through their clothes. Kit's head had been shaved, which made his ears stand out even more. He'd been stripped of his normal clothes, and wore the shapeless suit all prisoners did, printed with black arrows to make him visible should he manage to escape. Toby didn't like to think how many men had worn that rough uniform before Kit; or what had become of them.

'What happened to the special coin Theo gave you?' he asked. 'Have you still got it?'

'I don't know.' Kit twitched a little. 'No. But I had it before.' He turned anxious eyes on his brother. 'Will Theo be cross with me?'

'Will *she* be cross with *you*?' Toby had to stop, settle himself. 'No, Kit. She won't.'

'I didn't mean to lose it.'

Toby put his arm around his brother, and Kit huddled into him, hiding his face, though he was too big for that, really. He'd done it as a child, when he was sorry for something.

'You mustn't worry about it at all,' Toby said. 'I'm sure it'll turn up. And if not, then it really doesn't matter.'

Kit said nothing. Toby felt the ground shifting; the fear rising; the sickness in his stomach. From next door came the faintest sound of Oxcott singing what sounded like an old sea shanty: *Shave his belly with a rusty razor, early in the morning!*

'"*Hooray and up she rises*",' Toby sang softly, until Kit joined in – he couldn't help it, it had always been one of his favourites.

'"*Hooray and up she rises, early in the morning!*"'

They sang it over and over, louder, until a warder rattled his baton across the rivets of the door to silence them.

'Is there anything you'd like, Kit?'

'I want to go home.'

'I know.' Toby swallowed. 'Is there anything else, though? Something from home that I can bring to you? Or . . . something to eat?'

Kit thought for a moment. 'Will Theo come to see me?'

'Theo? I don't know, Kit. I don't think—'

'But she's my friend. She's always nice to me.'

'I know. But . . . Lately, since . . .'

'But will you ask her?' Kit insisted. 'She's my friend.'

'I'll ask her.'

It was true. Theo *had* always been nice to Kit. Right up until the moment she'd turned her back on him.

When he got back to Hallewell, Toby tried to make himself walk up to the big house and knock again. He knew he'd be turned away, but some bloody-minded part of him wanted to try it anyway. *Mrs Hallewell is very keen for nothing to disturb her daughter*. Well, he *wanted* to disturb the wretched Hallewells, tucked away safely in their sprawling mansion while Kit shivered in a cell so small he could touch the walls on either side with his outstretched hands. Theo *ought* to be disturbed. She ought not ride out the storm *she'd* created in safe harbour, while the Meriwethers foundered.

He hovered by the garden gate for a good long while. Staring along the path at the imposing door, and up at the windows; searching out the shape of her behind the glass. Waiting for her to see him, and come out. Then it started to rain, and he turned for home.

Theo, he wrote, *Kit has asked to see you. They will hang him in one week's time so I suppose you could call this his dying wish. Or one of them, in any case. I beg you to do as he asks. Summon that part of you that gave him Lord Abrecan's coin for courage, rather than whichever part let him be convicted. He wishes to see you because, he says, you are his friend.*

The gaol is not a pleasant place but you would be quite safe. You need not travel alone or see him by yourself, if you'd prefer not to. I will go with you, or my parents, or anyone else you wish to take. Timothy Crudge would travel down for it, I am certain. He has been to visit Kit more than once, so is well acquainted with the place. In any case I will make all the arrangements; all you need do is agree to it, and find a few kind things to say to Kit, when he is facing the end and is so very afraid.

I begged you to speak up for him, but you did not. Now I must beg you again, and this time implore you to do as I ask. Please come with me to see him, Theo, and say some words to comfort him; even if you cannot forgive the way I spoke to you before, even if no friendship remains between us. Send word, and it will be arranged as soon as may be.

He delivered the letter to the same servant who'd sent him packing the last time.

'It is of critical importance that Miss Hallewell receive this,' he said.

'Is it indeed?'

The young man took the envelope with a scornful expression, and closed the door.

Crudge came to tell Theo the outcome of the trial – the first time in weeks he'd been allowed to visit. Sitting by her bed, holding her hand, tears rolling down his cheeks. Theo was still blunted by narcotics. She tried as hard as she could to speak, and say sorry; but nothing came out.

Whatever Fortescue had prescribed made time both fast and slow. She lost track of it. She did nothing, saw no one; rehashed it all, over and over, as though she might solve it somehow. Like Toby with his notebook of symbols, always hunting out their meaning. She wondered if she might somehow disintegrate, and be released from her pain. Like the burnt paper of her invocation: little black flecks, coming apart in water. Like Abrecan's body in the holy well – a different state of being. *Abrecan the owl!* How she yearned for a different state of being.

Towards the end of an afternoon, when Theo had been watching rain snake down the windowpane, her mother burst in with a piece of paper clenched in one hand.

'Is that a letter?' Theo said. 'Is it for me?'

'No. It is nothing. We . . . have been burgled, Theo.'

'Burgled?'

'Indeed. Though I have only just noticed it. The King Alfred silver coin has been taken from the display case, and a dummy put in its place – a cunning thing for the thief to do, in an effort to conceal the crime. And the case is quite undamaged, so a skilled picklock has been at work.'

Theo was silent. Diana stared at her.

'I shall send for Constable Pryce, of course,' she said. 'I only wanted to ask when you last recall seeing the coin in its proper place? If we can ascertain when it was taken, then I may furnish the constable with a list of those who were staying with us at the time.'

'I—' Theo sat up straighter. 'Is . . . is it worth troubling the police?'

'Worth troubling them? I should say so, Theo. That coin is precious, for its provenance as much as its monetary value. It belongs here, at Hallewell.'

Diana didn't blink.

'I took it,' Theo said.

She sensed that her mother already knew, and didn't have the strength to dissemble. Besides, there seemed little Diana could do to make things any worse than they already were.

'You took it,' Diana echoed flatly. 'What for? And where is it now?'

'I took it because . . . I wanted something of Lord Abrecan's. It seemed . . . magical.'

Diana shook her head. 'How ridiculous you are at times.'

'I don't know where it is now,' Theo lied.

The last thing she wanted was for Diana to find some way of getting it back from Kit. She only hoped he still had it, and that it helped him, even a little. The thought of him in gaol made her stomach churn. If she hadn't been so certain of the Meriwethers' disapproval, she would have gone to see him. Despite the guilt, and the shame, she would have gone and held Kit's hand for a while. She thought that he, at least, would be happy to see her.

'I lost it,' she said. 'At the castle, at midsummer.'

'How careless of you,' Diana murmured. 'Perhaps you might stir yourself to go and look for it, one of these days? Though I daresay some lucky passer-by has pocketed it by now.'

Her mother's eyes pinned her for a few more seconds, then she turned for the door.

'Tidy yourself up, Theo. It's breaded veal for dinner.'

On Sunday the third of November, Reverend Nimrod spent an hour alone in the cell with Kit, while the Meriwethers stood out in the corridor like captured chess pieces. When he came out, the vicar took Mona's hands and bowed his head.

'Take heart, Mrs Meriwether,' he said, as Mona's eyes flooded. 'Gather your courage, and your faith. Show your boy that you are not afraid; that he is going to a place of safety and forgiveness. A place of mercy.'

'I . . . I *can't*, Vicar!' Mona whispered. 'I'm trying, but—'

'My dear woman . . . God sees your son for who he truly is,' Nimrod said.

Toby felt sorry for him. He was as powerless as they all were, and no amount of faith could make what was happening any better.

'Thank you for coming, Reverend,' David said.

'Call upon me at any time,' he said, as he took his leave. 'You are in my prayers, all of you.'

The governor had given them an hour, instead of the usual thirty minutes. The last hour they would ever spend with Kit.

'Mona, my dear . . .' David said gently. 'The vicar is right – it will frighten Kit to see you so distraught.'

'How can I not be distraught when my boy is being stolen from me like this? It is too cruel!'

'I know, I know. But just for now. Just for Kit.'

Mona took a few gulping breaths, trying to smother the sobs.

Toby couldn't stand it. 'I'll go in first,' he said. 'You come when you're ready, Mum.'

She nodded, her face twisting in pain.

The vicar's visit seemed to have calmed Kit. He was sitting on his stool like an oversized schoolboy – knees together, big, ungainly feet apart; hands clasped as though still in prayer.

'How are you, Kit?' Toby said.

'Will I . . . will I see her in heaven?' Kit said.

'What? Who?'

'Missy. Will I see her in heaven? The vicar said only sinners go to hell and I'm not a sinner, not very much. And Missy's in heaven now, isn't she? So will I go to heaven, too?' He glanced up, eyes enormous.

'Yes,' Toby said tightly.

'Because *God* knows, doesn't He? The judge said I did it on purpose, but God *knows* I didn't, doesn't He?'

'Yes. God knows everything,' Toby said; though, when it came down to it, he wasn't sure he believed in God any more.

Kit nodded. 'Will I find her, then, do you think? When I get there?'

'Yes. I expect you will.'

'Then perhaps it won't be so bad. I'd like to see her again. She's very pretty. Isn't she? Will she look like that in heaven? Like she always looked? Or will she look like . . . like . . .' Kit couldn't finish.

'She'll look just the same,' Toby said. 'What will you say to her?'

'I'll say, "Sorry, Missy." I'll say, "I never meant to bang you on the head." Because I *didn't*! I never meant to! She said climb up there, bet you can't, so I did! I did!'

Kit got up in a rush, his calm evaporating. Windblown emotions flew across his face – fear and hope and indignation. Mostly fear.

'It's all right, Kit,' Toby said. 'Sit back down. It's going to be all right.'

'Will it hurt?'

Tremors jerked through Kit's body, and Toby was close to choking.

'No, it won't hurt a bit.'

'I . . . I want to go home, Toby! I don't want to be dead like Missy!'

'I don't want you to be dead either, Kit,' Toby managed to say, anguish blurring the words. He shut his eyes and refused to be sick. 'But it won't be bad at all, I promise.'

'Oxcott says it will be like going to sleep quickly, like when I'm very, very tired,' Kit whispered, leaning in close. 'Do you think that's right?'

'Well, Oxcott knows about a lot of things, doesn't he? So I'm sure he has it right.'

'Yes. Only . . . I won't ever wake up again.' Kit's face contorted as he wrestled with it. 'I wish Theo had come to see me. Perhaps she'll come a bit later on?'

'I . . . I think Theo is poorly at the moment, Kit.'

'Oh. Poor Theo.'

'Poor Theo,' Toby echoed hollowly. 'She . . . she told me to say hello,' he lied. 'And to give you a hug. She said not to worry about the coin. And that she's very sorry for what's happened, and she'll always be your friend, and say her prayers for you.'

'That's good, then, isn't it?'

'Yes. That's good.'

David and Mona came in then. Mona's face was dry, but her eyes were red and gleaming. What could any of them say? They didn't dare shatter the fantasy they'd painstakingly constructed, that tomorrow would not bring a rope of coarse hemp and the racket of the others, banging their dented spoons on the floor; it would not bring a sharp pain in the neck and a release of the bladder and bowels. No: tomorrow morning at nine, Kit would close his eyes and fall asleep, and fly up into the clouds to see Missy Cartwright again.

The hour became an hour and a half, but after that the door squealed and a warder appeared to evict them.

'Just a little longer, I beg you,' David said.

'You've already had longer,' the man said, not without sympathy. 'Rules is rules, else I'll have the whole place up in a riot.'

'A' ye no pity in ye, man?' Oxcott called from behind his door, which earned him a loud clang of the baton against the metal hatch.

Toby could hardly speak by then. His throat had closed completely. He watched his mother and father hug Kit, and this time no one bothered telling Mona not to cry.

'Don't go, Mum!' Kit followed them to the door, snatching at their hands. 'Don't go, Dad. I want to come home with you!'

'I'm so sorry, my boy.' David sounded broken.

Toby held Kit tightly; rubbed his hand across his stubbled scalp, where the skin was soft and vulnerable.

'Be brave, Kit, and it'll all be fine,' he whispered.

He didn't want the last thing he ever said to his brother to be a lie, but he couldn't think of anything else. He kissed the top of Kit's head and fled.

'Missus! Missus!' Oxcott hissed at Mona as Kit's door was locked behind them.

They saw the gleam of his eyes behind the hatch.

''Ave a sing-song later, the bey an' I, geddon? Won't let 'ee all by hisself, will I?'

'Thank you,' David said, when Mona could not. 'You are a kind man, and we're grateful.'

Kit pressed his face to the bars of his hatch as they left. Strained to reach them with his fingertips.

'We can't just . . . *go*,' Mona said, once the prison gates had slammed behind them. 'We can't just leave him here!'

'There's nothing else we can do,' David told her quietly.

'Well, I'm staying. I'll wait here, on the street. I shan't sleep anyway. How could I? And I'm not leaving him.'

David hung his head, adjusting his weight on his cane, and Toby saw how close he was to giving up.

'My dear, they will not let us back in to see him. They will not let us. And it won't help him if you make yourself ill.'

'Will it help him if we abandon him?' she said. 'I can't bear . . . How can we just go home and . . . carry on, when he . . . When our boy . . .' Her face crumpled.

'It will help him to sing songs with Oxcott later,' David said softly. 'It will help him to remember what the vicar has said, and how very much we love him. And he knows it, Mona. He does.'

She sagged, and they held each other. A cold breeze fluttered around them, and Toby stood to one side. Separate again. Excluded by their pain, with no one to help him shoulder his own.

They went to bed that night because they didn't know what else to do. None of them slept. They'd decided to sit at the table together shortly before nine the next morning, to join hands and pray and remember happier times. It had been David's idea: they needed a structure, a ceremony of some sort. They needed to brace themselves, to survive the terrible moment of losing Kit. He had burned so brightly in their hearts since the moment of his birth, none of them could imagine life going on with any semblance of normality without him.

In the end, Toby couldn't do it. The slow march of the night ended in a grey dawn, and at ten to nine Toby knew he would go mad if he stayed. Sitting at the table like fools at a seance, while thirty miles south the best of them was extinguished. The idea of Kit's fear was insufferable. The knowledge that he had caused it was excruciating.

'Toby? Where are you going?' David said, as he ran for the door.

But he couldn't stay. He could *not* look into their faces as the clock struck nine.

He followed their footsteps from Midsummer's Night. Through the village, past the Roman Cross, and up the steps to the castle mound. He didn't drop a coin into the box by the gate. He didn't go near the Anglo-Saxon chapel, or the symbol of Uroboros. Instead, he went across the courtyard to the section of wall Kit had climbed, and sat down with his back to it. Tipped his face to the blinding white sky. Tiny spits of drizzle hit his eyes, and the wind was chill. He thought he heard Kit's hooting laughter, and the flap of his clumsy feet. *He's so full of joy, isn't he?* Then came an image of his brother crouching in the vegetable patch, holding the tip of his tongue between his teeth and pricking out baby radishes with an excess of care.

Toby's chest clenched. He stared, until his eyes ached, at the spot where he'd dithered like an idiot instead of saving his brother.

He could have prevented it all, if he'd only moved faster. Then the wind carried the tenor bell of St Mary's up the valley from West End, as it struck nine times.

Toby had no idea how long he remained there. Eventually, he found himself looking down at Hallewell House, hunkered against the autumn weather, lights burning in several windows. Theo could have saved Kit. She could, at the end, have gone to see him, and made him feel better. But she'd done nothing – not even replied to Toby's letter with some paltry excuse. Anger came like a flood, sweeping Toby up and momentarily drowning out the pain. He flexed his stiff hands into fists at his sides.

Then the front door of Hallewell House opened, and a female figure emerged. For a second Toby thought it was Theo, but no. He watched Diana make her way down the path, out into the lane. Unusual, to see her leave the premises. Even rarer for her to go alone. Without thinking, Toby set off to follow.

Diana turned in at the Meriwether cottage. Toby couldn't imagine why. She'd never called on them before, not in his lifetime.

'Mrs Hallewell,' he heard David saying. 'You must forgive us. I'm afraid today you find us . . . indisposed.'

He was grey-faced, leaning heavily on his cane. Behind him, Mona was sitting on one of the settees as though cast in stone. She hadn't even turned to see Diana Hallewell, standing there in her maroon dress with its matching cape, her hands stuffed defensively into a sable muff, gazing around the parlour as though she couldn't quite believe people lived like this.

'What I have to say will only take a minute,' she said, starting slightly when Toby appeared.

'Well, it's a minute that will have to wait for another day,' Toby said. 'You heard my father.'

'Toby, there's no need to be rude,' David murmured.

'I think there is,' Toby said.

Diana lifted her chin, eyeing him coolly. 'Young man, I have a simple enough question to ask.'

From a distance, Toby had always thought her beautiful, but now, close to, he saw the powder on her face and the creases along her top lip. He saw her arrogance like a tarnish, dulling the surface.

'*Really?*' he snapped. 'On the very day my brother has been hanged, for a silly game initiated by *your* daughter, you stand there when you have been asked to leave, because you have a *question*?'

Diana paled. 'I . . . I had no idea that today was—'

'No? Well, I suppose it's of scant interest to you.'

'I shall leave you,' Diana said.

'Say what you have come to say,' Mona whispered.

Diana wavered. Toby folded his arms and glared at her, and his hostility seemed to galvanise her. She looked him straight in the eye.

'My daughter has alerted me to the loan of an item that she made to Christopher some weeks ago. We wish for the item to be returned.'

'Item, Mrs Hallewell?' David said. 'What item is this?'

'A silver coin, of ancient origin. As I understand it, my daughter loaned the coin to your boy as a . . . talisman, of sorts. She had managed to convince herself that it possessed magical properties. A childish game, nothing more. And now—'

'She wants the *coin* back?' Toby could scarcely credit it.

'Young man, I would not have made such a request on this very day had I been permitted to withdraw. But yes. It is valuable, and it belongs at Hallewell House. And with Christopher in such . . . an unfortunate situation, there is a danger it could be lost.'

'"An unfortunate situation"? He's *dead*, Mrs Hallewell.'

The words winded Toby momentarily. Diana stared at him without a flicker.

'I offer my condolences for your loss. But he has met this sorry end by his own actions.'

'Leave us alone,' Mona murmured.

David simply stared at the floor.

'We want neither your condolences nor your opinions,' Toby said. 'I thought for a moment you'd come to say you were sorry. That *Theo* was sorry! But I should have known better.'

'I'm sure I haven't the first idea what you believe we ought to apologise for. In any case, my daughter is not well.'

'She got my letter, then? Is that what reminded her about the coin? And instead of going to visit Kit like I asked, she sends you to fetch it *back*?'

'That's not—'

'It was the *only* thing he asked for, other than to come home. He wanted to see Theo before he died, and she wouldn't even do that for him!'

'Toby, that's enough,' David said.

'No, it *isn't* enough!' Toby's fury was suddenly thrilling; he felt invincible.

'My daughter has been most deleteriously affected by this whole affair,' Diana said. 'Whether she will ever fully recover, only time will tell. But it was not *she* who cast that stone, and I shall thank you to write to her no more.'

'Well, you needn't concern yourself on that score.'

'Very well. And my property?'

'Gone. Lost,' Toby declared. 'They took Kit's clothes, shaved his head, and put him in a freezing cell. I suppose some warder has your precious coin now, and I expect he'll pawn it for half a crown and drink until he falls over. Or at least, I hope he does.'

Diana bridled, twin blotches of colour appearing beneath the powder on her cheeks.

'I see. Then I shall take my leave. Mrs Meriwether; Mr Meriwether.'

She left Toby desperate to say more. To shout her down, and make her sorry. To break her world apart.

Theo learned the day and hour of Kit's hanging by eavesdropping on Peterson and Kitty Shoat. That morning she lay unmoving in her room, paralysed by the impossibility of it. No longer drugged, but still incapacitated. She could not sleep, and she could not get up. She watched the hands of the clock on the mantelpiece tick towards nine in the morning, and then carry on past. Five seconds past. Ten seconds past. And somewhere, between those heedless ticks, Kit's life ended. The world was no longer a place she knew.

They held a memorial for Kit on the village green, clustered around the Roman Cross, which at least had an air of the sacred. There was no funeral, since, with the best will in the world, Reverend Nimrod couldn't hold a church service for a convicted murderer. Kit's body had been interred in the prison yard in Dorchester. Their appeals had fallen on deaf ears: they could not have him back for burial. Many of their close neighbours attended the gathering; people who'd seen Kit every day, and had known him well. But many others stayed away.

The Hallewells had not been invited to attend.

Toby didn't look at anyone. Whether they looked sympathetic, or solemn, or uncaring, he wanted to hit them all.

David spoke when Mona could not. He thanked them all for coming. He cleared his throat. He had a piece of paper but the wind kept crumpling it, so he smoothed it out, again and again.

'"*Suffer little children to come unto me*",' he said eventually. 'I suppose that is what the good reverend would be saying, had we been admitted to church today. If Christopher were lying in his casket before us, in a . . . clean place. We are supposed to find it in ourselves to be joyous at the passing of a loved one, and grateful that their cares on this Earth are over. We are to picture our boy with his maker, in the Kingdom of Heaven, but I . . .' His breath hitched. 'I am finding it hard to do as I should.'

He shifted his weight on his crumpled leg, adjusting his stick.

'On the very day that this . . . this catastrophe began to unfold, I had cause to say to my elder son that nature does not often allow beautiful things to grow old. I only wish I had been wrong. I . . . I wish that nature – God – had not chosen to break our hearts like this, by taking our beautiful son.'

Mona took his arm, her hands skeletal against the black broadcloth of his sleeve. David glanced down at his wife's sunken face, her unblinking eyes.

'Because they are broken,' he said. 'Our hearts are quite broken, and we . . . we do not understand.'

Toby stayed in bed instead of going to church on Sunday, since there seemed very little point in him being there. He was leaving for Durham on Wednesday, and wanted to go without seeing Theo. Without seeing anyone, but most especially her. He wanted to leave and never come back.

On Monday, Kit's toothbrush, comb and grubby, worn-out clothes were delivered, wrapped in brown paper. Toby buried his face in them, breathing in the familiar smell that was already fading.

Then his fingers found something hard, tucked carefully into the lining of the waistcoat. *Elfred Rex*. Abrecan's silver coin. He flung it at the wall as hard as he could, taking a small chip out of the plaster. Then he fetched it, and put it in an envelope with a scribbled note.

Under cover of darkness, he tramped up to the big house and shoved the envelope beneath the door. An autumn storm was building.

◆ ◆ ◆

The wind howled through Hallewell in the black hours before dawn, bringing down two of the big elm trees. It was a week since Kit had been hanged. The window was snatched out of Theo's hand when she opened it, and hurled back on its hinges, shattering the glass. The power of the storm was mesmerising. Leaning out as far as she dared, with her hair in her eyes and the wind in her mouth, she felt something release, at long last, and sobbed until her throat was sore.

When she went down early in the morning, she found Toby's envelope. She couldn't imagine he had anything kind to say to her, and yet she couldn't help but hope. *There is always hope of a reprieve*. Perhaps this was the first, fragile sign of a thaw. He hadn't left for Durham, though he should have gone in October. Theo didn't know if his plans had changed, or were merely delayed; she didn't dare ask anybody.

She slid the note into her pocket. She didn't want anyone near her when she read it. Even Amy's room was not private enough, so she headed outside.

Nobody would be at the castle that day, with the wind still carrying cold flecks of rain. Theo passed the corpses of the elms on her way, and their vast root balls reared above her. A small crowd had come to see the fallen trees, and to watch the gang of men set about clearing them with axes. Theo met nobody's eye as she carried on past. At the top of the mound, she looked across at the green lane she so loved. Had once loved. Now it was merely a track through a field, muddier at this time of year. It was a farmer's route, nothing more. She couldn't feel anything now, when before it had spoken so loudly of freedom, and adventure, and wonder.

The letter was a single folded sheet, wrapped around Abrecan's coin. Tears burned her eyes as she opened it.

> *Have the coin back, if that is all that matters to you. It did my brother no good – it could not make up for your abandonment. Your presence would have served him better than a token. I will not write again. TM.*

Toby didn't sleep. He doubted whether anyone in Hallewell did, with the racket of the gale. He heard a chimney pot come loose and shatter on the garden path. In the morning his parents slept in, so he stoked the stove quietly, and put the kettle on to boil even though he didn't want anything to drink. He sat at the table and looked out at the puddled lane, and saw Theo. Waiting by the gate.

The sight of her drove him to his feet. He was amazed that she would dare. And then angry. He hadn't *wanted* her to come; he hadn't wanted to *see* her. He set his jaw as he went out. Her face was streaked, eyes and nose reddened with cold. She had his letter in her hand; opened her mouth and then froze, as if forgetting what she'd planned to say.

'What do you want, Theo?'

'Your letter. How can you . . . how could you . . . ?'

'How could I what?'

'How can you be so *cruel*?' she managed. Fresh tears slid down her cheeks. 'Why would you ever think the coin was all that mattered to me?'

'By your actions, Theo – or the lack of them.'

'But I don't . . . I didn't . . .'

'There's nothing you can say to make up for it! And I have nothing to say to you. I don't think there's anything else *to* say.'

She wiped her face with her hands. 'I *did* try, Toby . . .'

'I heard your testimony read out in court, Theo. The first thing – the *very* first thing you said was that it was too dark to be sure. Who would take the least notice of anything, after that? When Joanna stood in the box and told everyone what *she* saw, with no prevarication!'

'I *couldn't* tell them what I saw!'

'You could have spoken up for him. You could at least have *been* there,' he said. 'He'll rot in that prison yard forever, now, alongside the murderers and defilers. Is that where he belongs?'

'Oh, *no*! Of course not! Toby, I . . . I want to tell you—'

'And you wouldn't even go and see him before the end, when it would have meant so much to him!'

She shook her head. 'But I didn't think you—'

'Just *go*, Theo. Go away! Go back to your own people.'

He went inside and shut the door, and only dared to look out again long after she'd gone.

◆ ◆ ◆

Peterson told Kitty he'd seen Toby early that morning, loading his trunk on to the back of a farm cart. 'Poor sod. Can't blame him for wanting to be elsewhere, can you?'

Theo had paused by the kitchen door, and his words caused a shiver. When she stepped into view, both servants straightened.

'Peterson, will you . . . I need to go to the station,' she said.

'Going somewhere, Miss Hallewell?'

'I don't think your mother—' Kitty began.

'Please,' Theo said. 'I need to go *now.* I'll come with you to the stables. There's no need to bring the trap to the front.'

Peterson inclined his head, and Theo followed him out.

She hadn't meant to try and see Toby again, when he was so obviously done with her, but she *couldn't* let things end as they were. The feeling of being cast off was too terrible. She gripped the side of the trap as they rocked and jolted along the lane. If he would only promise to come back, then she might survive him going. Some tiny sign.

The train was already at the platform when they arrived. Clouds of steam and noise. Theo scrambled down before the trap had even fully halted, and ran on to the platform as Toby swung open a door and climbed aboard. He took his seat and tugged at the window strap, all without looking back, and Theo could only stare, already bereft.

If he looks up, and he sees me, then he loves me and will be mine.

The words, so feeble and hopeless now, came into her head unbidden.

All Toby wanted was to be far away from Hallewell. He wanted it with a desperation that bordered on panic, though he knew his guilt and sorrow would go with him. Perhaps the distance might make them easier to bear. As the train drew in, Toby heard hooves in the lane – a horse trotting fast, and the rattle of wheels. Someone about to catch it by the skin of their teeth, he supposed. He refused to look, but his skin prickled, thinking that it might be *her*. Half expecting to hear her voice, or feel her grabbing at his sleeve. He would *not* look over his shoulder.

While he chose a carriage, while he climbed aboard, Toby still waited for her to call out, or try to stop him. He was ready to reject whatever it was; in fact, he almost *wanted* to be given the opportunity to do so. Heart thumping like a drum, he found a seat and put his small bag up on the rack. The train smelled of grubby wool and tobacco smoke, and as it pulled away somebody *was* on the platform. Itching in the corner of his eye. A pale figure pushed by the wind, standing all alone. But he still refused to look.

PART II

Chapter Eight

1891

Theo woke from a nightmare with a sense of towering dread, and spent the first few minutes of her eighteenth birthday reminding herself that there was nothing in particular to be afraid of. The day held no terrors, beyond the ordinary. Her mother still watched closely for any sign of relapse into the nervous collapse that had blighted the first full year after Missy's death, so Theo was careful to show nothing of what she felt.

She'd written to Toby every week, to begin with. Secret, rambling letters, penned in a scramble of guilt and anguish, the contents of which she could only guess at now. Begging for forgiveness, desperate to explain. Her letters had gone unanswered, and his silence, though expected, was still crushing.

But today would be a better day. Timothy Crudge was down from London, and coming to collect her at two for a birthday tea in Shaftesbury, and the only thing she loved more than seeing him was being allowed to leave Hallewell for a while.

After breakfast with the guests, her mother drew her into their private sitting room and gave her a neatly wrapped present. Inside was the pair of elaborate ruby drop earrings that had belonged to Diana's sister, who'd died before Theo was born. Theo had never liked them, whatever their value. She still wore Rosalind Mackie's butterfly pendant: simple and meaningful.

'They were my grandmother's, originally,' Diana said. 'She always intended them to be passed down the female line. You must give them to *your* daughter on her eighteenth birthday.'

'Thank you, Mama.'

Theo closed the box, feeling the weight of that expectation: that she would marry, and produce children. Diana got up briskly, as though pleased to have the small ceremony over with.

'Now, go and get dressed for visiting. We have an appointment.'

'But . . . Uncle Crudge . . .'

'He's not your uncle, Theodora. In any case, we'll be back in plenty of time.'

Theo did as she was told, surprised when they set off on foot, and even more surprised when they went directly to St Agnes's. She hesitated on the step, confused. She hadn't been there since she'd tried to talk to Joanna Bowen; hadn't set foot inside since she'd come to visit Missy and found her bored in bed, with her head in a bandage. The memory swarmed over her. That familiar tumbling sensation, like someone pulling a string attached to the back of her brain; the sudden flash of aimless panic that came with it, sending her pulse racing. Theo fought the urge to turn and run.

Diana took her by the arm. 'Whatever is the matter? Stand up straight.'

Mrs Vine nodded curtly as she opened the door. Theo had no idea why they might be there. Had the girls made something for her birthday? Why on earth would they?

The matron rang a tuneless handbell.

'Girls! Assemble.'

The Friendless Girls filed in. They eyed the visitors surreptitiously, passing whispers behind their hands. Scrubbed faces and tidy hair; plain, hand-me-down cotton dresses. Seventeen of them in all, bringing a smell of laundry starch, wool stockings and rosemary. Theo was relieved to know that Joanna Bowen would not be amongst them. She'd found a position as a dairy maid out on one of the farms, the winter before. The girls lined up in two rows, and all eyes turned to Theo. Some curious, some sullen, some anxious. She sensed their expectation and glanced at her mother, perplexed.

Diana made an impatient noise.

'Perhaps you might make a suggestion, Mrs Vine?' she said. 'Somebody who might make a suitable lady's maid for my daughter.'

It was Theo's turn to stare. Her mother didn't even have her *own* lady's maid. They simply shared Kitty Shoat – Diana taking the lion's share, with hair dressing and costume changes throughout the day. Theo didn't need a lady's maid; she didn't *want* a lady's maid. She was about to say so when she realised what was happening: it was a misguided attempt to cheer her up. Her mother was trying to buy her a new friend. Someone to replace Missy.

Heat flooded into her face. It was outrageous, and she drew breath to tell her mother so. But there were too many watching eyes, and they silenced her. The girls were expectant, all waiting to hear what their lives would be after that day: more of the same, or completely different.

'Well, let's see,' Mrs Vine said. 'Jemima's our eldest now. She's ever so good with delicate fabrics and mixing up beauty compounds. All the girls use her rosemary hair tonic.'

Jemima made the slightest of curtseys. Theo knew her fairly well, and could guess why she was still there at the age of seventeen. She and Missy had come to blows a number of times. There was something sly and smirking about Jemima. She was the kind of girl who reached at once for the biggest slice of cake on the plate. Theo said nothing, so the matron continued, giving a short résumé of each girl's achievements. *Susan has an excellent hand at pastry. Doreen has the neatest stitching.*

The girls weren't supposed to be ladies' maids – they weren't being trained as ladies' maids. And if some strange girl were to wander into Cook's domain and start making pastry, she'd certainly get short shrift. Theo didn't want any of them. How absurd to have to choose a person to have close to her, when all she wanted was to be left alone.

The last girl was the smallest.

'This is Audrey. She's only come lately, so we don't know too much about her, do we, Audrey? And she's had no training yet,' Mrs Vine said dismissively.

But Theo paused near Audrey. She was short, and birdlike – not particularly thin, but with a tiny waist and narrow shoulders. She had straight brown hair and olive skin, which made the unusual colour of her eyes stand out – a mottled mix of hazel and green. Her face tapered to a pointed chin, which was lowered, but she regarded Theo calmly.

'Audrey, is it?' Theo said self-consciously.

'Audrey Wagstaff, miss.'

'How old are you, Audrey?'

'Fourteen, miss, or thereabouts.'

'Don't you know?'

'Audrey came to us from Salisbury,' Mrs Vine interjected. 'She'd been apprehended for begging, and had no family as could be found. She was bound for the workhouse, before luck – and Lady Wilton's intervention – brought her here.'

'You're an orphan?' Theo asked her.

'I suppose, miss,' Audrey said, without self-pity or apparent rancour at being discussed like a heifer at market.

Theo hated the whole situation anew. She wanted to turn on her heel and leave, but found herself still standing by Audrey. The girl had lived through things, Theo saw. It was true of all the girls there, to some extent, but in Audrey it was obvious. Her voice was tiny, and she wasn't bold, but she also wasn't afraid.

'Do you . . . would you *like* to be a lady's maid?' Theo asked.

'I don't really know, miss, never having been one.'

'Audrey!' Mrs Vine barked. 'Perhaps Doreen might suit you, Miss Hallewell?'

Theo shook her head. She'd seen the flicker of good humour in Audrey's eyes, buried deep beneath the things she'd had to see and do. The girl was unbeaten – just like Missy.

'Audrey will suit me very well,' she said.

The other servants at Hallewell House were already two to a room, and, Theo argued, Audrey needed to be able to hear when Theo called her.

'If she is to be my lady's maid, she must be close at hand,' she said, more to cause a nuisance than for any other reason.

It backfired somewhat.

'Very well.' Diana sighed. 'We shall have to do out your sister's room for her.'

Theo's sanctuary. But she'd more or less stopped going in there. Like everything else, it had lost its power to comfort her.

Crudge took Theo to the Grosvenor Arms Hotel in Shaftesbury. It was an elegant Georgian building in the middle of town, away from the crenellated Town Hall, which Theo couldn't look at without a shudder. The proprietor's wife was Austrian, and her hot chocolate was made with proper chocolate, rather than powdered cocoa, and topped with thick cream. It was too rich for Theo these days but she usually ordered it anyway, out of nostalgia for the precious few outings she'd had there as a child – all of them with Crudge.

'It had to be champagne this time,' Crudge said, as the tea arrived on a tiered platter: tiny sandwiches and cakes, penny-sized scones. 'If you mightn't drink champagne on your birthday, then when on earth might you?'

He beamed at her and raised his glass. 'A toast to you, dearest girl: happy birthday. I wish you nothing but joy. And here,' – he brought out a wrapped parcel – 'this is for you.'

'Thank you, Uncle.'

It was a new illustrated edition of *The Rihla*, by Ibn Battuta, with a cover of peacock-blue calf hide. Theo thumbed through it carefully, seeing pyramids, deserts, ancient cities.

'The fellow went everywhere – simply *everywhere*,' Crudge said. 'Though perhaps he didn't go in person to *all* the places he claims to have visited. But a better and more entertaining account of the medieval world beyond Europe we simply do not have.'

'It's wonderful,' Theo said. 'You know how I *long* to travel – and reading about it is the next best thing.'

'Indeed, I do know,' Crudge said. 'Arnaud and I intend to travel to the Alhambra Palace, in Granada, next spring, to make a study of the various phases of its construction. I do wish I could bring you with us.'

Theo sighed. 'Mama would never allow it. I can hardly imagine seeing such a place! Though you could take me to Lyme and I expect I'd be just as thrilled. Anywhere that isn't Hallewell.'

'My poor Theo – is it so very bad?'

'It's only . . . To be the last one remaining. It's . . . how I imagine it might feel to be marooned, on a barren island, watching your ship disappear out of sight.'

Crudge squeezed her hand. 'Courage, dear one,' he said. 'This too shall pass.'

Theo didn't want to spoil things, so she sipped her champagne and drummed up a smile.

'You'll never guess what Mama has given me for my birthday.'

'No?'

'A servant. A lady's maid, all to myself.'

Crudge's woolly eyebrows shot up.

'Oh yes,' Theo said. 'We went down to St Agnes's this morning to pick her out. Like a hat in a shop window.'

'Really, Theo!' Crudge chuckled.

'It's true! Her name is Audrey Wagstaff. She's very small, and quiet, but I liked her better than the rest of them.' She thought about it for a moment. 'Perhaps Mama plans to make the girl her spy?'

'I'm sure that can't be it.'

'But she watches me all the time. As though I might suddenly do something terrible – and by terrible, I mean anything to discomfit the guests.'

Crudge looked thoughtful. 'Yes. I have often reflected upon the misfortune of your being raised in an hotel. You're simply not suited to it. The constant company of strangers must be wearing indeed.'

'You know me very well.' Theo paused. 'But – *tush*! For shame, Uncle! We are *not* an hotel.'

The day after Theo's birthday, Dr Anscombe paid a visit. Diana had invited him so many times during the two years since Kit's death that it sometimes wasn't clear whether he'd come to examine Theo, or simply on a social call. Theo was always pleased to see him, and they walked around the gardens, along the damp paths beneath the weeping birches, past the ornamental pond where the goldfish hung stationary near the bottom.

'And how have you been, really?' he asked.

Theo glanced at him, then away. The same strange blurring of his role was in their conversations as well. An uncertainty as to whether he was her physician or her friend. Whichever he was, she found it easier to speak to him than to anyone other than Crudge. It felt like he was on her side.

‘Has my mother said something?’ she asked.

‘She mentioned that you reacted badly, yesterday, visiting the Friendless Girls’ home.’

‘It . . . brought back a memory, that was all.’

‘Of Melissa?’

Theo nodded. They stopped at the furthest point from the house, where they were nevertheless still visible to Diana, out on the terrace with a number of the guests. Dr Anscombe reached for a tall, dried stalk of verbena flowers, snapped it off and began to shred it with restless fingers.

‘You really oughtn’t,’ Theo told him. ‘Mama likes the stems to remain through the autumn, for their height.’

‘Oh!’

He dropped it at once, embarrassed, and brushed his fingers on his waistcoat. His eyes were extra blue against the colourless sky that day.

‘You felt afraid to go back there?’ he said.

‘Not afraid, exactly . . .’ Theo found it hard to explain. ‘It is more like . . . an aversion. It’s quite . . . physical. And there need be no rational cause for it whatsoever.’

Dr Anscombe studied her closely. ‘I see.’

‘I’m fine, now,’ Theo said uncomfortably.

‘It’s good that you’re able to identify the reaction you are having, and to some degree separate the feeling from any source of real, physical danger. That’s an important step, Miss Hallewell.’

‘Oh? Am I cured?’

‘Of your melancholia? I think not. But you are improving.’

‘Well, please tell that to my mother. She doesn’t help. Constant scrutiny might put anybody on edge.’

The doctor, who frequently heard but never endorsed Theo’s criticism of Diana, remained silent.

'Does she still think I should be consigned to the lunatic asylum?' Theo asked.

She tried to say it lightly, but the idea caused a flash of the exact feeling of danger the doctor had just described. *The Laverstock Sanatorium for Hysterical Women and Girls.* It was just outside Salisbury, and Diana had first mentioned it early in 1890, when she'd intercepted a letter before it was sent, and discovered that Theo had been writing to Toby all the while. The storm had blown for days. *Dear God, Theo, have you lost your mind?*

All it would take was Dr Anscombe's prescription and her mother's consent, and she could be sent away for an indefinite spell of treatment.

'I have told you, I will not let that happen,' the doctor said with quiet emphasis. 'There have been tremendous advances in the treatment of acute melancholia; also with hysteria and the like. Cold-water therapies, and some using electricity that appear most promising. But you are not an hysteric. And your melancholia is lifting.'

'Is it?'

'A little more each time I visit. You may not feel it yet . . . not altogether. But I see it.'

'Oh,' Theo said, surprised that hearing him say so made her feel a touch better.

'Sometimes, time is the best medicine of all,' he murmured, still gazing down at her. 'You experienced a significant trauma, and it shocked you badly. But you are young, and you are mending. And . . . you will always have me to talk to, should you need to.'

It didn't sound the sort of thing a doctor would say. Theo looked away, suddenly shy.

'We'd better go in, I suppose,' she said. 'No doubt Mama will want to hear all about your latest surgeries.'

'For such an elegant lady, she does show a remarkable interest in the more visceral side of my work.'

'Well, we hear precious little of the sensational here in Hallewell,' Theo said. 'Though I'm sure it has more to do with the visiting ladies liking very much to converse with a handsome doctor than with any particular interest in medicine.'

He looked down, and Theo saw a smile playing on his lips. With sudden mortification, she realised she'd accidentally called him *handsome*. To her, it was merely a fact; something everybody said, rather than something she thought personally.

He stayed for dinner, in the end, and a youngish widow named Mrs Birch, travelling with a spinster aunt for company, made sure to sit beside him, and leaned towards him every time she spoke as though he were hard of hearing. Letting their sleeves and shoulders brush.

'Dr Anscombe only recently saved the life of a neighbour of ours,' Diana declared, to their end of the table.

She was almost proprietorial, Theo noticed. As though the doctor were a favourite possession of hers that she liked to show off.

'Poor Mrs Cox had suffered terribly for years, and no physician had been prepared to treat her. For the longest time, the poor thing thought that the swelling was a child, growing slowly because of her advanced years.'

The other women murmured in sympathy. Diana tipped her glass towards the doctor.

'But Dr Anscombe identified the problem in an instant, and Mrs Cox is quite recovered.'

Theo, watching without particular interest, caught her mother dipping her eyelashes at the doctor, the exact same way Missy had. She saw him pretend not to notice.

'It was a large cyst, in fact,' he said. 'Growing upon her right ovary.'

There was a slight collective wince. Diana's expression turned wary.

'The abdomen is a straightforward enough place to operate,' he went on. 'If the correct aseptic measures are followed, there need be little expectation of difficulty, in most cases. It is really in the fields of heart and cerebral disease where we must improve – the latter being where I hope to make advances.'

'I understand that your father, too, was a noted physician?' said Mrs Birch.

'A physician, yes; but not a surgeon. He did important and pioneering work into the treatment of diseases of the kidneys and liver.'

Diana smiled graciously. 'So it would seem that excellence runs in the family.'

'I simply cannot imagine anything more terrifying,' Mrs Birch confided, leaning in close again, 'than performing a surgical operation.'

'It is no small thing,' the doctor agreed. 'And there is still much to be learned. But we mustn't let the fear of failure stay our hands. It is by pushing against the edges of our knowledge that we will succeed in treating ever more serious diseases. While we remain so very ignorant about the particular structures and diseases of the human brain, people will continue to die. We must be bold enough to seek solutions, where at present we have only theories.'

Theo dropped her knife and fork with more of a clatter than she'd meant to. A shiver ran down her spine. Those sitting nearest to her turned to look, and she stared at her plate, wishing she could disappear.

'Forgive me,' Dr Anscombe murmured.

Theo glanced up, and saw the stricken look on his face.

'Forgive me,' he said again. 'Such things ought not to be discussed at the dinner table.'

'Well, I think it's extraordinary,' Mrs Birch declared, dismissing Theo with a sideways glance. 'Heroic, in fact.'

She laid her fingers on the doctor's sleeve. He reached for his glass.

'I only do what I can,' he said. '"*As far as power and discernment may be mine*", to quote the oath.'

'I wonder that you don't go up to London and work in one of the large medical institutions there. Surely you might find greater opportunity, and better facilities?'

'Well.' Anscombe smiled modestly. 'There have been offers, but I have always been of the opinion that *all* patients deserve the very best surgical care, whether they happen to live in London or the provinces.'

Theo remembered the doctor's distress when he'd told her about Missy. How intensely he had felt his own failure. He'd made it his life's work to alleviate suffering and save the lives of others. She couldn't imagine being possessed of such learning, or dedication. For a moment she was awestruck, and felt herself a lesser species than he.

Diana showed little emotion about the clearing of Amy's room. Only the dressing-table set made her pause – the brush with strands of pale hair still tangled in it; the oval mirror with its small, ghostly thumbprint. She stood holding them for a long time, then took them away without a word.

The drapes and pictures were changed; the mahogany tester bed heaved out in pieces on to an auctioneer's cart. In came a narrow bed with a plain candlewick bedspread; a chest of drawers with a broken foot; an old Ottoman rug that had once been good but was now faded and spotted with burns. And in came Audrey Wagstaff.

Neither of them knew how to behave, to begin with.

Theo sought her out, the first few mornings, only to find her curled up asleep on the rug, because the bed, she said meekly, was too soft and too hot. One of the kitchen maids came and told Theo that Audrey hadn't eaten all day, because she hadn't known where or when to present herself for meals, and was too shy to ask. Audrey had no idea of her duties and neither did Theo. Diana made a few pointed remarks, and then Kitty, whose nose had been put out of joint about the new girl getting her own room, got over it and took Audrey under her wing. Audrey began to bring Theo's cup of tea in the morning, and the jug of hot water for her to wash, and took over the spot-cleaning of her dresses and jackets, and the brushing and arranging of her hair. At this, Audrey had real skill.

'I used to do Michaela's hair, and she liked it all up and fancy,' Audrey said, then pursed her lips and wouldn't say who Michaela was.

Theo didn't press her. Missy had taught her that people who had nothing ought, at least, to be allowed to keep their secrets. So, her usual lopsided combs and loose plaits were transformed into creations with elaborate twists that criss-crossed the crown of her head; or into voluminous rolls that were fastened invisibly and didn't fall down all day.

Theo's suddenly elegant hair mollified Diana about the choice of Audrey Wagstaff. The fact that she cost the household next to nothing also helped. Many times, in the first few weeks, Theo found herself regretting that she was now responsible, in many ways, for this other person. Despondent at the thought that Audrey would always be around. But gradually she noticed that Audrey's presence in the room didn't make her feel self-conscious, or anxious, or as though anything were expected of her.

Audrey was self-contained; she seemed to need to occupy only a specific amount of space in the world, and no more. She didn't ask why Theo almost always wore her gold butterfly pendant, when she had so many others to choose from, or why she often sat down to write a letter only to never finish or send it. She didn't ask the meaning of the strange silver coin she often found under Theo's pillow, or in the pocket of her dress.

'What's Salisbury like?' Theo asked her one day.

'Haven't you been, miss? I thought rich folk went visiting all over.'

'Well, we're not so very rich. And with people coming here to stay, we don't often go anywhere ourselves.'

'Oh.' Audrey thought about it for a moment. 'Well, it's known to be a handsome city, and plenty do holiday there. But I don't suppose I've seen the Salisbury you'd see, if you were to visit. And I don't suppose you'd see the Salisbury I know, neither,' she said.

'Yes, you're probably right,' Theo said.

That was the end of it, and typical of their conversations.

One morning Theo woke too early, stared at the ceiling for a while, and then around at the four walls of her room. So very familiar, and secure. Like the walls of a cell. From next door she heard the gentle creak of the floorboards as Audrey got up. Already, her maid appeared to have developed a sixth sense: however ungodly the hour, she always knew when Theo had woken. And perhaps had learned that, left to their own devices, her mistress's thoughts would tread a resolute path towards dark places.

With the softest of knocks Audrey came in, carrying a single candle to push back the dark. She was still in her nightdress, her hair in a plait hanging over one shoulder.

'Pardon me, miss,' she whispered. 'I will get myself dressed quick, but is there anything you need?'

'No, thank you, Audrey. I'm sorry to get you up so early.'

'No need to be sorry, miss. I'll be back in just a moment with some tea.'

'No – no tea yet. Audrey . . . do you feel like a walk?'

'Certainly, miss.'

'Hurry and get dressed, and so will I. Dress warmly.'

They went up to the castle, just visible as the sky paled. Past the stumps of the elms that had fallen just before Toby left. Past the spring, where Rosalind Mackie had said her prayers. Through the shadow of the broken west wall, where Kit had climbed – too high – to impress Missy. *Look at me, Missy!* Past the window with the circular mark, where Toby had looked at her at last – holding her heart, as well as her face, in the palm of his hand. Everywhere was loaded with memory, and with loss. She missed them all with unabated intensity.

'I *must* leave,' she said quietly. 'It's only . . . I don't know how I shall ever do it.'

Audrey looked at her and then away, calm and undemanding. They had never discussed the summer of 1889. Theo spoke of it to nobody except Crudge and Dr Anscombe, and then only haltingly, in brief and broken phrases. She supposed the other girls at St Agnes's had filled Audrey in on the scandal, if not the moment she arrived then the moment after. She wondered what version Audrey had heard.

Theo needed to be somewhere else, where there was a chance life might feel more bearable.

'My uncle says that travel broadens one's horizons, and reminds us of our place in the grander scheme of things. Perhaps that would cure me.' She heaved in a sigh. 'A change from the everyday.'

'Are you bored, miss?'

'Bored?' Theo glanced at her maid. 'I'm worse than bored, Audrey. I'm . . . *mired.* And everything here . . . *everything* here makes me think sad thoughts.'

In silence, Audrey took her hand.

'Mesopotamia,' Theo said. 'That's where I should like to go.'

'Where's that, miss?'

'A very long way away, east of the Mediterranean Sea. Do you know where that is?'

Audrey shook her head.

'I'll show you on the map when we get back. My uncle once said he'd take me there, but he never did. Not yet, anyway.'

'Why not?'

'The usual reason. Mama would never allow it. Mr Crudge isn't truly my uncle, you see.'

'Yes – I've heard Mrs Hallewell say that.'

'She says it often.'

'What's in Mesy . . . Messa . . . ?'

'Mesopotamia?' Theo smiled. 'I've no idea. A lot of sand and palm trees, as I picture it; lost cities and . . . And I really don't know. That's why I'd like to go there.'

'But . . .' Audrey hesitated. 'It's not such a bad home, is it? The one you've got? And I'm sure Mrs Hallewell only wants what's best.'

'Yes, possibly. But best for whom?' Theo took another deep breath. 'And you're right – the problem is with me, not Hallewell.'

The sun rose higher, bright on the scabbed yellow leaves of the willows down by the stream. Theo tried to remember how it had felt to be the girl who'd stood in that same spot at sunrise more than two years before, full of hope and love and plans. But that version of herself was a stranger now.

'Let's go back,' she said. 'I . . . I need to write a letter.'

Toby read in his room until the Chapter Library in the cathedral opened. That was the best place to study – it was impossible not to concentrate in the reverent hush of near a thousand years of history.

Hours could slide by without him even noticing the hard bench, or the draught around his ankles. When it closed at lunchtime he went to the university's own library, nearby on Palace Green, but he was far more likely to be interrupted there. He didn't like to have his reading schedule set back. He followed the advice in the university guidebook, to always read first what he liked least; to work steadily for at least eight hours a day (he usually increased this to ten); not to take too many notes in a lecture, and never to assume that what was in his notebook was necessarily in his brain.

He read until a meal interrupted him, or Womersley thumped at the door, or he'd booked to take a boat out.

From his room in Hatfield Hall he could see the River Wear through the trees, and the boat house down below. He'd tried all sorts of clubs and activities in his early days in Durham, when his mind had been chaotic and he'd had few friends. There'd been so many new rules to learn, so much information to take in. He'd reeled from day to day, pillar to post, barely holding himself together. Sitting in silence at meals while his fellows got acquainted; feeling as though he spoke a different language to them.

How he'd passed the matriculation exam he had no idea. He hadn't won the foundation scholarship he'd needed, but the Principal had made allowances because of his personal circumstances. He'd been permitted to delay paying his first battels until the beginning of the Epiphany term, by which time he'd had the chance to win an exhibition at the Michaelmas collections – the end of term exams. Which he had won, because by that time he'd discovered boxing, and could once again focus his thoughts for more than an hour at a time. Then he'd taken the two-year Classics scholarship at the start of the second year, and, with Nimrod's continued contributions, he'd managed to scrape by.

Hatfield Hall had been founded with the specific aim of making the university more accessible to those of limited means.

Servants were employed and rooms were furnished by the college, rather than by individual students; all meals were taken communally; breakfast and wine parties in student rooms were not permitted. And how the students of the fractionally older and grander University College, housed in the Norman castle, looked down their noses at Hatfield Hall – never mind that the *entire* university had been founded as a cheaper alternative to Oxford or Cambridge. Snobbery was alive and well, when Toby had supposed that the love of learning would trump all that. He was shocked to discover that a proportion of the students were there because they could be, not because they particularly *wanted* to be. He found the pointless jibes, the tossing of coppers and the silly songs infuriating.

In the two years since his brother's death, Toby had developed a temper that flared quickly and disproportionately. Black thoughts gathered inexorably in his head, sparking violent impulses like flickers of lightning. He tried to ignore them, since his scholarship depended on continued reports of discipline and clean conduct. Though he must compete with his fellows for library books, for marks and for scholarships, he still needed to rub along with them. But he got into fights. He needed an outlet for his animosity, and boxing was the first thing he found.

He wasn't very good at it, but since it turned out that getting hit was as effective as hitting someone else, that hardly mattered. It also gave him a ready excuse for the cuts and bruises he frequently sported, should anyone in authority happen to notice. Boxing, he could say; not a scuffle with local boys, or with Castlemen, when someone said the wrong thing to him, at the wrong time.

'I say, Meriwether,' Womersley said on one occasion, as he hauled Toby up, belching blood, off the cobbles of the Bailey. 'You keep this up and they'll start coming from far and wide to have a go. People love a berserker, best of all one with more fury than skill.'

He'd passed his handkerchief, while Toby spat and checked the integrity of a tooth.

'Seriously, though. Word will get about.'

Toby heeded his friend's warning. He couldn't risk rustication, or a fine; and if he carried on as he was, his own mother wouldn't recognise him the next time she saw him. After that, he tried harder to turn the other cheek. He didn't always succeed.

Toby had met Tom Womersley by chance, on day one, by sitting next to him at the matriculation service. They'd become friends purely because Womersley went through life assuming that a person met was a person befriended. For him, it was generally true. He had an easy, buoyant personality that Toby's reticence and black moods had no power to dampen.

'What's the matter, Meriwether?' he said one day, when Toby was at his worst. 'Are you practising to become a poet?'

Tom wasn't a natural scholar but he planned to be a lawyer, so he stuck at it, passing his exams with no particular distinction. He had curly, light-brown hair that he wore long; a broad, open face and blue eyes. His perpetual good humour might have been annoying, but somehow never was. Sometimes, Toby envied him intensely.

After boxing he tried fencing, but the toffs were unbearable – prancing about in their ridiculous white socks. Then he discovered rowing, and it quickly became something he craved.

He rowed in the university VIIIs and IVs for a time – not the strongest man or the longest lever, but one who kept on pulling in a race, even when the exertion was making him retch. But the single scull was his favourite. Just him in a skimpy boat with an oar in each hand, rowing by faith with his back to the direction of travel. The weir made it impossible to go downstream, but he could scull right out of the city upstream, as the river looped through woods and fields.

Alone with his rhythmic, unchanging stroke; the surge of power when he straightened, the spatter of water when he turned the oars. The pounding of his heart. He'd find his head completely empty for that blessed while.

So he'd made it through the first year, his marks improving all the time; and through the second, when it became clear that he was on course to take first-class honours. *Honours in Classics*, the handbook said, *are evidence to all the world of ability and industry*. So he dug in. As to what he would do when the final year ended, and he went out into the world with his honours, he had no idea.

Most of the old city of Durham – the Bailey – was located on a steep, rocky promontory surrounded on three sides by a large loop of the River Wear, giving it the feel of an island. The vast Norman cathedral gazed down, dwarfing everything else. It sat along one side of Palace Green – a large, neatly mown square, enclosed on the other three sides by medieval buildings belonging to the Dean and Chapter, and by the castle. The streets were narrow and cobbled, but a wide, sunny footpath ran along the riverbank around the promontory. There, students and members of the university walked and picnicked and watched the boats. There were even punts, though the current was too strong for the most part.

Beyond the Bailey, the city spread out to the west and south in more ordinary industrial fashion, with streets of red-brick terraced housing climbing the hill towards the railway station. There, gangs of barefoot children played in the streets, and the men all worked in the nearby coal mines, and coughed.

Town and gown, side by side but worlds apart.

Every time Toby felt glad to be on the more rarefied side, it came with a hefty measure of guilt. Whenever he was happy to belong to a world of libraries and learning, where his bed was made for him and he could spend his leisure time rowing, he hated himself a bit more. He felt like a traitor. It was all so very far from Hallewell – but that was exactly what he'd wanted.

'Don't be ridiculous,' Tom said. 'What should you have done – stayed at home forever? Followed your father's footsteps into the army, or the teaching of farmers' children? I mean no slight in that.'

'I know you don't,' Toby said.

They were walking towards the market square after lunch, to check the latest second-hand stock at the bookshop. Toby went along for the fun of it; he only ever borrowed books. He pulled his coat tight around himself, hands deep in his pockets, still not used to the bite of the northern wind.

'I don't know, exactly,' he said. 'But I can't bear the eager *parvenus* you meet here: middling sorts who start affecting the vowels and the . . . *ennui* of the nobs. No offence.'

'None taken.' Tom grinned. 'Personally, I don't suffer from *ennui*. And I don't think anybody could mistake *you* for one of that sort. Everyone knows you're here to actually *learn*, not to kill time and make connections. So why feel guilty?'

'Because I . . . I don't miss it. I don't miss home.'

Toby wasn't sure that this was the point, exactly, but it was what sprang to mind.

'What, not even a little?' Tom sounded faintly outraged.

Toby shrugged. 'Well, perhaps my mother's cooking.'

It was true – the fresh vegetables from the garden, all the herbs, and the wonderful puddings. The food in Hatfield Hall was of the standard institutional variety: fatty cuts of meat with vegetables so stewed they lost all identity; steamed puddings with shamefully thin custard.

'Heavens, me too!' Tom said with a laugh. 'Not that *Mama* ever cooked.'

'Of course not. Let me guess – you have a cook, named "Cook"?'

'Doesn't everybody?'

Toby pulled a face. 'Nob.'

'Speaking of nobs – you are coming tonight, yes? To Franke-Grosvenor's wine party?'

'You don't need me there. He sounds a terrible boor.'

'Campbell Franke-Grosvenor? Not a bit of it! He's a damned good egg – not in the least bit snooty, I give you my word.'

'You think everyone's a "damned good egg", Womersley.'

'I do, I do. But then, most of them are, and it gives the ones who aren't something to live up to. Come along, do – you can't study all the time. What does the guidebook say?' he teased.

'That there should be some holidays *entirely* free from work,' Toby conceded.

'There, then. I'll knock you up at eight.'

The truth about Toby's lack of homesickness was that when he thought about Hallewell, it gave him an empty feeling; a sudden washing out of everything inside him, like someone had pulled the plug. So he did his best not to think about it at all. It had happened involuntarily in a collections exam, once – Latin elegiacs, and the poetry they were given to translate was, by chance, a piece of Tennyson: *Howe'er it be, it seems to me, / 'Tis only noble to be good. / Kind hearts are more than coronets, / And simple faith than Norman blood.* Toby had read it with his scalp crawling, to be dragged so unexpectedly back to Hallewell, and to Theo. He'd had to shut his eyes and sit entirely still for two terrifying minutes, certain he was going to be sick.

Campbell Franke-Grosvenor was a Castleman, and once they'd signed in at the porter's lodge they had to climb a horrible number of steps up to his digs in the keep. It was standing room only, jammed with people all talking over one another, and reeked of the large wheel of Stilton that had been plonked on a side table with a silver scoop stuck in it. Tom was absorbed into the crowd at once, slapping backs here and there, delighted with it all. Toby gulped his first glass of wine with unseemly haste, and it got easier after that.

'A *village school teacher*?' said someone whose name Toby hadn't heard, the primary openers of any conversation being what one's father did, where one's *people* were from, and what school one had gone to.

'That's right.' Toby glared at the fellow until he stopped laughing.

'Well, jolly good,' he mumbled, cheeks mottling, embarrassed and a bit cross about it.

It was no way to make friends, Toby knew, but then he wasn't sure he wanted to be friends with anyone who found it genuinely funny that one's father had been a teacher. How would such a person cope if they ever met a farmer's son? Or a tailor's? They might die laughing.

'Are you the Meriwether who keeps winning every blasted exhibition?' someone else asked, shaking his hand.

'Well. Not *all* of them.'

'Near enough. You keep pipping me to the post, you dog.' This without rancour. 'Eric Phillips. You cost me a trip to Paris my old man had promised me, when I didn't top out the first year.'

'Sorry about that,' Toby said, liking him.

'You can start to make amends by reaching through there and passing me some bread. If I don't eat something, I'll fall down. How's your eyesight holding up? Mine starts giving up by about seven in the evening . . .'

They drank more wine and talked more loudly, then drank *more* wine and ended up playing a game that involved standing on a chair and reciting a list of items backwards, and drinking when you got it wrong or fell off. The room was stifling; cherry-red faces, gleaming eyes.

'Air,' Franke-Grosvenor declared, at one point. 'I must have air!'

'To the roof!' somebody suggested.

'To the roof!' several voices seconded.

'Is this a good idea?' Toby asked Womersley, as they waited their turn to climb out through a bathroom window. He had the nagging feeling that he was about to do something truly stupid.

'Probably not.'

Tom climbed out. Toby followed.

The window opened on to a wide gutter, which Toby scuttled along, crouching low. At the end, a narrow ladder climbed six feet up and over the parapet, on to the sloping acreage of ribbed lead that covered the Norman gallery. It was an alien place to be, and exciting because of it. Still, Toby felt a low murmur of disquiet. These other young men could afford a fine. They could afford to be sent down for a few weeks as punishment; they did not have scholarships to lose. But his blood was racing with the wine, and he heard the stifled laughter and wanted to be part of it all. Steeling himself, he left the shelter of the parapet and followed the others over the ridge.

They lined up along the far side of the roof, where the Bailey dropped away below and the city's lamps speckled the darkness. There was a tang of urine, and a guffaw; at least two of them were relieving themselves over the edge. Then the scratch and flare of a match as somebody lit a cigarillo. It was very still and deathly cold; a thin fur of frost made the stone and metal slippery. Franke-Grosvenor threw his head back and took huge, noisy gasps of the crystalline air; there was some wrestling, more stifled giggles, like children out of bed. Then someone clambered on to the parapet and stood with his toes over the edge, arms windmilling for balance, face cracked at his own daring.

'Come down before you fall down, Beresford,' Womersley said, with no great urgency.

With a sudden kick, Toby saw the danger. It stabbed through his hazy, drunken brain. He splayed his hands against the cold stone. The drop was dizzying, the fall would be fatal.

'Meriwether? What's happening?' Tom breathed boozy fumes into his face.

Toby couldn't reply.

The sky whirled above them, the empty air waited below like an open mouth, and he was right back there, in the ruins at Hallewell, with Kit balanced on a broken wall. *Look at me, Missy!* The same shock that had paralysed him then, the sudden proximity of a terrible danger against which he was powerless. *Look at me! I told you I could do it!* He heard Theo's gasp again, saw her running across the candlelit grass towards his brother.

'Meriwether's gone green – is he scared of heights?' Franke-Grosvenor said, to general sniggering. 'Life is forfeit, you know, if a Hatfielder pukes on the castle roof!'

Then lamp beams flashed up behind them, from over near the gatehouse. They all ducked; Beresford jumped down from the parapet and the immediate danger passed, but Toby still couldn't move. Fright held every helpless muscle tight; his knees were weak, his fingers clawing numbly at the parapet. The others scuttled back towards safety.

'Come on, Meriwether!' Tom hissed in his ear. 'Time to shake a leg.'

'I can't.'

'You'll have to, I can hardly carry you.'

'You go. I'll stay.'

'For heaven's sake. Shut your eyes then, if the view bothers you, and I'll lead you.'

And so they went, slowly, keeping low, Toby partly on all fours, partly on his behind, letting Tom direct him like a blind man, one wobbling inch at a time. They were the last ones back through the bathroom window, by which time there was no sign of the party. They'd scattered like mice.

Toby made it down the keep's spiralling steps and outside before throwing up into the ornamental ivy. Luckily, there was nobody around to witness it. He was cold to the bone, and disgusted with himself.

'Come on,' Tom said. 'Final furlong.'

They went back to Tom's room in Hatfield Hall – a far less grand building, which had been a coaching inn in the eighteenth century. They were both shivering by then; Tom pulled a blanket from the bed and threw it around Toby's shoulders, then lit some lamps and rattled a poker in the remains of the fire.

'What was all that about?' he said. 'If you're afraid of heights, why on earth did you follow?'

'I'm not afraid of heights,' Toby croaked, his throat raw from vomiting.

'What, then?'

Toby stared at his grubby hands, pale with cold. Nobody knew the full story, not even the Warden of the university. Most people knew nothing at all, and it was far better that way. Once the story was out, there would be no way to get it back. But there, in the circle of lamplight, brought low by drink and exhaustion, Toby couldn't be bothered to keep it in.

'It was . . . my brother. I had a brother,' he began.

He told the whole story, not once looking up for Tom's reaction. Kit and Missy and the trial and the hanging, and the way he could hardly stand his parents to look at him any more, let alone go home to them. The silence when he finished lasted a long time. There was no right thing Tom could have said in response, and a great many wrong things. But eventually he stood, reached out to grip Toby's shoulder, and said:

'That's the saddest thing I have ever heard, my friend.'

Which was the best of a very narrow field.

Toby could only nod. He was already falling asleep.

He woke when the room was still pitch black, and listened for a while to Tom's gentle snores. When he remembered how much he'd revealed, he felt precarious again. Exposed; like he was still up on the roof. It was far too cold to go back to sleep so he decided to walk instead, setting off across Palace Green towards the steep path down to the river's edge. It was bitter, the path barely visible by the light of a setting moon. At the bottom was a lamp-post and Toby stopped beside it, listening to the hiss of the gas. When he looked up he saw snowflakes spiralling down, caught in the light as though that were the only place they were falling. Through that shaft of light, and on to him.

He stared up at them for a long time, watching their silent dance, feeling them touch and instantly perish on his face. Christmas wasn't far away. He would be expected at home, in Hallewell, but knew he'd find some excuse not to go. The snow twirled and dizzied him. He supposed he was probably still at least half drunk, which might explain why he felt like a set of badly matched parts that would never make a whole.

Chapter Nine

1892

After the third time, Theo realised it wasn't a coincidence. Families of their vague acquaintance – cousins of the Fitzwilliams; a god-daughter of the Smith-Copelands – began to visit. Families with unmarried sons in their twenties, next to whom she found herself seated at dinner. Their scrutiny was unsubtle. Usually, Theo was quite capable of seeming to take part in a conversation when her mind was elsewhere, simply by saying *oh* and *yes* and *really* when instinct nudged her to. But these new visitors wanted her *opinion* on things; to know what she had read, what she played, whether she liked to dance or travel or hunt.

'Of *course* she's trying to marry you off,' Audrey said, late one evening after just such a dinner. The guests had been a family out of Dorchester, owners of a publishing firm that had once put out a book of her father's. The son and heir – Bertram – had kept asking her how she found the food, and smirking at her replies as though they had a joke to share. As though he knew her.

'But did you *see* him?' Theo said, turning on her dressing table stool as Audrey held up Theo's skirt and examined it for marks.

'I did. They looked like money.'

'Money and . . . well . . . not much else.'

Audrey smiled. 'If he'd been handsome and witty, would you have liked him any better?'

'Yes. Maybe.'

'But wanted to *marry* him any better?' Audrey shook her head. 'That's the trouble, isn't it, miss?' she said softly.

Audrey knew Toby's name from the letters she smuggled out to post for her mistress, but they had never spoken about him. Theo didn't know how much Audrey had gleaned from gossip.

'In any case,' Audrey went on, 'your mother is a determined sort of person. Dr Anscombe had best hurry up. She'll see you wed before this year is out, else I'm Queen Vicky herself.'

'What do you mean, about the doctor?'

Audrey tipped her head. 'I think you know what I mean, miss.'

Theo did, but she didn't want to talk about it. Her friendship with Dr Anscombe had grown gradually. His was the only company she looked forward to between Crudge's visits, though the faint sense remained that, on some level, he was still treating her disordered nerves. In any case, she didn't want their relationship to change, or for things to grow strained between them. She wasn't sure how it would feel to know that he thought of her that way. He'd asked her to call him Ralph, in private, but she couldn't bring herself to do it.

'I think my mother would like to marry Dr Anscombe herself,' Theo murmured. 'The way she looks at him sometimes. I don't think he notices it.'

'Oh, I think he does,' Audrey said. 'But he'd far rather marry you.'

'He's closer to her in age.'

'What does that matter, with men?' Audrey paused to consider. 'I think he'd make a fine husband. Lord knows he's nice to look at, and he'll never want for an income. He might even be famous one day – everyone says how good he is. Did you hear about the mayor's wife?'

'What about the mayor's wife?'

'Cook was telling us. The Mayor of Shaftesbury's wife, last year – I forget her name. Might've been Violet. Anyway, she started all of a sudden to lose her breath and cough all the time, and it turned out she had a tumour growing right on her windpipe.' Audrey tapped two fingers on the notch at the base of her throat. 'Just here. Her husband took her to see the best surgeons money could buy, but all of them said they couldn't take it out without killing her.'

'But Dr Anscombe did?'

Audrey nodded. 'He said there was danger in it, but he was willing to try since the lady was slowly being throttled. She's right as rain now, though she wears a high collar, to cover the scar.'

Theo considered this. 'Perhaps he might have been able to save Rosalind,' she murmured.

'Who's that?'

'Rosalind Mackie – who gave me her butterfly necklace when she died. She and her husband came to stay here, three years ago. She had a tumour in her lung, and even though her husband was a doctor he couldn't save her, nor could any of the doctors they'd seen. She came here to pray to the goddess for healing, but that didn't work either.'

'Poor her. I bet Dr Anscombe could've helped her.'

The idea of it was very sad, but also thrilling.

Theo turned to Crudge's latest letter from Granada. His letters provoked equal measures of longing and delight; she read each one over and over until the next arrived. *I woke early this morning and saw the sunrise as it reached the Alhambra. Ah! But the colours were incredible, Theo, simply incredible. There is still snow on the highest peaks and it is dazzling, all rosy pink; then the deep chasms between the promontories are blacker than night. How I wish you were here! You will see it one day – somehow, I shall make certain of it.*

Theo tried to picture a feeling of such wonder. Her imagination flickered tentatively, but she couldn't sustain it.

Dr Anscombe came for dinner most Saturdays. Sometimes, he stayed the night then went to church with them in the morning. His visits were so regular that he generally informed them when he *wasn't* coming, rather than when he was. His being needed at the hospital was the most common cause of absence. But he arrived that Saturday afternoon, just as the publishing family were leaving and Bertram, still smirking, was pressing a kiss on to Theo's hand. His lips left a smear of moisture that she itched to wipe away.

After dinner, Theo played gin rummy with the doctor in a corner of the library, while a foursome of guests played bridge at another table.

'They look in deadly earnest, don't they?' he whispered. 'I wonder what the stakes are?'

'Hush – they'll hear you!'

'Nonsense – I think we could perform an operetta and they wouldn't notice.'

'It's your turn,' Theo pointed out.

Anscombe drew a card, frowned at it, discarded it.

'I think you have both of the kings I'm waiting for, Miss Hallewell.'

'You aren't supposed to tell me – now I won't ever discard a king for you.'

'Cruel lady,' he teased.

'Perhaps I am.'

'Perhaps that poor fellow you were seeing off when I arrived would agree with you.'

Theo's face got hotter. 'What do you mean?'

'Only that he seemed keen to make a favourable impression, and you left nobody in any doubt that he had not.'

Theo fidgeted her cards uncomfortably.

'It is whispered of amongst the guests,' he went on. 'Mrs Hallewell's steady stream of suitors, and how bravely young Theodora holds her nerve.'

'Perhaps she means for me to simply . . . pick one out,' she said. 'The way she took me to pick Audrey from two rows of girls at St Agnes's.'

'It might be quicker if she *did* line them all up at once. Then you could assess each one, form an opinion and name a favourite.' He tapped one finger to his lips for a moment. 'I *think* that's called a "coming-out ball".'

'Really, Dr Anscombe. We don't have such things here in Hallewell.'

'I wish you'd call me Ralph. Aren't we friends?'

'Of course we are. But I don't think Mama would approve.'

Ralph leaned towards her, eyes sparkling. In the candlelight, he was russet and gold – skin and hair and lips.

'She need not hear you,' he said mischievously. 'You might try it out. Just once?'

Embarrassed, Theo looked away. She sensed that he was flirting with her, and didn't want, accidentally, to say anything of significance. To that end, but without conscious thought, she strove to make herself his patient again.

'Earlier, at tea, someone asked about one of the legends of Abrecan,' she said. 'The one about how he returns at midsummer, on the anniversary of his death.'

She felt rather than saw Ralph's subtle withdrawal. He discarded the eight of spades.

'And what was your reaction?'

'Almost nothing at all at the time – I even remember thinking to myself that you would be pleased with me.' She smiled briefly, not holding his gaze. 'But afterwards, for some hours . . .' She took a breath. 'I sometimes feel a terrible urgency that I can't suppress.

As though it's all still happening *now*, and I have a chance to prevent it if I am only to *act.*'

'Miss Hallewell . . .'

'If I'd stopped Missy setting off for Shaftesbury, for example. If it was the exercise that made her worsen, then I could have saved her by stopping her, and that way saved Kit as well.'

'I don't think so,' Ralph said gently. 'And in any case, it's impossible to know.'

'But if—'

The doctor suddenly dropped his cards and took hold of her free hand in both of his. His skin was hot to the touch.

'Please, Theo,' he whispered. 'Such thoughts will flourish like weeds, if you let them. They will turn to obsession, to the exclusion of everything else.'

He squeezed her hand tightly, and seemed almost afraid.

'You will make yourself unwell again. I *beg* you not to do it.'

Theo was shocked. 'I'm sorry.'

Ralph sat back, and stared down at the table. Then he stroked the back of her hand with his thumb, just briefly. It sent a tingle over her skin. When he let go, Theo felt too aware of her abandoned hand, and was unsure where to put it. He picked up his cards and looked blankly at them.

'I didn't mean to startle you,' he said. 'Forgive me.'

They finished their game, but the fun had gone out of it. Only afterwards did she notice that he'd called her by her Christian name.

Dr Anscombe didn't come again for three weeks, and sent his apologies in a note. Theo wondered which part of their conversation had so offended him, but she couldn't fathom it.

More suitors came.

'You *must* make more effort,' Diana said, wearing a bitten-back expression after one particularly awful dinner. 'Or do you wish to remain here forever? A spinster with a reputation for frailty of the mind?'

The question sent a lance of dread through Theo. To grow old in Hallewell House; to one day take over from her mother as guests came and went; to see nothing new, do nothing new, go nowhere new. The thought weighed her down – a frightening reminder of the lethargy that had taken hold in '89.

In the dead of night, she wrote another letter to Toby.

She knew she shouldn't. She might perhaps have got away with it at the age of sixteen; but now, at eighteen, the repercussions of being discovered writing personal letters to an unmarried man of a similar age would be terrible. She wasn't sure if it would be worse for people to assume that there was a secret engagement or for them to discover that there was not: that Theo was merely a huntress. The visiting suitors would vanish, given that the Hallewell good name – and the prospect of inheriting the house one day – was all she had. She supposed her mother would finish with her. They had no useful relatives in faraway corners of the country where she might be sent in disgrace, so if Diana cast her out, it would be into ruin.

But it had been two months since she'd last written to Toby, and she craved the small flame of hope lit by every letter she sent. The possibility that, *this* time, he might reply. Her desperate apologies and utter supplication had, by now, grown more measured. More conversational, in fact. She wrote of life in Hallewell, of missing him and Kit, of her struggles to make sense of it all. He had just weeks remaining in Durham. After that, Theo would have no idea where to write to him. He would slip forever beyond her reach.

On the third Sunday, Dr Anscombe came to the service at St Mary's in West End, though it was far from being his nearest church.

Theo didn't see him there until afterwards, when she went to stand by Missy's grave. The day was mild and bright, the churchyard covered in daisies. It seemed such a peaceful place to sleep. She recoiled from thoughts of the prison yard where Kit was buried. Stony and cold, with nothing green growing and nobody ever passing by to leave a token or think fondly of him. Her guilty heart ached.

It was her habit to bring a little something to decorate Missy's headstone every week, and this time she'd picked bluebells from the woods and tied them with a white ribbon. She adjusted the bow before setting them down.

'As pretty as Melissa herself,' Ralph said, appearing beside her with his hat in his hands.

Theo looked up, startled.

'How do you do, Miss Hallewell? I'm sorry to have stayed away.'

'What has . . . kept you, Dr Anscombe?' she said.

'I . . . There were . . . reasons,' he replied. 'None that matter.'

'Oh.'

'You are a good friend, to come and lay flowers for her.'

Theo looked down at the grassy mound, which sank a little more every year.

'It's one thing to simply miss a person, but quite another to feel responsible for their death,' she said. 'And I shall always feel responsible, at least in part; no matter what anybody says.'

'As will I,' he said softly. 'But . . . I believe we both did all we possibly could.'

'Yes. Yes, I know.' She touched his sleeve.

'Theo?' Diana waved from over by the lychgate. 'Come along, we're leaving.'

'May I walk with you?' Ralph asked.

'Of course.'

They stayed some distance behind the others, talking easily enough about the season and the current guests at Hallewell, and a trip to York Ralph planned to take that summer, to visit his only living relatives, an aunt and uncle.

'Uncle Crudge loves York,' Theo said. 'He says the minster is the finest Gothic building in all of Europe.'

'And what do you think?'

'I have never seen it, or any to compare it to. I've never *been* anywhere.'

'Perhaps you might, in the future.'

They'd reached the gates to Hallewell House, and Ralph stopped.

'I . . . I wonder if we might carry on walking a little further?' he said. 'Perhaps up to the castle—'

'Not there,' Theo interrupted him.

She sensed the moment coming like a train, and no way to avoid it. But the castle belonged to her and Toby, and to Kit.

'Then . . . the orchard, perhaps?'

There was a wrought-iron bench at the far end of their small orchard, hidden from the house by the high wall of the kitchen garden. The apple blossoms had long since fallen, and the branches had tiny green fruit and sprays of new leaves.

'Shall we sit here for a moment?' Ralph said.

Theo nodded, tense in every sinew. It was all going to be ruined.

Ralph smiled ruefully, as if sensing her dread. 'Is it really such a terrible thought?'

'Pardon?'

'Very well. Theo . . .'

He took her hand in both of his again. Hands so much bigger than hers. She fixed her eyes on the sharp crease his housekeeper had pressed into his trousers, and the way his knees pulled the fabric taut, obliterating it. He carried the faint scent of the hospital beneath some kind of cologne.

'My dear Theo. I'm sure you must be aware that . . . my feelings for you run much deeper than those of a doctor, or a mere friend.' He paused, his face tightening. 'Though, of course, I *am* your friend . . . You are still so young, I had hoped to give you more time . . . time in which I'd hoped your feelings might grow in parallel with mine. But your lady mother has left me little choice but to act.'

He tried to catch her eye, but Theo couldn't look at him.

'She seems quite determined to parade you around like a . . . a . . . Well, to parade you around until you accept one of these young men she has truffled out, and I simply cannot *stand* it. I have tried to keep my distance but . . . You are not some frivolous girl who will be made happy by a callow youth! You are so very much better than that. You are . . . you are *rare*, Theodora Hallewell.'

He swallowed, his throat sounding dry. 'I know that, to you, thirty must seem terribly old. But my heart, when I see you, is as young as a child's! And how it *soars* . . .'

He let go of her hand and fumbled in his pocket, fetching out a small leather box, which he turned repeatedly in his fingers.

'I know you do not feel for me what I feel for you. But, I must ask . . . do you think you might, ever? Could you come to see me as more than your friend?'

'I . . . I value our friendship very much, Dr Anscombe—'

'Please.' He closed his eyes momentarily. 'Please, if on no other occasion than this, call me Ralph.'

'Ralph,' she said, and it did cause a shift, however slight. 'You are far too kind, to say such things. I am not special; not at all. I fear I could only disappoint you.'

'You never could!' He took her hand again. 'Your purity . . . your virtue, dear Theo; your kindness and sensitivity . . . You are *peerless*,' he said fiercely. 'If you could only find it in your heart to love me then I would be a man born anew.'

He dropped to one knee in front of her, opening the leather box. Everything she had been taught to expect, from novels and gossip. A cluster of diamonds around a single red ruby, like a flower with a drop of blood at its heart. Sunshine glittered in the stones. It would match the earrings her mother had given her for her birthday. Two pieces of jewellery that she did not want, however ungrateful that made her.

'Ralph . . .'

'Theo, please, look at me. Look at me, and *see* me!'

His choice of words struck her. Hadn't she once longed for that very thing? She did as he asked, and searched his eyes for the truth, because she didn't understand how anyone could love her.

'Missy loved you from the moment she saw you,' she murmured. 'Did you realise?'

'Yes. The poor child was far too forward.' His voice fell flat. 'I could not help her, but if . . . if you will be mine, then I shall devote my life to bringing back your smile.'

He pressed his forehead to her hand, and such supplication made her feel terrible.

'You would want for nothing. I *swear* that I would do whatever was in my power to make you happy.'

'I . . . I need time . . .'

He looked up. 'I am not sure you have it. If it were up to me, and I had cause to hope, then I would give you all the time in the world. But your mother . . .'

'She cannot force me!' Theo said vehemently. 'But I . . . I need to think about everything you have said.'

'Yes. Yes, of course.' Ralph was quiet for a moment. 'That's very sensible.'

He studied the ring for a second longer before getting to his feet. The grass had left a wet patch on the knee of his trousers. He tugged his jacket to straighten it; handed her the little box.

'Keep this for now; look at it from time to time, and be reminded of how much I love you. Because I do love you, Theo. I do not think I could continue to call, if it were to watch you . . . interviewing other suitors. It would be too painful. Even worse than separating from you. I hope you understand. But, I shall come again next week; you may either return the ring to me then, or – as I so keenly wish – I will find you wearing it.'

'Aren't you coming up to the house?'

His smile was wan. 'Not today.'

He walked a few paces, then turned back. 'Love may grow, given fertile ground. It may spread, from one heart to another.'

Toby was to have lunch with Womersley and his parents at the Dun Cow at midday, which gave him five hours to write two thousand words on Merivale's statement that *Tiberius did injustice to his own reputation*; and to revise the physical geography of Greece north of the Isthmus of Corinth, and its influence on Greek and Persian troop movements; and to compare Aristotle's Ethics and Bishop Butler's sermons on the differing principles of action of Men and Brutes. Well, perhaps not all of that, but he could try.

He was working his way through past papers of the final examination, which he would sit for real in one month's time. There was none of the panic and anxiety of the early days any more. He knew he would pass; in fact, he knew he'd take a first. But he wanted the ten-pound prize for Classics, and possibly the one for Hellenistic Greek as well, since they'd be the last of all the exhibitions he might win.

He sometimes worried that studying had become less about knowledge and more about winning. But then again, so what if it had?

At a quarter to twelve he shrugged on his gown – black, with a white-lined hood – clapped his mortarboard on to his head and legged it along the North Bailey towards Elvet Bridge. The only time that academic dress was *not* required of students was during the afternoon, and off university or church premises. But the afternoon didn't start until one o'clock, and it ended again at dusk, so Toby hardly ever risked it. Since the near disaster on the castle roof, he'd stuck tight to the rules he'd promised to obey at matriculation. He was only allowing himself to go to an inn that day because Womersley's parents were staying there, and because he'd got written permission from the censor.

That was the *real* him, he told himself: the one who studied, and won prizes; who kept to the rules and didn't smuggle wine or sherry into his room, or fool about with the local girls. The part of him that needed to hit things – to hit *people* – was an aberration. Something to be crushed. He was older now – a man – and determined to crush it.

The Dun Cow was on Old Elvet, a wide street of Georgian houses across the river. Toby arrived, out of breath but on time, just as Tom Womersley came out to look for him – wearing a jaunty blue waistcoat rather than his gown.

'Nick of time, Meriwether,' he said with a smile, pocketing his watch as the church bells began to strike noon.

'When have I ever been late?'

'Ha! Come on – everyone's already in.'

'Everyone?'

Womersley only raised his eyebrows in reply, so Toby guessed who'd come to join them.

They wound their way through the fuggy warmth to the table where Tom's parents were waiting. Mr Womersley, with greying whiskers and lively eyes beneath heavy black brows, and Mrs Womersley, dumpling-shaped, cheery and vague. And, as Toby had expected, there with them was Tom's sister, Lily. Had he merely expected, or had he hoped? It was hard to say. Her parents were good people, and Toby valued Tom's friendship more than anything. Instinct told him the situation was delicate.

Lily wore her fair hair parted in the middle and smoothed into a shiny knot at the back of her head. She had dark-brown eyes in a heart-shaped face, and an ironical tilt to her lips. Everything about her was soft and gently rounded.

'On the stroke of noon, naturally,' Tom said, as they sat down.

'Mr Womersley, Mrs Womersley,' Toby said. 'How do you do? And Miss Womersley. What a pleasant surprise.'

He shook her hand, and she gripped his firmly.

'Am I a pleasant surprise? Well, that *is* good,' she said, gently mocking, as she often was.

Lily was also a student at the university, in the first year of a degree in Physical Sciences. The Womersleys were local. They had a large house near Bishop's Auckland, and during term time Lily boarded with several of Durham's thirty female students in private lodgings with a beady-eyed landlady. *Of course, they won't actually award me a degree*, she'd told Toby when they first met. *Apparently, my aptitude for the subject is too amply concealed by my skirt.*

'Of course you are,' Toby said, his attempt at gallantry spoiled by having to look down and fiddle with his gown as he said it.

'Wearing the colours with pride, I see,' she said.

'For the next hour, at least,' Toby said. 'We aren't all as dash-it-all as your brother.'

'What *will* you do after graduation, without all these rules to follow? Perhaps you'll fly apart.'

Mrs Womersley tapped her daughter's hand. 'Don't tease poor Toby. I think it's commendable, the way you keep to the letter of the law,' she told him.

'Men do so love a law,' Lily said.

'Lily,' Mr Womersley said, 'shall we at least raise a glass to the boys, before we descend into political debate?'

'Oh, very well, Father.' Lily waved her hand, suppressing a smile.

Mr Womersley poured Toby a glass of wine, then raised his own. 'To Toby and Tom. Two finer young men I have never known, about to be launched upon the world. We wish you *every* good fortune. May the wind be ever in your sails . . .'

'May barnacles never grow upon your—'

'*Lily!*' Mrs Womersley cried. She leaned towards her son, eyes shining. 'We're so *very* proud of you, Tom.'

'And you, Toby – isn't it your birthday in a couple of weeks?' Mr Womersley asked. 'Will your parents be travelling up to see you?'

Tom shot a glance at Toby. He was still the only person who knew about Toby's family. Revisiting that time – even now, three years on – only fanned the flames of Toby's anger, a feeling so corrosive he thought it best to smother it. Tom hadn't mentioned it at all since Toby's drunken confession, and Toby had no fear that the story would go any further – the look Tom had given him now, at the mention of his parents visiting, was the most indiscreet he'd ever been.

'It's difficult for them to travel this far,' Toby said. 'My father has a crippled leg – an old war wound, from the Crimea.'

'Oh, the poor, brave man!' Mrs Womersley said.

'A long journey by train would not suit him.'

'Yes, I see.'

'But I shall travel to visit them after the exams.'

'Now, you cannot spend your twenty-first birthday at your books!'

'It's just another day, when you think about it,' Toby said. 'Just another birthday.'

The Womersleys exchanged a look.

'Then that's settled,' Mrs Womersley said. 'You will come to us at Fairton Hall, all three of you – and anyone else you care to invite. We'll play tennis, and charades, and eat too much and have a simply *splendid* time.'

'Really, you're too kind. I couldn't possibly impose—'

'Better not argue, Mr Meriwether,' Lily said. 'There's no point. Mama will not be put off if there's the chance of a party.'

'I won't, you know,' her mother agreed.

'There. That's settled.' Mr Womersley topped up their glasses. 'Be sure to get permission to be out overnight, the pair of you. And if it transpires, after all, that your parents feel equal to the journey, then the more the merrier.'

After lunch they strolled along the river, and Toby tried not to chafe to get back to his revision. Tom walked ahead, with his mother on his arm, leaving Toby and Lily to follow behind, keeping a seemly twelve inches between them. Sunlight came dappled through the trees above. Lily stopped by the weir, where two skinny boys were fishing with home-made rods.

'What do you hope to catch?' she called to them, and they turned to squint at her.

'Trout, miss,' one said. 'Salmon if oo'r luck's in.'

'Salmon? Goodness me!'

There followed a brief discussion on the sizes of fish, and when they walked on Toby wondered if Lily had engineered the conversation to allow the gap between them and her family to widen. She smiled at him, unabashed.

'We should go out in a punt one day. You could pole me about while I drape myself over the seat in a diaphanous dress, reading a novel.'

Toby wasn't sure how to reply.

'I saw a punt go over the weir last year,' he said. 'The current took it. There was a lot of yelping, and several ruined hats.'

'Well, we'll wait until summer, then, when the river's low.' She sounded faintly exasperated. 'It'd be more restful than rowing by yourself like a metronome, as you normally do. And a lot more sociable.'

'Sculling,' Toby corrected her, with a smile.

'All right, sculling.' She sighed. 'Why don't you row for the university? Tom says you're very good.'

'I did for a while. But I just . . . like doing it. I'm not bothered about winning.'

'That's not what I hear.'

'Well, I'm not bothered about winning at sculling, in any case,' he conceded. 'I find it . . . very soothing.'

He didn't want to say too much about it; didn't want her to ask what inner commotion he needed to soothe.

'It's a pity your parents can't come up for your birthday,' she said. 'But we'll have fun at Fairton, I promise. My mother will spoil you rotten – she *adores* having guests.'

'She's very kind. They both are.'

'I wonder . . . do you not get along with your family, Mr Meriwether?' Lily asked.

Toby kept his eyes to the front. The dry mud of the path; a pair of magpies tearing up tufts of moss.

'I love them very much, in fact,' he said, as neutrally as he could.

'Are you their only child?'

'No. That is, yes. I had a brother. We . . . lost him.'

Lily laid her fingers on his arm for a moment. 'I'm so very sorry. Forgive me.'

'For what?'

'When Father asked about them, during lunch, I thought I sensed some difficulty about the subject . . .'

She trailed off, but there was nothing he wanted to say about it; not then, not there, and not to her. But she wasn't embarrassed by his reaction; like her brother, she had no social diffidence, and there was nothing scheming about her. She only wanted to know him better, and he felt bad for being cagey.

They'd reached Prebends Bridge, a stately trio of half-moon arches spanning the river, wide enough for carriages to use. Toby turned on to it.

'Come on,' he said, when Lily hesitated.

'Where are we going?'

'Just to the middle,' he said. 'There was a footbridge here before, did you know? Very old. It was washed away in a flood in 1771, and this one was built to replace it, but further upstream than before, so there'd be a better view of the cathedral.'

'Is that true?'

'Men have built far bigger things than this, just to have a nice view.'

'I suppose you're right.'

Lily followed him to the centre of the bridge, where they leaned on the parapet and gazed up at the cathedral.

'One of the girls in my class is very upper, daughter of Lord Someone-or-other, and her grandfather moved their entire house, stone by stone, fifty feet to one side, to improve the view of the lake from the drawing room.' She smiled at his incredulous expression. 'Or so the story goes.'

'It would have been easier to move the lake, surely?'

'Well, money never could buy good sense.'

After a while they moved to the other side of the bridge and waved to the Womersleys, who were looking for them back along the path. Lily peered down at the lazy river, flat and green. The sun caught in the fine hairs at the nape of her neck. A single stray wisp moved in the breeze, tickling her, and she tucked it in at once.

'"*Still glides the stream, slow drops the boat*",' she said softly. 'Perhaps, one day, you'll tell me more of your stories.'

'Who's that? Dryden?'

'Matthew Arnold.'

'I didn't know you liked poetry.'

'Oh, heavens, I *don't*. So desperately dramatic, most of it. Or else so sweet it rots the teeth.'

She rolled her eyes comically, and a thought occurred to Toby, out of the blue. A thought loaded with pleasure and guilt: how nice it might be to belong to a family like the Womersleys. Unscathed. A family he could look in the eye, without shame. Lily's throw-away remark at lunch had hit home – asking what he would do after his degree. He had no idea. But, perhaps here was an answer. Perhaps it would not be so very bad to be married to a girl like Lily Womersley.

On his return from Spain, Crudge picked Theo up for an outing in a hired trap. With stones rattling beneath the wheels and a wake of pale dust behind them, her spirits rose. The hedges were decked with dog rose and pink hawthorn, and teams of men and women were out in the fields, pulling the wild oats from the wheat.

'Everyone dresses so darkly these days,' Crudge said. 'Cheap woollen cloth, made in large manufactories. When I was a lad, farmers wore linen smocks and canvas hats. A harvest was a sea of billowing white.'

'How old *are* you, Uncle?'

He gave a bark of laughter. 'Ha! I suppose to you I just look ancient?'

'Fairly.'

'Well, there you are then. I'm ancient-and-three.' He looked at her fondly. 'Your eighteen years have gone by in the blink of an eye to me, my dear. That's what happens as you get older. One day you'll look back and be astonished at how time has flown. It's so very important not to squander it.'

In the pause, Theo felt his question coming. She wasn't ready to answer it.

'And Mr LeRoy?' she said. 'Is he well?'

'Ah, now,' Crudge said.

Theo glanced across, and saw a deep sadness in his eyes.

'Arnaud has left me, I fear.'

'*Left* you?'

Theo registered his pain without fully understanding it. But then, he and Arnaud had been constant companions for over three years.

'Whyever has he left you?'

'He was offered a position at a university in Cairo. Though, I rather suspect he'd simply grown tired of me.'

'But how could he tire of you? And if he has then he's an ingrate, and a fool. Nobody could have taught him more about history, and digging, than you!'

'Thank you, my dear,' he said heavily. 'But . . . he is a young man and I am an old one. It stands to reason that he would want to make his own way in the world.'

Theo put her hand over his, and his smile was careworn.

'There it is,' he said. 'Now, forgive me, Theo, but I simply *must* know if you are engaged?'

Theo turned to stare out over the pony's ears. 'Not exactly. Not altogether.'

She described the conversation in the orchard. How it had been everything a proposal should be, apart from the lack of conviction on her part.

'Isn't that rather an important ingredient?' he said.

'My mother doesn't think so. She thinks the best thing would be for me to move away and begin a family.'

'Well, in this instance, I have to say I agree with her.'

'Sometimes I do, too,' Theo murmured. 'But she married my father for position and security, not for love – she told me so. And look how that turned out.'

'But some *do* grow into love. And their union produced two beautiful daughters, one of whom is a particular favourite of mine. So, it wasn't all bad.'

'I want to leave. I do. Everything at home reminds me of . . . what happened. But is getting married truly the only way? What if it doesn't work? What if I always feel . . .' Her head felt hot. 'I don't know what to do, Uncle. I just . . . I miss them so horribly.'

'Oh, Theo, of *course* you do! You loved them, and they are gone. There's no cure for that. But it mustn't direct the rest of your life. It *mustn't.*'

'So, I should marry a man I do not love?'

'I never said so. But the young doctor seems a fair prospect, if you ask me. And if there's a chance the union might, in time, bring you a measure of happiness . . .'

'But I don't *know*. How can I know? He's a good man – everyone says so. The things he's able to do . . . the way he saves people. He says he won't be able to continue as my friend, if I turn him down.'

'You must surely understand how difficult it would be for him to do so?'

'But it only makes the decision all the harder! Either I choose him, and hope to fall in love with him, or I turn him down and lose my only friend.'

'Not your *only* friend.'

'No. Not my only friend.' She smiled sadly at him. 'And Mama will make me marry *someone*, that much is clear.'

'I cannot advise you, my dear. I wish I could, but the decision must be yours alone.' Crudge paused. 'Perhaps I will venture to say that marriage to a good friend might be a better point from which to start than many do. And it would mean *change*. Which might be exactly what you need.'

'Audrey says the same thing. She says, "It's better the devil you know, especially if the devil is as comely as that one".'

'Young Audrey is wise beyond her years.'

Theo thought back. 'Dr Anscombe said that if we were to marry, he would be "a man born anew". What do you suppose he meant by that?'

Crudge looked faintly troubled. 'That you would be a good influence upon him, I suppose.'

'Why should he need me to be that?'

'I simply do not know.'

At length, Theo asked: 'Do you hear from the Meriwethers at all?' She tried to sound offhand, but Crudge wasn't fooled.

'Toby has still not replied?'

'He told me he wouldn't. I know I should stop writing to him, especially if I am to be engaged.'

'You really must,' Crudge said gravely. He gave her hand a squeeze. 'I haven't heard from him, but Mrs Meriwether writes from time to time. Toby will be sitting his final examination soon, and is in line for first-class honours.'

Theo listened closely, trying to glean every scrap of information from what was said, and what was not.

'And is he . . . happy?' she said. 'Does he enjoy it there?'

'He has made some firm friends. He rows – they row at Durham, as they do at Oxford and Cambridge. For a while he practised boxing, but he gave it up.'

'*Boxing?*' She pictured his hawkishness, his anger. 'Will he come back to Hallewell once it's all done?'

'What would he do here?' Crudge said gently. 'There's no suitable work for such an educated man.'

'Is he . . . does he . . . have a sweetheart?'

'My dear, I do not know. Mrs Meriwether did mention the sister of one of his fellows—'

'Who?' Theo was winded. 'Are they engaged?'

'I know nothing more, I swear it. You could always call upon Mrs Meriwether yourself. But I would *hate* to think of you hanging any hopes on Toby, my dear. He has moved *away*. You do see?'

Theo flinched, because those hopes were the real reason she hadn't answered Ralph. Marrying Dr Anscombe – or anyone – meant that she could never marry Toby. It made no difference that she was as likely to marry Toby as she was to fly to the moon; she still didn't know if she could bring herself to destroy the possibility altogether.

'Of course I see!' she cried.

'My poor, dear girl,' Crudge said, but found nothing to add.

Theo stared ahead in silence, no longer seeing the pretty views or the passers-by with their handcarts and bushel baskets. She remembered Missy stroking her hair when she first heard that Toby was going away to study, and was distraught. *He'll meet some sister of some new chum of his, and he'll get married!* What a cruel joke, to have been so completely right. And then the time Missy had read Theo's palm, and told her she'd marry a handsome man whom she already knew. Theo had thought that meant Toby, but now saw that Ralph Anscombe also fitted the bill.

Perhaps it wasn't too late – perhaps Toby wasn't *firmly* engaged. She could write again, and ask him outright. As soon as she decided on it, she changed her mind. He hadn't answered a single one of her letters, and on the two occasions he'd been back to visit his parents, he hadn't tried to see her. She hadn't even known he was home until after the fact. For a moment she entertained a wild fantasy of travelling to Durham to confront him, but it was not something that was actually feasible.

Her mind jolted back to the platform at Semley, standing there, *willing* him to look at her as the train pulled away. Which he hadn't.

She clenched her hands into fists in her lap, and Crudge left her to her thoughts.

At home, Theo went to the library to be by herself. She paced, surrounded by the rows of books with their faded spines, then bowed her head and sobbed quietly for a while, as a hornet bashed itself wearily against the leaded diamonds of the window.

When the worst had passed, she let the creature out. A thought had occurred, and she dragged a heavy album from a shelf, flipping through it until she found what she was looking for: a photograph of the Hallewells plus acquaintances assembled on the terrace, with a large crowd of people behind them. It had been taken at the summer fête; *August 1888* was written beneath it in Diana's neat hand. A day that had started out well and descended into chaos, when a storm had boiled up from the south: thunder and lightning and torrential rain. The clouds were there in the picture – an ominous smudge on the horizon. The *Lords v. Louts* tug o' war had been called off, and several of the gazebos ruined – brought down by the weight of water.

Theo looked more closely at the crowd of villagers and there they were, tiny but recognisable. Her heart clenched. Toby with his arms folded, squinting into the sunshine. And next to him, half blurred by motion, was Kit, his face dominated by an excited grin, and his hair a mess. Theo's eyes swam with tears. Carefully, she took the photo out of the corners, and studied every line of Toby's face and body – the way his eyes were thrown into shadow; the slight tilt of his mouth that was perhaps impatience, waiting for the photographer to get on with it.

Every detail choked her with longing. She pressed the picture to her chest for a moment, then got up and made for the door.

The Meriwethers' cottage looked the same, the garden just as tidy. There was no outward sign of the torment that had gone on within its four walls, but everybody knew about it. It would become Hallewell lore, Theo supposed; a tale passed down by word of mouth, like those about Abrecan the Wolf. That was how villages worked, with scant thought for those living at the centre of the story. Theo knocked at the door.

Mona had become gaunt, with hollow cheeks and lines across her forehead that aged her.

'Miss Hallewell,' she said, without apparent surprise or pleasure. 'It's a long time since we saw you.'

'How do you do, Mrs Meriwether?'

'Well enough.'

David was at school, so Mona was alone. Neighbours would have called around to begin with, Theo supposed. Well-wishers, sympathisers, bringers of cake and preserves. But perhaps those visits had dwindled after the memorial, as other people's lives had gone back to normal. The thought of Mona trapped in that empty house all day was wretched.

Eventually, she stepped aside and said woodenly: 'Won't you come in?'

The cottage was tidy, well swept and far too quiet.

'Would you like some tea?' Mona said.

'Oh, no, thank you. Please don't go to any trouble.'

Mona didn't insist. She motioned for Theo to sit down on one of the small settees, and perched herself on the opposite one. Theo brought out the photograph and handed it over. Her pulse was ticking in the back of her throat.

'I wanted to give you this,' she said. 'I remembered it just now. It's of the fête a few years ago – the one that turned into a complete fiasco.'

Slowly, almost reluctantly, Mona looked at the picture. Then she put the knuckles of one hand to her mouth and ground them into her lips.

'My boys,' she murmured. 'My beautiful boys.'

For a moment, Theo thought she'd done the right thing by bringing it. But Mona's face, when she looked up, said different.

'I lost them both, you know,' she said. 'I lost them both that day. Toby's . . . changed. When he comes home to visit—' Here she had to break off, gather herself. 'Those precious, rare times he comes to visit, he can barely *look* at us, for the shame he feels. When we were so thick before, the four of us . . . Everything was as it was *meant* to be. Not like now.'

'But Toby wasn't to blame!' Theo said.

'What does that matter? None who *were* to blame got punished, did they?'

Her stare was so bleak that Theo had to look away.

'I know, deep down, that it wasn't your fault, Theo. You were just a girl . . . A lonely girl with a head full of dreams. But I *do* blame you – I can't help it!'

In the silence, the staircase creaked as the cat went up.

'I blame myself, too,' Theo whispered.

Mona went back to staring at the photo – a moment of a happiness that would never return. Theo got up to leave.

'Mrs Meriwether,' she said, a tremor in her voice. 'Is Toby engaged? Mr Crudge mentioned someone . . . the sister of a friend. Up in Durham.'

Mona looked up, incredulity dawning. Theo felt painfully exposed but she didn't care. The need to know was greater.

'Is it your business at all, Miss Hallewell?'

'No. But, please, I . . . Is he engaged?'

Mona had always been so kind; now the cold look in her eyes hurt almost as much as what she said: 'He is.'

Theo excused herself from dinner because her head was aching, and sneaked out alone.

'What is it, miss?' Audrey whispered. 'What's happened? Can I come with you?'

'No. Thank you. It's nothing.'

In the failing light, Theo sat by the spring and poured her pain into a letter to Toby. All her love for him, unchanged since childhood; how she never wanted to marry another, and was stricken to hear that he would. How much she'd loved Kit, and how sorry she was. Her vehement wish to travel back to that night, and keep it all from happening; to have found the courage to speak at the trial. Page after page she wrote, resting the paper on her copy of Tennyson; a hasty scribble that would be hard to read.

She concluded with a verse that had struck her, and in some ways comforted her: *I have not look'd upon you nigh, / Since that dear soul hath fall'n asleep. / Great Nature is more wise than I: / I will not tell you not to weep.*

The darkness deepened beneath the trees, until the words were barely visible. Theo dropped her pen.

How foolish it seemed, all of a sudden. There was nothing *wise* or *natural* about Kit's death. Or Missy's. How pathetic to steal from Tennyson – a poet Toby had never liked – to lend herself gravitas. She saw how ridiculous it was, how ridiculous *she* was. She touched the gold butterfly at her neck. *There is always hope of a reprieve.* But it wasn't true. Toby was twenty-one, come of age, holding a degree and engaged to be married. And what was she? An hysteric, writing scandalously inappropriate letters when he had told her in no unclear way that he blamed her, and despised her, and did not want to hear from her.

Theo was too tired to fight the despair that crashed over her. He would not read her letter. He had gone.

She fumbled about in the darkness for a rock of a suitable size, then crumpled her letter around it. Dirtying the paper, smudging the ink. She tossed it into the deepest part of the pool, where it landed with a gulp and vanished. The words would never be read. Not by Toby, the goddess, or anyone else. Theo stood up to leave, then turned and threw Tennyson in as well.

◆ ◆ ◆

After the final written papers came a few wonderful weeks during which there was nothing to do but relax by the river, go rowing, and have picnics with friends. Toby tried not to worry. He knew the exams had gone well; there hadn't been a single moment when he'd stalled, or been blindsided by a question. But anything less than first-class honours would feel like failure, and it made no difference how many people told him it only really mattered if one wanted a fellowship. He didn't want a fellowship. He just wanted to be the best.

'Why does it matter so?' Lily asked him, walking side by side across Elvet Bridge one day. 'I won't even be awarded a degree when I finish, no matter how well I do. But it's still worth it, isn't it? The opportunity to learn?'

'It is,' Toby said. *For you*, he added silently. 'I just . . . A lot of people worked very hard and . . . made sacrifices, to send me here,' he said. 'If I do not do the very best I can, I'll feel that I've let them all down.'

That wasn't it at all, really; but it sounded good. The real reason, he suspected, was that he had nothing else.

'Ah. So it's *duty*?' Lily said, and he could see she didn't believe a word of it. 'Any advances on what you might do next?'

‘No,’ he confessed, hiding the nervous jolt that always came with that question. ‘Something will come along.’

She sighed. ‘Indeed.’

All Toby knew was that he wasn’t going back to Hallewell.

Franke-Grosvenor hired a carriage and invited Tom and Toby on a day trip out of the city, to hike across moorland swathed in yellow gorse and pink heather. They walked for miles, then flopped down beside a stream to a lunch of pork pies and gherkins. Toby watched cloud shadows slide silently over the distant hills, and felt his mind unfurl. The world was still there, waiting for him. He need not be anxious about it.

He knew he needed to get on and propose to Lily, so he took her out in a punt the next day, as she had once suggested. The river was low, and he poled them upstream with no real effort, and Lily kept her side of the bargain by draping herself very elegantly over the seat, though with her nose stuck in a book. Cramming for her first-year exams. She seemed put out, as though the punt wasn’t all that she’d hoped for. Or, he began to suspect, as though *he* wasn’t all that she’d hoped for.

It clearly bothered her that he hadn’t decided what to do next, or even where to go when the time came to vacate Bishop Hatfield’s Hall. Then there was the fact that he still hadn’t proposed, despite an over-enthusiastic letter he’d written to his parents, primarily because he’d been desperate to send them good news. And despite a note he’d dashed off to Lily, after one of his tutor’s sherry parties, suggesting that she and Tom travel down with him to meet his family. He hadn’t mentioned it since.

He punted them along in silence, trying to ignore the growing sensation that he was acting in a play, the script of which had been written by someone other than himself. It was the perfect moment, the perfect setting to propose.

‘Lily . . .’

She looked up, eyes shaded by the brim of her hat, unreadable. Toby swallowed. The words would not come. Lily cocked an eyebrow, and went back to her book.

She had every right to be expecting it by now; failure to do so would inevitably disappoint her, and cause affront. Tom might never forgive him. And he liked her well enough – she was clever and witty, and somehow both very forward and very decorous, which was never dull. There'd been a moment, during a tennis tourney on his birthday, when she'd come to shake his hand with her face flushed and her hair coming loose. His nostrils had filled with her hot skin and fresh sweat, and the smell had shot directly to his groin in an alarmingly animalistic way. He'd turned away abruptly, but not before their eyes had met; not before she'd seen the flare of desire.

When she finished studying Lily wanted to teach, which she could do until they wed. But Toby had no idea what work he would be doing to support himself, let alone her. And however rationally he turned the idea about, the fact remained that he didn't feel ready to be married. Not practically, not financially, not mentally. It was a thing to be done down the line, when he'd made something of himself. When he'd mastered himself. Lily had only ever seen him when he was in the mood for company: she'd never experienced the uproar that could sweep over him without warning; she had no inkling of the agonies that confined him to his room sometimes, or made him pull the oars until he couldn't breathe.

Tom had, and didn't seem worried by it; so Toby supposed it didn't look as bad from the outside as it felt on the inside. He decided that was a good thing.

Three days before the results were due to go up, Toby was called to sit a *viva voce* in Latin – an oral examination before of a panel of three professors. It meant he was hovering between grades with his written papers. Not far enough clear of the watershed to be awarded his first. And it was *his* first – he'd earned it.

'Don't look so horrified, Meriwether,' Tom said easily, clapping him on the shoulder. 'The world's doors won't slam shut on you if you take second class.'

Tom was in line to scrape a second, if he was lucky, and was perfectly reconciled to that. It would get him where he wanted to go.

'But I *must* take first class,' was Toby's terse reply, at which point Womersley decided to pick his battles.

Toby went directly to the library and started to revise. He had four hours. He did exactly what the guidebook said not to do. *Working at high pressure is ruinous.*

Standing outside Professor Kemble's room when the time came, Toby thought about throwing up. He was completely sure that he was *going* to be sick, so it seemed better to get it over with out there in the vestibule. There was a large Chinese vase in one corner, holding a few umbrellas and a riding crop. It was the perfect size. Toby was standing over it, breathing deeply, when the door opened and Kemble poked his head out.

'Ah! Meriwether,' he said. 'Do come in.'

So, the opportunity for a strategic spew was missed.

Toby's ears rang with a continuous high note. He had a vague sensation of floating. Then he sat down and became very, very calm. It was a strangely serene, almost dissociated state, in which he watched himself from one side, answering all of their questions, translating everything he was asked to fluently and with little apparent effort. A touch of arrogance, even – not enough to be obnoxious, but a good facsimile of a confidence he didn't feel. For those fifty minutes, he knew it all.

Afterwards, standing on unreliable legs on the cobbles of Palace Green, he felt spent but liberated. It was now completely out of his hands. Eric Phillips and Tom found him there.

'Well?' Eric said. 'How did it go?'

Toby shook his head. 'I have absolutely no idea.'

'But you must have *some* impression?'

'I can't remember it at all.'

Tom peered at him. 'Right. Come along – brandy is required.'

At around two in the morning the night before the results were due, Toby gave up trying to sleep. He lit a lamp and put on his coat against the perpetual chill of his room. Stilled by the peculiar loneliness of being wide awake in the dead of night, he sat silently in his chair for a while. Then he reached into the bottom drawer of his desk for his journal – his Hallewell journal, of the castle's symbols. He couldn't bring himself to throw the book away. It wasn't only because the sketches and jottings represented so many hours of thought and effort. It wasn't only because the puzzle was still unsolved. It was because looking through it felt a little like going home.

He hardly ever let himself do it. He didn't *want* to be comforted by thoughts of Hallewell – it was surely perverse, given all that had happened. He certainly didn't want to *be* there. And yet the journal cleared his mind, and set his feet squarely on the ground if he was drifting. The symbols, which might be runic or alchemical or figurative or nothing at all, were rich with abstract memories of warm stone and the smell of trampled grass; wide afternoon skies, the thump of Kit's running feet, and catching sight of a willowy figure with unbound hair, wearing a pale dress and ugly boots.

Full, conscious thoughts of it were too painful; the journal gave him just enough.

A stack of envelopes slumped to one side in the drawer: Theo's letters. She'd sent so many to begin with; then there'd begun to be gaps of weeks or months, before another flurry. He tried not to expect them; thought only absently about why she persisted, and wished she would stop. In the early days the arrival of a letter from her would ruin his day – a churning stomach, and poor concentration. Anger billowing up, disorganising his thoughts. But their effect had weakened over time, and now he barely looked at the envelope when one arrived.

He never read them.

He didn't want to hear anything she had to say. He didn't want news of home. And if she'd included any poetry, he might suffer a fit of some kind. The self-same anger made him keep them. There was something satisfying about shutting them away in a drawer, silenced. Not opening them was vengeance of a kind – one that he managed to feel equally justified in and faintly belittled by. Besides, if he never opened one, he couldn't be tempted to reply.

He straightened the pile, shut the drawer, then began turning the pages of his journal. The forked symbol that might be antlers, or a strange kind of crown. The circle with the cross overlaying it, like the addition sign in mathematics; another circle with a notched vertical line bisecting it, like the eye of a goat – or of the devil. The arrow pointing upwards that might be just an arrow, or the Anglo-Saxon rune *tir*, meaning glory. A triangle that might be a banker mason's mark, or the alchemical symbol for fire. No one symbol had any one meaning. Toby was matching them up, trying different pairings, when he fell asleep.

The results went up on the noticeboard. Toby not only had his first but also the Classics exhibition, which meant that his *viva voce* must have been to determine who had the highest mark outright:

his first-class honours had never been in doubt. Toby grinned sheepishly as he was barracked and thumped on the back, even by Phillips, who was far more magnanimous in defeat than Toby would have been.

'There you are, then!' Tom said, delighted. 'You've beaten *everybody*. Now, for heaven's sake let's hear no more about it, eh?'

'All right,' Toby agreed, still smiling.

There was to be a reception with the Principal that evening, and wine with supper, but until then Toby ducked away from the whooping and cavorting and throwing of caps. His relief was so huge he felt fragile, almost tearful, and needed time alone for it to settle. He was meeting Lily for a walk in the terraced gardens behind Hatfield Hall, so he went there, very early, to sit on a bench. He realised he hadn't even asked about Tom's degree. He also realised that his first didn't solve the problem of what to do next.

A letter had arrived from his mother that morning. He took it out of his pocket, thinking it would be wishes of luck that had come a fraction too late. So, the news that Theo was engaged to Dr Ralph Anscombe blindsided him completely.

It landed a stunning blow. That high-pitched whine was in his ears again; that pressure building in his head. The very man who had stood in court and testified against Kit – not directly, perhaps, but damning him nonetheless by refusing to allow that *anything* else could have caused Missy's death. Theo had begged him for an iota of doubt, as had Noah Cornwallis, but to no avail. Toby didn't know how she could conceivably *marry* him; how she could *dare* to. He thought bitterly of Anscombe's Byronesque profile, his flouncy curls of hair. The debonair doctor. But he was so *old* – so very much older than Theo. But then, Toby still pictured her as a girl, when in fact she was rising nineteen. Only a few months younger than Lily Womersley.

He read Mona's letter three times, but it kept saying the same thing. There'd been a reception at Hallewell House to celebrate the engagement, with a display of fireworks that the whole village had enjoyed. Toby stood. He paced. He crushed the letter in his fist. He shouldn't care, yet it felt as bitter a betrayal as her refusal to visit Kit or speak at his trial. Her request that Abrecan's coin be returned to her. And all the while she had carried on writing to Toby – albeit far less often these days. He'd thought, at least, that her letters were proof that she hadn't forgotten what had happened, and why. Yet she must have absolved herself completely, to dare marry the doctor. It was sickening. He'd been right to ignore her letters. Did they contain details of their courtship? Their plans? He would burn them, the second he got back to his room.

'Toby?'

Lily touched his arm and he spun around. Her smile faltered.

'Goodness, that's hardly the face of a man who's just won the . . .' She trailed off. 'Toby, what on earth has happened?'

'Nothing,' he managed to say.

'Is that a letter?'

'From my mother.'

He couldn't look at her; he felt humiliated, and didn't know why.

'Has something happened? Is she well?'

Lily laid her fingers on his sleeve and he snatched it away.

'I'm sorry, Lily – forgive me. I . . . I must go.'

'Toby, please wait! Won't you tell me what's happened? Perhaps I can help?'

He almost laughed at the idea of explaining it to her – or trying to. Her eyes were round with concern and he couldn't stand it.

'Forgive me,' he muttered.

'Sit down,' she instructed. 'Exhale. You do not have to tell me.'

He did as she said. Elbows on his knees, head down until it was bearable. The pressure eased and his heart slowed. He began to question why he should care, and answer that he did not. What Theo Hallewell did was no concern of his, and never would be. She had not loved Kit, she had not loved *him*; and if he hadn't known it when she'd refused to testify, then he knew it now.

Toby looked up. Lily was sitting beside him with a large leaf in her hands, tracing the veins with her fingertips, thoroughly absorbed in its design and not at all impatient.

'Lily,' he said quietly, taking her hand, though his was damp and unsteady. 'Would you . . . will you marry me?'

Chapter Ten

1893

Tout Hill House was a handsome, symmetrical Georgian building. It had huge sash windows that poured in light; high ceilings and square, airy rooms. Ralph had secured it the moment Theo agreed to marry him – he'd had his eye on it for months. Tout Hill was a peaceful lane on the north-western edge of Shaftesbury, a ten-minute walk from the Westminster Memorial Hospital, so Ralph could return home for the midday meal – patients and emergencies allowing. Uphill on the way to work, downhill on the way home.

'Just as it should be,' he said. 'And I won't have to go all day without kissing you, because that' – he held her face in his hands – 'would be unbearable.'

The house was let unfurnished, apart from a few huge pieces like the china cabinet in the pantry and the canopied bed in the master bedroom. Ralph had been living in quarters at the hospital until then, so had few things. The pieces of furniture they did possess scattered to the four corners of the house and apparently vanished.

'Where does one go to get furniture?' Theo asked. She had no idea – nothing new had ever arrived at Hallewell House; the things that were there had been there for centuries, and were only ever repaired, or recategorised from *good* to *back*.

'On our income, we shall go to the sale room,' Ralph told her. 'And might we beg a few pieces from your mother? The more we spend on furnishings, the less we shall have to spend on our honeymoon. What say you to a tour of Italy?'

'I say it would be *wonderful*.'

'Anywhere you wish to go – except, perhaps, Mesopotamia. I'd like us to have comfortable beds and excellent food, rather than sandflies and bandits.'

Theo smiled. 'All right.'

Ralph looked around with an air of approval. 'There's something rather fine about being the master of Tout Hill House on Tout Hill, isn't there?' he said. 'You were Theodora Hallewell of Hallewell House, and now you are Mrs Anscombe of Tout Hill House, Tout Hill. A pity we are mere tenants, and can't change it to Anscombe House.'

Theo missed her old name, which felt like who she really was; and she found the first few nights there deeply unsettling. She'd never before slept anywhere other than in her old room, and every strange sound roused her, from the rumble of carts in the street to the differently pitched squeak of the doors. For a full week she woke bewildered, and had to wait to remember where she was. For a fortnight she turned right at the bottom of the stairs, as she always had at home, even though that was no longer the way to the breakfast room.

The servants established themselves far more quickly. Mrs Meredith, who'd been Ralph's housekeeper at the hospital, jumped at the chance to run a private home instead, and soon took to presenting Theo with firm suggestions rather than open-ended questions on the topics of menus, parlour maids, and the sending out of laundry. Theo sensed her impatience, which bordered on disapproval; but after nineteen years of her mother's constant correction it hardly touched her. She was grateful to have Mrs Meredith take the reins.

Compared to the grounds of Hallewell House, their new garden was small. It stepped down behind the house in two deep tiers; parallel rectangles of lawn surrounded by flowerbeds, with matching ornamental bird baths in the centre of each. There were apple trees, and an orangery against the wall where a grapevine and tomato plants grew. The gardener came with the house: Seth Litton, an elderly man as strong and weathered as an oak, who'd been there forty years. Theo took to him at once. Whenever she asked him something he would look up, his eyes far away, and she'd have to wait for the answer to swim up from the depths of him. His calm eased her sudden flurries of anxiety.

From the garden, and even more so from the oriel window of the master bedroom, there was a wide view westwards, from the Blackmore Vale to the coaches and carts on Sherborne Causeway. The hill between them and Shaftesbury prevented any view of the town, or of the hospital, but Theo wouldn't have wanted one. It would always be the place where Missy had died; where her husband had battled to save her – and lost. Sometimes, it struck Theo to realise that *that* Dr Anscombe was the same one she'd married. In her memory, they seemed like two different people.

Once Ralph had gone to work, Theo's days were long. She had no friends in Shaftesbury, and few people to write to, so she wrote long letters to her mother, and to Timothy Crudge. Then she either read or haunted the echoing rooms of her new home, trailing her fingers along the dado rails and staring for long spells from each window.

She and Ralph had married in St Mary's, in West End, some six months after Theo had pushed the ruby ring on to her finger to try it out. To see how it felt to have made the decision. It had given her no firm answers, but with each day that passed after that, each day nearer to her escape from Hallewell, she'd felt better. She'd let Diana organise the whole thing, standing firm only on Uncle Crudge's invitation, and on her wedding dress. It was not to be white, or ivory, as had become the fashion since the Queen's wedding. Diana protested but Theo wouldn't budge, and in the end they opted for a lavender-blue velvet, trimmed with fur since it was a winter wedding. Theo didn't explain her insistence. She had always pictured a dress the starry white of wood anemones, but it belonged at a different wedding, to a different bridegroom.

In their marriage portrait, Ralph wasn't smiling – it was too hard to sustain a smile for the length of an exposure without looking strained – but his expression was one of clear and complete contentment. Theo wore almost no expression at all. Her eyes had a faraway look.

What she loved first and best about married life was not having to eat her breakfast with strangers. To constantly meet and converse with, inform and defer to, strangers. There was more freedom in it than even she had anticipated. For the first time in her life, her thoughts, her company, and her time were her own. And there were no memories anywhere. There was no castle. No view of the Meriwethers' house, or St Agnes's, or the spring where she'd finally scuttled her dreams. She had Audrey, and she had Ralph; she had the rest of her life ahead of her, and she was determined to look forwards.

Diana gazed about in horror when she next came to visit.

'What on *earth* have you been doing, Theo? The place is like a tomb!'

'I did write to you that we have few things, as yet.'

'But *weeks* have gone by!'

'Ralph wondered . . . that is, *we* wanted to ask whether there was anything you could spare from home?'

Diana didn't need to be asked twice. She swept from room to room, sizing up the windows and the space; tutting at the wallpaper and the bare floors.

'There's the green brocade settle in the music room – it has always been too big for it. And there are other things I can assemble, I'm sure. But first you need carpets, and wallpaper, and . . .' She waved a hand at the austerity. 'Some pictures! Really, Theo, I do despair of you, at times.'

'Yes, Mama. I'd gathered that.'

Diana and Ralph agreed a budget between them, and soon after that things started to arrive. Carpets from the Orient, via a dealer in Yeovil; fashionable wallpaper in wide stripes of green, or patterned with climbing vines; pictures for every wall, ceramics for every surface. More chairs than they could ever hope to sit upon. For weeks, crates and boxes turned up unexpectedly, for Theo to open with trepidation: another ugly lamp with a tangerine glass shade; figurines of shepherdesses and spaniel dogs; painted fire screens, and bamboo fans from French Indo-China. A small bust of the Queen, carved from translucent marble the exact colour, Theo couldn't help noticing, of mucus.

As the clutter piled up, the rooms seemed to shrink, and Theo realised that the simplicity of it half empty had been far more to her taste. It was too late, though, and Ralph seemed delighted.

She kept one room that was just for her: a small sitting room with almost nothing in it, just a damask *chaise longue*, a writing desk, and a sturdy bookshelf full of novels, journals and travelogues. One day she found Audrey in there, staring at the spines, tapping her fingernails against the fabric and hide.

Audrey jumped back. 'Oh! Beg your pardon, miss!'

She was supposed to call Theo *madam* now that she was married, but it wouldn't stick. Ralph had taken to correcting her.

'It's all right,' Theo said. 'Did you want to borrow a book? You'd be welcome to.'

'No, thank you, miss. I was just wondering . . . about books, I suppose. How you can spend so many hours staring at one the way you do, quite content.'

'Well, haven't you ever been carried away by a story?' Theo asked.

Audrey shook her head.

'No? Or . . . travelled to a place you might never see in person, just by reading and imagining?'

'No, miss.'

In the pause that followed, Theo realised that Audrey meant never. That she had never been told a story, nor read one for herself.

'Audrey . . . did anyone ever teach you how to read?'

Audrey dropped her chin, as if shamed.

'No, miss. Not much call for it where I was before.'

'Well, this is *wonderful.*' Theo smiled.

Audrey looked up in puzzlement. 'Why's that, miss?'

'Because I can teach you, of course; it will speed us through the winter, and give me a way to repay some of the . . . the help you have given me, since you came.'

Audrey smiled tentatively. 'Really? Can you? But . . . maybe I won't take to it.'

'Nonsense. You're more than clever enough, and I *know* you're going to love it.'

Ralph had reservations, when she told him.

'What cause has she to read, my love?' he asked, from the far end of their new dining-room table.

Theo ducked her head to one side, to see around the new candlesticks and the elaborate arrangement of wax fruit in the centre of the table.

'Well, the same cause as anyone, Ralph. Ease of day-to-day life, and the enjoyment of a good book on a rainy afternoon.'

'Hasn't she sewing to do then, or suchlike?'

'Before bed, then.'

'She has got this far in life without it.'

'She's never had a letter, Ralph – imagine that. Nor a written invitation. She might like to write to Kitty, back in Hallewell. She's never read a poem, or a newspaper . . .'

'What was that, my dear?'

'I said, she's never even read a newspaper, or a . . . a handbill. She relies on word of mouth for everything, and Mrs Meredith can't send her on any errand that requires a list – unless she manages to memorise it all . . .'

'Theo, wait – this is ridiculous.'

Ralph picked up his plate and glass and came to sit beside her.

'That's better,' he said. 'It's a very grand table, but I despise anything that places me at such a distance from you.'

'It's a mere minnow, compared to the great whale at Hallewell.'

'Well, that's as may be,' Ralph said stiffly. 'I hope the reduction of your situation isn't too disappointing.'

'Oh, no – that's not what I meant at all,' Theo said hurriedly. 'This is far, far better.' He still looked hurt, so she tried again. 'I am happier by far here, with you.'

'Are you?'

He searched her face and she saw hope in his: that he was on the brink of full happiness, and yearning to topple. That his own contentment depended upon hers. That was love, she supposed.

'I have but one worry.' She gestured the length of the table. 'How many children will we need to have, to ever fill all these chairs?'

Ralph laughed. 'I would never put you through such travail. But . . . three? Perhaps four?'

Theo smiled to hide her sudden nerves, because it *would* happen, sooner or later. She would fall pregnant, and they would become parents. That was the way of it. Nineteen was young to start, but not the youngest by far. She wasn't sure she was ready. To be a mother seemed a fixed point, an unchanging state, when she felt shifting, uncertain, and often at odds with herself – fighting against feelings that arose naturally, and trying to cultivate others that would not come at all.

One thing she was sure of, however, was that when she had a child she would love it completely. She would hug it whenever she could, praise it often, and never make it feel as though it were in any way a disappointment.

'Anyway,' Ralph went on. 'This table is for guests, not for children. Is there anyone you would like to invite?'

'My Uncle Crudge?' Theo said, without hesitation.

'Well, yes, perhaps,' he said, with a subtle creasing of his brow. 'I was thinking more of . . . fashionable society.'

'Oh.' Theo felt a flush creeping up her neck. 'I'm afraid I . . . I don't know anybody to invite.'

Ralph stared at her for a moment.

'How tactless of me,' he said, covering her hand with his own. 'Of course you don't. I am too much at my work. I'd thought that, in my absence . . . But no – I see it now. I shall help you, of course. We'll go together, and begin to know our neighbours. Forgive me, Theo.'

'For what?'

'For forgetting how very different this all is for you, and leaving you to simply . . . get on.'

'But I *ought* to be able to simply get on. Mrs Meredith despises me, I can tell.'

'Mrs Meredith is your servant,' Ralph said firmly. 'And you mustn't reproach yourself. To have lived all your life in such an out-of-the-way place . . . But, fear not – we shall conquer Shaftesbury society together.'

Theo pictured a procession of dinner guests, and long hours of polite conversation, and carefully hid the way her heart sank.

Their honeymoon, which was finally organised in the spring, was a week at a hotel by the sea in Lyme Regis.

'We'll have another, I promise,' Ralph said. 'A proper one – Italy, or wherever you want. But if we wait any longer for me to be able to take sufficient time away from my patients, we shall have our first anniversary before we make our escape.'

'I once said to my uncle that he could take me to Lyme and I would be every bit as excited as if it were some far-flung place,' Theo said, 'and it was entirely true.'

'Indeed.' Ralph considered. 'Mr Crudge is not *actually* your uncle, though. Is he?'

'Not by blood, or marriage. But we adopted one another a long time ago.'

Theo smiled fondly, but Ralph's expression had cooled, and it gave her an uneasy feeling. But he couldn't possibly distrust the innocence of their affection, and would surely like Crudge better once he got to know him.

The hotel overlooked the sea, very near to the Cobb. A weak sun lit their arrival but the offshore breeze had teeth, and made Theo's nose run. Bundled up for warmth, they hunted for fossils in the rocks along the beach, and hiked the cliff path to the top of Golden Cap, and bought cider from a farmer's wife through a hatch in her wall to drink with their picnic lunch. As she sipped it from the flagon, Theo tried not to remember a warm night at the castle, the ruins half gold with candlelight and half as black as ink. *Uroboros. Endless return.* It felt so close.

'A penny for your thoughts?' Ralph said, sitting shoulder to shoulder with her on a borrowed rug with a view of the dazzling sea below.

'Oh . . . they aren't worth that much.'

'Tell me them anyway.'

'I was thinking . . . I was thinking how far I am from Hallewell. From all that happened there,' she lied, with a prickle of unease. Waiting for Ralph to guess the truth.

'It is all behind you now,' he said. 'Like a bad dream.'

Theo smiled, but the truth was that it was *now* that sometimes felt dreamlike. A dream she couldn't escape from – the kind where events follow one another in what seems to be an orderly manner, and yet the whole makes no sense at all upon waking. She took her husband's hand and meshed their fingers together, wanting to feel for him what he felt for her. But where that feeling should have been she had an emptiness instead, that nothing seemed to touch.

That night, she noticed a subtle shift when Ralph made love to her. In the first few months of their marriage he'd been almost reverent; undressing her breathlessly, with hands that shook, and watching constantly to see that she was not frightened, or in any discomfort. And she hadn't been, despite her mother's cursory warning that there was likely to be blood and pain to begin with. Instead, there'd been a peculiar kind of embarrassment that here was Dr Anscombe, her physician – her friend – stark naked. As though he'd stripped off between the fish course and the meat at dinner. But she hadn't felt pain and she hadn't been afraid; it had been strange and after a while almost pleasant – like having her hair brushed. But that was all.

It had been similarly embarrassing to witness Ralph's growing excitement: his handsome face turning the colour of gammon, mouth gaping, eyes sliding out of focus. She'd put her arms around his neck and pulled him closer so she wouldn't have to see, and so that he wouldn't see she was unstirred, and not at all ecstatic. But it didn't seem to matter, so she supposed it only happened to men.

It had carried on like that for weeks, two or three times each night to begin with, until Theo got a bladder infection. Once that had cleared they'd resumed, most nights at least once, and his trembling reverence diminished in a steady curve – which she supposed was bound to happen, once the novelty had worn off. But he was always gentle, until the final moments, and he always asked her first; though she had no idea what would happen if she refused.

Sometimes she felt that pleasurable sensation and repositioned herself, focusing all her attention on it, trying to make it increase. Mostly she felt nothing at all, and foresaw a time when it might all start to seem a bit of a chore. Unless she did begin to love him, as people had said she would. There was nobody she could ask, and no book she could read, to discover whether any of this were normal. Ralph was a doctor, she reasoned, and he seemed perfectly happy.

So, it was ironic that it was on their honeymoon, six months after the wedding, that Theo first noticed his lovemaking becoming . . . perfunctory. A means to an end – the end being Ralph's pleasure, and the conception of a child. He remained gentle but he didn't take his time. There were still kisses and smiles, but he didn't check how she was faring, and he dropped off to sleep on top of her while she sweated underneath. It was late afternoon. Theo watched through the window as the sky lost its colour, and the sun dropped into haze towards the horizon. Gulls criss-crossed on the wind, and she allowed her thoughts to stray.

On the third day a telegram arrived, and Ralph was called back to Shaftesbury to treat a man who'd been kicked in the head by his horse. He went down at once to summon a cab, then packed hurriedly.

'Forgive me,' he said.

'Can't Dr Fortescue see to him?' Theo said.

'Hardly, my darling – he's not a surgeon.' He kissed her knuckles. 'I *am* sorry. You wouldn't have me leave the fellow to die?'

'No, of course not.'

She felt the same gentle awe as whenever he was called to an emergency; a startled pride that this man, who had such skill and knowledge, had chosen *her*. A tantalising glimpse of what it might be like to eventually fall in love with him.

'I'll be back tomorrow, or the day after. As soon as he is stable. And I'll send Audrey down to you . . .'

'There's no need. I'll be perfectly all right.'

'If you're sure?'

He was already halfway out of the door.

A kick in the head, Theo thought, as she went down to dinner alone. A percussive injury to the skull. Just like Missy's. Though, surely, Kit's stone had had nothing of the power of a horse's hoof. He hadn't thrown it with any great force – it had been more of a fling than a shot. He hadn't taken aim, or wound back his arm. The memory sent a shock up her spine. She wondered if this man would undergo the same operation as Missy; if he would emerge safely from the chloroform. Thus distracted, she spoke little at dinner, and afterwards declined an invitation to play canasta with a couple celebrating their golden wedding anniversary.

Ralph did not return the next day, so Theo walked along the shore and out on to the Cobb. It had been a long time since she'd done *anything* by herself, and she loved it. She bought a small, polished fossil of a long-dead sea snail for Audrey, and a postcard, which she wrote to Crudge in a café. *Here I am on my honeymoon, all by myself,* she wrote, and explained about the patient. *The sea is the most beautiful thing I have ever seen.* Even as she wrote it, she thought of Toby's smile. One of the sudden, rare smiles that transformed his face. She missed a breath, realising she'd never see that smile again. *Poor Ralph*, she wrote. *We were having a lovely time, and he was so disappointed to leave.*

A telegram came in the morning to say that Ralph would stay on at the hospital, so Theo travelled back alone. She wasn't upset about it. When she got home she was surprised to find Ralph already there, slouched at the desk in his study with a bottle of wine beside him. He looked so utterly dejected that her heart went out to him.

She crouched beside him. 'Ralph? What is it?'

'Mr Jackson died.' He peered foggily at the clock on the mantelpiece. 'At about the same time as you were leaving Yeovil Junction.'

'Oh, Ralph . . . I'm so sorry to hear it.'

'I failed him. The operation . . . did not go well. I thought it had, but . . . He *did* wake, and was able to say a few words, though weakly. It lasted only an hour, and then . . .'

He shook his head.

'But you *tried*,' Theo said. 'His injury must have been very bad indeed.'

'It was severe, but . . . the operation *should* have released the pressure of the clot. It should have *worked*!'

'Ralph, you mustn't—'

'What's the use of my trying, Theo?' He stared down at her, wide-eyed. 'What's the use, if I am to fail, over and over again?'

'The *use*?' She searched for the right response. 'The use is that you give them a chance! That you endeavour to save them, when otherwise they would surely die. And you do *not* fail, over and over. Far more often, you succeed.'

'But I should have been able to *save* him! Don't you see? When *everything* was performed correctly this time.'

Theo flinched as his voice rose; as it abandoned sorrow for frustration.

'Ralph, you have said to me before – you have said *about* me – that the human brain is not a Swiss timepiece, where each part fits neatly into its place, and may be replaced if fault is found.'

'No.' Ralph slumped back, frowning. 'No, it is a maze that I cannot map. Time, though . . . now that you mention it, perhaps *that* is the key. Perhaps I simply did not get to him in time. Perhaps the bleeding had already caused damage that relieving the pressure could not undo.'

Theo tried again. 'What you do is *astonishing*. You must not blame yourself! You might not have saved this life, but you have saved many others – and you will save many more, I know it.'

The look he gave her hardened, and she faltered.

'Platitudes do not interest me, Theo.'

He pushed back his chair, got unsteadily to his feet. 'Time – yes. If I had got to him sooner . . . If I had been here when he was first brought in, rather than off . . .' – he waved one hand – '. . . taking the sea air . . .'

He left her there, crouching by his desk, stung by the possibility that he blamed her, somehow, for the fact that they'd been on their honeymoon when Mr Jackson was kicked by his horse.

Late in the night, when she awoke in their bed to find herself alone – Ralph's pillow rumpled but cool – it was something else that struck her. Something that Ralph had said: *When everything was performed correctly this time.*

The loss of his patient affected Ralph badly. His self-recrimination manifested as long silences – conversation floundered, whatever subject Theo attempted to launch into. He was not cold towards her, nor angry, only absent. After a fortnight it got heavier, like something unwieldy she was forced to drag around behind her, and after three weeks she was ready to scream just to break the silence. It was worse than a four-hour dinner with reticent guests; worse than squirming beneath her mother's stony gaze when she had caused offence. The tension knotted her guts, and made her feel sick.

'You are such a good man, to feel for your patients the way that you do,' she tried, at dinner one evening. 'Such a . . . kind-hearted man . . .'

Her voice dried up.

'Kindness will not save lives,' he murmured. 'Only skill and knowledge will do.'

They got up in silence once the food was finished, and Ralph stopped her, touching his fingers to the gold butterfly at her throat. Rosalind Mackie's pendant, which was still her favourite.

'You wear this so often,' he said. 'Rather than either of the necklaces I have given you.'

A silver locket for her nineteenth birthday, engraved with a bird with a tiny sapphire eye, and the pearl choker that had been her wedding present.

'Well . . . those you have given me are far more precious. I would fear to wear them every day, and risk them.'

His mouth twisted unhappily. 'So, it is not simply that you do not care for them?'

'How could I not care for them? They're beautiful.'

'Well. Scant point in my buying them if you never wear them.'

The following day Theo wore the silver locket, but Ralph didn't seem to notice. Only after dark, in bed, did she have the courage to beg him to relent.

'Help me to understand it, Ralph.'

'But how can you?' he said. 'How can you possibly grasp the anguish of failure, when you have not the burden of responsibility, and never will?'

'But I . . . I felt responsible for Missy, and for Kit. I remember full well the pain of my failure towards them. So, I do know it is terribly hard.'

'That was different. You were not responsible for them; your role in it was entirely passive. And the trauma quite undid you, as I recall.'

Theo didn't press the point.

It was pure luck that, a few days later, nature provided a solution. Theo had never been one to count the days, or the weeks, and usually relied on Audrey to remind her when the time of the month was coming. So, it was Audrey who brought a supply of clean towels, and found the previous ones untouched.

'Miss . . .'

She pointed to the wads of white muslin still neat and tidy in the drawer. Theo didn't follow her at first.

Audrey spelled it out. 'And it ought to have come on this month, if it was going to.'

'Oh,' Theo said, the realisation emptying her head completely for a moment.

'"Oh" indeed.' Audrey gave a grin. 'That ought to buck him up,' she added, almost to herself.

She was right. Theo told Ralph the news at breakfast, and he stared at her quite as emptily as she had stared at Audrey before delight dawned on his face like a sunrise.

'Are you quite sure?'

'As sure as I can be. All of the signs . . .'

The nausea she had put down to anxiety; the tiredness she'd thought was due to Ralph's mood.

'On our *honeymoon*?' he said.

'Before that, I think. Perhaps eight weeks, though . . . it is difficult to tell.'

He hugged her tight, then held her at arm's length. 'And you didn't tell me?'

'I didn't know! Audrey has guessed it, else I still wouldn't have.'

'But this is *wonderful* . . . My clever, *clever* girl!'

Ralph dropped to his knees in front of her and stared at a point between her hip bones.

'Hello,' he said, and Theo laughed.

'Ralph, what *are* you doing?'

'It is only polite.' He pressed his ear to her skirt. 'It's a boy!'

'Ah, I'm told men always want boys.'

'I want girls, too, but nothing is better for a girl than an older brother.'

He stood up and hugged her again, smoothing back her hair.

'You have made me very happy,' he said.

'I'm happy, too.'

It was true. Whatever doubts she'd had, and however startling the news, she *was* happy. It seemed utterly bizarre, and entirely miraculous, that a child had simply . . . appeared inside her, conjured into existence from pieces of her, pieces of Ralph. It felt like a magic spell had been cast; something far older and wiser than she would ever be. A tingle of that old feeling from childhood, of the world being full of wonder and mystery and journeys to take. A journey, she suddenly understood, did not have to mean travelling to a different place. The space in her heart that had so worried her was already filling up. Within days of finding out about the baby, it had vanished altogether.

Revitalised, Ralph distributed their calling card, and they were duly invited to various teas and dinners. Theo met the neighbours with the same formulaic good manners she'd learned at Hallewell, and in turn their hosts seemed to find her dull, or else the wrong kind of interesting. She felt an affinity for just one person she met: Hermione Abbott, who lived a few houses further down Tout Hill. Hermione was not much older than Theo but had three young children already, whom she openly adored and rarely disciplined. She quickly guessed about the pregnancy.

'You look a little green about the gills, Mrs Anscombe,' she whispered, as their husbands talked about the Boers and Theo tried to eat a piece of cake though her hand was shaking and she was fairly sure she wouldn't be able to put it in her mouth even if she succeeded in getting it on to the fork.

'Are you ill?' Hermione asked. 'Are you . . . in a happy condition?'

Theo nodded, teeth clamped too tightly against the onslaught of nausea to reply.

'Oh, how wonderful! And you poor, poor thing – I know *exactly* how you feel.' She collared a passing servant. 'Myrtle, have we any ginger? Do see if you can dig some out, and bring a hot infusion for Mrs Anscombe. It's quite the best thing for it,' she said, returning to Theo. 'I drank nothing else the whole nine months with my first.'

'Thank you. You're very kind.'

'Nonsense. We women must look after one another.'

Hermione was plump and lively; her face was dominated by big brown eyes and an expression of curiosity and general good humour. She befriended Theo quickly and deliberately, and Theo didn't mind at all. She sensed no scrutiny from Hermione; no judgement or hidden opinions. She also seemed to belong to an inordinate number of clubs and committees, and immediately set about recruiting Theo on to them.

'What about politics?' she asked, at a subsequent luncheon. 'Are you at all interested? I've been trying to get up a women's reform group, but it's been all uphill so far.'

'I'm afraid I don't know.' Theo really didn't.

'Well, you must come this Friday – we're having a bring-and-buy. Alms for veterans of the African wars. Then we can talk without our menfolk,' she said, *sotto voce*, as though Theo must be brimming with secrets to tell.

Ralph got along well with Hermione's husband, Frederick, who was an actuary and sports enthusiast, and so the two couples met often.

'Which crusade has Mrs Abbott volunteered you for this week?' Ralph said at the breakfast table one day. 'The Ladies' Society for the Protection of Newts?'

'Don't tease,' Theo said. 'I like her. She has so many ideas. She says that, as women, we mustn't allow ourselves to be looked upon as little more than brood mares and the sewers-on of buttons.'

Ralph pulled a face. 'Doesn't she enjoy being a mother?'

'Of course she does. That wasn't—'

'And you will too, my darling.' He kissed her hand.

'I already do.'

'There, then. It doesn't do to overreach oneself.'

By June, Theo's middle had started to fill out; there was no abrupt bump as yet, just a subtle outward curve. They guessed her to be about four months along, close to halfway.

'Like a snake that's eaten a frog,' Ralph said, running his hand the length of her in bed.

'Dr Anscombe, please tell me this is not a frog I'm incubating?'

'In my professional, medical opinion . . .' He put his ear to her naked skin. 'Time will tell.'

They shared a laugh, but the moment was slightly spoiled by him then counting her pulse and listening to her heart, though it had been only an hour since he'd last done so.

'It's a little fast. You must rest tomorrow.'

They also dined regularly with Ralph's partner at the hospital, Dr Fortescue, and his wife, Margaret. Theo remembered him vaguely, from the morass of lost time around Kit's trial and execution. The man who'd sedated her, and quashed any possibility of her going to Dorchester to speak.

Fortescue was a generation older; he had washed-out sandy hair and dry, mottled skin. His face was gaunt, with wattles beneath his chin and flinty grey eyes. He was the senior physician, pharmacist and pathologist at the Westminster Memorial, where Ralph was junior physician and in-house surgeon – in such a small institution, combined roles were necessary. When he looked at Theo, she felt naked. There was nothing sexual in his gaze – nothing admiring whatsoever – but it penetrated her, coldly, dismissively. As though she were a painting he didn't care for, or a tedious child. His wife, Margaret, barely spoke at all. She took tiny bites of food, her back never less than brutally straight.

'Our neighbour, Mrs Abbott, plans to establish a branch of the English Ladies' Cycling Association in Shaftesbury,' Theo announced, into an especially large hole in the conversation. 'I have always wondered about trying it.'

'In your condition?' Fortescue was indignant.

'No, but . . . perhaps one day.'

'Women should not ride bicycles,' the doctor declared. 'Their physiology is wholly unsuited to the pressures and exertion of the pedalling action.'

'Oh, but Mrs Abbott says she enjoys almost nothing so much as cycling,' Theo said. 'She says women aren't quite the gossamer creatures poets have made us out to be, and that the exercise is thoroughly invigorating.'

Ralph frowned slightly, and Margaret looked up in slow outrage. Fortescue fixed Theo with his frigid stare.

'Mrs Abbott would do well to heed expert opinion, rather than persisting in such deleterious behaviour. A woman has no need of *invigoration*. Quite the opposite. They tend far too easily toward hysteria.'

Theo took this to heart, and felt tarnished. But some inner part of her also bridled at being chastised at her own table.

'I don't believe—'

'My dear,' Ralph interrupted her stiffly. 'That will do.'

Theo flushed, and said no more.

Her husband was different around Dr Fortescue; deferential, as though, despite their being equal partners, his position were in the older man's gift. She wondered whether, having lost his parents, Ralph looked upon Fortescue as a father figure, and sought his approval.

'Fortescue? As a *father*?' Ralph laughed, when she asked him later on. He shuddered comically. 'Heavens, no. I can't imagine anything more terrible for a child.'

He took her hands, still smiling. 'No, my love. It was just rather ill-mannered of you to disagree with him like that.'

Theo didn't even notice the date until afterwards. She was out in the garden helping Seth train a rose up the side of the house. Her role was very minor: she held a basket containing scissors, twine and vine eyes, and passed him whichever he asked for. It was a beautiful day, with a warm breeze out of the south and the air full of birds, and Theo's mind had been gathering wool when a sudden pain and a wash of cold made her gasp. Like she'd fallen into icy water.

She dropped the basket and sank to her knees. Audrey and Mrs Meredith came running, and took her up to bed, and Ralph was there within the hour.

'What's happening?' Theo demanded, the second she saw him.

'Hush, Theo,' he said, as he examined her. 'Try to be calm.'

'I cannot be calm!'

A midwife arrived, one that Ralph knew and trusted, and he left the room with his face rigid. Theo thought he looked afraid, but couldn't tell. She was too frightened herself. Audrey held her hand and didn't let go.

'Make it stop,' Theo ordered the midwife, as pain beat through her and she knew, without being told, what it meant. 'It is far too soon.'

The midwife looked grave. She put her hands on Theo's middle, and felt the ripples getting stronger.

'A bit of grit is what's needed now,' she said, with a nod and a not-quite smile. 'Nowt to be done about it, and you've plenty of time to make more.'

'But I want this one!' Theo panted through clenched teeth. 'Audrey, tell her! You must do *something . . . please*!'

'Best just get it over with,' the midwife said. 'This one weren't meant to be.'

'No . . . Call my husband back . . . He is a doctor, he'll do something – he'll make it stop!'

'Oh, miss . . .' Audrey said, distraught.

'Now then,' the midwife said. 'That's enough of that pother. What do a man know, be he doctor or not? This babber's lost to you. I've seen it a thousand times.'

She wasn't trying to be cruel, but Theo had never heard such terrible words. The woman washed her hands, and parted Theo's knees.

'Soon be over,' she said.

Theo never saw the child. She drifted away towards the end of the labour, and by the time she surfaced the bed was clean and the room had been aired, and a fire lit despite the summer. She herself had been washed and put into a clean nightdress – there was a vague memory of Audrey combing her hair. It stayed light until late in the evening, and Ralph came up to lie behind her, wrapping his arms around her.

'Where's the baby?' Theo asked. 'Where have you taken him?'

'Theo, my darling . . . The foetus has been removed. Try not to think of it.'

A sob shuddered through her. 'He was dead? But . . . where have they taken him?'

'It . . . was a girl.'

'You saw her?'

'Shh, now. Yes, I saw her. It . . . she was never meant to live, my darling.'

Misery clamped its teeth into Theo. Her tears ran constantly, unnoticed.

'What shall we call her?'

'Call her?' Ralph echoed. 'My love . . . at so early a stage, the child cannot be said to have truly *lived*. Try to think of that – we have lost the possibility of a child, this time, not a substantive one. A foetus—'

'Please, don't say that word.'

'It is the proper word, my darling.'

'But I hate it. I cannot hear it.'

'Hush now. I will give you something to help you sleep.'

'I don't want to sleep. I want my baby. And if you will not name her then I will – Amelia, after my sister.'

'Theo, please—'

'Oh, *Ralph*,' Theo breathed. 'Can't you feel it? Can't you feel how empty it all is, now?'

'It will fill again, my love.'

He smoothed his hand over the slack skin of her abdomen. But she hadn't meant that her womb was empty; she'd meant the world. She'd meant her heart.

'Why? Why did she die?'

'You must not blame yourself.'

Theo sat up abruptly, turning to him in the half-dark.

'Blame *myself*? Why? What have you not told me?'

'Nothing, Theo.' He looked away, seeming undecided. 'Only that, sometimes, stress and . . . nervous exhaustion in the mother can cause—'

'Nervous exhaustion? But I haven't been nervous – I've been fine. Better than fine!'

'Truly? Even today?' Ralph hesitated. 'I . . . I cannot think that the date is a coincidence.'

Theo stared at him; she didn't understand. 'I don't . . .'

She fell silent. The soft silver light outside, the warm breeze that had blown. It was the twenty-fourth of June. Midsummer's Day.

She lay back, the weight of responsibility knocking her flat. She hadn't noticed the date – she was *sure* she hadn't. And yet, she was not sure. Because how *could* she forget it? It was four years to the day since she'd brought them all together at the castle, and everything had been destroyed. And now, somehow, she had made *this* happen, too. Amelia. Gone, like the wonder out of the world.

Ralph fetched a tincture to make her sleep, and she swallowed it gladly.

Toby's arrival in London was marked by equal measures of wonder and revulsion. Durham had seemed huge after Hallewell; now London made Durham a speck. He walked for miles, trying to get his bearings, somehow imagining that he could create a mental map of the whole city, as he had with Durham. He soon admitted defeat, and simply walked to take it in. He was frequently lost. The sheer scale of the place astonished him. Whole rows of buildings that rose up and up, four storeys high, five, six; turning the street below into a canyon. Every now and then he would stumble across some wonder at the end of such a channel – Westminster Abbey, or Big Ben, or the brand-new Tower Bridge, not yet open to traffic.

The roads thronged with more shapes and sizes of vehicle and person than he'd ever imagined. Trams and omnibuses and wagons and traps; the rich, the poor, the shifty and strange. There was a constant blare of noise; an assault on all his senses, not least his nose. He soon learned that a butcher's shop could be found by following the evil reek of rotting blood from three streets away. A fishmonger's the exact same way. The smell rising from the open sewer grates seemed to climb up his nose and into his throat, where it lodged. On still days, a thick pall of smoke hung in the air. All the buildings, however grand, were black with smuts, as were the shop awnings and park benches, and the hawker boys' faces.

The city had endeavoured to clean up the Thames since the Great Stink of '58, but the river still wound through it like a turgid, murky animal, thick with effluent. Agglomerations of unidentifiable filth gathered wherever the current was slow. At low tide the mud had a fishy, almost sweet aroma that Toby found particularly nauseating. He sometimes wore a handkerchief over his nose, with drops of camphor.

As the weather got colder, and Womersley and the rest of Toby's cohort took up their positions in law firms, financial institutions and family businesses, Toby was still walking, as though he might make a career of it. He had his last bit of money from the Latin exhibition, plus a small engagement gift from the Womersleys, and was eking it out as slowly as he could. But it wouldn't last the winter. Toby felt chaos nipping at his heels. He didn't dare turn and look it in the face.

He didn't want to rely upon connections to advance; he didn't want to rely on anyone. He felt, deep down, that nobody could be truly relied upon. But no matter how far he walked, no solution presented itself. He recognised that the abstract idea he'd had, of steadily increasing influence, had been a childish delusion of grandeur, and that he ought to have given more consideration to a career of some kind. It was no longer enough to be an excellent scholar, but since that had defined him up to that point, it was hard to see beyond it. Trying to formulate any kind of plan was like trying to stick pins in mist.

Some nights he lay awake, spinning helplessly into that void Lily had alluded to. Robbed of the twin goals of studying and attaining the highest marks, with nothing left to structure his days, he *did* feel himself coming apart. It was terrifying.

Every couple of weeks Tom treated him to a steak supper, which was very welcome. Most nights his evening meal was bread and dripping, with a slice or two of bacon or a hard-boiled egg if he was lucky, and a cup of cocoa or beer. Some of this feast, provided by the landlady at his boarding house for an extra shilling a week, had to be saved for breakfast. By bedtime his stomach was always howling for more, and it took an iron-clad will not to polish off the lot.

'Any plans?' Tom asked.

Had he not been engaged to Tom's sister, Toby might have broken down and told the truth.

'I'm . . . exploring a few avenues,' he said.

'I hear there's always call for tutors,' Tom said. 'To coach the sons of the wealthy for the Oxford entrance. And their daughters too, these days.'

'Like Reverend Nimrod coached me.'

'There you are, then. You should put out a notice.'

'Perhaps.'

The sewers stank less once the frosts started, but the haze of smoke got worse. People coughed, all the time. Toby noticed that born and bred Londoners were small and weedy; they had permanently blocked noses, and died young from lung disease and dysentery. Young men fresh in from Ireland or the countryside stuck out like sore thumbs with their ruddy complexions and sturdy limbs.

If, in Hallewell, class was a question of whether you sat on a terrace at a fête or stood in the crowd, then in London it was a question of whether or not you ate. Whether your children would live, or you would make it to the age of forty. Slums were everywhere, and you could smell one upwind like you could a butcher's shop. In Hallewell, nobody went hungry for long. In hard times, there was always a kindly farmer's wife willing to give out milk and bread crusts. The vicar's wife would open a soup kitchen, or arrange a collection. There were rabbits to snare, pigeons to net, apples to scrump. In London, the poorest had nothing. Nothing to wear, nothing to eat, nothing to sleep on or warm themselves with. However much Toby had read, nothing had prepared him for the reality of such hardship. There was no safety net.

He had no safety net, other than to make himself a burden to his friends. He supposed the Womersleys might take him in if he fell into utter destitution; or else compel Lily to release him from their engagement. Toby couldn't tell what he felt about that. It turned out that being engaged to Lily was very easy. Once the initial shock of it had worn off, it appeared that not much was expected of him, or even needed to change. He wrote to her every other day – tales of the city – and she wrote back about her studies, and the possibility of a position at a boys' school when she finished, teaching physics and chemistry. She was looking forward to it, she wrote, and might be sad to leave it off once they were married. But she longed for that happy event, nonetheless. *With love, I am yours, truly, Lily.*

Her letters were always far longer than his.

For the first time in two years, Toby went back to Hallewell for Christmas. He wasn't able to buy gifts, or turn up laden with chocolates and Turkish delight as he'd imagined when a place at university was first mooted. All he took with him was a head cold, which Mona promptly caught. Toby was shocked by how small and frail his father looked, and how pinched his face had become. He was shocked at Mona's quietness – speaking only with a visible effort.

'My boy,' she said, taking his arms and gazing up at him. 'My Toby.'

She seemed far away; not quite present in the room.

'I'm sorry to come empty-handed,' Toby said to his father.

'Nonsense. You being here is all that matters.'

David patted his shoulder, and Toby saw him notice the frayed cuffs of his son's shirt, his untrimmed hair, and the fact that his jacket had gone through at the elbows.

'Any leads on a position?'

'Some, yes,' Toby lied.

He was getting used to lying about it. He *had* answered a few adverts, and been to a few meetings. But he never seemed to fit. His stellar education coupled with his lack of breeding; his obvious intelligence marred by the apathy he could not shake.

'It will not simply happen of its own accord, I think,' David said gently, cutting directly to the heart of the matter. 'Not for a man of your . . . background.'

'I have irons in the fire.' Toby hated the doubt on his father's face. 'You don't need to worry. I've been doing some tutoring, in fact.'

It was true, though he knew it wouldn't last long. He was a terrible teacher, irrepressibly impatient. The boys – and one girl – ended up hating him, staring in mute fury at their books. One lad had even burst into tears at one point. He had yet to last a month with any one student, before being thanked and dismissed. And perhaps word had got about, because he wasn't exactly inundated with enquiries.

'What we really want to know,' Mona said, 'is when we might meet your Lily? I'm sure she's a wonderful girl.'

Toby swayed a little, and sank into a chair. 'I don't suppose there's anything to eat, is there?'

Mona gave him a critical look, then headed for the kitchen. 'Tea's brewing, and I've made some mince pies.'

'A mince pie. Thank you. That would be perfect.'

'And as for tomorrow,' David said. 'You'll never guess? The vicar has sent us a rib of beef. How about that?'

'Will we be required to change our name to Cratchit?'

'Hardly. He had it from Lord Stitchcombe, but it's too much for Mrs Nimrod's digestion; they always have turkey. He wants to see you – Nimrod. To congratulate you on your honours, I suppose. Well, you'll see him at midnight Mass, in any case.'

Toby winced inwardly. Nimrod would also want to know what he planned to do with his degree. Why he hadn't applied for a fellowship. Why he was penniless and aimless and squandering it all. So, he steeled himself and they went to Mass, and he spoke to the vicar, and sang 'O Little Town of Bethlehem'; then the next day they roasted the beef and opened their presents by the fire – socks and a notebook for Toby – and did their very best to enjoy the time. It was as flimsy as a house of cards.

Kit had loved Christmas; the magic of it got him every time – hook, line and sinker. Starry-eyed at the decorations and presents; rapt at the singing of carols; greedy for the feast. Now it turned out that he'd been the source of all that magic. Without him they were just going through the motions; and though nobody said it, Toby knew they all felt it.

Once they'd eaten, Toby set off into the afternoon darkness, through the village and up to the castle. His breath made clouds, and he didn't have a ha'penny for the box. There was nobody around to see. The ruins were just as he remembered them, yet seemed smaller too. He'd thought he might sense Kit there, but there was nothing. It didn't feel like home any more; none of it did. A sliver of moon hung in a sky the colour of glass. Hallewell House was down below, casting a golden glow from every window. Faintly, he heard a piano playing, and voices singing. Perhaps Theo and her husband. They hadn't been at St Mary's, much to his relief. He stared and he listened, until he hated himself for doing it. The figure he must cut, shut out in the cold like a stray animal. *Take a hint, fella.*

His anger bubbled up, and it felt good.

Toby travelled back to London the day after Boxing Day, ostensibly because snow was forecast and he couldn't risk getting stuck in Hallewell, but really because he *needed* to go. The Meriwethers simply didn't work as a threesome, and the longer he stayed the more painfully obvious it became.

When he got back to his room, which he shared with three other men in two sets of bunks, it was freezing. There was a letter from Lily, but he didn't open it. He had a supper of cold beef and potatoes wrapped in paper, and four of Mona's mince pies, and beyond that, he realised with sudden, shocking clarity, he had nothing at all.

He spent a precious shilling on a bottle of truly awful gin, and drank in the new year with it.

Tom had invited him to a dinner at the apartment he shared with another junior solicitor, but Toby had lied and said he would still be down in Hallewell. He drank until the gin blotted out the tobacco-stained wallpaper and the baleful glare of the gas light; until it smoothed the knots from his shoulders and the lumps from the stained mattress. He went to bed at five past midnight with a pillow over his head to muffle the snores and farts, the yells and slammed doors of his neighbours.

In the middle of January, Toby's money ran out – he had to hide from the landlady. Lily wrote to say she was coming to visit. Toby panicked.

'You're an idiot,' Tom said, when Toby finally confessed to his situation over a lunch that Tom would pay for. 'Did you think we'd let you starve? Hm?' He poked his fork at Toby across the table. 'You're a Womersley now. Or as good as.'

'I believe in advancement through merit, not in asking for favours. I wanted to make my own way.'

'Meriwether.' Tom sighed. 'I mean this with tremendous affection, but you just aren't a . . . you aren't . . . *convivial.* I know you're a damn good chap underneath it all, but upon a first encounter . . . Well, put it this way: you're just not the sort who will ever charm his way into anything.'

'Thanks.'

'You have plenty of other good qualities,' Tom assured him, and Toby almost laughed. 'You're diligent, loyal, moderately bright . . . But you don't warm to people, so they won't warm to *you*. And you don't even know what sort of position you're looking for. Do you?'

'No.'

'Well, then.' Tom loaded his fork with ham pie and gravy. 'Let us help you.'

'Us?'

'Your friends. You do have some, you know, though you seem to have forgotten.' Tom was serious. 'And whilst one might not necessarily need friends in high places, Meriwether, one does need *friends*. No man is an island, and all that.'

'Womersley, I . . .' Toby shook his head. 'I'm a complete flunk.'

Tom nodded. 'I'm inclined to agree with you. When did that shirt last see soap? And you've lost two buttons. But it's a *temporary state*, Meriwether. It's nothing that can't be set right; and it must *be* set right.' He aimed his fork at Toby's chest again. 'Can't have you marrying my sister looking like that.'

'How do I look?'

'Like Oliver Twist,' Tom said, then laughed.

'Not even Bob Cratchit, then.'

'Hm?'

Toby sighed. 'Getting to university was everything,' he murmured. 'It was *everything*, you see. All through my school days, and the dreadful time when my brother died . . . Through all of it, my focus was on simply *getting* there.'

Tom blinked rapidly, and behind his bluff good humour Toby saw sympathy. He saw care, and something that bordered on pity. Which only made it worse.

'I do understand,' Tom said quietly. 'And few in your shoes would have had the . . . the grit to achieve that aim. Now we must simply turn that grit to some other task. And I shall find it for you.'

Tom loaned him the money to visit a barber and buy a new shirt and jacket. He said he would put out a few feelers. It took less than a week. It turned out that Campbell Franke-Grosvenor, their Castleman friend from Durham, was godson to the owner of *The London Daily News*. A few messages exchanged hands, and Toby was slotted into the post of junior copy editor and court news reporter. He didn't even attend an interview; he just had to turn up and do as he was told, and he would be paid a hundred and thirty pounds *per annum*. The ease with which it was all arranged appalled Toby, as well as coming as a huge and guilty relief.

The London Daily News was a liberal paper, at least.

He confessed to the help he'd been given in a letter to Lily. He supposed it would make her think less of him; as a woman, she would certainly be given no such advantages. *I must say I'm glad to hear it*, she wrote back. *I've been on at Tom for the longest time to persuade you to be helped. And don't go thinking less of yourself because of it. You aren't the son of an earl, Toby. You'll still have to do the work.*

So, he got stuck in. The copy-editing was easy enough, and quite satisfying. Weeding out spelling and grammatical mistakes, and reordering sentences for clarity before articles went to be typeset. The court reports were more interesting. He didn't have to attend every hearing – that would be impossible. But he toured the Crown courts weekly, collecting the schedules and verdicts as they were reached. These he was supposed to summarise to an extreme of brevity – which court, which judge, the plaintiff, defendant and verdict. *The London Daily News* certainly had no time for the lascivious gore of the *Illustrated Police News* or the penny dreadfuls. There were plenty of frauds, thefts and assaults. Plenty of failed petitions for divorce, and men sued for breach of promise of marriage; plenty of men suing their wives' lovers for compensation. A scattering of murders.

One day, curiosity got the better of him, and Toby ducked into the public gallery of the Old Bailey during a trial for murder. The clerk called them to order and the judge sat, and Toby broke into a sweat. All he wanted to do was leave but he made himself stay, as his mind spat up images of Kit in the dock below, rocking from foot to foot as Lord Paxton-Nevis leaned forward beneath his tasselled canopy and fixed Dr Heinemann with a stony eye. *Either the young man is of sound mind, and a murderer through and through, or else he is a cretin, a danger to all who encounter him . . .*

Toby ground his teeth and let the memories come, hoping to purge himself of them. The torment of being powerless as it all went wrong. Kit looking up at him, anxious and trusting. Theo's desertion. The guilty verdict. He remembered being dragged out by two bailiffs. He remembered Kit calling to him as he was taken away. The agony of impotence.

'You all right?' said the man next to him, forcing Toby back to the present. He had a hank of the man's coat in his fist, and was panting for breath.

'I beg your pardon,' he muttered, and got out as discreetly as he could.

He wasn't purged. Images of Kit's trial followed him into his sleep, and sharpened into nightmares.

Still, compiling the court listings became the thing that engaged him most, though his colleagues called it a dogsbody job. His round-ups were squeezed in towards the back of the paper; cramped, minuscule paragraphs amongst the abridged minutes of public meetings, the governesses looking for positions, and the adverts for Elliman's Embrocation without which, it was claimed, no stable was complete.

At noon, he and the other staffers poured out of the paper's premises on Bouverie Street, off Fleet Street, and into the chop-house on the corner, where a plate of hot food could be had for a few pence. Irish stew, or steak and kidney pudding, or sausages and onions. Baked apples and Bird's Custard. It wasn't a million miles from the food at Hatfield Hall, and Toby had developed a taste for it. It stuck to the ribs, and kept him warm, and hunger was by far the best seasoning.

By spring, he was able to move to better lodgings. He got his own room on a longer lease, in a house of multiple occupancy with a high turnover. The privacy felt like a luxury. There was no bath-room, just a shared outhouse, and no hot water unless he bought more coal, lit the tiny fire and heated a kettle himself. But it was cleaner and quieter, and the food the housekeeper provided was a bit better than before. He might have afforded something a step up, but he'd decided to save as much of his salary as he could. Lily was due to visit soon; he wanted to take her to a restaurant.

Lily stayed with Tom whenever she was in town, but Toby went to meet her off the train at King's Cross, full of inexplicable nerves. It had been three months since they'd seen one another, but he had no fear that she might have changed, or that he might like her less. It was not even that she might like *him* less – though that was a distinct possibility. So perhaps, deep down, it was the suspicion that he should never have proposed in the first place. That something was lacking in him, though he couldn't name it.

But being engaged to Lily gave him a reason to earn, and to save. It gave him an end point to work towards: finally marrying her, and providing for her. Her visits marked the distance to be travelled, and he'd learned that he needed that – a destination, and a waymarked route. They walked along the river, and around Hyde Park, and talked a great deal. They went for tea, and to the opera – Gounod's *Roméo et Juliette*, standing pit only – and Toby steadfastly refused to let her see his lodgings.

'They're not at all what you're used to,' he said. 'I'm saving all my pennies, you see.'

'How bad can they be?'

'Dreadful.'

He didn't say that the only women he'd seen there tended to stay for an hour or less.

'I'm not as shockable as you think. And what do I care, in any case? We could be alone together,' Lily said boldly.

'Yes. And then your brother would shoot me in a duel.'

'But he would shoot to miss.' She smiled. 'Tom loves you.'

'In that instance, I'm not sure it'd help me.'

'Dear Tom,' Lily said fondly. 'He seems to be getting along all right as a lawyer, doesn't he?'

'Better than I thought,' Toby agreed.

'Surely you never doubted his ability?'

'Not his ability, no. What I find it hard to picture is him ever being *stern.*'

Lily laughed. 'No, I can't either. But then, don't you remember what he told us that time? That they'd celebrated the birthday of a colleague by filling his umbrella with pencil shavings? So, I'm not convinced how very po-faced it all is there.' Lily laughed. 'How far are we from your rooms, anyway?'

But Toby would not be moved on the issue. They could not marry until he was able to keep her in something at least approaching comfort. And who on earth knew when that might be? Until then he would behave properly, and do nothing that might upset Tom, or call Lily's virtue into question. But he was learning the subtle ways in which Lily showed her disappointment. The press of her lips. Her long silences.

'So very proper – and stubborn.' She gave him a sideways look. 'Then walk me back to Tom's. Slowly.'

She looped her arm through his, leaning close, and felt the notebook in his inside pocket.

'What's this? Something to read, in case we run out of conversation?'

'No. It's just work. I've been noting some thoughts on a few of the cases I've seen coming through the courts. The ones that trouble me most, I suppose.'

It was those where some moral question was raised, or a particular social ill was illustrated. Often, they were murders. Capital cases where things were not clear cut; where the means and motive were unclear, or were so pitiful that to convict for murder seemed profoundly wrong. Like the factory worker who'd smothered to death his young sister. She'd been dying of a lung condition that was drowning her a bit at a time, and had begged him for a swifter end. He was sent to the gallows. But the gentleman who'd used his silver-topped cane to beat to death an elderly pauper who'd begged for a farthing was acquitted of murder on grounds of self-defence.

'You see,' Toby explained, 'it seems to me that some judgement of *intention* ought to factor into the apportionment of punishment. At least as much as the outcome does.'

'Isn't a murder a murder?'

'I suppose I would say not,' Toby said.

Lily still didn't know about Kit. She hadn't seen with her own eyes that causing a death was not the same as being a murderer.

'And if the charge must be murder,' he said, 'then must all murders weigh the same? Do some not tip the scales of justice more steeply than others, and more readily?'

'I do not know. But it sounds as though *you* do.'

'Too often I see wealthy men, men with powerful friends, let off or given a lighter sentence when they have committed some crime – even if that crime is murder. Provocation is pleaded, or self-defence, when, for the common man, the same judges will turn entirely deaf to any extenuating circumstance. If the mitigation is valid at all, surely it must be valid for all?'

'Agreed.'

'And yet it is not. The system is skewed. Justice ought not to have bias, but anyone who follows the courts will see plainly that it has.'

'And what does your editor say to this? At the newspaper?'

'The *editor*? I have no idea. I hadn't discussed it with anyone, until you asked just now.'

'Toby.' Lily stopped walking and turned to face him. 'Why ever not?'

Chapter Eleven

1895

It took a long time after losing Amelia for Theo to feel well again. The sadness followed her around like a shadow. After a few weeks she began to dread Ralph's approach – be it to medicate or to kiss her. His kisses often led to other things, and she was scared of falling pregnant again. She'd proved herself unfit for that, and accepted the constant, dragging heartache as her just deserts.

Ralph's face was terrible when she pulled away from him.

'Theo, don't,' he whispered. 'I simply cannot *bear* to have you recoil from me!'

So she would relent, and take whatever he wished to give. None of it was his fault, after all.

'Another child will mend this hurt,' he said. 'You mustn't be afraid.'

His certainty was a mystery to Theo. They could not say why it had happened with Amelia, except that Theo had been too anxious, or had failed physically in some other way. So why should it not happen again? Fear was the very thing that might bring about what she most feared, and she could tread that merciless spiral for hours unless Audrey interrupted her with a query, or with a word in the newspaper that she didn't understand.

Audrey had taken to reading like a duck to water. Theo had started her off with an ABC, borrowed from Hermione, just as her nanny had done with her: *D is for Daisy's Dolls; H is for Harry's Hobby Horse*. It was all so childish that Theo was embarrassed, but Audrey didn't seem to be: she traced the shape of each letter with her fingertip, frowning in concentration. And the first time she read a word by herself – *fry*, from one of Mrs Meredith's recipe books – her smile was one of sheer triumph. Theo listened to her read aloud as much as possible, and her vocabulary grew all the time.

'Serendipity,' Theo said, on one occasion when Audrey interrupted her reverie. 'It means . . . a happy coincidence. A well-timed stroke of luck.'

'Thank you, miss,' Audrey said. 'And what's the reverse?'

'The opposite. It . . . I don't think it has one. Not a particular word, in any case. Just . . . misfortune. Something that happens by ill luck instead.'

'I see.' Audrey fidgeted the paper in her hands. 'And one might just as easily have good luck as bad, I suppose.'

Theo looked up, noting the conviction in Audrey's voice. 'Was it only bad luck, then?' she asked, barely a whisper.

'You'd never have done a single thing to harm your baby, miss. Knowingly or not. Is that not true?'

'It's true.' Tears ached in her throat. 'It is.'

So, Theo dared to believe it. Still, it took more than a year for her to fall pregnant again – long enough for her to think that Amelia had been her only chance. Ralph sent for a specialist from Southampton, Dr Ogilvy, who examined her with metal instruments that seemed better suited to a veterinarian than a doctor. He probed inside her with a lamp and his fingers as though she were a machine with a fault, muttering complaints when the discomfort made her fidget. The intrusion left her feeling less than human, and she hated the way Dr Ogilvy then spoke to Ralph, not to her.

He recommended a further examination under sedation.

'No,' Theo said, dry-mouthed. 'I do not want that man to touch me ever again.'

'Theo, my dear—'

'No. This is *my* body.'

Ralph gave her a steady look. 'I am both your husband and your physician,' he said. 'It is in my care to do what is best for you.'

A shudder of fear, that Theo was careful not to show. She'd learned that her nerves reduced her, in Ralph's eyes. They gave him cause to overturn her decisions. So she held his gaze, and did not raise her voice.

'If you love me, you will not force me.'

Ralph frowned and looked away. He seemed torn, but then nodded. 'Very well.'

In due course another child took root, and Theo felt the wonder of it again. It shone such a bright light that the shadow of fear all but disappeared. All but. Traces of it lurked in the corners of her mind, and caught her unawares. A twinge of indigestion, an ache in her back; any tiny mishap and the fear leapt like a flame given air. But midsummer had passed before they realised she was expecting, so that could not be a factor. The fifth anniversaries of Kit's trial and execution loomed ahead of her; then the date that Toby had left for Durham. Each came and went until there was nothing else to fear from the calendar, and she breathed a little easier.

The bump was bigger than before, and the sickness a little less, but her mouth tasted strange, and the list of things she wanted to eat grew short. These subtle differences reassured her: this was a different pregnancy; a different child. Then the baby began to move – the first time in response to hot cocoa. Theo felt the nudge of a tiny fist or foot, a wriggle no stronger than a minnow, and her heart thumped in recognition. She told no one. Ralph would be happy, but she wanted it to be hers alone for a little while. The secrecy felt safer, somehow. She waited three days before showing him, putting his hands in position as she sipped her cocoa.

His delight made her feel bad for having kept it to herself.

'This one is strong, my love,' he said.

The pains started on New Year's Day. Sitting rigid with fear at her writing desk, Theo tried desperately to believe it was indigestion, or back-ache. But there was no mistaking the horribly familiar feeling. She sat with it for a while, head bowed, until the blood started and she knew she'd have to move, and call for Audrey and Ralph. Tears slid down her face. It hurt to breathe.

When the labour was over she pushed herself up from the pillows, peering down before the midwife had the chance to wrap and remove her baby. A tiny boy about as long as her forearm, with translucent skin and smears of blood on his swollen eyelids. With a helpless moan she positioned her hands around him, not quite daring to touch him. She gasped when he stirred – when he moved his arm. An arm no thicker than her finger.

'He's alive!' she cried.

The midwife was pulling at the corners of the bedsheet, ready to gather it all up and take it away; the blood and the sweat and her baby.

Theo glared at her. 'Stop it! He's *alive*!'

The woman left the room, and came back with Ralph. Theo made a shield of her own body, crouching over her baby. She didn't dare pick him up, but she put the tip of her little finger into the palm of his hand, willing him to close his fingers around it, willing him to move again. But he did not.

'I saw him move,' she said, when all trace of him had been scrubbed away.

'You cannot have done, my love.'

'I *did*! He . . . he moved his arm . . .'

'It's just not possible, Theo. No foetus so . . . unfinished—'

'Do not use that word!'

Ralph put his arm around her but she sat rigid, her knees drawn up tight. It felt as though she would come apart if she relaxed even a tiny bit.

'He was our *son*,' she said. 'He should have a name, and a funeral.'

'Theo, he was not . . . *here*!' Ralph shook his head.

'But he *was*! He moved, and I . . . I held his hand. And I *loved* him!'

'You must try to be rational.'

'Does it . . . does it make it easier for you? Is it easier to think of him not as a child, but as a . . . medical condition?'

'Theo, *no*. Of *course* I feel it! But you must not allow yourself to be overwhelmed. These things happen, and life must go on. Why, even Princess Helena, the Queen's own daughter, failed to carry a baby to term on one occasion! I have heard of women miscarrying seven or even eight times before succeeding.'

Theo stared at him, confounded that he could expect that fact to be a comfort. Ralph shifted as if her gaze were too heavy.

'Perhaps if you had let Dr Ogilvy continue . . .'

He didn't finish the sentence. Theo turned away from him, curling on to her side. She closed her eyes.

Ralph suggested that Theo stay in bed for several weeks, and she didn't argue. He forbade all visitors except Diana, who came, muffled up from the cold, and sat at her bedside for a while. Theo found herself sitting up straighter and trying to hide her grief. Knowing that her mother would find it uncomfortable.

'How far along was it, this time?' Diana said.

'Around six months, I think.'

Diana looked away across the room. There were touches of grey at her temples now, and the cold light from the window aged her skin.

At length, she drew in a breath. 'It is not uncommon.'

Theo sensed a subtle gravity to the words. 'Do you mean . . . did you lose a child, too? Besides Amy, I mean?'

Diana glanced back at her, mastered herself, and the moment passed.

'It doesn't do to dwell, Theo,' she said briskly. 'Think of it as of anything else – practice makes perfect.'

This Theo could not allow. 'It isn't like anything else,' she said softly.

Diana turned away again. 'Well. What we cannot change, we must simply bear.'

The weather turned raw. Theo's convalescence was monochrome: black silhouettes against a flat white sky. She felt smothered by her grief. Audrey lit candles to banish the gloom, and read aloud even when Theo turned away and put her hands over her ears like a child. Only very gradually did the pall begin to lift. She spoke a little more, ate a little better. Listened to Audrey's voice, and to the words she was reading.

'Quay,' she said quietly one day. 'I know it looks like "kway", but it's pronounced "key". It's just one of those illogical words that come from the French.'

Audrey looked up from the page, and smiled.

By February the world was still frozen, and a storm blew in like nothing Theo had ever seen before. She went to stand at the window. Thunder ricocheted from hill to hill like the echo of vast ordnance; lightning blanched the sky; and snow fell all the while, in violent flurries on a spiteful wind. Theo's breath clouded the freezing glass. It was as though the heavens were raging.

The door creaked behind her and she startled, but it was only Audrey, wearing a woollen shawl and carrying a lamp even though it was nearing midday.

'Miss, you shouldn't be up! You'll catch cold, and the doctor will be upset.' Audrey still struggled to call her *madam*.

'I'm fine, Audrey. Have you ever seen anything like this weather?'

'Mrs Meredith says no one's ever seen anything like it. She says it's a sign.' Audrey draped a jacket around Theo and tried to turn her towards the bed. 'Thundersnow, the paper calls it.'

'Thundersnow? Apt, I suppose; but not very imaginative.'

'Dying weather's what they ought to call it. Please come back and lie down; it's too soon for you to be up and about. I'll get some more coal brought up.'

'It's not too soon,' Theo said. 'I can't stay cooped up much longer. The walls are beginning to close in on me.'

'Well, it's not like you could go outside, in any case. I'll read to you, if you like. Then there's chicken soup for lunch.'

'All right. Has the *Royal Geographical* arrived yet? Uncle Crudge's report on the supply of water to ancient Ephesus ought to be in it.'

'Oh, yes.'

Audrey didn't sound keen; she preferred novels. They'd been through most of Jane Austen during Theo's first confinement, after Amelia died; then moved on to the Brontë sisters, and George Meredith. But Theo always preferred to hear about foreign places, and imagine herself there. Far away.

She climbed back into bed. Audrey poured her a glass of water to take her pills. Ralph had prescribed them for her; Theo had no idea what was in them, or what they were supposed to do. There were different ones for morning and evening, and neither had much effect other than to make her head heavy and give her indigestion. She met Audrey's gaze as she swallowed them, and for a brief, startled moment they acknowledged their unhappiness. Then Audrey glanced around as the wind shook the window sashes and moaned in the chimney.

'Is it really dying weather?' Theo asked quietly.

Audrey frowned. 'I shouldn't have said. I'm not supposed to upset you with anything.'

'Never mind that.'

'Two yesterday,' Audrey said. 'An old lady slipped on the churchyard path and couldn't get up. She was perished by the frost before the verger found her. And the other . . .' Their eyes met again. 'A little boy of six. His brothers took him skating on a dew pond out Motcombe way, and . . . he went through the ice.'

'That's terrible.' Theo's eyes burned.

'See – I shouldn't have said!'

'Anyone would find it sad, Audrey. Now, run and fetch that journal.'

With Audrey gone, Theo could screw her eyes shut and wait for the disproportionate heave of sorrow to pass. The cutting short of another small life, far too soon.

After lunch, she began a letter to Timothy Crudge. *Ralph does not think I ought to have visitors, but I am much better and would so love to see you, and hear all your latest adventures. In any case, it's impossible in this terrible weather. I hope you have plenty of coal.* Theo longed for one of Crudge's big, whiskery hugs. The old-cloth smell of his jacket; the trace of bergamot from his shaving cream. She knew it would do her far more good than any pills. *Do you realise it has been over a year? Since my birth, I think this is the longest I have gone without seeing you. I miss you, Uncle.* She didn't write much of her grief, since it would only cause him pain. *I wish there could have been a funeral. My son lived, though it was only for a moment. Ralph will not even have him named, but I have done so anyway. He is Timothy, after you.*

She slept for a while in the afternoon, and Ralph woke her when he got home from the hospital, as the light was failing. She pushed herself straighter as he sat down beside her, taking her hand in one of his and pressing the other to her forehead.

'How are you, my darling?'

'Perfectly well. I should like to get up, in fact.'

'I know it's boring, but it's necessary. You must give your organs time to recover fully.'

'There was a woman called Mrs Brownlea over at Hallewell. She had one of her babies during the harvest – at the edge of the field. She put it in a sling and carried on with her scythe. It was a famous story—'

'And one that has no doubt grown considerably in the retelling. I don't believe a word of it. In any case, you are not some baggage of a farmer's wife.' He brushed her cheek with the backs of his fingers. 'You are my own dear girl.'

Theo smelled the phenol on his hands, and undertones of something stronger, well-scrubbed but not quite gone. Perhaps chloroform, or formaldehyde.

'How was Mr Oadby today?' she asked.

'Better all the time.' Ralph smiled.

He'd been treating Mr Oadby for several weeks. Cancer had eaten away his jawbone; Ralph had operated three times to cut out all of the disease. Since then, he'd been endeavouring to rebuild the left side of Oadby's jaw using slivers of bone taken from his shin, and splints of prepared ivory. It appeared to be working, though not all the grafts had survived. The idea of it fascinated Theo. That bone was *alive*, and could be persuaded to grow in a new place. Few had ever attempted the surgeries Ralph was performing; he had no map to follow.

Sometimes, when her husband listened to her chest or probed his fingers into various points of her abdomen, Theo felt like the drawings in the medical books at Hallewell: reduced to strips of muscle and sinew, and mysterious, seething organs. She had to remind herself that it was only his way of caring for her.

Ralph's face was still young, still handsome. Eyes that lively blue; no grey in his tawny hair. His shoulders were broad, and when he rolled up his shirt sleeves, the muscles of his forearms moved smoothly beneath the skin. But it didn't seem to matter; nothing could make her flesh crave his. More than ever, she had to be careful not to pull away from him, involuntarily.

'What weather,' he muttered. 'No horse or carriage could tackle the hill – it's sheet ice. I all but slithered home to you on the seat of my breeches just now. And we'll be inundated with broken legs and arms in the next few days, just you wait and see.'

He fetched a match from the mantelpiece and lit the bedside lamp, uniting them in an orb of warm light. The gas hissed steadily.

'How are you in . . . in yourself?' he asked.

Theo studied the twin bumps of her knees beneath the bedspread. It wouldn't do to beseech.

'I think it would do me good to get up, Ralph. I crave a change of scenery . . . a distraction. Life must go on.'

She echoed the words he had said to her himself, on the very day that Timothy died.

'It must.' He looked troubled. 'Please understand that if I were to let you up too soon, and some damage occurred as a result . . . it would be my fault. If you were to persuade me against my better judgement.'

'But I'm well; I *know* I am. Surely, nothing too serious could go on inside me without my being aware of it?'

'My dear girl, a terrific number of things are going on inside you all the time, without you knowing the least thing about it.'

'It is this forced confinement that brings me low. Not at the start, perhaps. But now.'

He frowned in thought. 'Very well, tomorrow then—'

'Oh, thank you, Ralph—'

'But it must be for one hour only. And you must wear your stays properly laced. On this I must insist. Were it merely a question of fashion it wouldn't matter at all, but your organs *must* be supported; it is *critical* to their recovery, and to your chances of a successful pregnancy in the future.'

'Very well.'

He lifted her chin with two fingers. 'I'm so glad at your recovery, Theo. I know it's different for women – you are less resilient to adversity. But I do think sometimes we must just . . . *try* to be happy. And in the trying, make it so.'

Theo raised a smile, but said nothing.

She itched to go outside and feel the bite of the wind on her skin. When she was sure Ralph had gone downstairs, she crossed to the window again and lifted the bottom sash. The blast of freezing air snatched her breath away; flecks of gritty snow blew on to her eyelashes and melted on her lips. The world was so deadened with ice it was impossible to imagine it green again. Down below, carrying a shovel and thickly wrapped against the weather, Seth Litton trudged slowly along the path. Theo had the sudden urge to climb down to him and run away barefoot through the snow. Away from her bedroom, her home, her grief. Her husband.

The cold didn't break for twelve weeks. Frost crept so deep into the ground that roads heaved and pipes burst. Water pumps froze solid, and people thawed icicles to drink. Work on the land and in industry stopped, and soup kitchens opened to feed the unemployed. Coal prices rose. Horses slipped on the roads, broke their knees and had to be shot. The elderly and poor died in their beds, as night after night the mercury showed fifteen degrees below zero. In London, the papers reported, men were riding their bicycles across the Thames, putting the ferrymen out of work.

Ralph's prescription of solitary rest finally ended, and Hermione came to visit. She hugged Theo tight.

'So pale!' She smiled guardedly. 'But you look well in spite of it. How are you?'

'I am quite recovered, thank you.'

'Are you?' Hermione leaned towards her, searching, and Theo couldn't hide it.

'Of course not. But perhaps . . . in time . . .'

'You poor thing. I have thought of you constantly; it's been torture not to see you, when I knew how heartsore you would be.'

'Well.' Theo took a quick breath. 'Life must go on, as my husband says. I must not let myself become overwhelmed.'

Hermione studied her for a while. 'Do you know,' she said, 'the moment our babies were born, Frederick was besotted? Oh, yes – they were never a nuisance to him, not even when they mewled and puked.' She smiled briefly. 'But whilst I was carrying them . . . it was as though they weren't entirely real. Naturally, he understood that they were *coming*, but in the meantime he treated me as though perhaps I had a slight cold, or some sort of dropsy that caused me to swell up.'

She reached for Theo's hand. 'We become mothers at the moment of conception,' she said. 'But I don't think a man becomes a father until the child is in his arms. It's not their fault. Only a question of perception, I suppose.'

'He calls them "foetuses", and won't let me call them by name,' Theo said. 'He wouldn't let me . . . see them. And I can't seem to forgive him.'

'I understand. But do try to; you'll both be happier if you succeed. Nobody can be forced to feel something they do not feel. It's difficult, of course; I expect you have felt very alone.'

'It has created a . . . distance . . . between us.'

'You will see – when the baby is here, when Ralph can see it and smell it and weigh it in his hands, he will love it every bit as much as you love the two you've already carried.'

'Hermione, I . . . I don't think I can do it. I don't think I can go through this again. I can hardly bear for him to touch me, in case . . .'

Her friend's face creased with concern. 'Just let a little more time pass.'

'The first time, with Amelia, Ralph—' Theo hesitated. 'There was a traumatic event in my past, and I lost Amelia on the anniversary of it. Ralph noticed, though I had not. He suggested . . . he thought perhaps my fear of that memory was the cause.'

'He said that?' Hermione frowned.

'Do you think he could be right?'

'No. I do not.'

'And now, this time . . . He brought a doctor to see me, a specialist, but I detested the man and wouldn't see him. Ralph thinks I should have done.' She took a shaky breath. 'He blames me, Hermione.'

'I'm sure it was only sorrow and disappointment that made him say such things.'

But Hermione didn't look sure at all.

'He blames me, and I . . . think he's right to. So, how can I try to have another?'

'Oh, my dear,' Hermione said sadly. 'How can you not?'

Theo told Ralph about Hermione's visit as he was reading the newest copy of *The Lancet*.

'She and the Charitable Ladies' Society are organising a skating gala at the end of the month, to raise money for those put out of work by this terrible weather.'

'Hm, indeed,' Ralph said.

'I would very much like us to go. It's been years since I skated.'

He looked over at her. 'A skating gala? I'm not sure that's wise, my dear.'

'I won't fall. I'm rather good at it.'

He smiled. 'Are you indeed?'

'It would cheer me no end, Ralph.'

'Then we shall go,' he said, distracted. 'We will do whatever will cheer you.'

'What is it, Ralph? What are you reading?'

'Oh, nothing . . . Well, in truth, something.'

He threw the magazine down and got up, crossing to the fireplace to jab pointlessly at the coals. 'A great breakthrough, in fact.' He gave a tight little smile. 'A man named William Arbuthnot Lane has successfully repaired a section of a patient's cranium with a steel plate. The area of skull had fragmented, and natural regrowth was impossible.'

'That's . . . *remarkable*,' Theo said. 'How did the patient come by such a terrible injury?'

'That's scarcely the point.' Ralph took a breath before continuing. 'It is a technique I have tried myself – only once with the skull, but with other fractured bones. I have tried without success.'

'Oh.'

'There is always some rejection of the plate, leading to infection and weakening of the bone at the anchoring points . . . But I feel certain I *would* have perfected the technique, if I'd only had more chances to attempt it.'

'But now this Dr Lane has managed it you may use his method, and—'

'The discovery ought to have been *mine*, Theo! Don't you see? Every time I am close to something . . . Every time I dare to think *my* time has come, I am pipped at the post.'

Theo didn't know what to say, but Ralph had turned to her expectantly.

'You have saved so many lives, Ralph—' She floundered. 'And . . . your treatment of Mr Oadby . . .'

Ralph silenced her with a flick of his hand. 'A jawbone. What is a jawbone? One could tinker at it for months. But the *skull* . . . The name of William Arbuthnot Lane will go down in history, don't you see? To achieve an historic first in one's field is *everything*, Theo! I don't expect you to understand. How can you, when there is nothing you have ever worked towards? But the constant *endeavour* . . . Trying and failing and trying again differently. And having to wait passively for cases to come along in order to be able to work, when I am *so* close!'

He dragged in a breath and sighed it out.

'It's exhausting. Sometimes, I think . . . I fear I will never succeed. I will never break new ground, or make my mark.'

Theo didn't know how to console him. He was right – she didn't understand. She had never had ambitions, only unfulfilled desires. But that was not what silenced her. It was the way Ralph had spoken about his patients, and his work. As though the relief of their suffering were secondary to the advance of medicine as a whole, and to his own place in that advance. As though those two aims were somehow disconnected, when she felt certain they ought not to be.

'Still,' Ralph said, almost to himself. 'It is early days for Lane's cranial patient; it has been but two months since the operation, he writes. There is still time for porosis to develop, or resorption of the fracture points to destabilise the anchors.'

He thought for a moment, brightening. 'Necrosis is a possibility, as is reduced cortical perfusion. Yes, it is early days. The patient may yet succumb.'

◆ ◆ ◆

Toby scraped his thumb down the window and watched the frost build up under his nail. It quickly melted to a sliver of water. Cold radiated from the glass, in spite of the rags he'd stuffed around the frame; he could see his breath in the frigid air.

He hated to think how cold the poorest must be, in this spell of brutal weather. That morning he'd had to break a film of ice on his water jug in order to shave, but he knew he should count his blessings. He had a room of his own, a roof over his head, and he had eaten that day. He went back to the fireplace, where a few coals softened the chill, pulled his chair nearer and propped his feet up, as close as he dared. Wedging his hands into his armpits, he looked across at the little table where his breakfast sat wrapped in a cloth. He was sorely tempted to wolf it down. With a sigh, he reached instead for the brandy on the mantelpiece and poured himself a tot. The heat of it sank through his gut and into his bones. He poured another; then a third. It was rough stuff – inexpensive – but he'd got used to it.

He'd been planning to write but hadn't the energy, and his fingers were too cold to hold a pen. It was too early to go to bed. Instead, he took out his notebook and read over a case he'd been following through the courts, which had reached its inevitable conclusion today. He'd seen the court's decision coming, and had already drafted his comment.

It was another 'Cain and Abel' case – as the papers insisted on calling any crime involving brothers. This was a family of bakers called Hibbert, living in Spitalfields. The younger brother, George, had killed the elder, William. They'd been in love with the same girl for years, a ragged orphan who'd been taken in from the streets at the age of eleven. The boys had been twelve and thirteen at that point, so had never felt her to be their sister. William had proposed to her, but her feelings had always been stronger for George. The brothers loved one another, and neither was a violent man; their feud had been one of hurt and silent frustration. But then one day a scuffle, and a single punch thrown so unexpectedly, and being so out of character, that William hadn't seen it coming. He'd fallen back, landed awkwardly, and died.

Today, they had heard that George would hang. He had wept. The girl had wept. Their parents had wept. The public gallery had erupted, mostly in outrage.

It was no mystery to Toby that cases like this took hold of him and wouldn't let go. This case in particular: he had got into fights at Durham, he'd thrown impulsive punches. Any one of them might have accidentally killed the recipient in the exact same way, and sent him to the gallows in Kit's footsteps. They might both have ended up hanged for inadvertently causing a death.

There was a narrow window of time in which the court's decision might be overturned, or George's sentence commuted, and there was an outside chance that Toby might make a difference by writing about it. He sketched a first draft in his head:

Has a murder been committed when there was no intention to kill? George Hibbert most assuredly did not mean to kill his brother. He could not have expected a single blow from his fist to be fatal, and his grief and repentance are plain to see. To hang him as a murderer is to compound this tragedy, rather than to assuage it. The law, in this case, has been misused; else the law, as Mr Dickens would have it, is a ass.

He'd shown his notes to the editor at the newspaper, just as Lily had suggested. He was told to stick to the round-ups. He'd persisted – written a draft of a comment, and left it on the editor's desk. Just one paragraph, flagging up an unjust verdict and asking readers to reflect upon the possibility that any one of them might at some point find themselves at the mercy of a capricious set of circumstances and a bad-tempered judge. He'd been made to rewrite it three times, but it had run. The next one too; and then it became a weekly column. He was paid by the word, and the amount had been increased twice.

Lily was teaching at a boarding school in Newcastle, and enjoying it thoroughly. She usually had to wait for one of the thrice-yearly holidays before she could visit, but the school had shut unexpectedly due to an outbreak of scarlet fever, so she was on the sleeper at that exact moment, and due into London the following morning. Toby thought he might take her skating on the Thames – he still hadn't got used to the novelty of seeing the river frozen solid. The cold had lasted so long, it felt like it would never thaw. Warped tracks between Waterloo and Salisbury had given him a good excuse not to go home that Christmas; he'd sent a card and some gifts, and had gone north to the Womersleys instead. Lily had still never been to Hallewell. It never seemed the right time.

He showed her his comment about the Hibbert brothers – in print – as they walked along Victoria Embankment three days later. Frost had carved the London planes in white, unearthly against a Wedgwood sky. The cold was dry that day, and the stillness made it bearable; the city seemed cleaner, the river sanitised. He'd been made to take out the remark about the law being misused, since that was a direct criticism of the judge in question, but there had been several letters to the paper, from men of influence, in response to the piece.

'This is wonderful, Toby,' Lily said, pausing her stride to hold the paper closer. The typeface was punishingly small.

The sun had no heat but it blazed on her hair, and lit her eyes like polished rosewood. Her figure, in her fashionable blue dress – narrow through the waist and hips, with gigot sleeves that widened like legs of mutton – drew surreptitious glances from several passing men.

She looked up at Toby, her face sombre. 'What a tragic, desperate case. Do you think the sentence of death may be changed?'

'I imagine every effort will be made.' Toby tried not to sound too pleased with himself. 'A lawyer has come forward to act on George's behalf, *pro bono*.'

'As a result of your piece?'

'The publicity can only have helped.'

'Oh Toby, well *done*!'

'I only pointed out what should have been obvious.'

'But somebody must point out such things, and nobody else did.'

Toby tucked the newspaper into his coat. He planned to send it down to Hallewell for his parents to read. There was a long pause, which Lily would normally fill with a funny story about a pupil, or about Tom. Instead, she stared straight ahead, eyes narrowed to the glare, with her lips pressed together in that way.

'Lily? Is everything all right?'

She opened her mouth as though to speak, but didn't. In the end, she simply nodded. Toby took a nip of brandy from his hip flask, then offered it to her. She shook her head.

They'd reached a pier where an enterprising couple were renting out ice skates.

'What do you say?' Toby said. 'Shall we have a go?'

Lily still seemed reserved, but she nodded. 'I'm game if you are.'

She was far more graceful on the ice than he was, swooping in wide circles around him with her hands clasped behind her back, while he scuffed along. Gradually, Toby improved, trusting his balance more, and after an hour he supposed they were making an attractive pair, arm in arm, hardly wobbling at all. The city on either side looked magnificent, with the sky so blue and the roofs so white. A thousand skeins of smoke rose from a thousand chimneys, straight up into the air. It all glittered, and was briefly magical.

'Have we had enough?' Lily said. 'These boots are giving me blisters.'

'Of course – you should have said something sooner.'

'Yes,' she said flatly.

Toby halted, turning to face her. 'Lily, what is it? You must say.'

She took a deep breath. Her face was paler now, despite the exercise.

'Perhaps it is time. Toby, I . . . I release you from our engagement.'

Toby stared for a moment, speechless. Once the meaning of her words had sunk in, panic shot through him. His heart lurched to full speed, and his stomach dropped.

'Lily—'

'There – I knew it!' Her voice trembled. 'I guessed that I would know from the look in your eyes whether I was right or wrong to do this, and I see that I am right. Aren't I?'

'Lily, I—' He had no idea what to say.

She made an exasperated sound. 'Must I always be the one to speak? Toby . . . you do not love me—'

'I do.'

'No, you don't. Not as you *should.* Not as a husband. Oh, I'm sure you *like* me well enough; I'm sure I'm eminently *suitable*. And I'm amply aware that you love my brother. But I don't want to be *liked*, Toby. I don't want to be suitable. I want to be *adored* – worshipped! I want the man I marry to dream of taking me in his arms and devouring me. I want him to be unable to resist it. And that isn't how you feel, is it, Toby? Tell me truthfully.'

Toby felt as though the ice were splintering beneath him. Protestations crowded his head, begging to be said.

'That isn't how I feel,' he confessed quietly.

Lily sagged, her chin dropping as she absorbed the blow.

'Damn and blast,' she murmured. 'I'd so hoped you'd be staggered, and contradict me in the strongest possible terms. I mean, I knew you wouldn't, but I still hoped.'

'Lily, I am so sorry.'

'Well, don't bother to be!' she said bitterly. 'It's my fault – I suspected from the start that what you liked most about me was that I was Tom's sister, but I . . . I let myself believe you would come to love me, eventually. But it's been three years, and only an idiot would wait another three years, and then another . . . So, let's call it quits while I still have my looks.'

'I don't know what to say. You are so . . . decent, Lily. And so wise.'

Tears glimmered along her lashes. 'Oh, God save me from being decent and *wise*! In fact, I've been an utter fool. I thought you were so strong, and principled. I thought you were brave, but you aren't! You're a *coward*, Toby Meriwether.'

This stung him to silence for a beat. Lily turned abruptly and skated away, back to the pier, where she climbed from the ice, batting away his efforts to help her.

'Stop it!' she snapped. 'Stop trying to be gallant, when you aren't!'

'Lily, please . . . I feel wretched—'

'Do you? Good!'

She laced her boots with fingers that shook, then set off towards Tom's apartment, refusing to look at him, her face pinched with misery.

Toby followed along helplessly. 'Lily,' he said, as she reached the building and thumped on the door. 'Forgive me. Please. I wanted so much to—' He searched for some way to make it better. 'I'll . . . I'll always be your friend, Lily Womersley.'

She paused, and eventually cast a glance back at him.

'And I so wanted to be yours, Toby,' she said tremulously. 'I . . . I hope you find one. Somebody you can tell all your secrets to. Perhaps then they won't weigh so heavily upon you. Or upon the people who love you.'

She didn't look back again as the door closed behind her.

Toby bought a bottle of brandy on the way back to his room. He lit the fire and pulled up his chair as the sun set behind the rooftops, briefly casting the window in a delicate rose gold. He felt relieved, in part; and grateful to Lily for releasing him. A weight of responsibility he'd hardly been aware of had lifted, and he felt incredibly light without it. But he knew he had failed – failed Lily, and failed Tom. Guilt and anxiety churned his guts. His engagement, and eventual wedding, had been the only fixed point in his future; without it, he felt himself stumbling back towards that shapeless, unnavigable morass. It frightened him.

He began a hasty letter to Tom, then thought he ought to let Lily speak to him first and allow the news to settle; then he wrote his letter anyway, in preparation. Apologising, begging to be forgiven, and to see his friend soon.

He drank glass after glass of brandy as his mind turned in circles. There was nothing in particular he needed to do just then, but he was certain he ought to do *something*. It felt as though the four walls of his very self had been undermined, and were crumbling. Skirting the edges of panic, Toby fetched his notebook of Hallewell symbols and tried to make some new sense of them. But it only made him homesick for a place and time that no longer existed, and could never be returned to. It only made him angry with himself for trying. He was surprised, an hour later, to find the brandy bottle empty. The wind had whipped up and more snow was falling. He crammed his hat on to his head, and went out to buy another.

Towards the end of February, Toby risked a journey down to Hallewell. The weather was unrelenting, and the village had been largely cut off for weeks, but Mona had caught a cold that she couldn't seem to shift, and David was worried. It had been two years since Toby had seen them; his visits inevitably saddened them all. He was riddled with guilt about it nonetheless, and thought he ought to tell them in person about the end of his engagement. So, he negotiated three days away from work, and caught the train.

He had to walk the four miles from Semley station to Hallewell – only an idiot would risk their horse on the steep hills in between. It took him over two hours, and he arrived exhausted, chilled to the bone, but still felt a sparkle of recognition as the castle came into view against the flat grey sky. A nameless longing from somewhere so deep inside him he couldn't root it out. London was home now, he told himself firmly; childhood was long gone.

His father hugged him with brief vehemence, and Toby went upstairs at once. Mona was propped up on pillows but fast asleep. He sat down beside her, shocked by how old and ill she looked. When he took her hand gently, she woke.

'Hello,' he said. 'What's all this? It's not like you to take to your bed.'

'Dear Toby. You shouldn't have travelled in this weather! I'm fine.'

She smiled wanly, but her chest wheezed, and she struggled not to cough.

'Then get up, lazybones,' he said.

'I will. I will now that you're here.'

'I'm teasing; you must rest. But I should warn you, Dad and I plan to cook supper. And whatever we create, you *must* eat it – and praise us for it.'

'I'll be sure to.'

'Sole meunière, I thought. Perhaps devilled kidneys, or ham rissoles.' He stood up, straightened his jacket. 'Or possibly cheese on toast. Go back to sleep. I'll bring some tea up in a while.'

'Thank you, Toby. Thank you for coming to see us.'

Toby hated himself for that. Hated that she was grateful for his presence.

He and David muddled through in the kitchen, and managed to produce a supper of various things on singed toast – cheese, tinned pilchards, bottled tomatoes – followed by jam tarts donated by a neighbour, which they warmed and had with condensed milk. It wasn't at all bad. Toby took regular pulls from his hip flask, as covertly as he could. The brandy gave him the cheer he needed in that sad, quiet house. He hoped that, at some point during the visit, it would give him the courage to tell them about Lily.

When his father caught him in a swig and frowned, Toby offered it to him.

'No, thank you, son,' David said evenly.

'Keeps me warm in this godforsaken weather,' Toby said, as lightly as he could.

'No. It brings the blood to your skin, and cools you all the quicker. The heat is an illusion.' Toby put the flask away and was more careful not to be seen from then on.

Next day, he caught up with a few friends in the village, boys he'd grown up with, and heard about a skating gala that night, to which half the village was going.

'You go,' Mona said. 'Dress warmly! David – why not lend Toby your old greatcoat?'

David went off to fetch it.

'You're sure you don't mind?' Toby said.

'Go and have *fun*,' Mona said. 'How I miss your smile!'

'I still smile, Mum.'

'Not the way you used to.'

David reappeared with the coat bundled under his arm. It dated from his army days, weighed a ton and stank of lanolin, but it was the warmest thing any of them possessed. He shook it out, scattering a confetti of dead moths.

◆ ◆ ◆

The skating gala was held between Shaftesbury and Hallewell, on fields where the River Nadder had flooded and then frozen. The idea was to help the poor and raise morale; the entrance fee would be distributed to those in poverty, and men without work were employed as stewards, ticket sellers, putters-up of bunting and lighters of the naphtha lamps that were strung about on wires. They gleamed in hundreds of eyes as the daylight failed and the races finished, and a general melee of public skating began. Those who hadn't had a square meal in weeks clustered around a tent where a whole sheep was roasting over coals, alongside steaming vats of soup.

A full moon rose, as cold and unfeeling as the frost.

Theo walked the two and a half miles with Ralph and Audrey, with her skates slung over her shoulder and her spirits rising to be outside at last. She hadn't been beyond their own garden wall since well before Christmas. They all three wore multiple layers of wool, from their stockings to their ears, but still the cold crept in wherever it could. Theo yelped when she slipped, grabbing at Audrey's arm, but they were so well padded by their heavy skirts that it didn't hurt at all to whomp down amongst the skeletons of cow parsley and thistle.

'It is wonderful to hear you laugh,' Ralph whispered in Theo's ear.

They met the Abbotts by one of the tents, and toasted to visions of the not too distant spring.

Audrey had never skated before. She had fun at first, but soon grew tired of staggering about, splay-legged. Theo and Ralph left her at a church stall with a cup of mulled cider and skated away, arm in arm. They gradually made their way to the furthest corner of the field, where the lamplight barely reached and there was only the moon to see by, as silver as the ancient coin in Theo's pocket. There, the Nadder narrowed between its banks, still frozen as it headed east.

Ralph peered along the dark river. 'We can't go much further.'

'Just a little,' Theo said.

She was drawn to that icy pathway, disappearing into darkness; tunnelling through sleeping trees into the hidden kingdom of foxes and mice. For the first time in years, excitement spread through her – that yearning to take a path leading who knew where. Unseen wings beat overhead, and some wild part of Theo longed to steal away; to disentangle herself from the human life she'd been given, and swap the bed in which she was so often confined for a burrow of dry leaves out in the cold, clean air.

Ralph caught her hand to stop her.

'That's far enough, my love. We cannot trust the ice.'

The excitement flickered out. Theo looked back to see Ralph's face soft with desire, and her pang of dismay bordered on anger – that he could love her, yet understand her not at all. She'd needed the distance; a moment of otherness. She took his face in her hands, caught in an upswell of a feeling she couldn't name. It might have been affection, or simply sorrow, but as he kissed her she thought, for the first time, that perhaps she *did* love him, in some way. He was the father of her children, and to love them was to love him, at least in part.

Holding her hand, Ralph returned them to the light and noise of the crowd.

'Let's find Audrey, and get ourselves a hot drink,' he said. 'Then perhaps home, to a fire and warm blankets?'

'You go ahead; I'd like to skate for just a little longer.'

Ralph frowned.

'A minute more,' she said. 'I will come and find you.'

'Well, do be careful.'

Theo pushed away, two strides, three, revelling in the sudden freedom of leaving Ralph behind. And in the next instant she saw Toby. The familiar turn of his head, his dark eyebrows, the smile – so precious – that creased his cheeks. A flash of teeth in the darkness, arms spread for balance as he skated away and the crowd closed around him.

Theo's heart kicked, and without a thought she set off after him.

He was *there*, if she could only reach him. She stumbled and was bumped; rebounding from strangers who reached out to brace her. *Steady on, miss; careful there.* She stared at the place up ahead where Toby had been, and where he had vanished. Eyes darting from face to face, with a mounting sense of loss, until she was at the other edge of the ice and wondered if she'd imagined him – seen an echo of him in the face of a stranger, wearing a battered old army coat.

It had been over five years since she'd seen him. Tears ached in her throat.

Ralph caught her arms. 'Theo? What on earth made you take off like that? And crash about like a fool?'

'I thought I . . .' Theo was still looking around. Still looking for him. 'I thought I saw somebody . . .'

'Somebody? Who?'

She caught herself, realising how close she was to betraying too much. But it was too late.

Ralph stiffened. 'Somebody from Hallewell? Toby Meriwether, I suppose?'

His gaze became a glare and Theo went hot with guilt.

'No, I— it was . . . somebody else.'

'I see.' Ralph did not blink. 'Who, then?'

'Just . . . somebody I used to know, when I was little.' She snatched a name from the air: 'Jeanette.'

'Jeanette who?'

Theo took too long to answer. 'LeRoy.'

'Please don't lie to me, Theo,' Ralph said quietly. He tightened his grip on her arms, and she turned her face away. 'Was it him? Did you speak to him?'

'No.'

'But you obviously wanted to.'

'Only to . . . only because I . . . still feel responsible. For what happened to his brother.'

'You must feel very responsible indeed. You . . . you say his name in your sleep. All too often for my liking.'

Now Theo looked at him, horrified. His expression was pained.

'Do you love him?' Ralph gave her arms a jerk as he spoke, and Theo shook her head.

'No.' She swallowed. 'He . . . he was very hard with me, after the trial. He blamed me, when we had been firm friends before it all – the three of us. He was hard, and we parted badly, that's all.'

'Then you still . . . think about what happened?'

'I can't help it, Ralph. Forgive me.'

'I remember him staring at me during the trial,' he murmured. 'Such a black look! I thought at the time he must be a man of bad temper. A cruel man.'

'I suppose he was,' Theo said. 'In some ways. Never more so than when harm came to Kit.'

'I did no harm to the boy, and neither did you! But you were all just children, I suppose.'

Theo said nothing. She was thinking of the frozen river as it tunnelled away beneath the trees; a secret path to a different world. How much she wished she hadn't turned back.

Ralph bent his head forwards, shutting his eyes for a moment.

'How I *wish* you would just forget about all that!' he said sadly. 'I thought he was the reason, you see. I thought *he* was the reason you cannot love me.'

'Oh, Ralph.' Theo shook her head.

He saw much more than she gave him credit for, and she felt foolish, and ashamed. He'd begged her not to lie but she had to.

'I do love you. I do. That . . . time, and any dreams I may still have of it, are only because it left such a terrible mark.'

'My poor darling.' Ralph let go of her arms and took her hands, now painfully numb in spite of her gloves. 'You look frozen. Let's go home.'

Later, as she undressed, Theo noticed ten round bruises on her skin, one on the front and four on the back of each arm: Ralph's fingers and thumbs, where he'd grabbed her. She pulled the sleeves of her nightdress over them quickly, so that he wouldn't be reminded of her inadvertent treachery. She hardly dared meet his eye as she lay down beside him, and didn't sleep for hours; too afraid that she'd betray herself again, after the glimpse of Toby that had shaken her to her core. It *had* been him, she was sure of it. Just a few feet away, and she could still feel that closeness. A thrill of anticipation, as though he were right there in the room. She lay rigid, eyes open, terrified that Ralph would notice him there.

The brandy was boiling in Toby's blood, blurring his brain and his eyes so that the lanterns left streamers through the air. He horsed about on the ice like a boy, playing bulldog with the others – crashing into each other, falling, finding it all hilarious while people tutted and swore at them. He drank and played the fool so that he could ignore that feeling again – that sense of acting in a play. He did it so that he wouldn't look for her. There were plenty of married couples there, of the middling and upper sort. The gala was as close to Shaftesbury as to Hallewell. He briefly wondered what he would say if he found himself standing in front of her. But there was nothing *to* say.

Still, he couldn't prevent the sadness that stole over him. It was nothing to do with Theo, he decided. It was all down to his aimlessness, and his sick mother; it was because of Lily, and Tom, who had not answered his letter. He begged his friends to stay on, later and later, even though they were cold and tired and still had a long walk home. He made them stay until the crowd had thinned right out, and she was not there. Mrs Theodora Anscombe. Even the name made his gorge rise; he did not *want* to see her.

He trudged back along the lane in silence, well behind the others; numb hands in his pockets, face all but covered by his scarf. The ground was pitching like the deck of a ship. He focused all his energy on putting one foot in front of the other and not throwing up.

But the dejection would not go. He shook his flask but it was empty, and when his friends peeled off towards their various homes he stood for a while, alone, mesmerised by the glow of moonlight on the snow. Meandering up to the green, he sat down at the foot of the Roman Cross. Its carvings made by ancient hands, so many centuries before. How bewitched Theo had been by that idea – as awed as any pilgrim at a shrine. *Mrs Theodora Anscombe*. The world was white and black and grey. Sepulchral; not a place for living things at all. Toby stared at the castle, outlined against the glacial sky. The stone at his back burned with cold, and symbols danced before his eyes: a triangle that might mean fire; a circle that might be a snake. Soon, he could no longer feel his body or his face, but he could feel his heart and it was beating off-kilter, with a disconcerting wobble.

It was better to stay there, Toby decided. Far easier to stay there than to find the strength to go home; to feign sobriety and good cheer, to feign success. *You're a coward, Toby Meriwether*. The faint stars wheeled, the castle watched, and there seemed to be nobody in the whole world except for him, alone in the snow.

His pulse slowed, which was a relief. Slow was probably better. And warm was better than cold – he was getting warm now, even starting to feel flushed. His father's greatcoat was incredibly heavy. Suffocating, in fact – beneath it, his skin was actually prickling with heat. Toby shook his head in wonderment, which made his brain slop around queasily. It took a moment to coordinate his fingers, but then he set about unbuttoning the coat, and fought his way free.

Chapter Twelve

Ralph came home for the midday meal excited to tell Theo about a new patient. The unfortunate Mr Miller had been out on his bicycle with deliveries of haberdashery when he'd made the foolish decision to coast down Gold Hill. Eyewitnesses had reported him gathering speed, the handlebars juddering over the cobbles, before the front wheel jacked and Miller was pitched head first to the ground. He was brought to the hospital immediately, unconscious, with his left ear and eyelid all but torn away and his skull gleaming through the wound.

Theo had a mouthful of chicken fricassee but couldn't swallow. Ralph was sometimes too detailed with his descriptions.

'He woke while the wound was being dressed, and I noted a vertical fracture with a shallow depression at its centre,' he said eagerly. 'But while he remains alert and can talk and move normally, there's no need to risk an operation.'

'Could he recover without it?'

'Perhaps. But if he loses consciousness again, if his speech becomes slow, his eyes sensitive, and he seems stupid . . . then I must act, and quickly.'

The food turned to ashes in Theo's mouth. Ralph was too preoccupied to notice. She put down her knife and fork.

'The same symptoms as Missy,' she said quietly.

'Hm?'

'Those must have been the same symptoms Missy showed, the Monday morning before she died. When you decided to operate.'

Ralph looked up, frowned briefly. 'Yes,' he said. 'That's correct. Though, in her case, an infection was also present.'

'She had a fever? I don't remember you telling me that before.'

He looked down at his plate, steadily loading his fork with green beans.

'I'm sure I must have done. In any case, infection is not an issue here. The man was brought straight to us, and his wound was dressed with sterile iodoform gauze. Quite unlike the initial treatment Melissa received.'

'But hers was only a graze.'

'Do not speak of it, Theo. It only upsets you.' Ralph's tone was final. 'But it's true, this *is* a far more serious wound, and far more likely to cause a rapid deterioration, if there is unseen bleeding beneath the skull.' He ate in silence for a while, then said: 'Meningeal haemorrhage is so hard to treat successfully, with trephining or any other means, because treatment is almost always delayed – the patient seems well, walks and talks as normal. By the time the pressure on the brain becomes serious and treatment is sought, it is too late. But, *this* time, I have a chance.'

'Then . . . it was too late for Missy? She should have had the operation sooner?'

'Regrettably so. But enough, my dear. Enough about that girl.'

Theo pushed the food around on her plate while Ralph shovelled his down with unappealing haste, and she tried without success to think of a topic of conversation unconnected to brains or bleeding or death. In fact, she couldn't find her voice at all. Her husband mopped up the last of the sauce with a piece of bread and hurried back to the hospital.

Soon after they'd gone up to bed that night, there was an urgent banging at the door and a message for the doctor to come at once – Mr Miller was showing all the warning signs. Ralph scrabbled back into his clothes and dropped a brief kiss on to Theo's forehead.

'I cannot say when I will be back.'

She lay sleepless after he'd gone, her thoughts circling as night turned slowly into day. *When everything was performed correctly this time . . . Trying and failing and trying again differently . . .* Mr Miller's grave injury was not a tragedy to Ralph, it was an opportunity.

'Who gives a doctor permission to act?' she asked Audrey, as they did her hair in the morning. She met her maid's eyes in the mirror, through a gentle haze of powder. 'Permission to give treatment, that is.'

'The patient, I suppose,' Audrey said, not seeking an explanation of the question. 'When the patient goes to him, or calls him out. Then he just gets on with it, doesn't he?'

Theo paused. 'And if the patient is a child?'

'Then the parents.'

'Yes. And if the child has no parents?'

'Then . . . I don't know. If they have a guardian or a relative, then that person. If not, then . . . well, surely the doctor will not perform any treatment, since the child won't pay him, and probably won't know to call him in the first place.'

Theo nodded slowly. 'Do you . . . did you know your parents, Audrey?'

'I never knew my father, and Ma died when I was little. She fell down the stairs.'

'How awful – poor woman!'

'Blind drunk, by all accounts.' Audrey lifted her eyebrows. 'I only remember little bits and pieces of her.'

'So, when you arrived at St Agnes's . . . did that make Mrs Vine, the matron, your legal guardian? Or was it one of the ladies of the charitable society?'

'Don't know, miss. All I know is a fashionable lady came to the workhouse one day, and fetched me to Hallewell. As to what was legal about that and what wasn't, I can't say.'

'No, of course you can't. Forgive me, Audrey.'

'What's it all about, miss?'

'Just . . . something that happened a long time ago. You know I . . . I first became acquainted with my husband when he treated a friend of mine. Another girl from St Agnes's.'

'Missy Cartwright.'

'That's right. She was turning fifteen when she was treated, you see. Still a child . . .' Theo shook her head. 'Never mind.'

Audrey finished her hair in silence, then tidied away the brushes and unused pins.

'Is that who you saw on the night we went skating?' Audrey said, cheeks flushing. 'Someone from back then?'

'You . . . saw him?' Theo tried not to say his name, even in her head, in case it spoke itself later on in her sleep.

'Not properly. I saw you take off after someone, and it looked to be the fellow with the dark hair and the army coat.' Audrey took a breath. 'Then I saw how upset it made the master and I didn't like to mention it.'

'It's all right, Audrey. He . . . yes. He was – is – someone I grew up with. A childhood friend. But we fell out when Missy died.'

'It was his brother who hanged for it.' Audrey gave her an apologetic look. 'The other girls told me, right at the start.'

'Then, you know it all,' Theo said bleakly.

'Not all, I think,' Audrey murmured.

After a pause, Theo asked: 'Did you see where he went? Or who he was with?'

Audrey shook her head. 'Sorry, miss. There was so many people, all moving about.'

Theo looked down at the box of hair combs and brooches on the dressing table, but all she saw was that dark hair, that army greatcoat, that glimpse of his face lit by naphtha lamps, all vanishing into darkness.

After breakfast, Theo decided to go to the hospital, to ask after the patient and – hopefully – to congratulate Ralph. She hadn't ever done so before, but she couldn't stop thinking about Mr Miller and his operation. She had a strong urge to meet the man, and to know more. So, she packed cheese, apples and some currant buns into a basket, and set off.

Sister Hendry, whose displeasure at having to defer to Theo, as Dr Anscombe's wife, was as plain as the nose on her face, showed her into his private room on the first floor of the hospital.

'Dr Anscombe is still with the patient, but I will tell him you've come.' Her lips pressed hard together for a moment. 'You've not chosen the best moment, Mrs Anscombe. He might not be able to see you. Perhaps it would be better if—'

'It's quite all right,' Theo interrupted her. 'Thank you, Sister. I will wait for him here.'

She'd never been in Ralph's room before. In fact, she hadn't been to the hospital at all since before they were married, but she remembered it so clearly that the intervening years shrank to nothing. The smell of carbolic and metal and starch; the peculiar hush made up of a thousand tiny echoes. Ralph's desk was crowded, but everything was in its place. There were piles of pens and paperwork, and instruments made of brass and wood, including a large microscope. The only incongruous thing was a pair of ladies' gloves: sky blue, small and elegant. Theo didn't recognise them as hers.

One wall was occupied by an enormous mahogany cupboard. It had wide drawers at the base, and double doors above them. Theo had no idea what was kept in it. On impulse she went to look, but the doors were locked. She stared at the cupboard. Her husband had a whole realm, there at the hospital, about which she was permitted to know nothing beyond what he chose to tell her. She thought of Fortescue's cold, knowing gaze over the dinner table, and the feeling it gave her of being allowed no secrets, no privacy whatsoever. She thought of Dr Ogilvy's unwanted examination. The way he had told only Ralph whatever it was he'd observed inside her.

She wanted to look in the cupboard.

After a full minute of careful listening, she was confident nobody was coming. She swept her eyes slowly around the room. A skeleton hung in the corner, its bones all wired together. He'd been a murderer in life, Ralph had told her. Hanged early in the century, when to be a friendless convict was to lose all rights to your mortal remains. The skull stared balefully, and Theo looked away. On the walls were Ralph's various degrees and qualifications, alongside an illuminated transcription of the Hippocratic oath. *Practise two things in your dealings with disease: either help or do not harm the patient.* His chair was solid oak, with leather upholstery; the bookshelves crammed with medical journals and anatomical works.

Theo's eyes lit upon a small vase on the windowsill, holding a bouquet of dried lunaria. They looked disarranged, and a few seeds had scattered. She crossed the room and held the stems in one hand as she tipped the vase up. A small key landed with a clink on the sill. It was where he kept the spare back-door key at home – in the empty vase on the console table. Theo listened again, then crossed to the huge cupboard.

The lock clicked and the doors swung open, releasing a scent that caused Theo to recoil. Something both stale and sweetly tangy, not overtly horrible but utterly repellent. She breathed shallowly, trembling in spite of herself. Inside was a set of shelves, and below them two columns of deep drawers. The shelves held jars, and the jars held fleshy things – unmistakably parts of a body, or bodies. Pieces of people. Mysterious organs, and lumps of bone with the flesh and skin still attached, suspended in preserving fluid. Theo supposed Ralph had bought or acquired them to aid his practice in some way; she supposed it was normal, and only seemed ghastly to non-medical eyes. She didn't look too closely, but one snagged at her gaze.

It was a large jar on the bottom shelf, containing a pitiful thing – a tiny baby, hardly bigger than Theo's hand; its fingers the length of her eyelashes, its eyes dark behind translucent lids. Theo swayed, and held the cupboard door for support. *Her* baby? Theirs? Surely, he would not. And yet, she wasn't *sure* he would not. *At so early a stage, the child cannot be said to have truly lived . . .* She wasn't sure at all, and noted, abstractly, how terrible that was.

She turned the jar as gently as she could, until she found a label. *Foetus; male, approx. 20 weeks; pauper mother, died by exposure; aged approx. 30 years.* Theo sagged. Not Amelia then; not Timothy. But *somebody's* baby. A poor woman who'd died of the cold. Had she given permission for her child to be preserved in this way? How could she have? No mother would, so who or what had given Ralph the right? Because the label was in his handwriting. She looked closely and saw tiny stitches closing an incision that ran all the way up the back of the baby's skull.

Light-headed, Theo turned the jar back the way she'd found it. She opened the first of the drawers. A skeletal hand, the bones fixed to a wooden plaque with a series of tiny pins and wires. There was something wrong with some of the bones – even Theo could see that. They were bulbous and uneven, and in places the surface had peeled away to reveal porous innards like honeycomb. The second drawer: a long leg bone, too thick, and warped into a bow-shape. *Sabre Tibia, Paget's disease of the bone. Leg removed at knee; subject Leslie Tregowan, male, labourer, aged 64 years, M.E.* Theo wondered if Mr Tregowan had survived the operation; if he was walking about on one leg somewhere, happy to have donated the deformed one.

She opened the third drawer and snatched her hand back with a gasp.

A skull, much smaller and smoother than the one hanging in the corner. Theo guessed at once that this one had belonged to a woman, and the empty eye sockets gazed up at her from the drawer with what looked like an accusation. Or a plea. Grinning white teeth, the bottom set overcrowded, and crossing slightly. Above the left temple, a circle had been drawn on the bone. Theo looked closer, her stomach curdling as she understood. The circle was not *drawn*, it was cut into it. Sawn, in fact, with a fine-toothed blade. A disc about two and a half inches across. With faltering hands, Theo turned the skull. The label was inked directly on to the bone: *Trephine to remove meningeal clot beneath concussive injury; subject Melissa Cartwright, female, pauper, aged 14 years, M.E.*

Theo reeled back, knocking the drawer. The disc of bone fell out of Missy's skull, leaving a hole in her head like a gruesome third eye.

'Oh, *no*,' Theo moaned.

She wanted to snatch the skull up and rescue it from that dark and lonely hiding place; she wanted also to slam the drawer shut and never see it again. Shivers ran right through her; every part of her recoiled from what she had found. But, how had it happened? Who'd given Ralph permission to keep Missy's head? To bury her incomplete? The thought of her headless body going into the ground while Theo and the other mourners had all stood around, unsuspecting, was grotesque. Had *anyone* given him permission, or had he simply done as he pleased? The questions hit her like stones.

Had he detached her head himself? Had he cleaned the flesh and skin and hair away with some harsh chemical?

Theo fought for control of herself, and didn't hear the footsteps approaching along the corridor.

'Theo? What are you doing?'

Ralph's voice sent a shock right through her. Hidden by the cupboard door, she had just enough time to shut the drawer before he was there, and she turned to him, speechless. He pushed her aside and closed the cupboard doors.

'You shouldn't have . . . These samples are very sensitive to the light. They are not play things, Theo!'

'*Play* things?' she whispered.

'You shouldn't have looked.' He rounded on her. 'This is my private room, and its contents are *no* concern of yours. Why did you open this cupboard? *How* did you? Do locked doors mean nothing to you?'

Theo shook her head. She was shuddering, her ears ringing.

'Oh, for heaven's sake.' None too gently, Ralph pushed her into a chair. 'Put your head on your knees for a minute. Breathe slowly.'

Theo did as she was told, as much to buy time as anything else. When she looked up at last, Ralph was at his desk, leaning back in the chair, staring at her.

'What did you see that upset you so badly?' There was suspicion as well as anger in his voice. Theo knew without thinking that she must not confess what she had found in the drawer. It was too terrible, and she didn't understand it.

'The . . . the baby . . .' she managed to say, and he softened a fraction. A flicker of what looked like relief in his eyes.

'Of course,' he said. 'Such things are upsetting for a woman to see. Especially—' He shook his head. 'But to break into a locked cabinet, Theo—'

'It wasn't locked,' she said.

'It most assuredly was.'

'Yes, but – the key was in the lock. I swear it was. So I . . . I didn't think you would mind. I'm very sorry, Ralph. I shouldn't have pried. I was only curious, but it was wrong of me.'

He frowned, perhaps weighing the possibility of having accidentally left the key in the lock against the chances of her lying. Theo's eyes swam as she awaited his judgement, and she let the tears drop to mask her fear, her outrage. After a moment, Ralph got up and took the key from the cupboard door. He dropped it into the pocket of his waistcoat, then fetched a bottle of Vin Mariani from a shelf and poured two glasses. He knocked one back in a single gulp and passed the other to Theo, laying his hand on her shoulder.

'Then we'll say no more about it,' he said, calmly now. 'Drink this. It will restore you.'

Theo did as she was told. The drink was dark red, and slightly bitter. Within moments there was a tingling in her blood; a rush of determination cleared her head and crystallised her thoughts.

'What is that?' she said.

'Just wine, fortified with an extract of coca leaf from South America. The leaves are a natural stimulant.'

As he spoke he poured himself a second glass, and swallowed it as quickly as the first.

'Forgive me for barking at you, it has been a long night. Why have you come?'

'I wanted to ask after Mr Miller – how is he? And I brought you some breakfast from home. You always say the food here isn't to be taken before noon.'

Theo managed to smile even though her hands were still shaking. *Female, pauper, aged 14 years, M.E.*

'It was a kind thought,' Ralph said. 'And I'm happy to say that Mr Miller is progressing well, though he is not yet out of danger. It was a close-run thing; his condition was not at all good as he left the table. His breathing was shallow and his pulse was very high, but a large enema of hot saline immediately lowered it to one hundred and forty. He woke around an hour ago and was able to converse without impediment, though I do notice some slight paresis of his left side.'

'I see.' Theo's tongue was sticky. She was desperate to leave.

'A great deal of bloody serum has been oozing through the dressing. Across one section where I have cut away the skull, there was no skin to re-cover it—'

'Ralph . . . please stop . . .'

'It is only the normal workings of the human body – a body no different to yours or mine.'

'A wound so terrible it has nearly killed a man is not normal.'

'That's true. But the healing process . . . what a body can survive, when treated correctly, is truly miraculous, Theo!' He leaned towards her eagerly. 'Every time I make an advance like this, I begin to conceive of what we might one day *come* to achieve . . . It's a *marvellous* thought!'

Theo hoped the man would live. There had been other times, with other patients, when Ralph had been optimistic after surgery, only for the unfortunate person to deteriorate soon afterwards. Like the man kicked by his horse, who'd died while she was alone on their honeymoon. Ralph's mood after each loss cast a shadow over the whole house for days. They were all made to feel his disappointment, and frustration.

'If he lives . . . if he *lives*, Theo,' – Ralph shook his head in wonderment – 'then *all* has led to this point. Do you see? All the times I have tried and failed, since—' He stopped. 'All my endeavours towards perfecting a technique for remedial intracranial surgery . . .'

'And his family? They . . . must be delighted at this outcome, since they agreed to the operation?'

Ralph said nothing for a while, staring so that she shrank from his scrutiny.

'They are delighted,' he said at last. 'But I did not need their consent.'

'You did not?'

'No. Mr Miller gave it himself, when he was first brought in. I explained what might happen and he was eager for the surgery to go ahead, if it became necessary.'

'I see.' Theo swallowed. 'Was Missy your first?'

She hadn't meant to say it aloud, but the tonic wine had loosened her tongue and set off tiny fireworks in her head.

Ralph stared again, his face unreadable.

'Was she . . . was hers the first operation of that kind you had performed?' Theo pressed.

'Do you mean to imply that I botched her operation?'

'Not at all!'

Theo thought that perhaps she had meant exactly that. Her heart pattered.

'I only wondered . . . how long you have waited for a successful outcome. With such a terribly difficult thing.'

Ralph considered her. 'You're still very pale, Theo. I will call for a cab to take you home. I'm afraid I can't come with you just yet.'

'I understand. But I'm quite happy to walk.'

'No,' he instructed. 'Wait for the cab.'

In the small hours of the night, Theo crept out of bed. Ralph had been up for almost thirty-six hours by the time he came home, and though he'd been almost feverishly talkative at first he was now sleeping like the dead.

She went downstairs to her writing desk, lit a single candle and began a letter to Albert Mackie, the doctor she'd first met in Hallewell, whose wife, Rosalind, had been dying.

Please forgive me, Dr Mackie. This will not be a letter of the ordinary sort, but I am in need of the opinion of a medical man on a particular matter, and although we are acquainted only a little, I believe that if you find my questions impertinent, or offensive, you will tell me so and let that be an end to it. I can only hope that my faith in your discretion, whilst instinctual, is well founded.

Her fingers went to her throat but found nothing there. She didn't wear Rosalind's butterfly pendant very often any more. She'd grown wary of injuring Ralph; conscious of the oppressive spell of awkwardness that would follow. It had taken weeks for his good mood to fully return after the skating gala, and his long, accusatory silences were like a yoke around her neck. But the gold butterfly was still her favourite. It was a talisman of sorts; a link to another time. Through it she might retrace her steps, and perhaps find a different way forward. A way to go back, and make repairs. A way, if one existed, to undo the fact of her marriage to a man she increasingly felt she didn't know at all.

Subject Melissa Cartwright, female, pauper, aged 14 years, M.E.

She thought back to the day she'd gone to ask for a lock of Missy's hair as a keepsake. The way Ralph had put her off, offering to go to the undertaker himself. *Forgive me, Theo. It just wasn't possible.* Had the problem been, in truth, that Missy's hair had already been stripped away and discarded by then? Angry tears burned her eyes. She felt betrayed. Worse, she felt that *Missy* had been betrayed.

When she'd finished the letter she took it to Audrey, woke her with an apology, and asked her to post it discreetly.

'I must ask something else of you, Audrey. For the next while, if the master is at home, please try to be the one to receive the post.

Keep back anything addressed to me that you do not recognise, and give it to me privately. I'm very sorry to make such a request.'

Audrey's eyes were huge in the dark. 'Don't be sorry, miss. I'll do as you ask.'

◆ ◆ ◆

In his fever, Toby saw Kit in the bed beside him. He struggled to focus his eyes, because he couldn't shake the feeling that his brother probably *shouldn't* be there. But after a while he gave up trying to understand it, and was simply relieved.

'Where have you been?' he said.

Kit didn't reply. He was asleep – Toby recognised the regular snuffle of his breathing. He thought it was probably time he himself got up, and got some reading done. He could have a go at tackling Euclid. The Durham matriculation exam loomed ahead of him. When was it? Tomorrow? The following day? Had he missed it altogether – had he slept through it? In a panic he struggled to rise, but his body was entirely uncooperative.

'Shh,' he heard his mother say. Or thought he did. The sound appeared to have no source.

'Don't wake Kit,' he said.

The next time he surfaced, he forced his eyes to open. The room jerked stickily around him. It was curious. More curious still to find Theo sitting in the chair by the bed, with her Tennyson open on her knees. He knew it at once – the brown cloth cover fraying at the corners, the well-thumbed pages. She, too, looked just as he remembered her. He had something terribly important to tell her, but drew a complete blank as to what. But she was absorbed in her reading, and didn't seem in a hurry to leave. So, it was all right, he decided; he'd rest a bit, and it would come to him. Watching her, he felt calm. The kiss of the light on her face, her eyes on the page with that faraway focus he knew so well. Exactly as she'd looked when she'd studied the symbol of Uroboros on Midsummer's Day.

What *was* it he'd needed to say?

He woke again because he was ravenous. Weak white light from the window stabbed at his eyes, but when he tried to lift an arm to shade them it appeared to be fixed to the bed. He couldn't work out where he was. There was movement nearby.

'Mum?'

'Yes, I'm here.'

'What's . . .' His lips were so dry they felt stiff. 'Thirsty.'

'Here.'

The rim of a cup touched his mouth, and a hand behind his head tilted it forwards.

'Don't try to get up. You've been very ill – you've had a fever. Pneumonia. But you're all right now; you're going to be all right. Lie back. You mustn't try to do anything yet.'

Toby heard her voice vaguely; sleep was already dragging him back under.

It was another two days before he was strong enough to sit up in bed. He coughed a great deal, and very painfully; every muscle in his body ached like an abscessed tooth. He was horrified to hear that he'd been insensible a full fortnight.

A doctor by the name of Sanderson came to see him. A woman doctor, perhaps forty, with an unflinching gaze and a streak of grey through her sooty hair, who charged less than half what a man would have done. She was brisk and contained, and Toby tried not to react to her as though she were a talking horse.

'How do you feel?' she asked, having listened to his lungs.

'"*Weak as the puny rillets of the hill*", as Paulus Syllogus would have it,' Toby croaked.

She raised an eyebrow. 'It sounds as though you're back in charge of your mental faculties, at least.'

'Almost, other than a perpetual urge to sleep. I had all sorts of odd visions. I saw people that I . . . couldn't have seen.'

'Yes, well, your hyperpyrexia lasted over a week.' Dr Sanderson noted his incomprehension. 'Your temperature reached a hundred and four degrees at one point, Mr Meriwether. I'm not surprised it did peculiar things to your brain.'

'How bad was I?'

With her fingers on his wrist and her watch in her other hand, Dr Sanderson smiled faintly.

'Bad enough to boast of it to your friends. And to give your parents quite a scare.'

She was quiet for a moment, then put his hand back on the blankets and packed her things away.

'Do you have many patients, yet?' Toby asked.

Dr Sanderson tipped up her chin. 'You are number four. In three months.' She left a pause. 'Number three only called me out to prove to a house guest that I was, indeed, a woman.'

'I hope you billed him anyway.'

'Too right I did.'

'People will get used to it. They're as stubborn as mules around here, but once news of your fee gets about . . .'

'We shall see. I may well be selling snake oil to support myself before then.'

'We will recommend you.'

'Thank you.' Her clipped tone told Toby that she hated to need any such favours. 'Rest is all you need now, Mr Meriwether. Eat as well as you are able to, but don't try to do too much. Your lungs will be weak for quite some time. If you overdo it, you risk a relapse.'

'Thank you, Doctor.'

She nodded in reply, and left.

David had sent a telegram to *The London Daily News* to explain Toby's absence. A short acknowledgement had come in reply, with no promise to hold his position or anything like that. Toby fretted about getting back, but the simple fact was that he couldn't. The first time he went downstairs, he nearly didn't make it back up again. The effort left him gasping. He wrote to the editor to apologise, promising to return as soon as he possibly could.

'They would not give your job away, surely?' David said.

'They would, if some other suitable person came along. Ambition is like an illness, in that place.'

'Well. Then let's hope no such person comes along – you heard what the doctor said. You mustn't do too much.'

Toby sighed anxiously. 'Is there any brandy? Or a glass of wine?'

His father gave him a steady look. 'No.'

So he had to be patient, and wasn't at all good at it. He felt like a prisoner, chafing at the thought of his life in London going on without him. He hated being in Hallewell. The vanishingly slim chance that Theo would hear of his illness, and come to visit while he was too weak to escape, gnawed at him.

Since he'd got back on his feet, Mona had been quieter than ever. She avoided his eye. He took her arm one evening, as she helped him back to bed.

'What is it, Mum? Tell me.'

She shook her head. 'It . . . The way we found you, Toby. By the Roman Cross, on that bitter night . . . Snow had settled on your face, and not melted! That's how cold you were. And you'd . . . you'd taken off your coat and hat.' She took a deep breath, looking down at his shirt as she folded it absently. 'Did you mean to do it, Toby? Did you mean to freeze yourself to death?'

'No!'

He was shocked at the idea, but when he looked back, when he tried to *think* back, it was blurry and he couldn't be sure.

'No, I just . . .'

He did remember the skating gala, but little afterwards. He remembered looking for Theo in the darkness between the lights, and was grateful she hadn't been there.

He cleared his throat. 'Lily ended our engagement. Not long before I came here to see you.'

'Yes, we know. We thought we ought to let her know what had happened to you, and she was very kind about it, but she told us what had gone on between you.'

'I suppose I was a bit broken up about it. Not that I planned to kill myself over it – I'm sure it's for the best. But . . . I drank too much, that was all. I was foolish. Again.'

Mona sagged in relief. 'Foolish! There's a fine understatement.'

'Mum . . . Was Theo Hallewell here? Mrs Anscombe, I suppose I should call her. Did she come to visit while I was sick?'

'*Theo?* Heavens, no. Why on earth would she?'

'No. I suspected not. Only, I saw her as clearly as I see you now. Isn't that bizarre? And I . . . I saw Kit.'

The look she gave him was full of longing. 'You saw your brother?'

Toby nodded. 'Right there in the bed next to mine, just like he always used to be. Breathing too loudly because he hadn't blown his nose.'

'That sounds like him.' Mona laughed a little, her eyes flooding. She rummaged in her pockets for a handkerchief. 'Well, I'm glad. I'm glad he came to visit you. He sometimes comes to visit me, too. Full of mischief, as ever – he hides around corners, out of sight, and if I try to catch him I hear him chortling as he runs away . . .'

Her voice trailed to nothing and all the gladness left her face, grief slipping back into place. She abandoned his shirt on the chair, unfolded.

Toby's anguish left him mute.

'Perhaps you dreamt of things you long for,' Mona said flatly.

‘I don’t know about that. I also dreamt that the entrance exam was coming up, and I wasn’t ready. It was terrifying.’

‘Get some sleep, love.’

Toby lay back, exhausted. His final thought before he slept was that Theo’s presence must be something he feared, like the exam; not something that he longed for.

There was a white froth of blackthorn on the embankments by the time Toby made it on to a train back to London. His legs and lungs would only take him a short distance at a time, but he could ride the trams and omnibuses, and give himself plenty of time to get wherever he was going. He could still think, and write. But when he got to his rooms it was to find them occupied by a skinny man with a wall-eye, who advised him, not politely, to move on. Toby found his things in a heap beneath the stairs, with a moth-eaten rug slung over them.

Furious, he hammered his fist on the landlady’s door. Mrs Dunn eyed him dispassionately.

‘But you weren’t ’ere, Mr Meriwether, and your rent weren’t paid. What would you ’ave me do?’

‘Oh, I don’t know, let me see – perhaps count my year-long good behaviour as your tenant in my favour, and wait to hear from me?’

‘It’s been best part of two months, and not ’ide nor ’air of you! Dead and buried for all I knew. This in’t a charity I’m running.’

‘And all of my things just abandoned there, where anything might have been stolen?’

‘I’ve been keeping an eye out, in case you came back. Made sure nothing went for a walk. Moved it all meself, I did – count yourself lucky I didn’t sell the bloody lot! Now go on – ’op it. You don’t live ’ere no more.’

'Mrs Dunn, I will not have this!' Toby cried, but was jack-knifed by a fit of coughing.

Mrs Dunn whacked her door against his foot until he removed it, then slammed it in his face.

Light-headed, Toby sat with his back to it until he'd caught his breath. Constellations of black mould spangled the walls of the dingy hallway. He coughed a bit more, and tried to come up with a plan. The day was all but over; it would be dark soon, and it was drizzling. He could hardly take all his books and his rickety furniture to a hotel, even if he could have afforded one – he was paid by the word, and hadn't published any since leaving for Hallewell.

He got up, eventually, and set out to find a cart for hire.

He traipsed a long way, following the suggestions of strangers, until finally he found a man who would do the job for the few coins Toby had on him. By then he was both sweating and shivering, which he took as a bad sign. They loaded the cart together – Toby wheezing and stumbling and not being much use. The only address he could give was Womersley's, so that was where they went, and while his things were unloaded on to the pavement Toby leaned heavily on the bell pull. He staggered inwards when the door opened, and collided with the manservant. By then he was so tired he could hardly mumble his own name.

Any ill feeling Tom might have been harbouring about the way things had gone with his sister apparently vanished upon seeing Toby in such a state.

'Good grief, Meriwether,' he exclaimed. 'You look half dead!'

'I possibly am, Tom.'

'What's all that junk on the pavement?'

'That would be all my worldly goods. My landlady relet my room in my absence.'

'Indeed? Well, that will happen if you rent a cubbyhole in a hovel, instead of a proper apartment.'

'I'm a cubbyhole in a hovel type of fellow.' Toby smiled weakly, then coughed some more.

'I'm calling the doctor.'

'There's no need. If I might just possibly . . . some sleep . . .'

'Oh, hell – Barker, come and give me a hand with him.'

Mercifully, the relapse didn't last long. By the third day Toby was on a settee in front of a generous fire, wrapped in a tartan rug, with a bowl of soup on a tray.

'That's better,' Tom said, on his return from the firm.

'I feel like an emperor,' Toby said sheepishly. 'Your man Barker is a saint.'

'Yes, he's a good sort. And you're beginning to look less like a cadaver.'

'You've resurrected me.'

Tom dropped into a nearby chair, turning serious.

'Lily told me what was going on, after your father wrote to her. I wanted to come and visit you, but I . . .' He trailed off, uncomfortably. 'Well, I was still endeavouring to be cross with you about the engagement. And for being such a damned flop.'

'You've never been able to stay cross with anyone for very long, Womersley.'

'Ha! Luckily for you. That was a very stupid thing you did, Meriwether. Nearly killing yourself.'

'I don't think I did it deliberately.'

'I don't suppose you remember much about it?'

'Not a great deal, no.'

'Was it because of Lily?' Tom looked away uncomfortably, into the low flames of the fire. 'Do you wish the engagement were back on? Is that it?'

'No . . . no, she is better off without me—'

'Oh, come on, now.' Tom shook his head in disgust.

'I mean it,' Toby said. 'And I'm . . . I'm so terribly sorry I disappointed her. And you. I would have married her, you know. Had she wished it, I would have kept my word.'

Tom nodded gravely. 'Well,' he said at last. 'Least said, soonest mended. Our Lily's made of stern stuff, and, infuriating as it is, she's almost *always* right. Perhaps it will be for the best, given time.'

Overcome by gratitude, Toby could only nod.

'I've got engaged myself, by the way,' Tom said.

'What?' Toby was stunned. '"You've got engaged by the way"? To whom, for heaven's sake?'

Tom smiled. 'To quite the sweetest thing I've ever encountered. Her name is Rita Bremen. You'll meet her soon enough – she's coming with her sister for dinner, tomorrow night. So you'd better be well by then. We plan to marry in June.'

'But who is she? How did you meet her?'

'It was the damnedest thing, Meriwether. It was at the theatre – our eyes met across a crowded atrium, like in the drippiest of romantic novels. She looks like a little bird – so perfect and round! Her eyes sparkle, and she has the most heavenly dimples when she smiles . . . What else can I tell you, except that the moment I laid eyes on her, I knew that I would love her? I spent the rest of the evening engineering an introduction, and have dedicated every moment since then to being as charming as I possibly can.'

Tom's obvious joy sent an unexpected rush of feeling through Toby. His friend's happiness made him feel that there *was* good in the world, and that it wasn't entirely failing and corrupt. Gingerly, he stood up and cast off his blanket.

'Shake my hand, Womersley,' he said. 'I am utterly delighted for you.'

Their handshake became a bear hug, and Tom laughed, clapping Toby hard on the shoulders.

'You'll be my best man, naturally,' he said, not waiting for a reply. 'Now sit back down, before you fall down. I'd better go and get washed and brushed. Supping with Leonid Sokolov this evening – terrifying man. Best behaviour and clean collars all round. God help me if he finds out I'm harbouring a pinko-lefty.' He pulled a face. 'But you must stay as long as you like, naturally. Has your position gone the way of your hovel?'

'I don't know. As soon as I'm fit, I'll go and find out.'

'I'll ask about, just in case.'

'No, thank you. If needs be, I'll find the next thing myself. I can't keep relying on you, Tom. You may not mind, but I do.'

'Well. Just don't *brood* about it, will you? Without doubt, the time will come when I shall need *your* help.' He waited a beat. 'Twenty pounds do it? Until you're back on your feet?'

'Tom—'

'Not a word about it, old boy.'

At the beginning of May, as Ralph was polishing an article for the *British Medical Journal* about Mr Miller's injury, operation and recovery, Theo went to visit her mother. It was a duty, rather than a pleasure. Sitting back to back with strangers in a four-seater trap, she spotted familiar faces as they neared Hallewell. A few of them greeted her more warmly than Diana did.

'You look well.' She kissed Theo's cheek, but they did not embrace. 'It's nice to see you dressed properly for once.'

'Ralph believes that tight lacing will help my insides.'

'Well, it stands to reason. You must do as he says.'

They walked slowly along the terrace, which was bathed in sunshine.

'And are you again . . . in a happy condition?' Diana asked.

'It's only been a few months,' Theo said.

'It's been six. That's plenty.'

'It will happen when it happens, I suppose.'

Diana sighed. 'Please tell me you're more animated than this at home? Poor Ralph. It can be *exhausting*, you know.'

'What can?'

'Your . . .' She waved a hand. 'Melancholia. Doldrums. Whatever you like to call it.'

'I don't call it anything. It's only the way I am.'

'There, now.' Diana looped her arm through her daughter's, a rare gesture of solidarity. 'Buck up, my dear. You're still only one and twenty – more babies will come, and you'll forget all about this sad time. You have a *wonderful* husband. Attentive, and brilliant. A great many women would give their eye-teeth to be in your shoes. Does that not hearten you?'

'I know it ought to,' Theo said. 'Ralph says I must *try* to be happy, and happiness will follow.'

'There – you see. I'm sure I've said the very same thing to you, before now. Practice makes perfect.'

Theo would happily never hear those words again.

'What news from the village?' she said.

Diana cast a measuring glance at her daughter. 'Well. Toby Meriwether nearly killed himself. That caused a bit of a stir.'

Theo flinched, turning her face away instinctively. 'What?'

'Yes. Drank himself silly at that ice-skating festival, then sat out in the snow until he was all but frozen. He was discovered purely by chance, and only just in time – it was *quite* the drama. He caught a fever and was laid up with his parents for several weeks. Word was he'd done it on purpose.'

'What? Why?'

'I don't know.' Shielding her eyes with one hand, Diana looked across the lawn and tutted. 'Those wretched peonies have collapsed again, when I *did* say they were to be staked.' She sighed. 'I heard that he is no longer engaged to be married, so perhaps that had something to do with it.'

Theo didn't reply while she absorbed the news. She clasped her hands to keep them still.

'It was a long engagement, was it not,' she said at length, in a small voice.

'Indeed. Perhaps the girl got tired of waiting, and I can't say I blame her. Such a . . . a *grim* young man he turned out to be. And terribly bad-mannered with it. When I think of that time I went—' Diana stopped herself short. 'Anyway, let's go in. Lunch won't be long, and I need to talk to Cook about dinner.'

'I'll sit out here for a little while,' Theo said.

With her mother gone, she shut her eyes. The image of Toby lying helpless in the snow was *horrific*. But he had recovered; he had gone back to London. He was well. She did not dwell on the fact that he was neither married nor engaged. It was too late – she *was* married, and could have no hopes in that direction any more. But the thought that he might have wanted to die was like a slow knife twisting in her flesh.

Theo had thought about her own death many times, confronted by the loss of her children, and of her friends. But she had never thought about Toby's. She *could* not. Toby must simply live, and be happy. That was all she wanted from him now. She didn't feel that she deserved or even needed to be happy, but if *he* was not then she could see no point in any of it. *Word was he'd done it on purpose*. But he *had not* died. Fear and relief competed for control of her.

Theo sat still until the news about Toby had run its course, like a sudden illness. Until she felt able to walk and talk again.

To Theo's delight, Timothy Crudge wrote that he was travelling down to visit a dig at Shaftesbury Abbey. She wrote back at once to invite him to stay with them. She planned walks, scenic drives, a picnic; to be taken on a guided tour of the abbey. But when she told Ralph over breakfast the next day he glared at her, with little white crescents appearing above his nostrils.

'You should have consulted me, Theo. Write and tell him it will not be convenient after all.'

'But . . . why should it not be convenient? We've no other plans, and they will understand if you have patients that call you away. I'm happy to entertain them myself—'

'*Them?*'

'He will have his new assistant with him. Mr Bourton – the slight fellow with the blond hair. I think you met him at the Yule Ball?'

Ralph's expression darkened further. 'I did not. In any case, it's out of the question.'

'But . . . what do you mean, Ralph? Why should it be out of the question? Mr Crudge is far more of a father to me than my real father ever was, and—'

'But he is *not* your father, Theo. He is not any kind of relative, and he is not a moral man. I will not have him in this house – least of all with his latest consort. Do you understand?'

Theo was outraged at hearing Crudge spoken of that way.

'You *mustn't* say such things! Mr Crudge is *very* dear to me. It's been so long since I saw him—'

'And it will be longer still. Forever, if I have my way. You will write back and tell him not to come.'

'I will not!' she cried, her heart racing.

'I say that man is not *welcome* here! Do you hear me, Theo?'

'I hear you, but I do not understand!'

Ralph's face reddened. 'Then be guided by me, as a wife should, and do as I say.'

But Theo would not. 'How can you say he is not moral, when he is simply the kindest of men, and entirely respectable?'

'*Entirely respectable?*' Ralph scoffed. 'You're a foolish, blinkered girl. You understand nothing. And you *will* rescind the invitation – immediately.'

'But I—'

'*Enough!*'

He thumped his fist down so hard that the teacups rattled and a piece of toast fell out of the rack. Theo was shocked into silence. Ralph reached for the newspaper, turned a few pages then slapped it down in front of her. He stood up and kicked his chair out of his way.

'Read. Perhaps it will elucidate.' His eyes were snapping. 'And do as I have said, whether it elucidates or not.'

Once he'd gone, Theo tried to steady herself. She looked at the paper. It was an account of the trial of the playwright Oscar Wilde, who'd been charged with gross indecency, and named as a sodomite by the Marquess of Queensberry. Wilde's eloquent defence of the innocence of his relationship with Lord Alfred Douglas, the son of the marquess – the platonic ideal of the affinity between an older man, full of intellect and experience, and a younger one full of hope and joy. How the court booed, and hissed, and cheered. Wilde had been convicted, and sentenced to two years of hard labour – the harshest term the judge was able to impose, though he lamented its inadequacy in what he called the worst case he had ever tried.

Theo sat with it for a long time. She'd seen Crudge's affection for Arnaud LeRoy, and the pain their separation had caused. Had it been *the love that dare not speak its name*? And if so, did that make it a lesser kind of love? She thought of

Nicholas Bourton, the young man now employed as Uncle Crudge's assistant. He had soft, dreamy eyes, and deferred to Crudge with obvious devotion; and for his part Crudge had seemed brighter, and happier, than he had in some time. The smile that she loved was big and horsey again. The thought of labelling it unnatural – even *criminal* – was unsettling, but she quickly decided that even if Crudge had loved Arnaud, and now loved Mr Bourton, in some way that went beyond friendship, then it was an entirely private matter, and one that altered none of her affection for him.

Suddenly, all the times she'd arranged to see Crudge only to have to cancel because Ralph needed her for something, or was busy, or had decided she was not well enough, were thrown into a new light. Her heart sank even further. And now that Ralph had finally named his aversion, she knew he wouldn't change his mind. Her uncle could not come to stay, and seeing him at all would surely be more difficult from then on.

Audrey found her crying, still at the breakfast table.

'Hush now, miss. We'll find a way,' she said, as Theo gulped, and nodded, and picked up her pen to write to Crudge. To tell him not to come.

It was a long time before a reply came to her other letter, the one written in secret in the middle of the night. Audrey dutifully spirited it away, and gave it to Theo once Ralph had gone out.

3, Springfield Villas,
Church Lane,
Chobham,
Surrey

Wednesday, 3rd July, 1895

Dear Mrs Anscombe,

I trust this finds you in good health. I must admit that your letter came as something of a surprise, arriving as it did so long after our last correspondence, and being so perturbing in content. I take no offence at either of those things. However, it has taken me some time to decide how best to reply to you. The questions you ask raise complicated points within the field of medical ethics; to answer succinctly will be a challenge. Let me first confess that, though you have included no names, I believe I know the case to which you are alluding, since it occurred during our stay at Hallewell. If I am correct, and it is the behaviour of your own husband you have cause to question, then I can only reiterate my surprise, and my discomfort.

However, I see no reason why I should not respond to you in general terms.

Firstly, the easiest to answer. I cannot say for sure, but my best guess at the meaning of M.E., in the context of the labelling of specimens, would be 'Mortuus Est', this being the Latin for 'it died'; i.e., the subject did not survive the procedure. Please understand that the impersonal, even callous, tone of such a notation will not be intended to slight the patient in question. It is merely a way for the physician to maintain professional impersonality. Person becomes object, and a distance is thereby created that is entirely necessary for calm and effective treatment to take place.

It is likely that a well-equipped hospital would have the facilities and substances required to prepare specimens of bone for preservation. As you appear to be aware, the retention of such samples, i.e., the use of mortal remains for the purposes of medical advancement, can, in most cases, be done lawfully only with the express permission of the donor or their legal representative. The dissection and retention of the cranium of a minor would be lawful only with the permission of their legal guardian. A foetus would be treated as tissue taken from the body of its mother, rather than as a person in its own right.

Any adult may, in life, give permission for their remains to be donated to medical science. Relatives may contest those wishes, and prevent the donation. Under the terms of the Anatomy Act of 1832, the remains of those who die as paupers or without next of kin in either a hospital, workhouse or prison, may be sold to a medical professional for dissection. So, in the case you describe, I suggest the most likely scenario to be that the proprietor of the charitable home where the girl was lodged gave permission, and probably received remuneration, for the donation of her body for dissection.

I understand the distress that can arise at the thought of a loved one being examined and dissected in this way. It is for that reason that the Anatomy Act allows for relatives to prevent the action. It does not, alas, allow the same right to a friend or acquaintance. To my mind, the dead can suffer no indignity. The person has ascended to a higher plane, and what remains is merely earthly matter, no different, in essence, to a rock or a tree. The dissection is done neither ghoulishly nor voyeuristically, but sombrely, and with the sole purpose of improving medical practice. No doctor may become a doctor without having studied, at first hand, the anatomy of the human body.

On a personal note, I should like to add that your letter saddened me. Perhaps as a result of my wife's affinity with you, I have liked to imagine you happy and well these days. When I think of my dear Rosalind, I often find myself thinking of you by extension. Two young women whose paths happened to cross. That she should be taken and you spared causes me to reflect upon the arbitrary nature of human fate. Your letter does not seem to me to have been written by a person who is happy or well. If I may be so bold as to counsel you, let it be to say that a life spent dwelling on past grievances, and past losses, is a life blighted. Do not poison yourself thus, Mrs Anscombe. However, should you wish to discuss these matters further, I am at your service.

I remain,

Dr. Albert M. Mackie

Chapter Thirteen

1896

Theo and Ralph spent Christmas and New Year at Hallewell House. The weather was cold, though nothing compared to the previous winter. By midday, the morning's frost had thawed to drab green and brown. A huge fir tree had been erected in the hallway, decorated with nuts and ribbons and gingerbread stars, and they sat down to Christmas lunch with the paying guests. A large chunk of roast venison, endless potatoes, and plum pudding with custard. Theo sat in polite silence while Ralph talked and Diana talked, and the guests all talked. Stuck there for the duration, she felt fifteen again, longing to make her excuses and leave the table.

Rain kept them cooped up indoors for two days, then Ralph went back to Shaftesbury. Theo stayed on without him, ostensibly for her mother's sake, but really because, for the first time since her wedding, she *wanted* to stay. She craved a little distance from Tout Hill House, from her husband, and the constant expectation of a new pregnancy. Just a few days away, in order to go home refreshed. Galvanised for more.

She went walking, and let her mind wander. It wandered, inevitably, to Missy's skull. Theo trusted Albert Mackie, and on his advice she had tried to forget what she'd seen at the hospital. *Mortuus Est.* She'd tried to forget that her husband had cut off her best friend's head, leaving her body to be buried without it. But it was impossible. The hands that held hers, that roamed her body in the night, that thumped the table when she disobeyed him, had done that terrible thing.

Dr Mackie had made it perfectly clear that Ralph had done nothing wrong, as long as he'd had permission from Missy's guardian. But when she'd discovered his cupboard at the hospital, the way he'd rounded on her had been frightening. The way he'd snapped, and ignored those questions it hadn't suited him to answer. He had not wanted her to know what he kept in there. Then again, given how they had come to know one another, perhaps that was unsurprising.

Theo's breath plumed as she squelched through drifts of rotten leaves. She walked right out of Hallewell to West End, and beyond; following the lane as it got narrower and muckier. The sky was the dirty white of an unwashed fleece.

Do you mean to imply that I botched her operation?

His words wouldn't leave her alone. She hadn't meant to imply any such thing, and yet he had leapt to that conclusion. She was reminded of her disastrous appearance before the magistrate in Shaftesbury, when she'd been so horribly aware of the lie she was about to tell that she'd accidentally proclaimed it – the involuntary expression of a hidden truth: *It isn't a lie*. The magistrate had guessed her true meaning at once. *I wonder why you should feel the need to make that assertion?*

So, was that what Ralph believed? Did he know he'd made a mistake during Missy's operation? The thought lodged inside her like an icicle. But perhaps it was only his sense of guilt that Missy hadn't survived, which he'd confessed to many times. *Everything was performed correctly this time*, he had also said. Which implied that there were times when it had not been.

Weary at last, Theo stood for a while by a field gate, beneath a dripping ash tree. Her toes had gone numb. The field beyond the gate was ploughed and empty. Nobody came past her, and no birds flew overhead. She stared across the furrowed earth but saw no gulls, not even any rooks. She had wanted to be by herself – and it *was* a relief. She just hadn't noticed, until then, how very alone she truly was.

On the way back, her feet took her to St Agnes's. She knocked without really planning to, and asked to see Mrs Vine. The matron looked surprised and not especially pleased to see her.

'Mrs Anscombe,' she said flatly. 'A happy new year to you.'

'And to you,' Theo said, without feeling.

'Is there some problem? Trouble with Audrey, perhaps?'

'Audrey is exemplary. Did you . . . Mrs Vine, did you sell Missy Cartwright's body to Dr Anscombe for dissection?'

'I *beg* your pardon?'

'I said, did you sell Missy's—'

'No! I most certainly did not.'

Theo stared at the matron, and knew that she was lying. The woman's throat was bobbing like a frog's.

'I know that you did,' she said. 'He is my husband, after all. The only way he could have done it was with your permission. How much were you paid, Mrs Vine?'

'Now, look here, I bade him *treat* her – cure her! And if he could not, then to . . . examine her, if he pleased, before she was laid to rest.' Mrs Vine tried to sound righteous. 'And so he waived the fee for her treatment. I was quite within my rights.'

'Your *rights*? Shame on you, Mrs Vine! You *never* liked Missy!'

The matron almost smirked. 'The advancement of medical science is a noble endeavour, Mrs Anscombe. I'd have thought you of all people would cleave to that. Why shouldn't some good come of that girl's sad end? Now, I must get on. I'll bid you a good day.'

She held the door for Theo to leave, but wouldn't look her in the eye.

Leaning close as she passed, Theo said: 'He took her head, Mrs Vine. It remains at the hospital to this day. She was buried without her own *head* – may it haunt you!'

And had the satisfaction of seeing the woman's face drain of blood as that sank in.

Theo knew Mrs Vine wouldn't mention her visit to anyone, least of all to Ralph, and she knew she couldn't confront him herself. There was nothing to gain. He didn't like her to mention Missy, or Kit, or the past. He liked her to be meek, and fragile, as she had been when they'd first met. He liked her to do as she was told.

Theo refused to join her mother and the guests for dinner, and didn't trouble herself to give an excuse. It felt good. She was no longer a child, and she no longer felt meek. Lonely, yes. Powerless, most certainly; and beset by doubts. But not meek. She asked for the fire to be lit in her father's old study and sat in front of it with Audrey, only half listening as she read from *The Island of Doctor Moreau*. The room, finally cleaned and stripped of all remnants of Seymour's solitary existence, was ordinary again, even cosy.

Theo stared into the flames, and she thought. She pictured Missy's skull, in the few stunned seconds before Ralph had interrupted, and could recall it as clearly as if it were in her hands now. Shock had fixed the memory: the whiteness of the bone; the blackness of the eyes. She saw the label written on one side: *Mortuus Est*. She saw the circle of bone sawn neatly through the upper left part of the forehead. Saw that disc of bone fall away when she disturbed the drawer. But what Theo didn't see was anything *on* that disc of bone. No crack, no puncture, no signs of a break. No visible injury whatsoever, to mark where Kit's stone had struck. *The fracture to her skull was more severe than it had appeared*, Ralph had said, in a conversation years before that she would also never forget.

From the safety of Hallewell House, she wrote a new letter to Dr Mackie.

Another gravely ill patient was rushed to the Westminster Memorial Hospital. It was only a broken arm, belonging to a lad of eleven who'd fallen out of a tree; but his parents were poor and had tried to reset it themselves, though the bone was out through the skin. When the wound went bad they bought a salve of primrose leaves from a wise woman. The boy had developed septicaemia – Ralph described the angry red tendrils of infection creeping under the skin, up towards his shoulder, reaching for his heart. Ralph had dosed him with arsenic, washed the wound with a copper solution, and amputated above the elbow.

Having lain insensible with fever for three days, the lad was now awake, sitting up, and learning to eat with one hand.

Despite this recovery, Ralph was morose.

'Rank stupidity,' he muttered, calling for wine though it was still early afternoon. 'If the parents had brought him to me the day the bone broke, he'd be as fit and whole as ever at this moment.'

'They didn't know,' Theo murmured.

'They didn't *think*,' Ralph said. 'Well, his disablement is upon their consciences now.'

'You . . . you did not tell them so?'

'Why not? People must learn.'

'But they must surely have felt it already? And been very afraid?'

'You think me cruel?' He gave her a look. '*You* were not made to witness the child's fear as his life ebbed away!'

'But it did not ebb away – you saved him. Modern medicine saved him.'

'"*Modern medicine*"*?* Modernity has an uphill battle against such ingrained, peasant ignorance. I could have saved the limb with ease; instead, I was forced to perform an act of butchery better suited to a barber-surgeon of two centuries ago.'

Hesitantly, Theo crossed to where Ralph was sitting and put her hand on his shoulder. He jerked away but then slumped, covering her hand with his. She sat down on the arm of his chair, and Ralph leaned against her.

'The utter, dispiriting . . . *mundanity* of it,' he murmured.

'But the boy *lives*, and he will learn to do without the arm. You *saved* him, Ralph.'

Theo cradled his head, smoothing his hair. She hoped to stave off the dark mood that seemed bound to follow the outburst. It was confusing; Ralph was usually made jubilant by success, but sounded as though *this* success had not been of sufficient quality, or magnitude.

The next day, she returned from visiting Hermione to find him standing by her writing desk. The drawers were all open, the contents spread in disarray across the top – pen nibs and envelopes and blotting paper. He looked up, wholly unabashed at being discovered, and Theo stared, outraged, her heart leaping to her throat.

'Ralph, what—'

'You still write to that man?' he said, eyes snapping. In his hand was her latest letter from Crudge.

'He is my—'

'Even after what I told you about him? Even though you know how I feel about him – him, and all men of his sort? Do you feel no loyalty to me whatsoever, though you are my *wife*?'

'Forgive me, Ralph, but I will always write to him,' Theo whispered. It was the truth, and she didn't know what else to say. 'He has been close to me since I was a little girl. Closer than my mother, in many ways.'

'Indeed? And do you not apprehend how *perverse* that is, Theo?'

'I do not,' she said, shaking a little. 'He is a good and kind man.'

Ralph screwed the letter in his fist and Theo darted forwards to snatch it back. He lifted it out of her reach, blocking her with his other arm.

‘Desist,’ he said, with such terrible calm that Theo obeyed. His arm remained raised, the fist hovering above her. She sank back. ‘That’s better,’ he said.

‘What possible harm can come of my writing to him?’ Her voice cracked as she spoke.

‘Do not weep! What cause have you to feel aggrieved? You are *secretive*, Theo – hiding in here, where I am not supposed to come!’

‘My letters are my private property, Ralph—’

‘In fact, this room is mine and this desk and everything in it. As *you* are mine, Theo.’

‘I have no secrets from you,’ she lied. ‘What has made you . . . do this? What were you looking for?’

Ralph glared at her. ‘You’ve never been able to lie particularly well, have you? I want to know what you do here, while I am out all day. And who you do it with.’

‘But . . . you cannot suspect me of . . . of behaving *inappropriately*?’

‘Why not? Plenty of women are adulteresses. And I know you feel more for that Meriwether man than you will admit.’

Theo’s face burned. ‘*Felt*, perhaps – a long time ago, when I was little more than a child.’

‘Indeed? But you ignore my wishes regarding your precious Mr Crudge, so why not in other matters?’

This shocked Theo to her core. ‘You . . . you *cannot* believe that I would *ever* behave in such a way? To separate me entirely from Timothy Crudge is cruel. Do you wish for my unhappiness?’

‘*Do you wish for mine?*’ he thundered.

Theo flinched, and shook her head. But she would not promise not to write to Crudge. She could not.

‘Upon my soul,’ she whispered, ‘I want only your happiness.’

It was true. Life was barely tolerable when Ralph was unhappy.

Her words seemed to break something in him; the anger dissipated. His shoulders drooped. He frowned down at the crumpled paper in his hand, then smoothed it somewhat before putting it back on her desk.

'I am . . . Am I not *worthy* of your love? Is that it, Theo?'

'You have my love, Ralph,' she lied without hesitation. 'You have it.'

'Do I?' A bitter little twist of his mouth. 'Theo . . .' He didn't look at her. 'You are my *wife*. You belong to me. Do not forget it.'

He left, and she heard his study door slam. Then she sank on to the small chair at her desk and tried to breathe normally. As quietly as she could, she tidied away her scattered belongings. Then she glanced at the bookcase, and her copy of *Le Morte d'Arthur*, in which she'd hidden Albert Mackie's first letter. His latest reply had come that morning, and was in her pocket. She didn't like to think what would have happened if Ralph had found either one of them; and it occurred to her that she had begun to fear her husband. This particular, unpredictable mood of his.

Eventually, ears still straining for Ralph's approach, she opened the letter.

Your question troubles me a great deal, Mrs Anscombe. The answer is that yes, in theory, it may be possible for a specialist to tell from the examination of a preserved skull whether a head injury was serious enough to have proved fatal. However, it would be all but impossible to give a definitive answer without having seen the condition of the patient prior to death. The implication, however, that an operation as dangerously invasive as an intracranial trephining was carried out in error, or without good cause, is extremely serious.

The cutting of the human body after death in order to further medical knowledge, and during life in the attempt to preserve that life, are both entirely justified. The cutting of the human body during life in any kind of experimental manner is wholly wrong. It is known as 'vivisection', a practice both rife and of particular concern in our present age. I myself have written to the medical press to condemn it, and to urge vigilance against it. It is the exploitation of poor and ignorant patients, who are offered free treatment by a surgeon bent upon personal advancement and 'gaining experience'. For any physician to undertake an operation as risky as a trephining were he not completely convinced of its necessity would be worse than reckless. It would, in my opinion, be criminal.

Mrs Anscombe, I can only reiterate my unease, given your proximity to the protagonist, and beg you to think carefully before talking to any other person about such things, or taking any action. For my part, I can assure you of my complete discretion.

Theo didn't sleep well for several nights. She hadn't meant to imply that Ralph might have operated on Missy without just cause, and she couldn't believe that he would. But she was troubled. It was something that happened, and it had a name: *Vivisection*. Her husband *was* determined to make advances, and to make his mark. He *had* offered to treat Missy without charge, in return for being allowed to dissect her afterwards. But he wasn't so hungry for subjects that he would operate where it wasn't necessary. She would not believe that of him.

But what, then, *had* she meant to imply? That he had made a mistake – that he had 'botched' Missy's operation? She had wanted to hear that there might be a way for Kit to be pardoned. That was the truth of it, barely acknowledged even to herself. But if that could only come at her husband's expense, what then? *You are my* wife. *You belong to me.*

It tangled her up. She was distracted, and wished she could discuss it with somebody. Dr Mackie was at a safe enough distance, but everyone else was too close. There was danger in even thinking such things, let alone in speaking them. She felt the threat in her bones, and blamed it, at first, for her decreased appetite, her tiredness, and her unsettled gut. Until she realised, of course, that she was pregnant again. Then the baby – and her fears for it – chased everything else from her mind.

Chapter Fourteen

1898

Cassandra stirred in her sleep, draping one arm over her eyes. The sun was throwing incandescent light through the crack in the curtains, right on to her pillow. It would wake her soon, which was good. Toby didn't like to leave while she was asleep – that was too perfunctory, even for him. It was three in the afternoon. From four o'clock, the risk of their being discovered grew exponentially, and Toby preferred to be gone well before that. He stared at the elaborate ceiling rose, waiting a few more minutes. From the street below came the whirr of wheels and quick clatter of hooves, and pigeons cooed on the windowsill.

Cassandra opened one eye. 'What time is it?'

'Just gone three.'

'Oh dear.'

With a sigh, she turned on to her side to face him, pushing back her mane of dark hair. Her family were Spanish on her mother's side, and her eyes were even darker than Toby's. A sloe-eyed society beauty.

'Then you'll be up and away like a jack rabbit at any moment,' she said. 'Won't you?'

'Well, I wouldn't want to outstay my welcome.'

She laughed. 'Go on then, get dressed. I can see you're itching to.'

Toby pretended not to notice her pique when he did exactly that. With a resigned expression she swung her feet to the floor, crossed to the basin and began to wash between her legs. She was still graceful, even then. At thirty-seven she was a full decade older than Toby, but there was little sign of it. Her skin was smooth and olive-hued, her limbs sinuous. But her face was her trump card – she turned heads wherever she went. She'd turned Toby's in an instant. Not just beautiful, but animated, knowing, and unashamed. Toby was under no illusion that he was her first extra-marital lover, nor that he'd be her last.

She put on a chiffon wrap and came to knot his necktie for him.

'It's a very clever trick,' she said, raising one eyebrow. 'Pretending not to care for me.'

She was only half mocking. The other half, he couldn't quite decipher.

'I do care for you, Cassie.'

'Lord Warburton's son sent me a poem. I think he possibly even wrote it himself.'

'Oh? Was it any good?'

'Hm. Not terribly. It compared me to Helen of Troy.'

'Oh dear. Well, your face might very well start a war – albeit a domestic one.'

'I thought it was rather sweet. Aren't you jealous?'

'How can I be jealous? You aren't my wife. If I let myself be jealous over you, I'd drive myself mad.'

'Oh? Then it's only control, Toby? Not coldness?'

He caught her eye. 'You tell me. Am I cold?'

'Not in there.' She nodded towards the rumpled bed, shrugging one shoulder. 'But out of it . . . Perhaps I shouldn't have you back again.'

'Perhaps not.'

'Oh, go away, then! Go and write something *worthy* for your socialist cranks, that nobody will take any notice of.'

'People might, one day. And they're not cranks.' He turned to her, relenting. 'Don't be angry, Cassie – you're the one with the husband.'

'A husband who could ruin you. Or shoot you.'

'And you as well, don't forget.'

He took her hands, kissing her knuckles, left then right. 'You are exquisite, Mrs Pridde, and I am not worthy.'

'No, you're not. Now go. I need to get dressed before my louse of a husband staggers back from the House.'

The bed in which they'd so recently rolled belonged to the Right Honourable Havelock Pridde, the MP for Greenwich, though the house with the fine bedroom was in Bedford Place, in Bloomsbury. Pridde was twenty-three years his wife's senior, and one of those men who saw no hypocrisy whatsoever in keeping a string of mistresses while flying into a fury should any whiff of a story involving his wife reach his ears. He'd actually taken a shot at one of Cassandra's former lovers, and had subsequently bullied a police superintendent into reporting that the gun had gone off accidentally. The horse pulling a passing cab had taken the bullet in the shoulder, and been put down. Pridde had paid off the driver.

Which, Toby thought, said everything that needed to be said about the man: a dyed-in-the-wool Tory, dripping with entitlement, who made his way through life by buying what he couldn't simply take. Toby was rather pleased to be cuckolding him on a regular basis. He sometimes wondered why on earth Cassandra had married a man like Havelock Pridde, but supposed the reasons were the same as whenever a woman married – wealth, status, security, children. Plus he'd probably bullied her into it. Small wonder she was becoming petulant, and took lovers both to amuse herself and to keep score.

Lily Womersley had married, Tom had written to tell him. After an engagement of only four months, to a man who owned a fair chunk of the Scottish lowlands. MacDonald? McDonnell? Toby had forgotten the name already. The tactful tone of Tom's letter suggested that Toby was expected to mind about it, but he didn't. Lily was far better off, and so was he. Still, there was a faint pang of . . . something. A distant whiff of the chaos he'd tumbled into when she ended their engagement. Rita was expecting again, Tom wrote in the same letter. Toby was godfather to their firstborn, a son also named Thomas; and after him had come a little girl called Penelope.

Toby shook off thoughts of Lily and babies as he trotted down the back stairs of Pridde's well-appointed home, nodded to the scullery maid as he passed through the kitchen, and exited via the tradesman's door. The soul of discretion. It was a twenty-minute walk up Tottenham Court Road to Osnaburgh Street, and the offices of the Fabian Society, where Toby was under-secretary, but since it was Saturday he went south instead, across the river via the granite arches of Waterloo Bridge, to his rooms on Cornwall Road, on the top floor of a small terraced house, conveniently located right next door to a pub.

He'd lived there for two years now, sharing the cost of a daily housekeeper with the couple downstairs. The pair weren't married – he was a senior clerk in a bank, and had left his wife to run away with their children's piano teacher. She had a charming laugh, and they laughed all the time – their voices drifting up through the floor, above the din from the nearby sawmill. It made Toby notice that he hardly ever laughed. The meals they cooked, on their new gas stove, helped mask the pervasive reek of a local linoleum works.

Toby didn't cook, beyond the boiling of eggs and occasional grilling of cheese. The housekeeper made him a pie or a casserole, if he asked the day before; else he ate in the pub, or in a café on workdays, in Regent's Park with all the nannies and their charges on the way to the zoo. Sometimes he snatched something from Pridde's kitchen; sometimes he missed a meal altogether and drank strong, penny-a-pint beer instead. He endeavoured to steer clear of wine and spirits.

Toby had a small bedroom separate from the sitting room, and a tiny kitchen with a sink and a range that often went out, and had to be coaxed patiently into heating any water. The privies – dank and smelly – and wash-house were in the backyard, shared with two neighbouring houses. In his sitting room Toby had a pair of upright armchairs he'd got at a kerbside auction, and a pedestal table with two ladder-back chairs where he spent most of his time, either eating or writing. The rest of the decor was sparse and functional. Beyond some hooks and a small mirror that hung by the door, he had no ornaments, no pictures. The housekeeper was a motherly sort, and he sometimes came home to find a few ox-eye daisies in a jar on the mantelpiece, or something like a decorative toffee tin, which he wasn't quite sure what to do with.

Later that evening he was marshalling at a public lecture of the Fabians, in Essex Hall – 'The Moral Aspects of Socialism'. Taking the register, minuting questions from the floor, and writing it all up for the society annals afterwards. But before that he wanted to proofread his own latest tract. It was going to be published by the London Society for the Humane Reform of Prisons, which had campaigned for years for an end to hard labour in prisons: men made to climb a giant treadwheel until their legs gave out. Men made to turn a metal crankshaft, stirring a paddle through sand, to earn enough food to subsist on. Men made to break rocks on Dartmoor until they simply died.

The national policy of *hard labour, hard fare, hard board* was finally on its way out, but had not gone yet. Men were still kept in silence, day in and day out, and refused even a few minutes a day to talk to anyone. They still slept on boards rather than on mattresses or in hammocks. They were still fed nothing but bread, suet and gruel, day in, day out. The policy had been designed to make prison life as miserable as possible. It killed hundreds every year.

The main focus of Toby's pamphlet was on raising the age at which the death penalty could be handed down. At present, there were no legal age parameters. Seventeen-year-old Charles Dobel, hanged for murder in 1889 – the same age, the same year, as Kit. Eighteen-year-old Samuel Smith, hanged in Winchester in 1896; eighteen-year-old George Nunney, hanged earlier that year, though the evidence against him was circumstantial at best. Toby's argument was that no person not yet twenty-one should be hanged for any crime. And if some of his arguments for that overlapped with a call for complete abolition, then so be it.

Are we to say that, at the age of eighteen, a boy may be so wholly condemnable that there is NO HOPE of reforming him? Who among us can look back at our younger selves and not see that we were still learning to master our selves; still lacking in our fundamental understanding of the world? Should the state not intervene with the purpose of SALVAGING that person, rather than simply extinguishing their life? Would a specific reformatory for the under-aged criminal not be the more rational, the more humane, course of action?

Toby tweaked the punctuation and changed the word order here and there as he went, before writing out a fair copy for the typesetter.

When one speaks out against the judicial death penalty, one often hears a quote from the Bible in reply: 'A eye for an eye, a tooth for a tooth.' But, surely, the imposition of such a penalty out of vengeance makes MURDERERS of us all? If there is a debt to be paid to society, and if society must be protected, then these twin goals may be amply met by the imprisonment, reform and transportation of convicted men. To rethink is to risk ridicule, but one must not baulk at ridicule if one longs for change.

In his closing statement, he'd wanted to distil his revulsion and anger into a single, unarguable paragraph. As he re-read it now, that anger surged – it always did.

All men are flawed, and ANY SYSTEM DESIGNED AND OPERATED BY MAN IS THEREFORE INHERENTLY FLAWED.

Mistakes will be made. While the death penalty remains, INNOCENT MEN WILL BE SENT TO THE GALLOWS, and this is a far more grievous injustice than a guilty man being treated too leniently.

Toby wanted to shout it from the rooftops. He wanted to pick the prime minster up by his lapels and shake him till he rattled. Instead, he slammed his palm down on the tabletop, which wobbled and slopped ink over his fair copy. Toby ground his teeth for a moment, then took out a fresh sheet of paper to begin again.

Essex Hall was off the Strand, a twenty-minute walk back across the river. Toby arrived an hour before the meeting and got to work setting out the chairs, hanging the banners and furnishing the ticket desk by the door. The room smelled overwhelmingly of wood – old wood, polished to a shine. It had strong schoolroom connotations that were comforting to Toby, though perhaps not to everyone. He set up a table on the dais for the three notables, and a chair to one side for himself. He'd spent some of Tom's twenty pounds on a course in shorthand notation, which was proving extremely useful.

Before long, the audience began to file in: mostly men, but not exclusively so. Thinkers, writers, left-leaning minor politicians. He saw familiar faces – enthusiasts who came to every meeting – as well as strangers. A few young working-class men in suits gone shiny at the elbows, tired-eyed at the end of the day.

Then, a pair of latecomers gave Toby a shock of recognition. The grey-headed man in the turquoise waistcoat, being helped to his seat by a younger fellow, was Timothy Crudge. Toby ducked. His immediate reflex was to hide, perhaps because of how much Crudge knew about him. But Crudge had only ever been good to the Meriwethers, and had done his best to help Kit. Toby ought not to blank him. He realised he'd missed Bernard Shaw's opening remarks, and quickly fudged something for the minutes. Then he barely looked up again until the meeting drew to a close two hours later.

As the volume rose and hats returned to heads, he went over.

'Good evening, Mr Crudge.'

Crudge turned, his face lighting up. 'Tobias Meriwether! How simply *delightful* to find you here!'

'How do you do?'

'Very well, very well. And yourself? Do let me introduce my *amanuensis*, Nicholas Bourton.'

As they shook hands, Toby relaxed. Crudge's magnanimous good humour was always contagious, and Bourton seemed pleasant enough – all smiles and diffidence.

'This is our first time at one of these lectures,' Bourton said. 'Are you a Fabian?'

'I am. In fact, they employ me – I've just been taking the minutes.'

'Really?' Crudge said. 'But how *marvellous* – jolly good show!'

He beamed with almost paternal pride, and Toby grew a little. In that moment, he *was* proud of where he had got to. For the first time since leaving Durham, he felt that he was doing well.

'The cause of social justice could have no finer champion,' Crudge went on. 'Young Toby here has always been an excellent scholar, Nicholas; fertile ground for liberal ideas to germinate. But you must dine with us, Toby, and tell us all about it – we've a table at Simpson's.'

'That's very kind, but I've no wish to impose—'

'Nonsense! It will be our pleasure to invite you. I insist.'

'Then I accept.' Toby smiled. 'Thank you. I'll need to finish up here.'

Crudge gave a nod. 'We'll go ahead and wet our whistles. You come along as soon as you're ready.'

Toby knew Simpson's in the Strand, but he'd never been in – couldn't afford it. The huge dining hall was opulent with chandeliers, marble counters and leather banquettes. World-famous chess players still met there for contests, but most people went to eat, drink, and be seen. White table linens, silver cloches, complicated cutlery. Toby tried not to feel self-conscious as he was loaned a dinner jacket and tie by the maître d'hôtel, but since neither Crudge nor Bourton seemed to notice that the jacket didn't match his trousers, Toby decided not to worry about it. And he could hardly turn down the wine, when it was the best he'd ever tasted.

He relaxed, and dared to feel that he belonged. They talked about the book Crudge was writing – a new anthology of the myths and legends of the South of England, with an analysis of their basis in archaeological evidence – then moved on to justice and politics and social reform, all without ever touching on how Toby might have come to espouse his causes. Toby knew, instinctively, that Crudge wouldn't have discussed his particular circumstances with Bourton. The old man had always shown perfect tact and discretion, and he was grateful for it. He also knew that Crudge wouldn't offer any unasked-for information about Theo.

But as the evening grew late and the wine swaddled Toby's brain, he began to almost resent it. It made little sense, but perhaps he *wanted* to hear some news of Theo without having to ask. Because he was damned if he was going to ask.

'And Mrs Anscombe? Have you seen her lately?' he heard himself say, when Bourton had excused himself from the table.

Crudge's face fell. 'I haven't actually *seen* her in quite some time, but she writes.'

'Oh?'

The old man looked uncomfortable, and turned his wine glass by its stem.

'Forgive me, Toby, but why do you ask? You cut yourself cleanly from Hallewell and all your old acquaintances. I completely understand why you did it, and perhaps you were right to. But you can't imagine your going wasn't painful for her?'

Toby picked up his glass, but it was empty. A waiter appeared at once.

'Lots that went on was painful,' he said. 'I suppose, as one gets older . . .'

He wasn't sure where the sentence had been going. *She wouldn't even go and visit Kit*, he wanted to say, like a child. His cheeks flared as blood thudded through his skull.

'Anyway, she clearly recovered from any injury well enough to marry that doctor,' he said. 'But you're right – it was wrong of me to ask. Only, I know how close the pair of you are.'

Crudge nodded. 'She's as dear to me as my own daughter. And expecting a child any day now, I'm happy to be able to tell you.'

'Only now? I'm surprised it's taken so long.'

Crudge winced minutely at the crass remark. 'Yes. Well. Others came, but sadly did not stay.'

Toby looked down at his plate – the globs of congealed gravy, the strip of gristle from his steak – and was suddenly awash with bitter, aimless disgust. He didn't belong there. He wasn't a man of intellect or urbane society, he was just scrabbling along, feigning composure and trying to stay afloat, like he'd always done. The wine turned to acid in his stomach, and they sat in silence until Bourton – who seemed boyishly delighted by everything he saw – returned to the table.

'I say, I've just come past the sweet trolley,' he reported. 'I hope you've left room, chaps, because it all looks stupendous.'

'Jolly good,' Crudge said.

'Tell me, Mr Meriwether, where do the Fabians stand on the subject of women's suffrage?' Bourton asked. 'My sister is terribly hot on it these days.'

'Well.' Toby marshalled himself. 'We're more concerned with social reform than political.'

'But surely social reform can only come from political reform?'

'Swingeing changes, perhaps, but that is not the essence of the Fabians. Personally, I think there are more pressing concerns than votes for women. Suffrage ought to be extended beyond landowners, first to all working men come of age. They're the ones living out the policies of ministers they haven't been permitted to elect.'

'But plenty of women work, these days – and not only on farms or in factories. Are they not subject to the exact same policies as men?'

Toby thought of Dr Sanderson, who'd treated him during his fever. It threw him right back to that night in the ruins of the castle, when he'd spoken loftily to Theo of *women*, and seen her recoil. He pushed back against the memory.

'Are women politically minded, for the most part? It seems to me that many are perfectly happy and fulfilled in the domestic realm, and that those agitating for the vote are a small minority.'

'Oh, but I couldn't disagree more! I don't think one should ever mistake silence for contentment, least of all from those who have been so long denied a voice they've likely forgotten how to speak.'

They argued back and forth without rancour until the dessert trolley arrived, and Toby was glad of the distraction. Though never less than genial, Crudge was subdued, and Toby knew that he was the cause. His disgust with himself was still churning, and got worse whenever he stopped talking. So he talked and talked, and drank and drank – port after the wine, then brandy after that, so that by the time they were saying their goodnights the greater part of his mind was occupied with staying upright. Bourton hailed a cab, and when Crudge offered his hand, Toby embraced him instead, because he was sorry, and ashamed. *You're a coward, Toby Meriwether*. The idea that he'd disappointed the old man was horrible.

Crudge patted his shoulders then gently disentangled himself, briefly holding Toby at arm's length. His eyes were sad.

'There now,' he said. 'Delightful to see you again, Toby, and to see you doing so well. I will look out for that pamphlet of yours! Do keep in touch. Here's my card – I've a new *pied-à-terre* in Chelsea.'

Toby decided to walk home to sober himself up, and set off towards the river, where the reek of the mud was the final straw, and he threw up over the railings. All that wonderful food, wasted. He tried to be tidy about it but managed to splatter his shoes; swiped at them with his handkerchief but couldn't keep his balance, so gave up and wove onwards. Trees, buildings and traffic all swam queasily around him.

The disgust came back even stronger. It made him angry. Angry at Crudge, angry with himself for having asked about Theo, angry with Theo . . . Theo, who was about to become a mother. Theo, who had lost other babies before now. How that must have saddened her – he registered the wound without feeling any pain. Not yet. But he didn't want to think about it, any more than he wanted to think of her with a babe in arms. Perhaps the proud husband standing by; slaps on the back from his chums; cigars all round. The anger spread until dark blotches crowded his vision.

He'd meant to go home, but it turned out he was in Bedford Place. Because he was angry with Cassandra too, lying up there with her disgusting husband – stinking of him between her legs, no doubt, when hours earlier she'd been *his*. He knew she was only marking time with him. When she got bored, she'd move on. Cast him off like a worn sock. And how dare she – how *dare* she? There was only one word for a woman like that.

'*Trollop!*' he shouted, then regretted it at once. 'Cassandra!' he called instead. 'Cassandra, come down!'

Was that what he wanted? Did he want her to choose him? Take him in her beautiful arms and kiss him and stop him feeling so . . . *paltry*? He didn't know, but he shouted a few more times – 'Please, Cassie!' – staggered a bit, and grabbed a lamp-post for balance, until a window slid open and a head and shoulders appeared: Pridde, with his eyes bulging and his face lit a ghastly hue by the streetlight. Toby recoiled.

'Who is that?' Pridde bellowed. 'Meriwether? You wretch!'

Toby had no idea how the man knew his name, but the fact that he did was faintly perturbing.

'Mr Pridde! A good evening to you,' he slurred. 'I wonder if I might have a . . . quick . . . word with your wife?'

'A *word*? I'll give you a word! How dare you turn up here, whining and sniffing like a dog! The brazen, bare-faced *cheek* of it! I'll teach you to make a spectacle on my doorstep, you *worm*!'

He ducked back inside and Toby thought he saw a brief struggle behind the drapes; he heard Cassandra's voice, raised and beseeching. He laughed briefly, as a hindquarter of his brain advised him to move along.

'I am a worm,' he mumbled. 'A worm on a hook.'

Cassandra appeared at the window, her hair hanging down in dark curtains. 'Have you lost your *mind*?' she hissed. 'Go away! *Go* – he'll kill you!'

'But you're so beautiful, Cassie . . .'

Seconds later, the front door was wrenched open and Pridde stormed out in his dressing gown, lips curled in a vulpine snarl. He had a rifle in one hand, which he set against his shoulder and levelled at Toby. That sensible corner of Toby's mind sent a cold twinge down his spine to tell him he was in trouble, but it was far too late to make any kind of escape, so he laughed again, manically, swinging himself around to the other side of the lamp-post as a deafening retort split the air.

◆ ◆ ◆

Arthur Ralph Seymour Anscombe had the most perfect face Theo had ever seen. She could stare at it for hours at a time, while he slept or gazed about with his bleary indigo eyes. Occasionally he frowned as though puzzled by something, but the nurse said it was most likely just wind. The pearly finish of his eyelids, and miniature wisps of eyebrow; the deep-red pout of his lower lip; his crimson flush when he wailed, revealing his ridged, slippery gums.

Theo hadn't wanted the nurse to stay on beyond the first week or so, but Ralph insisted she remain. Arthur had got the hang of feeding very quickly. He woke up several times a night and so did Theo – sometimes even *before* he started crying – so she got no more rest if he was along the hall in the nursery instead of beside her. In the end, she took to keeping him in a basket on Ralph's side of the mattress. The nurse – who didn't mind a bit – slept undisturbed in the nursery, and Ralph slept across the hall with scraps of gauze stuffed in his ears.

Theo's arms soon felt empty without Arthur's warm weight. She loved the smell of him – sometimes sweet, sometimes feral. He'd been conceived a full year after her last miscarriage, in the summer of '96. So early, that time, that there'd been no question of knowing whether it had been a boy or a girl. No question of a name. Theo's grief had been just the same, and it had not gone. But her love for Arthur was its antidote, and made it more bearable.

For his part, Ralph seemed delighted with his son. At first, in any case. He weighed him and measured him and kept a journal of his growth, and when he handled him it was with the intense circumspection of new fathers everywhere – in spite of his medical training. He liked to watch as Theo rocked him to sleep, and if she looked up and caught his expression – tender, almost confused – he would rise and touch her face, and say something like: 'My clever, clever girl.'

'Perhaps he'll be happier, now,' Theo whispered to Audrey, when Ralph was out of the room.

Audrey's reply was a weighted silence. She was smitten with the baby, and took every opportunity to cuddle him.

Ralph insisted that Arthur remain at home for the first three months of his life, and since the weather was glorious Theo took him into the garden every day, to lie on a blanket in the shade of an apple tree. He was fascinated by the dappled light flickering through the leaves. On those occasions, and in the still of the night while she fed him, Theo was perfectly content. The feeling grew slowly after the terror of the pregnancy and birth – like seeds sown into barren ground. But she didn't know if or when she had ever felt as happy as she was in those moments.

Those times of unalloyed wonder were fleeting. Tempering them were the five and a half years of her marriage to Ralph, and all the things she now understood about him. That he did not like his judgement called into question, on any subject. That his self-esteem was a fragile thing, to be nurtured at all costs, because when it was injured life could be unbearable. That he cared deeply for his patients, but not entirely because they were *people*. They represented a chance for medicine – for *himself* – to succeed. Every injury, every illness, every tumour and case of sudden paralysis were skirmishes in his personal war against ignorance and death.

He worked himself hard, dosing himself with cocaine to stay awake for days at a time if necessary. Then, when he came home with darting eyes and restless hands, he took Bayer's heroin drops to relax. The heroin was a new cure for toothache, menstrual cramps and hysteria. Also for the easing of a troubled mind, so Ralph sometimes prescribed it for Theo as well. If she was *overwrought*, and it caused her to disobey or to argue with him. When he caught her writing to Timothy Crudge, or laughing with Audrey about something. His nostrils always flared at the sight of them with their heads together, as though they could only be laughing at him.

'Well? What's the current conspiracy?' he'd say, with a humourless smile.

Once he added later, in private: 'You're too tight with that dratted girl, Theo. It's inappropriate.'

'Ralph . . . Audrey is my friend—'

'Well, she should not be! She is a servant in this house, and neither you nor she should forget it. Servants can be indiscreet if they are made too bold, and forget their station.'

'But I trust Audrey with—'

'Enough. Mind what I have said. If I believe she is getting above herself I will feel no compunction whatever in choosing a new maid for you, for my own peace of mind.'

Theo held her tongue.

The heroin tincture tasted bitter and made her feel like she'd fallen backwards into a billion feathers. She certainly forgot whatever it was she'd been unhappy about, and when the heavenly fog receded she found herself wondering if another small dose might not make the day – might not make *everything* – much, much easier.

But Ralph controlled all the medicines in the house, and Theo noticed that the craving eased after a day or two. That craving troubled her, until she began to avoid taking it at all. She would drop it into her mouth if Ralph were watching but spit it into the basin once he'd left the room. Arthur made her more determined. She must not be insensible, but ready at all times to protect him. Instinct told her to shore up and create safety, for him and for herself. To forget the past, and see only the best in her husband.

It was not easy. It required a continuous and exhausting effort of will.

Once or twice, Ralph made her give the heroin tincture to Arthur, too, when he was loud or colicky. And it did soothe him.

But there was no mistaking the lingering lassitude, during which time he would not latch on to her, and would not eat.

'I am the medical man in this house, am I not?' Ralph said, when Theo refused to give it to Arthur any more. 'Who knows better, do you suppose – you, or I?'

'You are the medical man,' she said, breathless with nerves. 'But I am the mother.'

A certain person has developed the habit of taking tonics, she wrote to Albert Mackie. *Indeed, he depends upon them. Cocaine to keep awake, and heroin to fall sleep. He has quite a different character when he has taken a tonic, compared to when he has not. Could these medicines change the very essence of a person? Are they really a cure, or are they merely a numbing?*

To which Dr Mackie replied: *If pain is the symptom, then may a medicine that numbs it not be called a cure? Such tonics are entirely safe, I assure you. I prescribe them to my own patients on a regular basis.*

But Theo wasn't reassured.

Her fear was an amorphous thing. She couldn't say what she thought would happen. There was nothing definite about it, only the growing conviction that she didn't know who her husband *was*, or therefore what he might do. She couldn't tell if it was because he'd changed, or because she'd never really known him. If she was careful then he rarely lost his temper with her, yet she increasingly suspected that this was not enough. That perhaps he *wanted* to lose his temper with her.

What Theo had taken for shyness on Audrey's part – the way she faded into the background when Ralph was around – she now understood to be something more. It was distrust. And the other servants had gone from openly adoring Ralph and resenting their young, unfashionable mistress to quietly going about their work with sombre expressions, shrinking from their master like water from oil.

Theo knew it was her fault. She had disappointed him, and she had not loved him – not in the beginning, and at no time since. And she was certain he knew it, and didn't understand. He was far better suited to being adored. Theo reminded herself that he was as tethered to her as she was to him. Only Arthur made that bearable for her, but perhaps she could make it better for all of them by being a better wife. By being all the things he wanted her to be – loyal and obedient and happy to see him.

Thoughts of Missy's operation, and her remains, became one more thing Theo kept hidden. So her world shrank a little more every day. *So she* shrank a little more.

'But this is not the *summit* of mankind's capabilities,' Ralph declared, pacing the length of the dining-room table one evening. 'Not even close! It is but a step higher.'

He'd drawn the curtains, declaring the evening sunshine far too bright. His pupils were huge, the whites bloodshot, and when he blinked it was too much – more like a sudden, rapid screwing-up of his eyes.

'This is only the *start* – Mrs Geary's recovery will be the first of many. I have begun to make inroads into areas of surgery that have until now been wholly out of bounds . . .'

Theo sat rigid with her dinner gone cold on her plate. He didn't need her opinion, only her ears. His elation was due to two things: firstly, another article he'd written – 'The Mechanism of Contra-coup and of Certain Other Forms of Intracranial Injury' – had been published in *The Lancet*, to a flurry of interested and congratulatory correspondence.

'How would you like to live in London, my dear?' he'd asked, looking up from one letter. 'It would be exciting, would it not?'

Theo was startled. 'There has been an offer of a position?'

'All in good time.'

The second thing was that a patient of his had survived an operation to remove a large bony growth from her skull, with partial paralysis to one side of her body the only apparent after-effect.

'God did not intend for us to live in fear and ignorance, Theo,' Ralph went on. 'He did not mean for us to be felled ahead of time by accident or disease. He has given us the wherewithal to *solve* these problems, and to cure ourselves – to cure others.'

He knelt down beside her, and she jumped. Staring into those vast pupils was like leaning over a well. Theo could see nothing at the bottom – no glimpse of reflected sky.

'It's wonderful, Ralph,' she said.

He grabbed her hands and kissed them furiously, then pulled her up from her chair.

'Come! Come into my arms, my darling girl.'

'Ralph – the servants!'

'Hang the servants.'

Theo managed to herd him up to their bedroom, at least, before he fell upon her, his face suffused with passion. This was her duty, she reminded herself; it was how they'd made Arthur, so it could not be so very bad. It was over quickly, in any case.

Later on, when Ralph's face sagged with exhaustion but he couldn't sleep, Theo watched him at his dresser, tipping his head back to drop the tincture into his mouth. His tongue repulsed her – curled out of the way, outlined by faint light from the window. There was something inhuman about it. Something reptilian.

The next morning he plodded into the nursery while Theo was feeding Arthur, and sank into a chair, unshaven, only half dressed.

The nurse excused herself, though for once Theo wished she'd stay. Ralph smelled stale and almost metallic. His hair was mussed, his skin still puffy with fatigue.

'It's very early,' she said. 'Why not sleep a while longer?'

He ignored her. The morning light was cool and crystalline; Theo had opened the window to hear the birds and let the dewy smell of the garden drift in. She wanted Arthur to experience every possible beauty, but with Ralph watching them like that her happiness withered. Arthur's cheeks were mottled, his eyes clamped shut with perfect concentration as he fed. A minute later, Theo wiped his chin and deftly switched him to the other side.

'Ups-a-daisy, little one,' she murmured.

'How readily you love him.' Ralph's voice broke the air apart.

Theo looked up, her smile fading. She opened her mouth but couldn't think of a reply. It was not a question.

'How very readily you love him, when in six long years you have not managed to love me.'

Theo knew she must deny it. She knew she must reassure him, but her tongue refused to move. His stare was nakedly angry. She tensed; Arthur broke off, and started to cry. Ralph grimaced, clapping his hands over his ears.

'Dose him,' he said. 'Dose him, if he carries on that din – or I shall.'

He lurched to his feet and left without another word.

Audrey, who'd been in a corner all the time, quite unnoticed by Ralph, came and took the baby. She put Arthur over her shoulder and patted until he burped.

'You've no better manners than your father, have you?' she said to him.

Theo didn't rebuke her. She'd never been more grateful to have Audrey.

A little later, when she heard the front door close behind her husband, Theo allowed herself to relax. Moments of calm were now islands in a restless sea – a sea that heaved with undertow. She could only ever swim for the next one, hoping, but not certain, to reach it.

In the afternoon she went into Shaftesbury with Hermione Abbott, to have tea at the Grosvenor Arms Hotel. She hadn't told Ralph about it, not wanting to give him time to find a reason why she ought not go. He was always far happier if she stayed at home. In any case, Theo planned to be back before he finished at the hospital. If she could get away without mentioning it at all, then so much the better. He didn't like her to be secretive, yet it seemed increasingly necessary to be so.

Hermione had given birth to her fourth child and youngest son, Percy, just three months before Arthur's arrival.

'However adorable little Arthur is – and my goodness, he *is*,' she said, as they walked side by side up the hill, 'I imagine you might be ready for an interlude of adult company. I know I am.'

'Oh, yes,' Theo said, though the truth was she wouldn't have left him at all, if she hadn't known Audrey was with him. There was nobody else she trusted enough, and she was already missing him.

'I begin to feel like a dairy cow, after a while,' Hermione said. 'Not that I don't love them when they're tiny – I *do* – but once I can pass an entire day without being gnawed upon, I'm not entirely *un*happy about it.'

'I just can't imagine being a mother four times over,' Theo said. 'Feeling this much love for four different children . . . isn't it overwhelming?'

'Utterly, in a delightful sort of way. But, Theo – you already *are* a mother four times over,' Hermione said, and Theo loved her for it.

They found a table in one of the big sash windows. The air was lazy with summer warmth, and petals were dropping from the pink roses on the table.

'I love this place,' Hermione said. 'It's so out of the modern day. Can't you just imagine Jane Austen sitting here to take tea, a century ago?'

'I came here on my eighteenth birthday,' Theo said. She'd just met Audrey, and Ralph had been merely her doctor. It felt like decades ago. 'My uncle brought me, as a special treat.'

'Your uncle? Not your parents?'

'My father was long dead by then, and my mother rarely . . .'

She trailed into silence, because through the window she'd seen Ralph across the street. There was another inn over there, a less reputable place more for drinking than high tea. A man had opened the yard gates to one side, and was rolling barrels out into the street. And there in the yard was her husband, holding the hands of a woman. Theo shrank back in shock, fearful of discovery, before remembering that *she* was doing nothing wrong. Ralph's medical bag was by his feet, but their pose told Theo that this woman was not a patient. Her clothes were respectable – too expensive for her to be an employee at the inn. She wore a peacock feather in a small straw hat, and had rolls of chestnut hair at the nape of her neck. Her face was feline, and she smiled up at Ralph, her expression both wry and helpless.

'Theo?' Hermione said. 'What is it? Have you seen somebody you know?'

There was no way Theo could prevent Hermione seeing them too.

'Oh . . .' she said, when she did.

After a while Ralph kissed the woman's mouth, and both of her hands, then checked the street before heading back towards the hospital, his medical bag swinging at his side.

'Oh, *Theo . . .'* Hermione looked horrified. 'Did you . . . do you *know* that woman?'

Theo was wooden with shock. Humiliated. 'No. Not at all. Do you?'

'No . . . That is, she did look a *little* familiar. Perhaps I . . . I could find out for you . . . ?'

Theo shook her head, swallowing against a sudden hollowness inside. *Your purity, your virtue*, Ralph had said when he proposed to her. *If you could only find it in your heart to love me then I would be a man born anew.* It had puzzled her at the time, but now she understood. The blue gloves on his desk at the hospital – in the shock of everything she'd discovered afterwards, Theo had forgotten all about them. And there were other things she'd noticed over the years, but attached no significance to: odd whiffs of perfume; the sudden giving of gifts; scratches on his shoulders one time, which he claimed had been made by a patient in a fit. Yet his shirt hadn't been marked at all. Each small thing dropped neatly into place. Ralph had been a rake, and now he was a faithless husband. A man, like so many others, who kept a mistress – or perhaps a series of them.

When he'd suspected her of infidelity, he had been judging her by his own standards.

'Well, I can't—' Hermione was aghast. 'I mean, how simply *terrible* to see . . . to discover such a thing! I suppose there are many men who . . . But . . . Had you any idea?'

'No. Though perhaps I ought to have had.'

Because, of course, she never had found it in her heart to love him.

'Should we go home? Perhaps . . . Yes, shall we?'

'Please don't speak of this to anybody.'

'My dear, I would *never*.'

So, that was the end of their afternoon.

For several days, Theo wasn't sure what she thought about it. She could hardly bring herself to look at Ralph, but he didn't seem to notice. In the end she decided it might be a good thing, if it fulfilled him in some way she could not – and had no wish to. Yet she still resented it. The probability of people knowing about it, and laughing at her. The way he did exactly as he pleased, but allowed her to do so very little. She said nothing, to anybody.

Theo missed Timothy Crudge intensely – his steady presence, his kindly outlook on the world. With Audrey's help, in carefully hidden correspondence, they made a plan to meet up.

Ralph had been invited to speak at a medical conference in London, in early September. Since he did not care to visit Hallewell, Theo asked to spend the days he was away with her mother.

'Of course, if you wish,' he said. 'I suppose she'd like to see Arthur. Though I'm not sure she likes the idea of being a grandmother.'

'I think she likes it very much,' Theo said.

Ralph grunted. 'All women like babies – the female brain is susceptible to such primitive instincts. But *grandmother* has a whiff of Bath chairs and mothballs about it, don't you think?'

Theo chose to say nothing about the primitive instincts of men.

In fact, she planned to go to Hallewell for only one day, and then return. Doubts plagued her at the thought of deceiving Ralph so completely, but his trip to London was too good an opportunity to miss. A rare pocket of freedom. Her anxiety grew as the time approached.

'He won't find out, miss,' Audrey said. 'He'll be miles and miles away, and none of the servants would report on you – not any longer. They see how things are.'

Theo wasn't so sure. Crudge planned to travel down on a train that would arrive just an hour after the one taking Ralph to London departed. They would pass on the tracks – the idea made Theo's knees ache with foreboding. She couldn't have him to stay; the chance was too great that a neighbour might mention it, quite innocently. Ralph had persuaded Diana to the opinion that Crudge was unwholesome, so these days Hallewell House tended to be fully booked when he wrote to reserve a room there. But there was a coaching inn at Sherborne Causeway that the old man had declared would suit him very well. They would meet early on the second morning and spend the day together, with Audrey and Arthur too. Something that Ralph had expressly forbidden.

Before their son was even born, Ralph had warned that he would not have him corrupted by *exposure to the wrong sort.* Theo had known exactly who he'd meant. She'd hoped for Ralph to mellow once the baby was born, but instead he'd repeated his injunction all the more explicitly. Arthur was not to be *exposed* to Timothy Crudge. Hearing that gentle old soul spoken of in such terms made Theo's face burn, but she was powerless to change Ralph's mind. She knew better than to try.

She was jittery with nerves that morning, as they loaded themselves and a hearty picnic into a hired trap, beneath a sky full of wheeling swifts. Theo drove, and Audrey squeezed her hand as they set off.

'It'll be all right, miss,' she said. 'He'll be *so* happy to meet Arthur.'

'Yes.' Theo exhaled. 'Yes, he will.'

And he was, coming to meet them outside the inn with his whole face lighting up. Theo had barely finished hugging him before he wanted to hold the baby. His huge, gnarled hands dwarfed Arthur's little body as he held him up and looked him in the eye.

'Goodness me, what a fine chap!' he said. 'What a jolly fine chap you are, indeed!'

Arthur made a grab for Crudge's whiskers, and Theo couldn't help her eyes flooding. This ought not to be prohibited; it was very wrong that it was.

'He's the very best of chaps,' she said.

Crudge's face fell. 'My dear Theo, don't cry. Come – we shall have a wonderful day of it. I've brought an apple cake to add to the picnic – your favourite, Audrey. The landlady sells them for tuppence and claims they're the best in Dorset.'

'Well, we'll see about that,' Audrey said.

They headed south to Melbury Beacon, an ancient hill with a flawless view in every direction: across the Blackmore Vale and Cranborne Chase, and of Shaftesbury, scattered on its hilltop like a child's building blocks. They left the horse with an ostler and hiked to the top, where Theo turned in a wide circle, gazing at the scalloped escarpments and dark wooded gullies, the meadow grasses bleached by the long summer, and the patchwork of fields that chequered the valley into the far, far distance. The breeze was warm, and bees were busy on the last flowers setting to seed.

'Glorious,' she breathed, meaning not only the view, but the sense of escape; of Tout Hill House being just a building, too small to see, rather than her whole life. That one house; that one bed; that creeping feeling of danger she had all the time. She took great lungfuls of air, wishing that the moment was not so irrevocably finite.

'"*Hail to thee, blithe Spirit*",' Crudge said, quoting Shelley as he squinted up at a skylark. Theo remembered another line from the poem: *Like an unbodied joy whose race is just begun*. How long it had been since she'd felt like that – since she could envisage something beyond or after her present situation. But *unbodied joy* was a good description of what she felt for Arthur. Her love for him seemed bigger and better than herself, with all her wrong choices, her cowardice, and her buried self.

'Are you ready for the picnic? I've set it all out,' Audrey said, unmoved by the view. Her opinion of the countryside was that it took an awfully long time to get anywhere. If there was an ants' nest around to be sat upon accidentally, Audrey would be the one to do it.

‘I’m always ready for a picnic,’ Crudge said, before Theo could tell Audrey to wait, that it was only just noon, that she wasn’t to rush the day.

When they’d eaten, Audrey fell asleep with Arthur draped across her, the pair of them snoring softly. Theo looked closely at Crudge, noticing that though he’d climbed the hill quite easily, his shoulders were more stooped, and his eyes couched in ever deeper hollows. He’d always seemed old to her, but was growing older still. The thought dismayed her.

‘How is Mr Bourton?’ she asked.

‘Nicholas is very well, thank you. I left him trying to decipher some of my more tangled notes, poor boy. *The Gentleman’s Magazine* has offered to publish extracts from the book, if I can only get them ready in time. A lifetime of scribbling things down in the field has quite destroyed my penmanship. But he tolerates it. He tolerates me, the dear boy.’

‘I’m sure he’s happy to,’ Theo said. ‘He’s obviously very fond of you.’

‘Yes.’ Crudge’s smile was almost shy. ‘Yes. I believe he is.’

‘I’m glad.’

Theo searched around for some way to say that not only did she understand, but that he could speak freely with her, if he wanted to. It would change nothing between them. But there was no way to say it, so she said:

‘It’s so wonderful to see you, Uncle.’

‘I’m terribly sorry Ralph doesn’t approve of me, my dear. And I understand some of his reservations – I am not a relation, after all.’

‘Perhaps not by blood, but in every other way. I wish he would understand it better.’

‘I fear that what a person does not wish to understand, they never will.’

‘He’s . . . he’s getting worse.’

Theo couldn't help herself. Tears stung again, and she struggled to hold them.

'Worse? In what way?'

'Oh, nothing! I didn't mean . . . Only, I'd so hoped that when we finally had Arthur he would be pleased with me.'

She saw the full scale of her unhappiness dawning upon Crudge.

'It's my fault,' she said. '*I* have turned him hard – he was so good-natured when I first knew him. I've tried, but . . . I *cannot* love him, and he knows it. I have wounded him deeply.'

'Wounded him, perhaps, but—'

'He has a mistress. I saw them together. I think it's been going on for some time – or else she isn't the first. And then he tells me that *you* are not a moral man!'

'Oh, *Theo*.'

'I . . . I should have *made* myself love him. He's a brilliant man, and he used to be so kind.'

'You might as well try to make the sun rise ahead of time,' Crudge said gently.

'Then I should never have accepted his proposal.'

'But how can you regret it, when it has brought forth this adorable little boy?'

'No. You're right.' Theo rubbed at her eyes.

After a pause, Crudge asked: 'Is he cruel to you?'

'He— not cruel, exactly. But I seem to disappoint him at every turn. I frustrate him. He works so very hard, and does such important work, and all he asks is that I cherish and obey him, as a wife should. But I fail constantly at those two things! Mother says I must try harder, and she's right. Because what choice do I have? I can't *leave*.'

'No. The law is most unkind on that score.' Crudge put his hand on her shoulder. 'It distresses me to see you so unhappy, my dear. I hadn't realised it had got so bad.'

‘I ought to be happy. I have Arthur, and Audrey, and a nice home . . . I must be a terribly ungrateful sort of person.’

‘Or one whose emotions are authentic, and won’t be marshalled here or there at will. Perhaps you are merely very honest.’

Theo thought at once of Toby; she suspected Crudge had been hinting at Toby. But it was impossible, so she suppressed it. He belonged in another world, from long ago, and it was painful to remember it. She never asked Crudge if he heard anything of the Meriwethers, since nothing he might report would bring her any comfort.

‘I don’t feel honest,’ she said. ‘I have gone against my better judgement at every turn, because I am a coward.’

‘You are *not* a coward – I will not have it! It’s so *easy* to look back and castigate oneself for decisions made and paths taken, but at the time of choosing we all simply do what we *can*. What we think is best, and what we can manage.’

‘And I must live with those choices forever.’

Crudge could hardly deny it. ‘Nothing is forever, Theo,’ he said. ‘Though, I appreciate it must feel that way. If you ever want to stay with me in London, for a short or a long time – whether under a cloud or otherwise – I shan’t ever turn you away. You must never think you have nowhere to go.’

‘Thank you, Uncle.’

She held his hand for a while, knowing that she could never visit him without Ralph’s permission. And that he would never give it.

After that, Crudge succumbed to the sunshine and dozed as well, and Theo stared into the sky and tried not to feel trapped. She knew she was blessed in many ways; and if she must inch through her days, forever on edge, then she would just have to find a way to live with it. *I do think we sometimes must just . . . try to be happy. And in the trying, make it so*. Ralph’s words, but she knew now that trying to be happy was like trying to be in love. *How readily you love him*, he’d said, watching her with Arthur. And he was right: *that* was love – an irresistible impulse that had nothing to do with effort or necessity.

Again, Toby stalked the edges of her thoughts; but he brought her no peace.

When Ralph got back from London the following evening, Theo knew at once. She knew from the way he slammed the cab door, and strode along the path without looking up at the house, or at the window from which she was watching. She knew from the way he dumped his hat and coat on the floor when the servant wasn't quick enough to take them, and the way his face was fixed as he came into the room. Dread coursed through her. She had no idea how Ralph had discovered her deceit, only that he had. The anger came off him like a smell.

Arthur was on her lap, chewing an ivory ring and drooling.

'Audrey, take him. Take him!' she hissed, standing up and handing her son to the startled girl. 'Go upstairs.'

'But, miss—'

'You will address my wife as *madam*, or you will be dismissed from this house!' Ralph shouted. 'How hard can it be, for pity's sake?'

The sudden noise set Arthur crying. With a worried glance at Theo, Audrey hurried him from the room.

Theo's heartbeat was like the quick ticking of a watch, and sweat prickled her armpits. Ralph took two steps towards her, drew breath as though to speak, and then hit her instead. A back-handed slap that sent her sprawling on to the couch.

A bright light exploded behind her eyes. She kept them shut as the world collapsed inwards and she was reduced, for a moment, to nothing – a mere collection of scattered sensations: the taste of blood between her teeth, the smell of dust in the cushion beneath her, and the racket of her pulse. *Person becomes object.* Seconds later she realised that although the pain was a shock, the violence was not. She'd seen it coming months ago – perhaps even years ago. A sudden memory of storm clouds caught in a photograph; of a creeping, inexorable shadow on the horizon. No amount of forewarning could keep a storm like that from breaking.

At length, she became aware of Ralph weeping. Looking down, she found his head in her lap, his arms around her legs. There were spots of blood on her dress and she brushed at them absently; her lower lip was stinging, swelling, and her neck ached fiercely.

'Theo, forgive me . . . forgive me . . .' he said, muffled.

Theo said nothing. Her mind would not stop picking at the issue of *how* he'd discovered her disobedience. Had her mother betrayed her? A chance sighting somewhere? Or had he arranged to have her watched from the very outset? The idea made her skin crawl.

'I'm so sorry,' Ralph went on. He looked up, face bloated with tears and regret. 'I never want to hurt you . . . Never! But . . . Why did you disobey me? *Why?*'

Still numb with shock, Theo told the truth. 'Because I *cannot* obey you. Not in regards to Mr Crudge.'

'But you *must*.' He got to his knees and took her hands. 'Don't you see, I only want what is best for you, and for Arthur?'

Theo stared at him. Her head throbbed. He was making no sense to her.

'But I . . . I should not have struck you. It was a *despicable* thing to do! My darling Theo, I will *never* do it again, I swear it. That is not who I am.' His tears began again. 'You do understand, don't you? That's not who I am.'

He looked distraught, so Theo dared to hope he could be telling the truth.

Chapter Fifteen

1902

The breeze whipping up the Thames was still more winter than spring. Toby squeezed his upper arm where the cold made it ache. A piece of shot remained lodged in his humerus bone; the surgeon had said it would do more harm than good to extract it. Havelock Pridde's shot, which had winged him the night he'd gone to serenade Cassandra like some drunk and dismal Romeo. By agreement, Toby hadn't pressed charges of attempted murder, and Pridde hadn't sued him for consorting with Mrs Pridde. Pridde had even pulled strings to keep the incident out of the press, though the rumour mill had done what it did best in any case. Toby had denied, denied, denied. Claimed to have stumbled against the spike of an iron railing.

Only Tom knew the full story, and when he'd finished upbraiding Toby for an idiot, he'd laughed until tears ran down his face. *Humerus indeed, old boy.*

Despite Toby's fears, it turned out that being shot by Pridde did wonders for his career. After three years with the Fabians he'd got frustrated with their drawing-room socialism, their softly, softly approach, and had decided to move back into journalism. He'd known exactly where he wanted to be: *The Star*. A newspaper that had been founded with the aim of championing the under-privileged, which highlighted the daily hardships and injustices faced by the working classes. It had grown rapidly to a circulation of over a hundred and fifty thousand, making it one of the most popular evening papers in the capital. *The Star* was radical in outlook, opposed to all military action, and even included a 'Woman's World' feature. Their writers included illustrious socialist and reformist figures like George Bernard Shaw, Thomas Marlowe and Annie Besant.

Toby decided it was the perfect fit. With only his relatively short stint at *The London Daily News* behind him, he'd sent in a variety of essays and pamphlets in support of his application. He'd been called in for a meeting out of courtesy, only to be told there were no vacancies on the staff.

'But we'll keep you in mind, Mr Meriwether,' the managing editor said. 'You might have to moderate your tone somewhat, were you ever to write for us.'

'I can do that.'

'Good. We're here to fight the good fight, but it doesn't ever do to froth at the mouth.'

'Ah.' Toby shifted uncomfortably. 'Of course.'

His arm ached and he put his hand up to press on it, a gesture that had become almost unconscious. The managing editor – tall, lean, extremely well-groomed – tipped his head quizzically.

'Meriwether . . . I thought that name was familiar.' He nodded at Toby's arm. 'Old war wound?'

'Well, it . . .' Toby had been on the verge of trotting out the story about the railings, but the other man looked so delighted he decided not to bother. 'Of a sort,' he said.

'The rumour was that Havelock Pridde shot at you.'

'Not so much shot *at* me, as simply . . . shot me,' Toby confessed.

The man chuckled, then stood to shake his hand. 'Well, any man who makes an enemy of that bloated oaf is a friend of mine. Leave it with me.'

A week later Toby began work at *The Star*, taking over the 'What We Think' column. He was getting on well. He wrote them some broader opinion pieces too, and now, after only eighteen months, there were rumours of him moving up to assistant news editor. He continued to write articles and pamphlets independently of the paper, and occasionally lobbied parliament on behalf of various reformist bodies. He did not yet have real *influence* – not like the upper-class reformers, the Oxford men, the politicians' nephews – but he was certainly being *heard*. His name was becoming known in certain circles, and not just for having been shot by Havelock Pridde.

He was on his way to speak at the annual conference of the Society for Social and Judicial Reform, about the new system for young offenders' prisons recently begun in Borstal, in Kent. He'd come to love the particular character of London's various meeting halls – the old wood and dusty plaster cornices; the portraits of long-dead notables; the susurration of a crowd settling down; the coughs and blown noses that obliterated the first five minutes of any speech. It all felt like home, and carried with it an addictive sense of purpose, of being part of the machinery of change.

His speech went down well – only two older men fell asleep, but the hall *was* stuffy by the end. Afterwards, he spotted Dennis Armstrong in the crowd. Stocky, ruddy, as quick to laugh as to argue, Dennis wasn't a university man but had read – and continued to read – practically *everything*. Five years ago, at the age of only twenty-one, he'd set up a small publishing company to circulate the works of various reforming bodies, and it had gone from strength to strength. He planned to publish Toby's speech as part of the SSJR's quarterly journal.

'What ho, Meriwether,' Dennis greeted him, shaking his hand robustly. 'Good job. You almost have me convinced.'

'Almost?'

'Hm. Can't quite swallow the idea of a murderer not going to the gallows, even though I agree with all your arguments. There's the rub, I suppose – that irrational streak we all have.'

'Which only proves my point. To err is human, *et cetera*.'

'I wanted to run something by you, Meriwether. The chap I live with, Edwards – you've met him, I think?'

'The architect with the boxer's nose?'

'That's him. He's getting married. Some girl he met three weeks ago – a dancer. He's quite lost his head, and it'll end in tears, but, anyway, he's moving out, and I need someone to take over his room. Any interest? Fetter Lane – far more convenient for *The Star*. It's a decent set-up, and the char has a dab hand for pastry.'

'Well . . . possibly.'

Toby was still in his rooms on Cornwall Road, south of the river. It was as noisy and smelly as ever, but he hadn't bothered to move.

'Splendid.' Dennis handed Toby a card. 'Here's the address. Stop by after hours sometime, and see what you think of the place. Now, come and meet a friend of mine – Mary Gladwell. She's asked for an introduction.'

'Oh?'

'Don't panic – she's one of us.'

Mary Gladwell was as tall as Toby in her heeled shoes, and possibly a year or two older. She was wearing the latest fashion, and had glossy hair the exact shade of the mahogany wall panelling. She was handsome rather than beautiful – more Athena than Aphrodite – with an impressive bosom, a wide, sardonic mouth, and lively green eyes. Toby picked them out as her best feature.

'How do you do, Mr Meriwether?' She shook his hand vigorously. There was nothing at all flirtatious about her, which put Toby at his ease. 'I enjoyed your speech. It will be very interesting to see how this new youth prison gets along – or rather, how its young inmates get along.'

'It will, indeed. Have you a particular interest in prison reform?'

'No, not a personal one. Only that the whole system seems inhumane to me – I shall throw my weight behind any move to drag it into the modern era. But my main field of interest is rather more political.'

'Mrs Gladwell is a universal suffragist,' Dennis told him. 'Central Committee of the National Society for Women's Suffrage, isn't it?'

'Ah, well . . .' Mary looked slightly sheepish. 'It was, until I had something of a tiff with Millicent Fawcett. A case of too many cooks, I suspect. In any case, we're all part of the National Union of Women's Suffrage Societies, now.'

'How *do* you keep track of it all?' Dennis asked.

'We are a new movement, Mr Armstrong, and constantly evolving. So don't poke fun.'

'But I am full of admiration, Mrs Gladwell, else I wouldn't tease,' Dennis said.

Mary went on: 'As with your own work, Mr Meriwether, there are a lot of petitions to parliament, a lot of meetings and conferences – and pamphlets, almost all of which are roundly ignored. I don't expect you to have read any, for example, though I have read a great many of yours.'

'Ah. There you have me,' Toby said.

'You needn't look so embarrassed. As a woman, one is used to shouting into a void.' She smiled quite amiably. 'I've written articles for the press, too. Most recently on the benefits of cycling for good health.'

‘As in . . . ?’

‘As in cycling, Mr Meriwether. You’ve heard of it, I’m sure? It’s both useful *and* beneficial, and yet it has taken until now – and rather a lot of hectoring on my part – to get a medical doctor of good repute to go on the record and say that a women’s internal organs are no more likely than a man’s to be harmed by the vibrations or the action of pedalling. Isn’t that patently absurd?’

‘It does seem to be.’

‘I sense an “and yet”, Mr Meriwether?’

‘I was only thinking that there must be bigger fish to fry. Is it really worth arguing about bicycle riding?’

Mary lifted her chin. ‘If *you* were told *you* could not, would *you* argue about it?’

‘I suppose I would, yes.’

‘Well then. Why should I not? Why should *women* not? Large walls are built of small bricks, Mr Meriwether.’

‘I stand corrected,’ he said, not actually minding at all.

‘You’ll find that happens a lot, in a conversation with Mrs Gladwell,’ Dennis said.

‘Well,’ she went on, ‘as I said, the campaign for the emancipation of women is young. We’re still at the stage where even men of sensitivity and learning must have their routine assumptions challenged on a regular basis.’

Mary studied Toby. ‘Not all of them like it.’

‘Who is publishing your article, Mrs Gladwell?’ he asked.

‘*The Englishwoman’s Review*. I plan to write something in support of the rational dress movement, too,’ she said. ‘Did you hear about that latest young lady in Esher, who just dropped dead? Laced up too tight. She bent over to pick up a kitten and ruptured her spleen – a simply *ludicrous* way to die. And you, Mr Meriwether? What will you write next?’

‘I’m not entirely sure,’ he said, then blurted out: ‘I have the outline of a book in mind – just rough notes, as yet. A collection of essays using specific case histories to illustrate our country’s gravest social and legal injustices.’

He felt faintly ridiculous to presume he could author a book, so he hadn’t told anyone about it until then. But he was caught out by the unexpected urge to impress Mary Gladwell.

‘With an eye to encouraging reform, of course,’ he finished.

‘That sounds very much the sort of book that *ought* to be written,’ Mary said earnestly.

‘Well. Perhaps. There never seems enough time to make a start.’

‘I’ve always found that time expands to fit whatever you put into it.’ She smiled. ‘But you must come to dinner one evening – I wouldn’t dare call us a *salon*, but we usually have a stimulating time of it, don’t we, Mr Armstrong?’

‘Without fail,’ Dennis agreed.

Toby moved into Dennis’s apartment two weeks later. It occupied the upper two floors of a spacious four-storey building at the top end of Fetter Lane. They had a sitting room and eating room on the lower floor, and a bedroom each on the floor above, with a bathroom crammed into what had been a linen cupboard. There wasn’t actually room for a tub, but there was a water closet that flushed, and a basin with taps. Toby struggled with the idea of emptying his bowels indoors. It seemed unhygienic, and more than a little unseemly. It was, however, considerably warmer.

The apartment wasn’t grand, but it was grander than anywhere Toby had lived before. He’d acquired a few more pieces of furniture, but his room remained sparse and functional. What he did have looked shabby alongside the ornate marble mantelpiece, and the heavy curtains with their pattern of heraldic beasts. Below them lived their landlord, a retired army colonel, who liked to play laments on the bagpipes on Sunday mornings; and at the back was a small apartment for the live-in housekeeper, who was indeed excellent with pastry. Toby looked around his new home, and saw that he was coming up in the world.

In due course, an invitation arrived to dine with Mary Gladwell at her well-appointed Chelsea townhouse. Toby was relieved to see that Dennis had one too. However confident he was now in his work, he still hated to walk into a social gathering knowing nobody.

'Where's Mr Gladwell?' he asked, as they jumped aboard a tram.

'Died of his heart,' Dennis said. 'Congenital. He was only twenty-two at the time. They married young – childhood sweethearts.'

The term caused Toby a barely-there memory of hurt.

'He left her with stacks of money – not that she was exactly destitute beforehand. She's from old money, in Surrey. Then her parents were shipwrecked off the coast of Rimini, and Mary inherited the entire estate.'

'A wealthy heiress, no less.'

'The genuine article,' Dennis agreed. 'Mary has money, property, and the freedom to decide what she wants to do with it all. And she's done a tremendous number of things. She's terribly clever, you know.'

'I'd gathered that.'

'Very determined, too,' Dennis added, with a smile. Toby began to suspect that his friend was enjoying a private joke at Toby's expense.

'What is it?'

'What's what?' All innocence.

Mary's home was fully staffed and lavish, with – to Toby's eye – far too many *things* in it, and more yards of fabric than could possibly be necessary for the exclusion of light or draughts. Swags and bunches and festoons of fabric; damask on the walls;

velvet on the furniture; embroidered cushions; twisted silk ropes and tassels *everywhere*.

'You must wake from nightmares about moths,' Toby said, after an initial glass of champagne had gone straight to his head.

'Sometimes,' Mary agreed. 'But I shan't take tips on decoration from a man – least of all one who just dropped the end of his cigarillo into Great-uncle Cedric's mortal remains.'

'Oh, good Lord.'

Toby was mortified – the urn had looked very like an ash-tray – but Mary only laughed.

'Don't upset yourself, Mr Meriwether – the old dear soul *loved* tobacco.'

Mary's circle were all thinkers or writers of one kind or another. Toby slotted in neatly enough, and found himself enjoying the evening.

'Aren't you the fellow who got shot by the Right Honourable Member for Greenwich?' someone asked him, once the wine had loosened everyone's tongues.

Toby smiled. 'I'm still standing. One shouldn't believe everything one hears.'

The other guest cocked his head. 'I didn't hear a denial in there. Did anyone else?'

'Havelock Pridde?' Mary said. 'I know him reasonably well, though I'd rather I didn't. I'm Lady Captain of the Hampstead Golf Club. *He*, unfortunately, is the Gentlemen's Captain. I find him so infuriating on the shortcomings of my sex that I challenged him to a round of nine holes last year.'

'Please tell us that you beat him, Mary?'

'Alas, no. He has a one-hundred-and-forty-yard drive. But I did come in under par, at least.'

'I can't imagine he was gracious in victory?' Toby said.

'He was *insufferable.*' Mary sighed. 'I was sorely tempted to brain him with my wedge.'

'No court in the land would have convicted you, Mrs Gladwell.'

She smiled at him. 'Would that that were true.'

Later on they moved to a cavernous drawing room, and Toby studied a series of pictures of ancient cities in the Levant: Palmyra, Samaria, Jerusalem and Petra.

'Have you travelled much, Mr Meriwether?' Mary asked, appearing at his side.

'No.' Toby pulled a wry face. 'The sons of country schoolmasters tend not to.'

'Ah. Well, should you ever get the chance, it is a wonderful thing. One returns not quite the same person as when one left.'

'You mean to say you've been to all these places?'

'I drew these pictures from life, Mr Meriwether.'

'Good Lord.' He was stunned. 'They're . . . really very good.'

'Thank you.'

'Wasn't it terribly hard going, for a—' Toby bit his tongue.

'For a woman?' She arched an eyebrow at him. 'No, not particularly. I went with a large train of mules and porters, to carry the expedition's camping equipment. We had a full kitchen array, and a bathing tent. It was perfectly comfortable.'

'But . . . the language . . .' Toby floundered.

'There are local guides one can hire, who can translate,' she said. 'Though, in fact, I studied Arabic before I went. Just in case.'

'You speak Arabic?'

'Enough to get by in a tight spot,' she said modestly.

'Have you heard of the antiquarian Timothy Crudge? He's explored a good deal of the archaeology of that area.'

'Yes – I'm sure I've read something of his.'

'He's a . . . family friend,' Toby said. 'Left-leaning. He dabbles, politically, though I don't think he has any *real* investment in it.

But he turns up at meetings here and there – I could introduce you, if you'd like?'

'I should like it very much, thank you.'

There was a pause, and Toby looked again at Mary's drawings. Ancient temple walls with broken pillars, and men in their desert robes, all captured with a few deft lines of the pencil.

'Mesopotamia,' he murmured.

'Well, no. Not really,' Mary said.

'No, I— I was thinking of somebody I used to know. She always wanted to travel to Mesopotamia. Though I don't suppose she ever did.'

'Why not?'

Toby looked down at his glass. 'She got married. Had children. The usual things women do.'

'Ah. You mean the usual things women are *constrained* to do.'

'You can't imagine that *every* woman would be off exploring the desert or . . . or . . . climbing the Matterhorn, if they only had the time and resources you have?'

'Oh, I don't think it, Mr Meriwether, I *know* it. Not the desert, necessarily, but whatever their equivalent passion might be.'

Toby smiled, not quite believing her. He thought Mary must be an exceptional sort of woman, to do all the bold and sometimes outlandish things she did. But could that be wrong? Perhaps, given a similar freedom, more women *would* be like her – adventurous, autodidactic, politically astute. The idea was unsettling. Like one of those optical illusions – a drawing that looked like a vase but transformed into two faces in profile without you moving your eyes one bit. The realisation that you'd been looking at it all wrong, or from one side only.

'Well, perhaps you could put in a word for your friend with Timothy Crudge?' Mary said. Toby stared at her blankly. 'Perhaps he might find a place for her on his next expedition, if she's a useful sort?'

'Oh, I see. Yes. Perhaps.'

At home, Toby rooted around in the cupboard under the stairs, moving clothes airers and broken lamps and shoes waiting to be re-soled, until he was able to drag out his old university trunk. In it was his notebook of Hallewell Castle's symbols. In it were Theo's unopened letters. He hadn't looked at them, or even thought about them, in a very long time. Now he took them to the table in the front window of his room, and poured himself a glass of wine. He counted the envelopes: thirty-seven, in total; the first from before he'd even left for Durham, the last – he squinted at the postmark – from June 1892. A decade ago. Of course, she could hardly have kept writing to him once she was married.

They spanned just three years. At the time it had seemed as though she'd kept writing for an age, and he was loath to remember being pleased about that. He'd wanted her to hurl herself against the fortress of his anger until she broke herself to pieces. And he *had* remained unconquered; he was just no longer sure whether that meant he'd won. He ought to open and read them all, or else get rid of them. He spread them out across the table, noticing the handwriting getting more sophisticated as time passed. She'd been fifteen when Kit had hanged. *Fifteen.* Yet he had made none of the allowances for her that he now argued for on behalf of young offenders everywhere.

Toby took a gulp of wine, selected a letter from the middle of the array, and opened it before he could change his mind.

I know I was cowardly not to do as you asked me. I let fear govern me, and I did not do as I should have done. You said that I'd given them a small piece of the picture and left them to misinterpret the rest, and you were right. I could have drawn that small part differently to make them see the truth of the whole. How I wish I had! But I only made things worse for him with the magistrate, and I didn't dare to try again in front of the judge. I was so very ill, by then. I think about Kit and Missy every day, and I think of you, too. Can you ever forgive me, Toby? Please, please do. It is agony to know that you hate me.

Toby dropped the letter and got to his feet. He paced, poured more wine and then stoppered the bottle and put it away, out of sight. The letters must be destroyed. He could no more undo the fact that they'd gone unanswered all these years than Theo could undo her absence from Kit's trial. He knew, now, why he hadn't opened them – because he would have forgiven her. Over time, he would have done; and he hadn't *wanted* to forgive her. He'd needed his rage. Back then, it was all that had kept him going. Now, at thirty-one, he saw quite clearly what his teenaged self had not.

But the letters were relics of another time. Theo would probably be mortified to know he still had them. She was a mother now; she was no longer the girl who'd dreamed of Mesopotamia. He pictured her with her handsome and successful husband, in their comfortable home, with their growing family, and doubted whether he or Kit ever crossed her mind any more. It was only natural. They'd been so young, and so much had changed since then. He picked up the letter he'd opened, intending to stuff it back into its envelope. Instead, more words caught his eye, and he found himself reading the whole thing.

Sometimes I dream about the moment you and Kit arrived at the castle that night, when it was all lit up by the moon and the candles, and you seemed so happy to see me even though it was just a stupid, childish game. I never want to wake up from that dream, but I always do.

And then, shockingly: *I still cannot understand why you said what you did in your last note to me, about the coin. I didn't want it back, I wanted Kit to keep it. I hoped it was helping him to feel brave.*

And I wanted to go and see him – I truly did. I would have gone, readily, but you had been so hard on me and told me I was no friend of yours or Kit's, so I didn't dare to ask you . . .

Toby sat back, winded, as it fell into place. It was blindingly obvious. Of *course* she hadn't asked for the coin back; of course she'd have wanted to see Kit. But, because it had suited him, he'd believed at once that she simply didn't care. He'd kept on believing it, and now saw that the underpinnings of his righteous anger had been pure fiction. The most probable explanation was that Diana Hallewell had intercepted his note, and retained it. *Mrs Hallewell is very keen for nothing to disturb her daughter.* That was how she'd found out about the coin, and why she'd come, so callously, to ask for it back.

That was why Theo hadn't answered his summons to visit Kit.

His fingers were shaking when he finally pushed the crowded paper back into the envelope. It was far, far too late now to take it back, or apologise. He gathered the letters together, took them over to the fireplace and put them in the grate. There were matches on the mantelpiece, and a few bits of kindling in the scuttle. He scattered the kindling, lit a match and waited for the flame to burn steadily. Staring at it, he was hurled back to the moment she'd described – climbing up to the castle at midnight, seeing her there with her candles and props and her air of nervous anticipation. He shut his eyes, and when the match burned his fingers he dropped it with a curse.

The memory was an ache, every bit as physical as the fragment of shot still lodged in his arm. He sighed, and opened his eyes. The letters were still in the grate, with the burnt-out match perched on top like a withered insect. He knew he wouldn't burn them, or throw them away; but he couldn't read any more of them, either. Her words caused flickers of the old chaos, when he liked to think he was the master of it now. He put them back in the trunk, then picked up his old notebook and sat leafing through the symbols, stacking his feet up on the windowsill and waiting to feel better.

Amazingly, perusing the notebook *did* still feel like catching up with an old friend. It was not because he wanted to go back. It was not because he missed that time, or Theo, or the person he'd been – gauche, and obnoxiously self-important. No, he decided: it was only because he might now be able to see something in the symbols that he hadn't before, and tie up that loose end. Not because he felt the beginnings of regret, setting in like rust.

Ralph came home in the particular sunken mood caused by the loss of a patient. The whole household sensed it, none more so than Theo. It had been twenty-seven days since he'd last hit her; she suspected it would not be that many before he did so again. She was torn, because asking him what was wrong could at times be as provoking as *not* asking him. She sent Arthur upstairs before approaching.

'Ralph? Is all well?'

'Is all well?' he echoed bitterly. 'No, it is not.'

'Will you tell me what's happened?'

'Do you care?'

He looked up with more sorrow than anger in his eyes, so she went closer and laid her hand on his arm.

'Of course I do.'

'Fetch wine first, I beg you.'

He gulped the first glassful with grim determination.

'Another one lost,' he said. 'When there was simply *no* cause for it that I could discern. What says that for my skill, and my knowledge?'

'What . . . Was the patient gravely ill?'

'Yes, though she did not seem so at first. Miss Breton. An elderly spinster. She slipped on a wet floor and hit her head against the wall, though she only called me out to reset her broken finger.'

Ralph poured more wine, slopping some on to the table. 'But, fortunately for her – or perhaps not, after all . . .'

He swept the spilled wine on to the rug. A scatter of droplets like blood.

'Fortunately, I noticed her blinking rapidly, as though unable to focus her eyes. I asked if her head ached, and she said that it did. So I invited her to attend the hospital, to be observed in case she worsened.'

'There was a wound to her head?' Theo asked.

'A bump, nothing more. Or so it seemed.'

Theo's mouth had gone dry. 'Yet she . . . worsened?'

'She did. I operated this morning – a trephining, to relieve the pressure.'

He was quiet for a long time.

'But . . . she did not survive it?' Theo whispered.

Ralph didn't answer, but she didn't need him to.

Only later, in the evening, did he speak again, by which time he was crumpled in a fireside chair, sodden with wine, staring morosely into the flames. Theo knew the shifts in his mood like a fisherman knows the tides. Such lassitude rarely led to violence; she was safe, for now, and sat nearest to the lamp, stitching Arthur's initials on to some new handkerchiefs.

A sudden flurry of words burst out of him: 'She was a spinster with *no kin*! That was what she told me. Mad, then, or a liar. It matters not which. The wretched man ought to be grateful I even tried, given how old she was.'

A shiver grazed the back of Theo's neck. 'Who ought to be grateful, Ralph?'

He waved a hand. 'Brother. Come out of nowhere. The old witch's neighbours sent him word.'

The fire popped; from along the back hall, the kitchen door closed with a muffled bump. Theo held her breath, hoping nothing would interrupt him.

'He saw her last night, and not a soul in the building saw fit to tell me! Well – let him run to the Council, as he threatens; let him claim he knows better! Foolish, ignorant man . . . They'll put him in his place, and make no bones about it.'

'What does it matter if her brother came to see her?' Theo said, but Ralph swivelled his groggy eyes towards her, so she returned to her sewing and pretended not to have spoken.

Her head thrummed with it. She could already guess at the story. Miss Breton's brother had seen her last night; Ralph had operated this morning. The patient was dead; the relative was aggrieved: he did not believe that she'd needed the operation. Theo felt the urgent need to act; as though, after thirteen years, she still had a chance to save her friends – to *do* something. She pricked her finger, and tasted her own blood.

It had been seven years since she'd discovered Missy's skull in the drawer of Ralph's cupboard. Seven years since she'd observed no sign of injury on the piece of bone her husband had cut away. Then she'd fallen pregnant twice, with an empty year in between, and then Arthur had come along to change everything. Soon after that Ralph had hit her for the first time, and since then she'd walked a daily tightrope between love and fear, joy and pain. There'd been little room to think of anything else. Her letters to Albert Mackie had concerned Arthur's health and her own, and nothing more about medical consent or vivisection.

But she decided to write again now, and ask him to relay anything he heard regarding a complaint to the General Medical Council about her husband, concerning a patient named Miss Breton.

Arthur had Ralph's blue eyes, and light-brown hair that turned almost coppery in the sun – Theo knew from one of the portraits at Hallewell that it had come from her own father. From her he'd inherited skin that freckled over the nose. *I see little enough of myself in him*, Ralph said once, drunk, and only half joking. *Are you quite certain he's mine?*

He was small for his four years, but not abnormally so, and despite his slightness and pallor he seemed robust – Theo could count on the fingers of one hand the number of coughs and colds he'd caught. He was quiet and biddable, and Theo wished he had a brother or sister to play with; an ally by his side should anything ever happen to her. She dreaded for him the loneliness of her own childhood. But every time she thought she might be carrying another child, it turned out she was not.

Arthur had a good friend in Percy Abbott, however. Hermione's youngest boy was a cheerful sort, with intensely carroty hair. He and Arthur were the same age, and similar in temperament, and had become friends at the instant of their meeting, in the way very young children often do. Whenever the Abbotts came to visit, or Theo took Arthur to visit them, the two little boys would disappear at once, and be found later in a den in the linen press, or under a bed, or up on the gallery of the library. They liked beetles, and marbles, and Snakes and Ladders. It filled Theo's heart to bursting. For her, a visit to the Abbotts' home was a welcome respite from Tout Hill House. There, she could speak without fear of an unforeseen reaction. There, she could breathe.

Hermione knew about Ralph's mistresses, but she knew nothing of his violence. Nobody did. Theo wouldn't have told her even if she hadn't feared Ralph's reaction to such indiscretion. Their marriage was her own private hell, and she had no wish to drag the Abbotts into it. To embarrass them, or have them pity her.

Hermione caught glimpses of Ralph and his lady friends around town. She heard whispers. The cat-faced woman Theo had seen was called Evelyn Duchamp, whom Ralph had met in secret for several years. Now she was gone, and it was Clare Fitzherbert who kept him out late. Theo had seen her, too – willowy, pale, and golden-haired. Younger than Theo. A lot like Theo, in fact – as she had been when they'd wed. Ralph had treated Clare for melancholia, too. Theo didn't want to know anything else about her, though. She was neither jealous, nor angry, nor curious. She was nothing.

'I'm certain he loves you, in spite of it,' Hermione said on one occasion, mistakenly thinking that what Theo wanted was to be loved by her husband. All she wanted, in fact, was to be left alone. 'Some men are simply . . .' She threw up her hands, at a loss.

Theo was standing by the brass cage in which a pair of African finches perched, cocking their heads, examining her with eyes like jet beads. Ralph had bought the birds for her after breaking two of her ribs. There was often a present to go with his apology – bottles of scent, a silk shawl, new stockings. He'd soon changed his mind about the finches, though, offended by the smell of their cage. Theo had gifted them to Beryl, the eldest Abbott girl.

'Some men are what, Hermione?' She turned with a sad smile for her friend, whose expression was dismayed. 'And why should he love me? I do not love him.'

'*Theo!*'

'But it's the truth. I never did, no matter how I tried. So I can hardly object if he seeks affection elsewhere.'

'Would *he* object if *you* did?' Hermione said.

Theo didn't answer. What Ralph might do if he caught her in a betrayal – any betrayal – was too terrible to imagine. She felt sorry for Hermione, having to cast about for something encouraging to say.

'I have Arthur,' she said. 'He is all I need.'

And all the while she was expected to entertain various Shaftesbury notables, and visiting surgeons, and neighbours, and the Fortescues; to smile and be polite and find things to say – just enough to be sociable; never enough to give herself away, or betray their fiction for what it was. In company, Ralph was gentle and solicitous towards her; he was an affable and generous host, and put people at their ease, while Theo laboured beneath Fortescue's cold, contemptuous stare. The older doctor gave the impression that he knew everything, and detested her all the more for it.

Some weeks later, she had a letter from Dr Mackie. She put Arthur down for a nap before opening it, and checked from an upstairs window that there was no sign of Ralph returning.

> *My dear Mrs Anscombe,*
> *Miss Breton's brother has received short shrift from the General Medical Council – which, alas, I was not at all surprised to hear. He now plans to take his case to the police, and will endeavour to bring charges of manslaughter against your husband. I am certain he will fail in this, too.*
>
> *If a surgeon deemed an operation necessary to the preservation of life, and in addition was granted permission by the patient to proceed, then there is little cause for any such complaint to progress – the police, sadly, can have no opinion as to whether or not the operation was appropriate.*
>
> *I suppose the very fact of Mr Breton's sister being able to give her consent supports his testimony that when he saw her the evening prior to her operation, she was not suffering from pain or confusion. Dr Anscombe's assertion that she'd been all but insensible by the morning, following a precipitous deterioration during the night, rings false. However, at the time of the operation Dr Anscombe had no knowledge of the existence of any relatives. Had she deteriorated*

badly – which, though unlikely, is not impossible – he would have given no thought to seeking further permission before proceeding.

The post-mortem examination found the cause of death to be a clot of blood upon the brain, though whether the cause of it was the original injury or the subsequent treatment, it is impossible to tell. I am certain the police will not touch it, and I can think of no other way in which Mr Breton might proceed.

I understand why this case has upset you, Mrs Anscombe. The similarities are marked. More is the pity, then, that similarities between two cases do not prove a pattern of behaviour. In truth, I am not sure how such a pattern might ever be proved. I will write again if I hear more.

I remain, at your service,
Dr. Albert M. Mackie

Theo sat rigid. She re-read the letter then got up and paced, trying to think it through. Because it was not about herself, or about Miss Breton or her brother; really, it was not even about Ralph or Missy. It was about Kit.

Time passed and she couldn't unpick it. She began a reply to Albert: *You mentioned to me some time ago that an expert in bones might be able to tell from a skull whether a head wound had been lethal or not. Are you acquainted with such an expert, Dr Mackie?* She broke off, fingers aching because she'd been clenching the pen too hard.

I do begin to see a pattern, most terribly perturbing. We have touched upon this before. It is a pattern of people with nobody to speak for them – paupers and widows, those alone in the world – being persuaded or coerced into surgical operations that they do not truly need. Operations mortally dangerous to them, that do more to advance the skill and reputation of the surgeon than their own well-being. But surely the needs and rights of the individual must outweigh, in every case, the needs and demands of medicine itself?

As soon as she'd written it, Theo was struck by the certainty that there must have been others, down the years. Not just Missy, not just Miss Breton, but other poor people, other elderly people, other people who would not be missed. *Mortuus Est.* Something hardened inside her. Yet she still didn't know what to do. Ralph had saved lives, undoubtedly. But what if those had been at the expense of others? She couldn't remain silent, but she couldn't denounce her husband. The very thought turned her blood to water. It would be an unforgivable betrayal if her suspicions, let alone a campaign of any kind, were ever discovered; no matter that he had betrayed her first.

But she did not want Mr Breton brushed aside and silenced, the way she herself had been. She wanted to help him.

Audrey knocked at her door.

'Miss? Are you resting? It's almost time to wake Arthur – shall I? And Mrs Meredith wants to know whether you want raspberries or dried coconut on—'

Theo couldn't keep it in any longer. 'Oh, *Audrey*! I don't know what to do!'

Audrey tried to sit her down. 'Shh, now – do about what?'

'Miss Breton, who died. I think . . . I think she died because of my husband!'

'You what?'

It poured out. Missy's skull; the way she'd died so suddenly; the way Ralph had bought the right to dissect her. Miss Breton, and how very similarly she had met her end. Ralph's ambition, and all the times he'd slipped up and said something careless about his failures, and about not having enough patients with head injuries to work upon.

'And if I'm right . . . If I am right, then Kit Meriwether didn't kill Missy at all! Do you see? He was *never* responsible, though he was hanged. And I . . . I don't know how I shall ever prove it. I don't know what to *do*!'

Audrey sat silent when Theo finished. Her eyes were glassy with shock, but behind them Theo saw her turning it over and over.

'You cannot bring him back, miss,' she said eventually. 'The lad that hanged . . . he's gone.'

'I know. But his family are still alive. They could have his good name restored, and bring home what remains of him, at last. Home from the prison.'

Audrey nodded. 'Yes. I see.'

Theo grabbed one of her hands, staring into her face. 'If I am right . . .' she said. 'If I am right about my husband, and what he has done . . . then how could I *ever* love such a man? A man who would do such things?'

'How could anybody, miss?' Audrey was grave.

'All this time I have thought the fault was mine, but . . . perhaps I have been right to keep my heart from him?'

'I've never thought the fault was yours, miss. Not once.'

And, as so often happened, Audrey came up with a solution.

Two weeks later, Ralph came home with a copy of *The Western Chronicle* in his fist, and his face twitching with anger. Theo recoiled when she saw him; they hadn't expected him back until the evening. The weather was humid; the sky clotted with clouds. She was in the garden with Arthur, playing with his building blocks, and before they could even say hello Ralph had grabbed Theo's wrist and hauled her to her feet.

'Leave that and come with me. I want a word.'

He hurried her indoors, leaving Arthur standing uncertainly with one blue wooden block in his hand.

'Ralph, please – you're hurting me,' Theo said pointlessly.

Inside, he spun around and held the newspaper so close to her face she could smell the ink.

'Was this you, Theo? *Was* it?'

'Was *what* me? I don't know what you mean.'

'Oh, really?'

He glared at her, a vein writhing at his temple. She shook her head desperately, but she *did* know. She'd written to the newspaper editor anonymously, as Audrey had suggested. A letter of support for Mr Breton, deploring the way his concerns had been ignored by the medical establishment; suggesting that, if the house surgeon *had* been reckless, there may well be other such cases in the hospital's recent history. Suggesting that Mr Breton – and the newspaper – put out an appeal for any similarly troubled relatives to come forward.

Her heart raced with the anticipation of violence. There was no way he could have found out; but then, she'd thought that about her day out with Timothy Crudge. Ralph screwed the newspaper in his hands, then cuffed her around the head with it, speaking through gritted teeth.

'You never could lie very well, Theo. I know all about your *concerns* regarding one such operation I performed. All your *insinuations* . . . Was this you? I will have the truth!'

She shrank from him. 'Ralph, stop!'

'Tell me the truth!'

'I know nothing about it!'

Ralph hit her with the paper again, which was more humiliating than painful; then shoved her so hard that she stumbled back and crashed against a table, where a vase fell on to its side and broke cleanly in half with a loud slop of water, scattering the flower stems.

The corner of the table drove into Theo's stomach and she gagged, sinking to her knees, as Ralph aimed a kick that caught her hip and flung her back against the table. She heard the wood splinter. All she could do was curl up, hands over her head, and try to protect herself until it ran its course. She fought for air; pain radiated from her hip, and the leg on that side was numb and useless.

'Get up,' Ralph said.

She felt him wrestling for one of her arms, endeavouring to drag her up.

Then Ralph grunted, and something clattered to the floor beside Theo. She opened her eyes and saw a small blue block, and looked up, horrified. There was Arthur, standing by the door, eyes huge and fixed on his father. He'd thrown it, she realised. Thrown it to try to stop Ralph.

'Run and play, Arty,' she gasped. 'Off you go! Run and play!'

But Ralph had him before he could.

'Am I to be attacked by my own *son*, now? How *dare* you? It is your *mother* who has asked for this treatment! Come here, boy!'

He dragged Arthur to a chair, sat down and threw him over his knees.

'Oh, Ralph, please don't!' Theo cried. 'Please – he's so little! He doesn't understand—'

Ralph fixed her with a furious look. 'Do you imagine that I enjoy this? *You* have turned him against me! But he must learn that I am to be obeyed.'

'*Mama!*' Arthur wailed.

Ralph took off his shoe and brought it down hard on Arthur's behind, three, four times. It made a terrible sound.

Only their breathing broke the silence afterwards. Then Arthur started to cry. Theo crawled towards him and he wriggled backwards off his father's lap, bolting into her arms. She looked up to check that Ralph had finished, and in that moment, she *hated* him.

'Are we raising a boy, or a snivelling little girl?' Ralph said. But perhaps something in her expression hit home, because he seemed less sure of himself. 'Theo . . .' he said quietly.

She ignored him, rocking her son, as Ralph put his shoe back on and left them there.

'There, now,' she said, setting Arthur back and finding a smile. 'Soon it won't hurt at all.'

She got to her feet, wincing. Her left leg was still dead from the kick, and the hip itself was throbbing, but the fire below her ribs was now only embers. 'There – see?' she said. 'I'm quite all right, too. Let's go upstairs, shall we?'

An hour later Arthur had recovered, and was looking at one of his picture books. But Theo knew, in her bones, that this was only the start of it for him. And she knew she couldn't stand it. She asked Audrey to send for a cab, and set about packing a bag.

Ralph stopped them by the front door.

'What's this? Where are you off to?' he asked conversationally, as though nothing had happened. Theo tightened her grip on Arthur's hand.

'Away,' she said.

'Away? Where? And why?'

'You know why.' Theo's voice shook. 'Audrey, please take Arthur to the carriage. I'll be along in just a moment.'

'Yes, miss.'

'You will address your mistress as *madam*,' Ralph snapped. Audrey ignored him.

Theo turned to face her husband. 'I will not let you beat him, Ralph.'

'I am the boy's father,' he said, his voice lacking conviction. 'Theo—'

'He is four years old, and he was trying to protect me. I will not let you beat him.'

'Where are you going?'

Theo's gaze slid away. 'Somewhere safe.'

Ralph stepped closer. 'I see. But if you intend to go to that man, Theo – to your *uncle* – then know that I will bring the full weight of the law down upon him. Mark my words. I shall have him hauled before a court to answer for his unnatural ways, and all the world will know his debauchery.'

Theo caught her breath. Of course she'd planned to go to Crudge – it was the only place she could run to. Triumph and anger turned Ralph's handsome face ugly.

'I plan . . . to see my mother,' she whispered. 'You must do nothing to harm Mr Crudge. He is perfectly innocent.'

'Is he hell.' Ralph spoke with quiet intensity. 'But I'll have no need to spare him a thought, so long as you keep away from him.' He leaned towards her before she could pull away, kissed her cheek and whispered: 'To Hallewell with you, then. A little holiday, during which time I suggest you think upon your duties as my wife.'

Diana was pleased, if bemused, to see her daughter and grandson. She pressed her cheek to Theo's without actually kissing her, and patted Arthur on the head.

'Had we a plan for you to visit?'

'No, I just . . . I wanted to come away for a while,' Theo said. 'And to see you.'

Diana clasped her hands. 'How lovely. We've a full house, so I'm afraid it's rather busy.' They turned to go inside, and Diana frowned. 'Theo, why are you walking in that peculiar fashion?'

'I've hurt my leg,' Theo said. 'I . . . tripped. On the stairs.'

'Well, you ought to be more careful. You'll want to go and unpack – I'm glad you've brought Audrey, because poor Kitty has quite enough to do. Now, I must get back to Mr and Mrs Collard, who wish to tour the castle. Unless – I don't suppose you might like to take them . . . ?'

'My leg is rather sore, Mama.'

She settled Arthur for a nap on the cot bed that had been set up next to hers. Audrey stayed with him – her nose in a book – and Theo, careful not to be seen by her mother, went out into the buttery light of the afternoon. She walked slowly to West End, thinking of David Meriwether, who made that walk every day with his far more severely lamed leg. The way seemed longer, the hills steeper. At St Mary's she paid her respects to her father, who lay in the Hallewell tomb, before going to stand beside Missy's grave.

The churchyard was as tranquil as ever, and a song thrush carolled from the top of an ancient yew, but Theo couldn't feel peaceful. Looking at the sunken mound only reminded her that Missy was not intact: she had been robbed of her skull as well as her life. *The dead can suffer no indignity*, Dr Mackie had said, but it didn't feel that way to Theo. Though she could no longer marvel at the sacred, she still felt the outrage of desecration. So, perhaps the indignity of the mutilation, and the pain, was all with those still living, who had loved that person. She didn't think that made it any less of an outrage.

'I'm so sorry, Missy,' she whispered, feeling more than ever that she had let her friend down. 'Dr Anscombe is . . . not what we thought him to be.'

She wondered if that was fair. If Ralph *had* been good, in fact, and the way she'd constantly disappointed him had changed him, and made him violent. But was it not violent to cut off a young girl's head, even if she were dead? A head that had surrendered to him trustingly, full of fantastical hopes.

'I will return it to you, I promise,' Theo murmured.

She felt lost and unsafe. Like she'd stepped away from the world and everyone in it, and was drifting out of reach. But she resolved not to go back to Ralph; not if it meant putting her son in danger. She could not tolerate Arthur being hurt, or frightened. She *would not*. But if she couldn't go to Crudge, then where?

After a week, Diana asked how long she intended to stay.

'I've had a letter from Ralph, you see,' she said. 'He misses you.'

'*You've* had a letter from him?' Theo said. 'Why should he write to you, and not me?'

'Why indeed?'

They were in their private sitting room, in the quiet hour before dinner.

'Mother, I . . .' Theo struggled to say it. 'I have left him.'

'Whatever can you mean?'

'I mean not to return to him. May I – may we – stay here with you? For the time being, at least?'

Diana gave her a long look. Her expression betrayed nothing, but her tone, when she spoke, was frigid. 'I'm not sure I understand you, Theodora.'

'This limp . . . I didn't trip.'

'Theo—'

'He beats me, Mama. He has done for years. And just last week he . . . he beat Arthur too, and I—'

'Ralph said in his letter that he'd been forced to discipline the boy.'

'*Discipline* him?'

'What on earth is the matter with you? Of *course* the boy must be corrected – how else will he learn how to behave? You mollycoddle him. He's not made of soap bubbles, you know.'

'Did Ralph tell you why?' Theo said, choking on the outrage. 'Arthur was protecting *me*. At four years of age, he was attempting to protect me from his own father!'

'Lower your voice!' Diana snapped. 'I won't have a scandal, Theo. If Ralph is cross, then you must simply not provoke him.

Surely you know by now what causes him to lose his temper? And so you may take steps to ensure that it does not happen again. A husband's happiness is a wife's duty.'

Theo didn't reply at once. 'Ralph caused me to fall, last year. I fell across the arm of the settle, and I – I started to bleed. I was carrying another child. Just the early beginnings of one, but still . . . I lost it.'

Diana softened fractionally. 'If so, then it's a pity. Men often do not appreciate their own strength. But these are private matters between you and your husband, Theo.'

'How can you be so hard on me?' Theo was bewildered. 'Though we have not always been close, I am still your daughter.'

'And I am your mother, so heed my advice. Go home to your husband, and behave in the proper way. Do not give him cause to chastise you. You were always wilful and . . . difficult. You married a good man, but even a good man may be driven to distraction by a disorderly wife.'

She stood up and gazed down at Theo; her face was pinched, but Theo couldn't guess what she was feeling.

'You cannot stay here. I won't have a scandal.'

'Yes,' Theo said woodenly. 'You said that already.'

She left the next day and took a room at the Grosvenor Arms Hotel in Shaftesbury, sending a telegram to Crudge to ask for help with the bill. She had very little money of her own – only a small amount of cash, which Ralph gave her each month for sundries. At any moment she expected word to reach him, as it always seemed to. She expected him to appear, wearing his smiling public face, and take her home to face the consequences.

A day passed, and another. The waiting was awful. She was known in Shaftesbury; somebody would see her, sooner or later. Whispers would pass from busy lips to eager ears – they always did. At mealtimes, she took a table far from the window and sat facing away from the room. Her skin crawled at each new set of footsteps, and when the door opened she didn't dare turn to look. Audrey, who had a view of the room, met her eye and gave a minute shake of her head.

Theo realised she'd made no kind of escape. She'd only put them all in worse danger. The one friend in the world she might run to she could not, for fear of taking trouble to him. But she couldn't go back.

The longcase clock in the foyer interrupted its ponderous ticking to whirr, and strike noon.

'Look, Mama,' Arthur said, making her jump. He had a sticky moustache of hot chocolate, and she couldn't help but smile.

'What is it?'

She'd borrowed the pencil and jotter from their room, and he'd been scribbling in it. He turned the page towards her. The lines wandered here and there in an unruly fashion, but in them Theo made out an animal of some kind. A neck, a body, skinny legs.

'That's very good Arty,' she said. 'What is it?'

'A hen,' Arthur declared. He pointed out through the window behind him, where chickens were scratching the bare earth of their coop.

'Of course it is,' she said. 'A most excellent hen, in fact.'

At that moment, footsteps did come towards them. Theo's heart lurched but it was only the clerk of the hotel, with a telegram from Crudge.

'What does he say?' Audrey asked.

Theo read it quickly. 'He's sending a lawyer to meet me here.' She glanced at the clock. 'He's travelling down today, and should be here by two o'clock.'

'A lawyer? Can he do something, then?'

'Well, I don't know. But I don't think my uncle would send him unless he thought so.' Theo took a deep breath, hope rising.

'Perhaps there's some way I might be granted independence . . .' She didn't want to say more in front of Arthur. 'Might you take Arty to visit the horses, Audrey, while I speak with him?'

The solicitor was a youngish man, with kind eyes in a broad face, and a ready smile.

'Thomas Womersley, at your service,' he introduced himself.

'Theodora Anscombe. Thank you for travelling all this way to talk to me.'

'My pleasure entirely, Mrs Anscombe,' he said. 'It's rather a treat, in fact, to be let out of London for a while. Now . . .' He unpacked a ledger, a pen and ink. 'Why don't we begin at the beginning?'

Womersley didn't hurry her; he waited patiently while she fought to explain her situation both honestly and discreetly. During one quiet spell the door banged across the room, and she couldn't help an involuntary gasp.

'May I interrupt you, Mrs Anscombe?' Womersley said.

'Please, do.'

'I fear I may be the bearer of bad news.' He spoke gently, but Theo sank inside. 'A petition for a period of judicial separation from your husband, on the grounds of cruelty, might only be sought had he been charged and convicted of an assault upon you. Have you ever . . . sought to bring such charges?'

'Charged as in . . . by the police?'

'Yes?'

'No, I . . . I haven't.'

'I quite understand. It is no small undertaking, and such accusations can be very hard to prove. Most do not end with success, unless some permanent and obvious injury has been done to the lady in question.'

'Then . . . the wife may be compelled to remain with her husband, though she has endeavoured to bring charges against him?'

'Yes. I fear so.'

Theo said nothing.

'Should you ever bring charges, and Dr Anscombe be convicted, we might then attempt such a petition. However, I feel I must warn you that it is a lengthy and costly procedure, which must pass through the Chancery Division.'

'My husband controls all of my money.'

'Well, Mr Crudge has offered to fund any such action. But . . . the fees could easily run into the hundreds of pounds, if not the thousands.'

'So much?' Theo breathed.

'Indeed. Which is why only the very wealthy proceed, though they are the least likely to wish to do so, given the inevitable damage to their . . . position.' Womersley gave her a rueful look. 'But there is worse. It strikes me that you are an attentive mother, and would not wish to be separated from your son?'

'Separated from Arthur? Not *ever*.'

'I understand. However . . . should your petition for separation from your husband be successful, you would not necessarily retain custody of the boy. We would have to petition against your husband, for both custody and access, until his sixteenth birthday. And such petitions can fail.'

Under Womersley's apologetic gaze, Theo's resolve crumbled. Twin tears slipped down her face, and Womersley gave her his handkerchief.

'Then it is impossible,' she said. 'Did my uncle send you here to that end? To make me see beyond doubt that it's hopeless?'

'I think he sent me to do whatever I could. And, regretfully, what I can do is very little. Marriage, within the law, is sacrosanct.'

'Though a wife is made to suffer fear and pain, whilst her husband does as he pleases?'

'In far too many cases, yes. I'm terribly sorry to disappoint you, Mrs Anscombe.'

He said it so sincerely that Theo believed him.

'You are a married man, Mr Womersley?'

He smiled involuntarily. 'I am indeed. And blessed with three delightful youngsters.'

'I can tell from the way you brighten that you love them. And would never hurt them.'

Womersley's smile disappeared. 'Indeed, I wouldn't harm a hair on their heads, nor tolerate anyone else to do so. And it grieves me that not all men feel or behave in the same way.'

'But at least there are those like you in the world. That is something to be grateful for.' Theo hung her head. 'If you met my husband, you would like him. Everybody does.'

Womersley took his leave soon afterwards.

Theo took one more night away from Ralph. She and Audrey lay either side of the bed with Arthur sound asleep between them. Before long Audrey drifted off as well, but Theo stayed awake.

She went through it from every possible direction, but the answer was always the same. She could not remain indefinitely in Shaftesbury. She might go to a hotel in a different town, or even take an apartment, but only if Timothy Crudge continued to foot the bill, which Ralph would certainly discover. She couldn't risk causing any trouble for the old man. Her husband's abhorrence of him was as strong as it was unreasoning. She couldn't bring charges of assault against Ralph until the next time he left her with visible injuries, and even then she didn't think she could face it. The gossip; the opprobrium. And all of it only to risk separating herself from Arthur.

Marriage was a steel trap. She'd been foolish to think she could prise open its jaws and escape.

Ralph enjoyed his reputation of benevolence and charm; perhaps of genius. Theo knew it from the way he behaved in company, the way he absorbed compliments with a modest glow but no embarrassment. Her short absence could easily be passed off as a visit to family, but still. Theo expected the potential exposure of the true state of their relationship to have enraged him. She expected bruises, perhaps fractures, and the taste of blood. She expected Audrey to be fired. When they arrived back, in silence, she went up to the bedroom to wait, wanting to get it over with.

But when Ralph came home and found her there he flung himself to his knees instead, gripping her skirts in his fists as he let out a single, loud sob.

'Forgive me, my darling,' he said. 'Please don't leave me . . . I do love you so!'

Eventually, steeling herself, Theo laid one hand on his head. His shoulders heaved.

'I have behaved like an animal,' he said. 'But I will be better. I *will* be better. I just . . . I love you both, so very much, and it . . . it hurts me to see how well you love one another, and how little is left for me.'

'Oh, Ralph! Of *course* Arthur loves you,' Theo said. 'You're his papa – he worships you.'

'Then why does he cringe from me?'

She didn't reply. Experience had taught her not to trust his contrition, and certainly not to rely on it. Anything she said now would be remembered, and perhaps used against her further down the line.

'He's just so very little,' she said weakly. 'That was what upset me so.'

'I won't lay a finger on him again, I swear it. Not without the most serious provocation.'

Ralph looked up, and she was shocked by his pleading face, his trembling mouth. There were lines around his eyes now, and grey strands through his hair. His neck was thicker than it had been, his cheeks mottled with broken capillaries. He was distraught, but she couldn't feel sorry for him. Once, perhaps, but not any more. *The most serious provocation*. Who knew how trivial a thing that might turn out to be?

She was offended by his mimicry of love.

'I won't be a brute to you any more,' he said. 'You do believe me, Theo?'

'Yes,' she lied. 'Of course I do.'

'You would never . . . work against me, would you?'

'Of *course* I would not,' she intoned, with a sudden thump of guilt that made her feel sick.

'I know it; I do. You must hate me. Oh, how you must hate me! When all I ever wanted was to be loved by you.'

'I don't hate you, Ralph.'

His resolution might last a week a two, she supposed; perhaps up to a month. He would be home promptly at the end of the day; he'd be sober, solicitous, gentle in bed. But it wouldn't last. She could not feign love any better now than before, and his anger would return.

But, much sooner than she'd guessed, he came home very late one evening, and undressed quietly, as though not to disturb her. He slid into bed beside her and whispered, tightly, close to her ear:

'If you *ever* do that again, Theo . . . If you *dare* to make a public spectacle of yourself, or of me, then I shall know you have become irrational. I am your physician and your husband; I would need no second opinion before sending you away for treatment. Your mother mentioned it once, before we were married, and perhaps I was wrong to dissuade her. I would do *whatever* was needed to restore you to reason, Theo. As is my duty.'

Theo held her breath. She knew he could do it. He could impose an open-ended stay at a sanatorium; take what freedom she had with a word, and separate her from Arthur indefinitely. She would be powerless to stop him.

She didn't dare to cry.

Two weeks later, a letter came. The envelope had been addressed first to *Miss Hallewell*, at Hallewell House; but it had been corrected in her mother's handwriting, and sent on. Theo didn't recognise the original hand, though it had a Shaftesbury postmark. The letter was scruffy, the paper thin and inexpensive.

5, Church Street, Motcombe
12th October

Dear Miss Hallewell
You do not know me but I know you. That is to say I remember you from a goodly time back. Now it comes to it I hardly know what to write or whether I should but I saw the bit in the paper about the Hospital and that fellow and his sister and it hant let me alone ever since.

I was a nurse at the hospital for a time. I was not married then and my name was Sarah Webster. Now I am Mrs Toller since I married Clarence Toller the grocer here at Motcombe. I was there when your friend was in for the cut on her head. Melissa Cartwright she was called. I hant forgot her name. I remember you from when you came to visit her. I was the one you saw who took you along to the ward tho we were halted there by the doctor. Another time

I heard you talking to Sister Hendry and the doctor about her. I was passing by looking for Sister and I heard you ask if there may be some other things that had gone wrong with Melissa other than the bump on her head and them telling you 'no' and what she had been suffering before they operated on her.

It hant ever sat right with me since I know it was not true. I asked Sister about it soon after or I tried to since she would not speak of it. And before long I was dismissed. Sister said it was because I was not cut out for it and maybe that was it. I did not make a good nurse really. I liked the people and wanted to look after them but I would swoon at the sight of blood or muck. To begin with they said it was normal and I would grow out of it but I never did so maybe that was the reason. But that she sent me off so suddenly perhaps was not by chance.

I cut Melissa's hair for her before they took her down for her operation. That was the Monday morn when she later died that same day. A section of her hair needed to come off so that Dr Anscombe could tell the full extent of the injury and where to make the operation. She was such a quick and jolly girl and we were of an age more or less. She made no fuss at all. 'The doc wants a closer look at my bonce' so she said. We had a joke and a laugh in fact. She bid me cut the hair neat so she should still look pretty for the doctor. 'Do not do it like the time Pip took the shears to me' so she said and she was all smiles. I did it as gentle as may be but she said not to worry for her head did not hurt one bit any more.

Then afterwards I heard them tell you she had gone much worse and was at deaths door. But that Monday morn as she was about to go down for the operation I had a laugh and a joke with her and she was right as rain. I swear my oath on it.

It has sat heavy on me all this while and tho it is thirteen years since it is fresh in my mind and I know I have it right. There never seemed much to be done once she was dead and then that poor lad Christopher hanged too. Dead and buried the pair of them. And I knew Dr Anscombe to be a good man so I said nothing thinking perhaps I had it wrong or else an honest mistake was made. But now I think it was none of that. I have written to you and not to the newspaper because I do not know what good or evil my saying so might do. It was not right and that is Gods own truth. And I have known in my heart since I heard you talking to them that you did not credit it either however much they would have it their way. So perhaps you will know what to do.

Yours truly in good faith
Mrs Sarah Toller

Chapter Sixteen

Toby accompanied Mary Gladwell to a talk Timothy Crudge was giving at The Athenæum, to launch his book on English folklore – finally finished after five years of endeavour. It was a wet, windswept evening at the fag end of October. Inside, the lecture room blazed with light, and the warmth of two hundred bodies.

Toby only half listened to the lecture; it wasn't really of interest. It was the end of a busy week, and he was content to let Crudge's familiar, sonorous voice lull him. Mary was paying enough attention for the both of them – no fidgeting, no people-spotting. She was the only woman in the audience. Somehow, the usual rules didn't seem to apply to Mary Gladwell, and she pointedly refused to notice when disgruntled looks were aimed her way.

Toby drifted pleasantly, his mind wholly off guard.

'Now, when we compare these prevalent tropes to the legends of Abrecan of Hallewell, in Wessex, as was,' Crudge said, 'we find, again, rebirth, endless life, a further iteration of the philosopher's stone . . .'

The memory engulfed Toby. The scent of warm earth and summer grass, of cider apples on soft breath. Candlelight reflecting in eyes that had filled with desire when they looked his way. Theo Hallewell, turning her face into his hand. Heat flooded him. A feeling like falling. Toby swallowed hard, tugging at his collar, and ignored Mary's enquiring glance.

Please . . . It is agony to know that you hate me . . .

For a few tormented heartbeats, Toby was consumed by the need to tell her that he didn't. That he never had.

The assault was mercifully short. By the end of the lecture he had mastered himself, and took Mary over to be introduced to Crudge, as promised. The room thronged with conversation, as waiters brought out glasses of champagne on silver trays.

'Delighted, delighted,' Crudge said, as he shook Mary's hand.

'As am I,' Mary said. 'I thoroughly enjoyed your talk, Mr Crudge. I do look forward to reading more.'

'Well, well,' the old man said modestly, accepting the glass Nicholas Bourton had fetched for him. 'You are too kind, my dear.'

'Mrs Gladwell shares your love of exploration, Mr Crudge,' Toby said. 'She has travelled to many of the ancient places of the Near East.'

Crudge's wiry eyebrows shot up. 'Indeed? But how wonderful!'

They talked for a while about where they had been, what they had seen, and where they might travel to next.

'Nineveh, if Nicholas and I can get ourselves organised,' Crudge said. 'The older one gets, the more *complicated* it seems to become.'

'Try being female,' Mary said, with a smile.

'Ha! Indeed, I am sure.'

'Speaking of which, Toby, what of your friend?' Mary said. 'The one who wanted to go to Mesopotamia? Perhaps Mr Crudge might have space for her on his trip to Nineveh.'

Her face registered puzzlement at the startled pause that followed, and the long look that passed between Toby and Crudge.

'Have I put my foot in it?' she said at length. 'I do beg your pardon.'

'Not at all, my dear Mrs Gladwell,' Crudge said. 'I was merely taken aback. I know very well who you must mean, you see. Mrs

Anscombe is a mutual friend of ours, of long-standing. I should like nothing better than to take her travelling, should she still wish to go. Alas, things are not so simple. If I – or anyone – might think of a way to free her up for it, then I'd be delighted.'

Toby took an inelegant gulp of champagne, and looked away.

'It was only a . . . passing thought,' he said tightly. 'A memory that surfaced.'

'Indeed?' Crudge said.

Tactfully, Mary changed the subject. 'Are you acquainted with Geoffrey Mortmain, Mr Crudge? I think I see him over there – now, *he's* an interesting fellow, by all accounts . . .'

But for the rest of the evening, Toby felt precarious. He kept catching Crudge's glances, which were as penetrating as ever. Seeing things that Toby didn't want him to see. Things he barely understood himself; things that were impossible. There was a faint tremor in his gut. He gripped his glass too tightly, and only half listened to the conversation. He wanted to leave the stuffy room, and the distinguished club. Take a breath of cold air. He needed reality – his true and present reality – to reassert itself, because this growing sense of aimless urgency was alarming. The sudden desire to grasp Crudge's arm, and surrender to what the old man seemed already to know. To blurt it out – something Toby had never thought could ever be true:

I want to go back.

That same evening, Theo sat for a long while by Arthur's bedside. A fitful wind threw bursts of rain against the window, and in the quiet lulls between she heard her son's soft breathing, as regular and reassuring as gentle waves on a shore. It lowered her heart rate, slowly restoring a sense of the calm she craved.

Her head was throbbing, but her cheek seemed to have stopped swelling. It would go down in a few days, then the bruise could be masked with powder and she might go outside again. Gingerly, she touched her ribs on the left side and felt the lance of pain. But she didn't think they were broken – she was learning how to tell: this time, it was too easy to breathe. Where – or to whom – Ralph had stormed off to, she had no idea. It hardly mattered. She counted her blessings instead: he was not there right now. Arthur had not been touched. He had not discovered her letters from Albert Mackie, or Timothy Crudge. He had not discovered her letter from Sarah Toller.

The nurse's letter was well hidden. Theo knew it by heart – every inflammatory, damning, miraculous word of it. She could almost feel it reverberating, wherever she was in the house. It was a weapon, and a key. A gift so precious she was terrified of the responsibility of owning it.

Arthur breathed, and slept, and Theo thought of Kit, and of Missy; of her fleeting, ephemeral sister, Amy, and of Rosalind Mackie. However hard she tried, she still couldn't grasp where the dead went. She'd been taught that the answer was to heaven or hell, but these days heaven seemed like a picture in a book, not a real place at all. And if there was no heaven, what then? Why put a posy of flowers on a headstone, if the person couldn't look down to see? Why fret about an unlovely grave? The idea that a person stayed with their decaying body, trapped in the darkness, was too terrible. But how, then, could they simply cease to exist? All that *life*; all those thoughts and feelings.

It would happen to her one day. And it would happen to Arthur – a quick stab of agony worse than any broken bone.

The dead can suffer no indignity.

So, did it matter what became of their earthly remains? Their memory? Logically, it did not, but Theo's heart wouldn't agree. It *mattered.* In the same way it mattered that Kit was buried alongside murderers, in the prison yard in Dorchester. It mattered that he had been executed for a crime he hadn't committed. It mattered that Missy had been robbed of her life, and then of her head, in the pursuit of surgical skill. Both so young, and so full of life; so deserving of the futures that had been taken from them.

And Theo had married the man who'd killed them both.

All any of us can do, in any situation, is speak truthfully. So Ralph had said to her, around the time of Kit's trial. And yet he had lied, and lied, and lied.

The proof was in Sarah Toller's letter, thrumming with portent, loaded with possibility. And with that proof Theo might find a way to clear Kit's name, and bring him home. A way to keep her promise to Missy. A way, perhaps, to free herself from a marriage that was slowly crushing her. The thought was tantalising, terrifying. Her knees ached as though she were somewhere very high; a place from which she might fall . . . or perhaps fly. The rain fell, Arthur slept, and the night wore on. With steady determination, Theo pulled her scattered thoughts to order, and searched inside for the strength to act.

Because she *had* to find it.

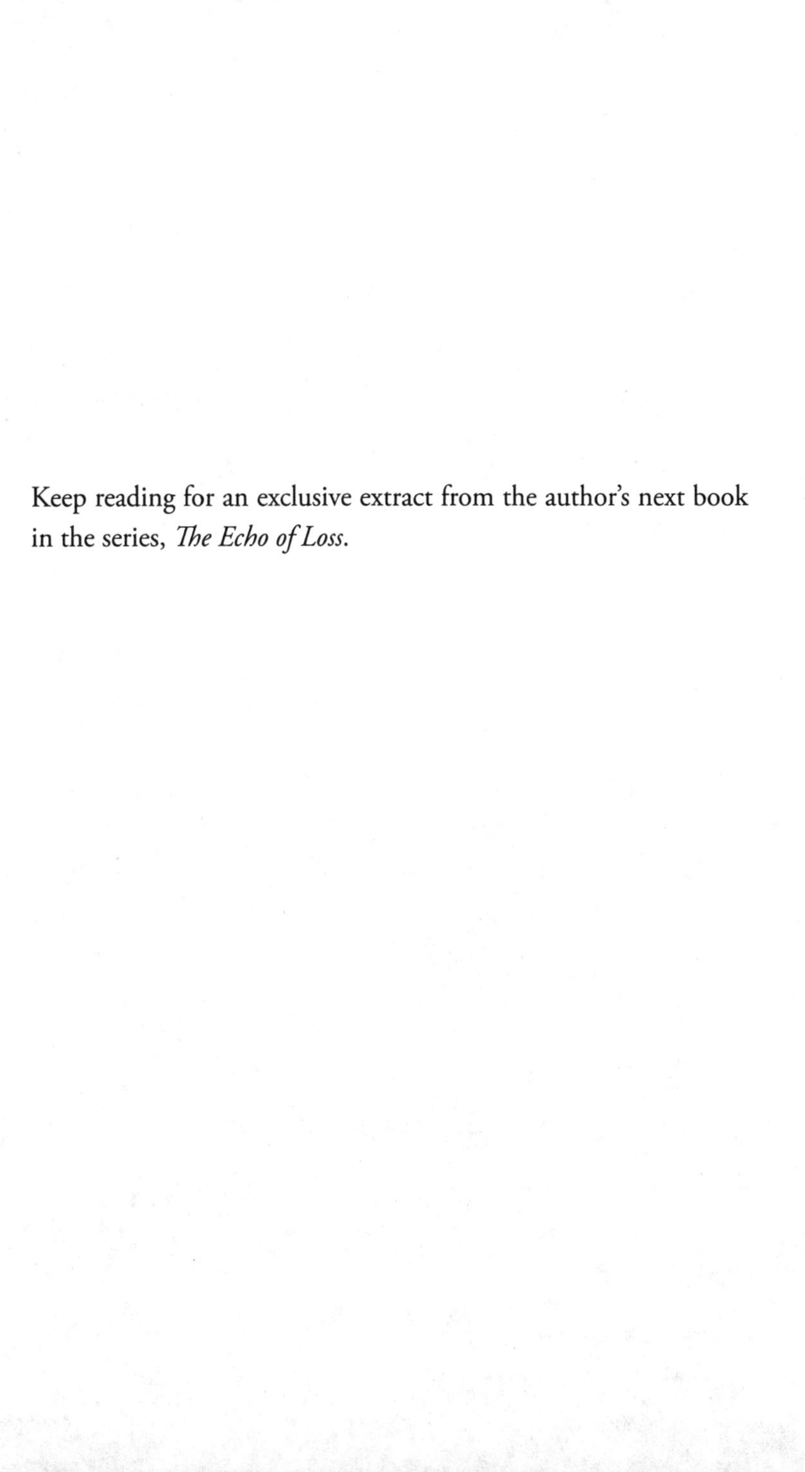

Keep reading for an exclusive extract from the author's next book in the series, *The Echo of Loss*.

It was nearing seven by the time Theo got home. The sky was a muted grey, with the first faint stars appearing and the gentle bite of the changing season in the air. She'd missed Arthur's bedtime but would go up and tuck him in anyway. And if Ralph were home . . . if Ralph were home she would claim to have been out for a walk, to have lost track of time. That's what Audrey was to have told him, if he arrived home ahead of her. She tried not to think about the time she'd taken Arthur to meet Crudge: that Ralph had found it out, and she still didn't know how.

So, when Betty, the parlour maid, opened the door with her bottom lip hanging and her eyes wide with fright, Theo blanched. The air emptied from her lungs. But he could not *know*, she told herself. He couldn't *possibly* know.

'Betty? What's wrong?' she whispered.

Betty swallowed before answering. 'The master said to send you to him in his study, as soon as you're back.'

'He's home?'

'These two hours past, madam. He . . . he's had a good deal of wine.' She looked down, unable to meet Theo's eye.

Head thumping, Theo took a second or two of stillness before walking along the hallway with the slow, resigned tread of the condemned. Perhaps this was better, she thought. Better to get it over with, and not wait weeks for him to spot the theft, and connect it to her.

She knocked, and pushed the door open.

Ralph was by the hearth, leaning against a mantlepiece cluttered with the gewgaws her mother had chosen, back when they were newlyweds. He had a glass of wine in one hand and the poker in the other, and was jabbing at the smouldering coals. Theo hung back by the door.

'Ralph, I—' The story about having been out for a long walk died on her lips.

He looked at her, and she was confused. He seemed calm, but not the kind of calm she could trust. His face was strangely slack, eyes liquid and huge.

'What have you done with it?' he said quietly.

Theo stared. As quickly and easily as that, he knew it all. Did he have spies, then? Despair swayed her like a strong wind.

Ralph didn't blink. 'Don't make me ask you twice, Theo.'

'I . . . I don't—'

'If you lie to me about this, I swear you will regret it.'

He put the poker down and came a few steps nearer. Theo smelt the wine on him, and the particular tang of his sweat when he was in a violent mood. All at once she was exhausted, and sorely tempted to surrender to whatever came next. She hadn't the energy to fight or scream. But something was not normal about him. She wondered if he meant to kill her.

'I saw you catching the bus in town this afternoon, with a basket over your arm. And Dr Fortescue saw you at the hospital, hurrying away. Where have you taken it?'

'I . . . I buried it,' Theo whispered.

'You *buried* it?'

Ralph burst out laughing, and for a moment Theo thought he might believe her. He drained his wine in a single gulp.

'I grant you, that's just the sort of ridiculous, childish thing you might do,' he said. 'But your hands are awfully clean, Theo; your skirt and shoes also. And where is your shovel?'

'I buried—'

'*Do not lie to me*!'

He hurled his glass into the fire where it shattered and hissed, and came towards her.

'What have you been plotting? *Tell me!*'

Theo said nothing.

'Is it too much to ask that you be *loyal* to me?' Ralph went on. 'That you honour and obey me as you swore to do, before God?'

This was too much. 'As you swore to cherish and protect me?' she cried. 'As you swore to keep yourself only unto me? As you swore *that*?'

Ralph's eyes widened. 'I need not justify myself to you. You are my *wife*, though you have never behaved as a wife *should*! And I will not be married to a shrew – a deceitful one at that. You will learn to respect me, if I must break every bone to teach you.'

'You can break my bones, we both know that well enough.' Her voice shook. 'But I shan't *ever* respect you. I know what you did, Ralph. I *know* what *you* did to Missy! And to Miss Breton. You *preyed* upon them!'

She was saying too much, but fear had derailed her and she couldn't stop. All thought of surrender vanished, leaving only the ringing clarity of the danger she was in. His face darkened and he came towards her, unsteady on his feet. He aimed a kick at a small table, and sent the wine decanter flying. Theo darted out of the way, nearer to the fire.

'Come here!' Ralph turned sluggishly. 'I will teach you . . . by God, Theo . . .'

The words sounded thick, almost slurred, and he lost his balance, lurching a step to one side. He was drunker than Theo had realised, and hope kindled – he might pass out; he might sleep it off, and forget what she'd said. What she'd done.

'You will do as I say, Theo,' he said.

Theo braced herself against the wall, ready to push away and run if he came closer. The iron poker was now within *her* reach; her fingers itched to grab for it, but words Toby had written shot through her mind: *Mrs Jeanie Absolom of Deptford – pushed beyond the limits of endurance – sent to the gallows*. She must do nothing to separate herself from Arthur. Ralph stood swaying for a moment. The door cracked open behind him, and to Theo's amazement Audrey's face appeared, her eyes huge. Theo gestured frantically for her to go, to close the door before Ralph noticed her, but Audrey was looking at Ralph, not at Theo.

The moment hung peculiarly. Theo was bewildered. She didn't understand why Ralph hadn't hit her yet; why he hadn't come and hauled at her wrists. She didn't understand why Audrey was hovering in the doorway, when all the staff knew to keep away when he was like this. Ralph rubbed one hand over his face, like a man just waking from sleep. He stared across at Theo with fury in his eyes, some deep turning force, but his body didn't seem to be obeying him. A thin line of drool snaked from the corner of his mouth, and hung, swinging, from his chin. Then, finally, he lurched forwards.

ACKNOWLEDGEMENTS

My sincere thanks to Hannah Shaw, Arzu Tahsin and the fantastic team at Lake Union for their enthusiasm for this book, their clear vision, and their invaluable input. I am so grateful to my agent, Mark Lucas, for believing in this story from the very first draft, for helping to make it the best it could be, and for being generally brilliant.

Thank you to my talented and lovely author friends for their opinions, feedback and unflagging support: Kate Riordan, Emylia Hall, Hannah Richell, Vanessa de Haan and Kate Lord Brown. Thank you to my friends and family for always being there, and to James, for everything.

AUTHOR'S NOTE

Details of medical and surgical practices at the time this story takes place owe much to various articles from the *British Medical Journal* archive, particularly: 'A Skull and a Book', unattributed, October 2nd edition, 1869; and 'Successful Case of Trephining for Meningeal Haemorrhage: Ligature of the Carotid', by Francis J. Shepherd M.D., C.M., April 11th edition, 1896. Also helpful was 'Risk, Responsibility and Surgery in the 1890s and Early 1900s', by Clare Brock, *Medical History* Vol.57(3), 2013.

Sir William Arbuthnot Lane was a pioneer of many medical procedures in the late nineteenth and early twentieth centuries, including the internal fixing of fractures with a metal plate that he himself had designed. However, in the case of skull fractures, experimentation in this period focused more on bone grafting than on artificial plates. It was not until the First World War, and the sheer number of head injuries resulting from it, that metal and other artificial materials began to be used more widely for cranial repair.

'A Skull and a Book' is a review of the fate of John Horwood, who died in 1821. It includes observations on the examination of the prepared skull of a girl named Eliza Balsam, many years after her death. Her attacker, Horwood, was convicted of her murder and hanged. This tragic case helped to inspire Kit's story.

One January day, his romantic advances having been rebuffed, Horwood threw a stone at Eliza while she was out walking with friends. It was a throw of forty yards or more, but, by good luck or bad, the stone hit her on the head. Over the next few days Eliza walked to and from Bristol Infirmary several times to have the wound cleaned and dressed. On 31 January she was spotted in the waiting room by Mr Richard Smith, the senior surgeon there. He insisted she be admitted for treatment. Eliza did well at first, but on 10 February she became feverish, and complained of a headache. Mr Smith operated at once, and trephined the area around the wound. Eliza died a week later, and John Horwood was charged with murder.

Horwood was repentant, and denied any intention to kill Eliza. Nobody at his trial seems to have queried whether it was the initial wound that had proved fatal, or the subsequent medical intervention. Horwood was hanged three days after his eighteenth birthday, but his sentence didn't end there. These events took place prior to the Anatomy Act of 1832, and Horwood's body now belonged to Richard Smith for dissection. Horwood was anatomised, his skeleton prepared and kept for display, and his skin tanned and used to bind a book into which Mr Smith put all his notes on the case, medical and colloquial. Eliza's skull was also retained as a specimen. Writing some forty-eight years later, the author of the *British Medical Journal* article concludes, with thinly veiled disgust, that Mr Smith was a man who *enjoyed work thoroughly*. The whole abhorrent episode has stayed with me since I first saw the book bound in Horwood's skin at the Bristol Museum some years ago.

ABOUT THE AUTHOR

Photo © 2022 Nell Mallia

Katherine Webb was born in 1977 and grew up in Hampshire before reading History at Durham University. Her debut novel, *The Legacy*, won the popular vote for the TV Book Club Summer Read 2010 and was shortlisted in the Best New Writer category at the 2010 Galaxy National Book Awards. Her seven subsequent historical novels include three *Sunday Times* Top Ten Bestsellers, and have been translated into twenty-six languages around the world. Katherine also writes crime fiction under the pen name Kate Webb. She lives in a farmhouse in Devon.

Website: katherinewebbauthor.com

Instagram: @kwebbauthor

Follow the Author on Amazon

If you enjoyed this book, follow Katherine Webb on Amazon to be notified when the author releases a new book!
To do this, please follow these instructions:

Desktop:

1) Search for the author's name on Amazon or in the Amazon App.
2) Click on the author's name to arrive on their Amazon page.
3) Click the 'Follow' button.

Mobile and Tablet:

1) Search for the author's name on Amazon or in the Amazon App.
2) Click on one of the author's books.
3) Click on the author's name to arrive on their Amazon page.
4) Click the 'Follow' button.

Kindle eReader and Kindle App:

If you enjoyed this book on a Kindle eReader or in the Kindle App, you will find the author 'Follow' button after the last page.